I0576102

Richard Savage

The Anarchist

A Story of Today

Richard Savage

The Anarchist
A Story of Today

ISBN/EAN: 9783743400023

Manufactured in Europe, USA, Canada, Australia, Japa

Cover: Foto ©Andreas Hilbeck / pixelio.de

Manufactured and distributed by brebook publishing software (www.brebook.com)

Richard Savage

The Anarchist

THE ANARCHIST

A STORY OF TO-DAY

BY

RICHARD HENRY SAVAGE

AUTHOR OF

"MY OFFICIAL WIFE," "THE LITTLE LADY OF LAGUNITAS,
"PRINCE SCHAMYL'S WOOING," "THE MASKED VENUS,"
"DELILAH OF HARLEM," "THE PASSING SHOW,"
"FOR LIFE AND LOVE."

———

F. TENNYSON NEELY
PUBLISHER
CHICAGO   NEW YORK
1894

PREFACE

THE story of active anarchism is a chronicle of th present time. The bells ringing out the nineteent century may ring in a conflict which, in its politic and social importance, will dwarf every other issue the day.

Socialism and communism moving blindly on pa allel lines are closely followed up by the were-wo of nnarchy.

This red propaganda has crossed racial and nation dividing lines, and watching the troubles of the weak governments for propitious moments—anarchism ha emerged from the shadows of midnight conspirac and now fights boldly in the open!

It has at last thrown off the mask of years! Franc Spain, and Italy have been added to the battlefield the "dynamitard," and the ominous growl of its parli mentary struggle is heard to-day in Germany, Austri and Switzerland!

The reigning family of Russia is no longer the on proscribed line of victims of this modern Vehn gericht.

As it leaves the shadows, anarchy must exhibit i true colors, move under its real leaders, and have a open and avowed creed! Any general movemer designed to tear down the fabric of society must cla with the affairs of varied classes. It needs mone skilled and plausible emissaries, and must, on the li of its battle against society, deal with the life

3

women—with the schemes of the "salon"—with active political effort and with all the priceless interests it would destroy.

Its projects will be varied. The possible preparatory manœuvres are lightly sketched in the following pages. Its future course will be bold and its vicious attacks must be firmly and promptly met.

No one can tell now, what crystallized form of modern society will survive the coming storm, but it needs not the wisdom of the seer to predict that the red flag of anarchy will never wave in triumph.

It will not fly over the wreck of the varied ties knitting together the whole useful element of a world unwilling to re-enter the mad chaos of a red whirlpool like the French Revolution.

The octopus feelers of an insane revolt against all law which guards Private Right are stealing to-day through every avenue of human life. Organized cosmopolitan repression will be the stern answer of the civilized world to the dark creed of Destruction.

·THE AUTHOR.

CONTENTS

BOOK I

AN AMERICAN HEGIRA

BOOK II

LOVE TOOK UP THE HARP OF LIFE

BOOK III

AT CROSS PURPOSES

BOOK IV

THE SPORT OF THE GODS

THE ANARCHIST

A STORY OF TO-DAY

BOOK I

CHAPTER 1

THE HARTLEY TRUST—PREMONITION

"Can you give me an hour this evening, Judge? I wish to confer with you on a matter which has been long troubling my mind," said millionaire David Hartley to his trusted lawyer.

Wilkinson Fox gazed in surprise at his client's gloomy brow. It was the close of a particularly cozy dinner 'en famille.'

"I am sorry, David, but I am down for the address at the Law School Commencement to-night! Can you come to the office to-morrow? I will be late, I fear, as it is!" replied the old counselor, glancing at his infallible watch.

"Wait a moment!" briskly remarked his host, touching the foot bell.

"Sampson!" Hartley cried, as the butler appeared, "send the carriage around at once! I'll ride down with you, Judge!"

"Beg pardon, sir! Mrs. Hartley, Miss Evelyn and Doctor Stein have just gone to the lecture. Will you have the coupé?" The functionary hastened his stately stride at the imperious nod of a master impatient of delay.

"Nothing serious, I hope, Hartley?" interrogated the advocate. "We got through the meeting very fairly, I thought."

"Ah! It is not current business. I. wish you to come up to-morrow evening. The fact is, Judge, I wish you to make some changes in my will! I must talk with you alone!"

David Hartley stepped briskly toward the door, for punctuality was a fad of his now anxious listener.

"See here! You are not looking badly! Why, Rheingold told me this afternoon you were at concert pitch." Fox eyed his client closely. "You have had no serious mishap? no personal trouble?"

"Not a cloud!" said Hartley, good humoredly, "only I have had a reminder! I will tell you all to-morrow night! There's the coupé!"

"Very good! I will come at eight! Count on me!" and Wilkinson Fox warmly pressed Hartley's hands as he walked out of the arched doorway of Cleveland's most princely residence.

"Hartley seemed worried! Money! Money! Master and slave at once" murmured Judge Fox as he sank back in the cushions and proceeded to mentally plot out the headings of a characteristically mordant lecture of advice to the fledglings of the law school.

"Will you have anything else, sir!" inquired Sampson, with diffidence, as David Hartley stood gloomily gazing out on the darkened waters of Lake Erie. With his hands folded behind him, he smoked in silence.

Take the coffee into the library! I will be late to-night!" abstractedly remarked Cleveland's business autocrat.

"Something up with the Guv'nor!" mused the butler, as he left his master standing by the window.

Hartley turned from the casement with a sigh. His quick eye had noted the gleaming lights of his favorite evening boat!

Below the aristocratic sweep of Euclid Avenue, the trains were screaming and whistling on the twisted lines of railway. The Union Depot was a blaze of light. Through the gathering gloom of night, fitful flashes of red flame spoke of the never satisfied gnawing of the hungry mill furnaces! An indistinct murmur of never-ceasing toil brought a smile to Hartley's face as he watched! "All on the move!" It was true! Around the capitalist's stately palace, shaven lawns, and beautiful gardens swept in emerald richness! Side by side, wealth's luxurious citadels reared their stately fronts along the famed avenue, but in far distant streets, crowds of men, roughly clad, with labor's drooping shoulders and sullen tread, trooped off or on shift! Tin pail, short pipe, carelessly buttoned coat, wolfish eyes gleaming over blue bearded cheeks marked the great army of toilers.

The able-bodied men were "all on the move," and in hundreds of prosaic shelter dens, weary-eyed women faced the varied phases of a never-ending drudgery or aimlessly exchanged sullen gossip around their humble doorsteps.

The sluggish carbon-laden air of the manufacturing city hung heavily like a pall over stately home and squalid tenement, daring even to cross the sacredly guarded line which separates patrician and plebeian in

Columbia—that invisible barrier which gives the lie to our boasted equality!

Where nature smiled, where wide streets, brilliant lights, gay crowds, opulent display, and life, vigor, amusement, dissipation, and animation clung around the "money end" of Cleveland, the very footsteps of the passers rang merrily on the well-kept pavement. Laughter, love, and animal spirits fled away before the brooding silence of the narrowed and darkened quarters of the generation "doing time" for their masters "on the avenue!" The pitiful shrinking up of the civic attractions in the labor quarter accorded with the narrowed foreheads, shuffling walk, and abased manner of the crowds jostling each other on the roughened pathways. It was an object-lesson in "Environments." They were results en masse!

All is on the move," mechanically repeated David Hartley, as he dropped the rich curtain and walked through the noble dining-room, down the superb hall to his spacious library. He wasted not a single thought on the thousands toiling under his industrial banner and plodding sullenly along in life's tread-mill, as he threw himself down in an easy-chair of Cordovan leather!

His eye coldly gazed upon priceless pictures gleaming in beauty on the walls of a room larger than the tenement he was born in! In serried cases, under the glow of a frescoed ceiling, reposed the scholar's weapons, the embattled books of four hundred years of Faust and Gutenburg's art.

When David Hartley thrust himself up from a haggard-eyed horde of his fellow-toilers by dint of sheer will power and a marvelous mechanical talent, he knew not the names of a dozen of the volumes now at his side.

"I must go to work! he thought. It was a self-applied goad! A memory of the days when the warning factory whistle called him hungry, from a cold and squalid room, to his machinist's bench and vise.

His eye fell upon a simply framed drawing placed between a Corot and a Fortuny. His face lightened with a glow of conscious pride. It was his patent of nobility! The first drawing of the Hartley engine valve!

Opening a safe ingeniously concealed under the pedestal of a massive bust of the Hon. David Hartley—Railroad President, Bank Director, Insurance Official, etc.—he drew forth a bundle of papers and seating himself at a working-table fit for a premier, was soon lost in calculation and the penciling of private notes.

The quarters chimed unnoticed from the great ormolu clock on the mantel as the self-made plutocrat toiled in silence. His cup of coffee and cigar were finished long before he swung the safe-door to its place.

David Hartley's brow was clouded as he took up a richly framed miniature from his desk. His lips moved in murmured tenderness when he laid it down after a long scrutiny. "Poor little man!" he muttered, as he began a nervous tramp over the tufted carpet. "He might have saved me this heart worry over Evelyn's future, if—if—"

He did not finish the sentence! His father's heart shunned the thought of the little mound at Lake View hidden by tons of sculptured marble!

Beneath that gleaming stone shaft, the hopes of a life lay buried. His only son! It was the bitterness of death.

In the haunting silence of the room the great capi-

talist forgot his intermeshed money machinery! Pipe
line, railway, rolling-mills, steam lines, shares, stocks,
and bonds were forgotten! Drifting back on the tide
of memory, a childish voice long stilled rang once
more on his ear! Two chubby arms seemed to press
his neck again—he waited for the quick rush of un-
steady little feet!

"What is it all worth? this daily battle—the struggle? Life's barren victory! Even my name will vanish. And Evelyn? Alone, young, inexperienced—
the prey of every sly fortune-hunter! It would have
been all different, so different, if Davey had not died!"

Some gentle angel of slumber brushed the tired
man's brow with a sweep of its shadowy wing and
alone, surrounded by his hard won wealth, David
Hartley slept.

As his tired head lay under the gleam of the crystal
globes, the man of fifty-six looked gaunt and worn.

His heavy, robust, angular frame spoke of the youthful hardening factory life. Dark, grizzled, wiry hair
surmounted a broad forehead beneath whose overhanging brows the keen eyes gleamed with intellectual fires
in his walk among men. High cheek bones, heavy
jaws, and a firm, clean-cut chin marked the resolution
of his massive face. Under the sweeping gray mustache his firm lips were as coldly stern as ever soldier
leading a forlorn hope.

In his slumber the hard face relaxed not a line.
His broad, knotted hands rested on his knees as if
ready to grasp the throttle at the clang of bell!

Severely plain in his dress, the ruler of an industrial army was of less 'swelling port' than his prosperous 'middlemen' basking at ease under the banners
of this victor, in the money riot of modern American
business life!

There was not a softened shade on the bronzed cheek of this apostle of work and syndicated energy!

Yet, in his uneasy slumbers the lonely man's voice betrayed the tenderness of a heart strangely moved, as he murmured, "Davey! my little boy!"

From his rest, David Hartley returned alert and energetic, swinging bolt upright as a beautiful young woman with the stride of a goddess swept into the room!

"So late, father! Must you work always? Is this right?" She was a picture of glowing loveliness as her rich, earnest voice waked the echoes of the room!

Her listener laughed as he held out his arms! "What do you know of work, Evelyn? I was merely looking over some papers! Thinking! Thinking of old times!"

Evelyn Hartley dropped the fleecy wonders of her wraps and, in an instant, was folded to her father's breast. Her quick eye had noted the displaced picture of the little boy who died! A tender gleam, a ray of sunlight on the wintry darkness of David Hartley's eyes lit up his face as he smoothed the fair head resting on his bosom.

"Did you enjoy the lecture, Little One? What was it?" He fondly gazed on her eager face, radiant in the golden light of youth.

"It was grand! 'The influence of Goethe on Modern Thought.' Professor Stein was more than satisfied!"

Evelyn Hartley pointed merrily to the clock dial.

'And your mother?"

"Has already gone upstairs! You know Doctor Rheingold's orders! Good-night, father!"

The beauty swept toward the grand staircase, pausing to throw a kiss from dainty gloved finger-tips to the rear guard of the first family of Cleveland. No fairer woman ever wandered by Lake Erie's shores than Evelyn Hartley. She stood, waiting, a living picture, at the head of the stair to beckon the Marshal Ney of the Army of Capital to follow her graceful movements.

Sure of her Empire, the lovely heiress noted the docile obedience of the stern man who, ever turning a defiant face to the world, was gentleness itself to his wife and the one child of his heart.

David Hartley's eye rested in delight upon the swaying figure of the girl. Tall and with an exquisite lissome form, her dark eyes, softened with the glowing light of eighteen, her shapely neck, firm in its gleaming contour, was swept with rebellious tresses mutinous of control. Her cheek was flushed with the rich tints of life's unsullied spring-tide, and an energy of hope and aspiration clung to her every movement. Fair brows unshaded by a sorrow, shone over the tender eyes gazing fondly on him! The happy ease of a gloriously dawning womanhood, a presence of thrilling charm and the laughter ringing from an untroubled heart were the characteristic gifts of kindly nature, softened from the unshakable virility of her father by the gentle graces of a delicate mother.

"Bright, brave girl! How can I make life's pathway smooth for you? My Evelyn! I had hoped some day to see Phil—ah!"—The strong man gasped as he clung to the carved rail. A sudden spasm tore his breast with anguish. He waited in an awful expectancy for passing moments as long drawn as a death sentence.

"That weakness! The old sledge-hammer days! I must hasten lest I be too late!" David Hartley slowly moved up the stair! No man shuddering under the

awful decree of the "Vehmgericht," no wretch awaiting the voice from the terrible "Lion's mouth," ever
walked under a surer sentence of death than David
Hartley!

His face was ashen as his trembling limbs bore him
past the door where, in her maiden bower, beautiful
Evelyn Hartley stood, a radiant vision before her
mirror.

"She must not know! Poor girl! I must find a
way! Judge Fox can aid me!"

And the stricken Crœsus stealing to his rest under
costly lace canopies, found in his vial of drops, a nepenthe of the night! It was the heart weakness gained in
the days of striking as a blacksmith's humble helper,
which beaded with cold drops the brow of the millionaire inventor!

On her knees, almost within hearing of the long-
drawn sighs of the resolute sufferer, Evelyn Hartley
faltered a fervent prayer for the dear one, under the
unsuspected sentence!

Long before the sun had pierced the suspended
blackness of Cleveland's overhanging smoke clouds,
David Hartley, brisk and alert, was on his way to the
headquarters of his financial body guard! Calm,
erect, his dark eyes glowing with earnest purpose, the
man of millions took his accustomed place among the
anxious-faced watchers of telegraph, telephone, and
stock ticker. He faced a relay of secretaries with
mounds of letters. The click of type-writers, the coming and going of the Ishmaelite messenger lads, and
hurried morning reports varied the occupations of
Hartley as he regarded a daily calendar of meetings,
interviews, and appointments. A smile lingered on
his lips, for in his button-hole a red rose spoke of the

bright-eyed one who had graced his usually solitary breakfast!

"A reward for watching for me last night, sir!" cried the willful beauty as she decorated him with the badge of victorious Lancaster.

"What do you propose to do to-day, Evelyn?" was his parting query.

"Drive out, after mother sees Doctor Rheingold. She thinks she can bear it to-day," his daughter answered, as David Hartley thought, with patient regret, of the fair-faced English wife who seemed to have been frightened into the inertia of invalidism by the rushing, jarring shocks of the nerve-destroying American life she had never learned to like! She yearned for the green lanes of merrie old England!

A quiet eyrie above the overhanging smoke pall sheltered Wilkinson Fox a few squares from where David Hartley's office was the mecca of the money-seekers of Cleveland. The astute old lawyer hung between heaven and earth in a great pile devoted to the parchment-faced Knights of the Greenbag. There was a grim smile on his face this pleasant summer morning, as he mounted the steps of the legal rookery.

"About as far as I could get from the clients," he mused. For Judge Wilkinson Fox, of national reputation as a jurist, enjoyed the delicious Indian summer of life. A veteran advocate, he lived in the intricacies of modern legal entanglements. Secure in a splendid private fortune, browsing at will in the desiccated pastures of his great library—his metier was, as adviser, to cry ware wolf—and to point out hidden pitfalls to his clientéle—resolute gladiators in the arena of nineteenth-century speculation. To a large family he had transmitted his wealth, not his brains!

Entrenched in his guarded study, he heard distantly of the social triumphs of his womankind through the carefully arranged cuttings in his daily posted scrap-books, or learned of the somewhat doubtful lustre added to the family name by a new football exploit or athletic feat of his wild sons, all judiciously tethered out at various colleges.

Gazing with an air of mild disdain upon the weather, having satisfied himself that the lake was in its usual position, he drew out a cigarette case, adjusted his spectacles, and sharply rang his desk bell.

"Codman!" he remarked, as a managing clerk of becoming gravity appeared, "Bring me 'Jarman on Wills!' Stay!—After that I will see no one but Doctor Ernest Rheingold. He has an appointment! Remember!"

"There are several matters,"—began the factotum.

"Never mind! Mr. Saunders will attend to all! I will see no one! Let no one but Mr. Saunders interrupt me!"

As the neat footed clerk laid the book down on his return, he closed the door softly. "It's a field day with the Judge," he murmured. The old spider was leaning back in his chair, wreathed in smoke and apparently examining several austere engravings of Daniel Webster, Jeremiah Mason, Chancellor Kent, Rufus Choate, and other legal word jugglers of dead and by-gone days! But, the radial lines of legal intrigue reaching out from that silent den swept over the vast territory under the star flag! The silent tide moved along daily!

"It is a pity!" soliloquized the old judge, as he absently turned the leaves of "Jarman." "Hartley is a fine fellow! A mainstay of many an enterprise! I wonder—I wonder, how it would affect the Superior

Iron Ore Company." The aged lawyer started as his eye rested on rows of green dispatch boxes! He had failed to define the "it!" David Hartley's death appeared more near as he read the inscriptions. "Estate of Rogers." "Winder Estate," and sundry other lugubrious endorsements. Mementos of vanished clients whose fortunes had paid him heavy toll!

"Gone! All gone!" Wilkinson Fox sighed. His sixty years weighed suddenly on him. Yet the gentlemanly vice of avarice held him in its spell as he ran over in his mind the stocks controlled by Hartley, in which his own golden gleanings were invested! There was the chance of a great "turn!"

"Perhaps Rheingold can post me! I may make some prudential moves!" was the advocate's last fleeting thought before the fragrant incense of his Cairo cigarette shut all the world out save the stilted intricacies of the treatise on "Wills."

Of the dainty port of the scholar, neat in attire, with slender, eager, yellowed hands, his whole manner accentuated by the furtive watchfulness of his craft, Wilkinson Fox was a modern Roman. An overhanging brow, under the silvered rounded dome of thought, an eagle air, cold gray eyes, glinting like steel, and carefully controlled pitiless lips marked his sphinx-like face. The hooked profile of the bird of prey gave an acerbity to the passionless face.

A Jesuit of the legal forum, patient, cold, sly, unerring in his intellectual conclusions, matchless in restrained force, indefatigable in labor, the old judge was a very Richelieu of the bar. The self-reliance of the experienced counselor was veiled in the exquisite diction of his sparkling conversation. It was only on great battle days in court when the lucid flow of his elo-

quence, the clean-cut logic of his argument swept
away in a resistless tide the banners of opposition.
Then he was incandescent!

"Show the doctor in!" said the plodding reader, as
he glanced at a card an hour later. "I wonder how
much he knows. Surely a house physician for years
must have noted Hartley's weak points. I will let
him talk," he smiled grimly.

When the genial German left the room a half-hour
later, Wilkinson Fox showed him out with deferential
politeness. Round of face, with beaming blue eyes,
a habitual bonhomie marked the prosperous physician,
Ernest Rheingold. Dreamily sentimental, faithful, and
sympathetic, the doctor's genial presence was the beacon
light of Caroline Hartley's uneventful life. The gold-
rimmed glasses, abstracted manner, and quaint way
of Ernest Rheingold told of the plodding years in the
Vaterland, spent in acquiring a vast fund of professional knowledge. An indefatigable worker, a zeal-
ous physician, and a valued friend, the very name of
Ernest Rheingold was an omen of good import in all
circles, from the rich who flattered and petted him, to
the poor who .paid him with fervent blessings. The
guarded secret of the Teuton's impressionable heart was
a fondness amounting to romantic devotion for the
woman, who, as David Hartley's gentle but useless
wife, was allied to the fierce chess play of her husband's gigantic money schemes. She was a social nullity, living in repressed awe of his soaring onward
flight.

Her recluse life was a mild protest against the energetic vivacity and brilliant dash of that budding
beauty, Evelyn, into whose firm white hands the household reins had dropped from her own slender fingers,
weighted down with gems!

"So!" mused Wilkinson Fox, as Rheingold vanished, "it is a matter of any sudden excitement! The heart walls are thinned with the brutal hardships of his earlier working days! A last flicker, then, 'out brief candle!' I must look into this at once! Would Hartley retire? I wonder if he knows all! He's a terribly resolute fellow! Working away with no sign of fear! I suppose he will die some day in harness! And I must now put his house in order! The girl is a noble woman! I always thought that Maitland might fancy her! But he's away at the uttermost ends of the earth. He seems to wish to verify the existence of every town named in the World's Gazetteer! Pity too! Phil had a decided legal bent!"

The afternoon shadows were gathering before Wilkinson Fox closed his familiar tomes. He was armed to the last triviality. "Jarman" was now hidden under a castaway pile of similarly formidable treatises cunningly devised to enable the intelligent to create legal jungles impenetrable to hostile attack!

"Now I wonder if that fellow Stein has an eye to the future! I must look into that! Singular man. His ability is marvelous! Is he a world rover, a free lance, or an intellectual renegade? I think I will watch Professor Carl Stein," and the old judge was weaving, weaving his silent web, while his superb horses bore him along the avenue on his constitutional.

As Judge Fox measuredly paced along the front of the Hartley grounds in the starlight, pondering over the division of the great estate, a springing step roused him, and a ringing manly voice set every nerve tingling.

"Confound the fellow! He always comes on one like an Alpine storm blast!" muttered the lawyer, as he gravely said "Good evening, Professor Stein! You are going in!"

"I am, Judge! Miss Hartley is extending her private library! I am classifying her books!"

"Does her studious enthusiasm still bear her up in her flights into the realms of German philosophy?" queried the old man.

"The only woman mind I have ever seen unfold and grasp knowledge broadly. There is nothing beyond her capacity!" replied Stein, with enthusiasm. "I can lead her no farther. There is nothing hidden to her aspiring intellect. Beyond comparison, the finest woman nature I have ever fathomed!"

"And the emotions? Has her lonely girlhood smothered the longings of a woman's heart?" There was a shade of expressed concern in the lawyer's voice.

"Evelyn Hartley is beyond the spasmodic fever of the love mania. She is destined to a higher empire than to be the Sultana of a fin-de-siecle marriage!" replied Stein, forcibly.

"Indeed—few women reach that exalted station!" remarked Fox, with a polite 'sneer, as he turned into the great lawn, "What is its special characteristic?"

"The personal and intellectual freedom of a glorious natural womanhood!" gravely replied Stein as they entered the great portals.

"This tutelage leads whither?" mused the judge, as he watched Carl Stein's erect figure disappear in the great drawing-room. Wilkinson Fox had caught the expression of Carl Stein's face in the great mirror as the German disappeared with a curt, snappy bow. A smile of contented pride played on Stein's lips as he had spoken. There was the light of triumph on his strong, masterful face. The real attributes of Doc-

tor Carl Stein were an enigma to even the watchful
lawyer.   For three years the director of Evelyn Hartley's studies in belles-lettres, the Heidelberg alumnus
was of unexceptionable bearing.

His forty-three years were not indicated by the freshness of his massively moulded face.   Defiant gray
eyes flashing under his waving locks, a restless physical and mental activity and singularly graceful cosmopolitan manners gave him distinction.   The reserve of
his daily life harbored no mystery, for in the intellectual world Stein of "Heidelberg" was not without clear
credentials and well-vouched laurels.

In accordance with Caroline Hartley's one resolutely
expressed maternal fiat, her daughter had been carefully instructed at home.   The reputation attained by
Doctor Stein, as an attaché of continental German
Embassies was a nimbus of glory.   Unexceptionable
in bearing and address, his position in Cleveland was
accentuated by the romantic stories of his determined
attachment to republican principles.   This alone fully
explained his sacrifice of diplomatic promotion!

A lonely life, an impenetrable social reserve and a
frank indifference to womanly charms piqued his patrician pupils and caused maternal hearts to rest untroubled.

"I hope Mrs. Hartley is well this evening," was the
gallant salutation of Judge Fox, as he bent with stately
old-fashioned courtesy over that lady's hand.

The visitor was rewarded with a graceful wave of the
fan and a welcoming smile from the lady who, propped
with silken pillows on a sofa, was the embodiment of
refined invalidism.   Caroline Walton's Indian nativity
may have suggested the languor of her womanhood.
She lingered in memory over the memory-painted

visions of her girlhood, before Captain Walton of the
Bengal Army fell into a snug Yorkshire property by
the death of a brother who obligingly broke his neck
in a stiff run across country. Still fair, and with the
fresh complexion of her Saxon race, it was easy to
divine the instant victory of the Anglo-Indian girl over
ardent David Hartley, flushed with the wondrous successes of the Hartley valve, showering English gold on
the talented American.

"You have business with Mr. Hartley, I presume,
Judge!" equably inquired the handsome matron.

"Some papers! yes!" interjected the master of the
house who had warmly greeted his friend, and now led
the way to the library.

The counselor cast a furtive glance at the eager
face of Evelyn Hartley, to whom with unusual animation, Carl Stein was eloquently painting the future
of the American woman.

"To lead her sisters in victory, past the barriers
built by man for centuries against her sex, will be
the fadeless glory of one great American woman! The
social structure of the world can not be changed without woman, invincible in her purity. It is to America
that the old world—"

Wilkinson Fox compressed his lips as he followed
his host. "Can Stein covet this girl's enormous individual heritage? On what road does he lead out
that fearless neophyte? She has passed out on the
sea of modern unrest, feverishly acquired knowledge,
far beyond her mismated parents!"

The lawyer chose a seat, in silence, as David Hartley closed the door. He easily divined it was of the
brilliant, ardent, inexperienced girl's future the anxious man would speak! Too well he knew by tacitly

established custom that the fair-haired English wife, with the unvarying placid blue eyes, was a domestic nullity.

Wilkinson Fox accepted a cigar in silence. He gazed expectantly at the earnest face of Hartley, who strode up and down the room, in some agitation.

Abruptly seating himself, the client faced his life-time friend and hurled a direct question at him.

"How am I going to tie up my daughter's fortune to secure to her alone its entire control?"

David Hartley placed a mass of papers on the table from a dispatch box at his side.

"It can not be done! Hartley," answered the lawyer in a dry voice. "State your wishes and I'll see how far I can aid you to carry them out."

"I will not hide anything from you, Judge!" retorted the anxious millionaire. "You know I am the whole of my own family. There is no one else! As regards my marriage I may as well admit that it has been a social failure! Mere accession of wealth, the temporary commercial value of a signature adds no polish to the self-made man! My wife has never drawn a shade nearer to me than on the day when the shy English girl placed her hand in mine! She has simply been transplanted, not transformed. It is different with my daughter! She is of my own blood! Her very soul is wrapped up in an inductive sympathy with my hard boyhood, my early struggles, my brain work, and the late flowering of my intellect! My wife judges me from a superior social standpoint. My daughter echoes every throb of my heart!" Hartley paused and buried his face in his hands. His labored breathing stilled as he lifted his head.

"I had hoped to live to see Evelyn a self-reliant

woman, married to a man of power and one who could direct my complicated affairs! If my son had lived, she would have known a brother's love!"

"But, my friend, I have lately received reminders of the coming stroke. I fear, I even predict a sudden death! It is here,"—he tapped his breast—"I went away last year to the metropolis. As a stranger I consulted leading specialists! The time approaches! The overtaxed heart action can never repair the wasted energies, the injurious strain of my 'slavery days'!"

He glanced with defiant pride to the window where the forge-fires lit up the horizon.

"It is to secure Evelyn's future I wish you to aid me now!"

The lawyer, in pity, tried to divert the concentrated energy of the brooding mind.

"Who is the head of your wife's family?" he asked.

"Admiral Horatio Walton, formerly of the English, late of the Italian Navy," replied Hartley, "an elder brother's son inherits the lands. He is a minor and a stranger to me! His father married late in life!"

"And the Admiral, his character and situation?" briskly followed up the lawyer.

"Walton is a singularly gifted man, a widower nearly sixty, and living in London in retirement. He was a Commander in the English Navy when Garibaldi captured Naples. For a friendly kindness he was offered an Admiral's commission by Victor Emmanuel. Resigning the English service, he accepted the rank and is now on the retired list. He is childless, his wife, an Italian countess, has been dead many years. He is a man of cosmopolitan gifts, arts, and of a vast experience."

Hartley paused.

"And would you trust him?" the suave counselor continued.

"Most decidedly! He is my wife's nearest relative and beyond any personal scheming. His retired pay as an Italian Admiral is ample for his needs. He is an authority in many special branches of science. We were quite congenial!" frankly said the capitalist.

"Now what is your wish, Hartley, as regards your daughter?' Fox was quietly watchful of every shade of thought flitting over Hartley's face.

"I would shield her from the jackal horde of fortune-hunters who would snarl over my grave before the grass was green upon it! If Evelyn were older, I would feel inclined to trust her absolutely! She is capable of great things! But, if called away, I know that her mother is utterly unfit to guide her in matters of moment! I wish my wife to have half of my property, absolutely. Her brother will advise her. But the other half will be a tempting bait for the wolfish American schemers! I fear the result of the awakening of Evelyn's emotional nature! She has passed beyond my ken in education! Her whole thoughts move on a higher plane than mine. I am tied to the practical. She wanders in the ideal world!"

"And her heart?" the counselor was alert.

"Once awakened, the flood of her emotional nature will bear all before it in its released energy! She has built up a world of her own! In the fierce play of the world's pleasures, in the pride of untrammeled power, she may be a victim to her own inexperience! My fortune is in negotiable shares and securities mostly. It is a great responsibility. Under a malign influence he might be despoiled! I have decided upon a general course. I wish you to create a trust to terminate when she is twenty-five. The properties I have here in this list can be transferred to the incorporated company. One-half of the stock can be placed in my wife's name, and the rest held for Evelyn by three trustees or their survivors."

Hartley handed his listener a schedule.

After a careful examination Wilkinson Fox, with a trembling hand, returned it.

"It is an enormous property! The trustees should be selected with the utmost care!" he gravely remarked.

"I have exhausted my circle of friends. The choice is a narrow one. I name them in order. Yourself, Admiral Walton, and my wife!"

The old lawyer started up! It was a crowning proof of the confidence of a lifetime!

"Not a word, my old friend! I shall feel armed against the future if you accept! Above all not a word to my child. I wish her to remain at present in ignorance of the whole matter! I have made notes here as to her allowance, to a suitable increase on her twenty-first birthday, and as to the delivery of the entire estate upon her reaching twenty-five! Let nothing delay this after you have covered the entire subject! I have retained ample funds for my personal use. They can take the course of the law!"

"And do you see no other clouds before your daughter in the future? Have you thought of every danger? There is yet time with these vast resources to cast out anchors in every direction! This property is all in the United States! Do you not note the signs of the times?" The advocate was eager.

"What do you mean?" demanded Hartley in wonder.

"These properties are industrial, manufacturing, rail-

way, and corporate stocks, franchises and privileges
representing the heaped-up labor of thousands, the
bond wage of a polyglot army! Do you not fear, in
these restless days, when through our open port the
world's refuse thing—the rising tide of socialism, bearing in the red fire-ship of Anarchy!"

Fox had risen, his eyes lit up with the glow of
prophecy.

"You are timorous, Fox!" cried Hartley.

"The anarchist in America is only an anonymous
coward!"

"I will not combat you with argument, Hartley,"
replied the counselor. "As an adviser, I urge you to
divert a portion of this great inheritance destined for
your child to England, France, and Germany for
investment in government funds! You and your fellow
millionaires forget flaming Cincinnati, sacked Pittsburg, and great New York under mob rule! The poison
of anarchy is daily infiltrated through every industrial
stratum! You do not hear the growl of the masses,
you can not follow the filaments of the poisonous lichen
of imported agitation!"

"We have the general government?" urged Hartley.

"Before it could act, the accumulations of a generation would be sacrificed! Be warned! I would divide
this wealth!" repeated Fox.

"The National Guard is ready always!" persisted
Hartley.

"How long would it withstand the wild rush of the
maddened masses goaded on by ingenious conspirators!" rejoined Fox.

"No National Guard has ever shown itself trust-
worthy as an organization. They join one side or the
other of a civil quarrel. Look at the history of France

for the last hundred years. Your militiaman is judge, jury, sheriff and executioner! when he is effective, he acts as a regular—a mere executioner! We want no thinking bayonets in a riot! We want Napoleonic handling of the artillery! Remember the Church of St. Roch! The Corsican shot first and talked later when he said 'My task is done!' Your guardsman reasons falters and does not shoot! You plutocrats will learn all this some day when blazing factories light up the 'Carmagnole' of the foreign scum drifting in here! They only need leaders! Human fiends, mad with the poisonous doctrines of Marx, Bakunin and Tchernicheffsky are now creeping to the front! They abandon the creed of Proudhon, the vagaries of Mazzini, the finely spun theories of St. Simon, Fourier, Owen and Enfantin! The red terror is nearing us! Its disciples are led on by men as careless of their generation as Jean Jacques Rousseau of his progeny! Dynamite is their argument! Purification by fire their cure! The modern world is sick! The old remedies of the law are seemingly useless! The shock of Anarchy will kill the patient if it does not cure." Fox was agitated.

"But, to your own affairs!" the crafty adviser returned. "You think you are safe in your property! I pass the subject! Your daughter has the glorious promise of royal womanhood in her sweet face! You may make your will as you please! Can you enforce a single wish! In the future, where will awakened passions lead her! There is no settled station in America! Do not hope to see her walk the path you fondly lay out, in a father's love! We are creatures of fate, Hartley; (the judge's voice trembled), God alone can guide and guard. Let me invest half her fortune in English lands and public funds! Old Brittania will make the last stand against the Red Spectre, thanks to feudal land laws and a strong aristocracy! Admiral Walton will watch over it."

"See here, Fox!" cried Hartley, rising, "I will not be persuaded to send a dollar out of the United States! Come to me to-morrow night! Bring up a skeleton of your proposed papers! I tell you the industrial masses of America are superior in comfort to those of any civilized land!"

"True! and because this great army can be turned against capital in resistless attack is why conspiring Anarchy seeks America as the open field to fight out its awful battle to a finish! When that day comes, as come it will, mercy will be laughed to the wind! The storm is drifting down on us, driven hither from Europe! Are you blind to the growth of organized resistance? Trades-unions, labor-unions, socialistic clubs, agitation, secret societies, anarchism, nihilism, in its drastic remedy of 'dynamite' for every political and social ailment!"

"My dear Judge! You are infected with the timidity of the scholar! You are an alarmist!" vigorously replied Hartley.

"I am not!" stoutly replied the awakened lawyer. "Here, alone, the toilers have freedom of movement, money, innate courage, a press free to the point of license—all they lack is a competent set of successful demagogues to light the fires of revolt!"

"Let us join the ladies" said Hartley, as he opened the door. "Ah, Doctor Stein. Going! Good-night!"

And that name haunted Wilkinson Fox's slumbers of the night!

CHAPTER II

"What a perfect morning! There is nothing sweeter than the breath of June in old New York!" Evelyn Hartley sighed as she turned from the windows of the faded drawing-room of the "Brevoort." Her splendid eyes were moist, as roses and violets in dainty freshness greeted her.

"Take them to my rooms, Ashford; I am going out to drive with Judge Fox!" She dropped the card bearing, in a boldly pencilled hand, the words "Carl Stein."

In a shaded corner of the room, the heiress sat, her face bowed in grief! The violets spoke of other blossoms now nodding at Lake View over the grave of her father!

Robed in deepest black, her eyes tinged with the first great sorrow of her life, Evelyn Hartley seemed a royal daughter of the Night!

"To-morrow will bear me even farther away from him! Out on the wild waves, a lonely woman on lonely waters of Life! It is too bitter, too cruel!" The stately woman wrung her hands in anguish.

Yet calmly, with the dignity of her grief she met grave-faced Wilkinson Fox, who ceremoniously escorted her to the carriage. It was only when the trembling leaves of the park shaded them, that her old trustee found his voice. He had been intently watching the noble face, proud and firm in its virginal beauty.

33

The carriage threaded the alleys at a walk, while in monotone, Wilkinson Fox assumed the Polonius. "My dear young lady," said the counselor, "it seems fitting you should know of the concern with which I see you go so far from me! Your father and I were old friends! I feel his loss daily even more! The testimonials still reaching me of his public worth and esteem are sad reminders of our loss! It is natural that your mother should desire to return to the land of her birth! She looks toward the sunset of life! I am sure that her interests will not suffer, and I shall assure myself that her bankers afford every facility to her of avoiding intrusion and mere detail! But you, my child, are a part of us! You call up to those who knew him, your father. I wished to talk alone to you of him, and of his wishes! In the months before his sudden death his very heart and soul seemed to be wrapped up in your future! You cannot ignore the duties of your high station at home to the thousands of toilers, to the charities David Hartley planted, to your own community. For you are an uncrowned princess of the Age of Gold! I would not wish you to mingle in new scenes, to be dazzled by a differently organized society, to gradually lose your heritage of interest in and duty to the army still marching under David Hartley's draped banners!"

"I am thankful, Judge! I will have you, but I feel I know, at last, the innermost workings of my dear father's heart! He did not have time to teach me to love him," the girl bitterly said, "money-slavery claimed his every moment, but I know his tenderness—too late —too late!"

"How, my dear child!" cried the astonished lawyer.

"Doctor Armytage handed me a sealed packet after

my father's death," softly said Evelyn. "He had not confided in Rheingold for fear the kindly German might alarm my mother, or that it would reach me! The words of gentle love he penned are sacred! I can only tell you, Judge," and the girl smiled through her tears, "that he bade me in matters affecting the estate to depend absolutely on your judgment! He was so brave! So self-denying! If I could have only told him once how I loved him for his thoughtful words, reaching me after he had passed beyond the veil! His hard life was heroic, a protest against the early eclipse of his wonderful talent!"

"Do Rheingold and your mother know of this?" asked the old lawyer, regarding her curiously.

"Not a word has reached them!" replied the heiress.

"Dr. Rheingold is engrossed with my mother's case! and it is strange that her placid nature is absolutely concentrated on herself! I feel my father's last confidence too sacred for others! It is all mine! My own treasure! I doubt even if my mother realizes his loss! It was a singular marriage!" the girl mused. "I know no one who could have been so absolutely unsuited to my father as my mother!"

"Judge! marriage is a strange relation!" The heiress was dreaming!

"It is the modern mystery!" the counselor dryly said. "Its greatest characteristic seems to be its usual utter uselessness in the union of discordant natures, warring souls, uncongenial tempers and alien tastes!"

"What causes this?" Evelyn Hartley was earnest.

"Because modern marriage is only a game of egoism, latent or expressed! It is a living problem of the future to you, my child, but to me the monument of a life's mistake!"

Wary as Wilkinson Fox could be, the return from the drive left him held at arm's length by the reserve which seemed to seal Evelyn Hartley's lips.

"I shall, of course, yield to my mother's wish to meet all those who are of kindred blood! We shall spend some time on the Continent, but my own future is undetermined. I shall follow up my studies! I am not tied by conventionality to any human being." The heiress was his match in self-control.

"One last effort!" thought Judge Fox, as he realized that his review of the whole situation left him in doubt. He suddenly said, "What of Professor Stein? Do you see him?" The heiress quietly answered, "I believe he intends to spend two years at Lausanne, engaged on his serious work on the "Political Future of the German Empire. My father's legacy enables him to use that period in his researches. Lausanne and Heidelberg are, I believe, the scenes of his future employment."

"Can you give me his address?" said Fox, as the carriage drew up at the "Brevoort".

"I presume Dr. Rheingold can send it to you at any time. They are great friends!" was the calm rejoinder of his ward.

"Till to-morrow, then, at the steamer," concluded the baffled lawyer. "She is indifferent to this man, it seems. I am glad to know they have drifted away from each other."

The aged diplomat did not observe Professor Carl Stein gazing at his retreating carriage, as he rolled toward the "Fifth Avenue."

"I must not let this sly busy-body see me at the wharf!" muttered Stein. "Now for the secretary. My friend, the judge, will not suspect the cause of his absence. I will sleep on the 'City of Paris' to-night!"

Carl Stein's brow was knitted in deepest thought as he swiftly strode along to the Cafe Hungaria.

"Ah! There's my man," he joyously exclaimed, as a young man carelessly lounged toward the table where Stein's cup of coffee was an excuse for dallying.

"All ready, Professor!" whispered the new-comer. "Shall we walk around the corner to Gramercy Park?"

"Certainly!" briskly replied Stein, as they rose. "The papers are complete!" He searched the face of his companion with a stern gaze.

"You'll find them right!" said his tool, as in the secluded by-street the faithless secretary gave the professor a bulky envelope. A few moments sufficed for a recognition of the enclosures. They had entered a basement groggery.

"You are sure the schedule is correct?" the German said, his eyes blazing in astonishment.

"I copied it from the engrossed trust-deed myself!" confidently rejoined the clerk.

"Just count that! I think you will find it five hundred!" coolly remarked Stein as he carefully hid the papers in an inside pocket.

"I think I will get back! It's all right!" With a careless nod the Judas disappeared.

Carl Stein, with furtive glance, noted the passers-by as he reached his hotel by a tortuous course.

"Money! money! Concrete force of the modern world! This fortune must be won for the 'Cause'! In our hands it would arm us for a victorious struggle! The way! The means! I will find it! It must be secured!" His gray eyes blazed in yellowish flashes as his burning thoughts drove him, like a goad, to the shelter of his chosen retreat. He was a dreaming, human tiger!

The great liner slowly swung out in the Hudson, under sunniest skies on the morning after Wilkinson Fox had vainly cross-examined his stately ward, under the pleasing subterfuge of a Park drive.

When the "City of Paris" gathering headway, quivered under the impulse of the huge engines, Evelyn Hartley recalled the last solemn words of the old judge who was still waving his parting signal on the pier.

"My dear child! May God speed and guard you!" were his last words as they stood alone, for Mrs. Hartley was already settled in a padded chaise longue, under the eyes of her maid, at the spot of minimum nautical disturbances. That excellent lady was buoyed up by the realization of a dream of years. Her return to England gave that resigned invalid new hopes! A sense of grateful relief seemed to accompany the removal of that energetic nature—her late husband!

"I know not what your noble father's last wishes were!" said the lawyer in parting. "It is for your loyal soul to prove that it is not the law but love which binds! May your life be all he would have fondly realized had his tenderness been spared to you! I shall watch you from afar! But you are now going out alone on the unknown seas of the future! Be not too trustful! And—God bless you always!"

When the clanging bell left her alone, Evelyn Hartley sought the deck from whence the babel of the New York was seen in the brightness of the golden day.

She turned her eyes westward to where the man, whose memory thrilled her now, was sleeping by the blue lake!

Lonely in death, as in life, David Hartley's sleep was dreamless, by the side of his little son!

The western breeze bore to her his message. So

strangely thrilling her with hope. "Love is the higher law! Love alone leads upward! Avoid the shadow-paths of life!"

And, with the beauty of life's morning on her sweet face, Evelyn Hartley looked backward in vain, when the sun sprang up from its gray and azure Eastern bed.

The old life was far behind her now, and in the cloudless glow of morning skies, the flying ocean wonder bore her on to the unknown future.

"Such a pleasant surprise, Evelyn!" equably babbled Mrs. Hartley as the heiress approached the coign of vantage, where Dr. Rheingold had marshalled the daily needs and conveniences of his gentle but exacting patient. It was the peculiar talent of Caroline Walton Hartley to keep her entire following continuously employed in ministering to her varied necessities.

Evelyn had early learned the benefit of a judicious Fabian policy, and a physical zone added to the social distance of mother and daughter. Their orbits were concentric, but their paths were separated by the neutral ether of indifference.

Rich in color, glowing in beauty, her hands clasping the first livre de voyage, so hard to attack, Miss Hartley was already an object of interest to a distant knot of society free lances! These club men, running vainly up and down the earth were visibly excited when Rennslaer Hayward, famed for varied useless acquirements, and his comet-like social path, murmured lazily:

"Rather nice woman! Western heiress! Rolling mills and all that—Miss Hartley—saw her at Cleveland when I was out West with 'Buster Fox'—my classmate."

"Deep mourning! Out of society for a season. **Must** find out how the land lies! I wonder who knows them," mentally noted Arthur Hobart, who had an eye to a "lass wi' a tocher!"

"Not in our line! She will wind up in lonely grandeur in some tumble-down English castle, with a new title, and her money will chink up the old walls! Turn iron into stone, then a gold coronet! That's the horoscope I cast!" murmured Jack Manners, who was going abroad "on general principles."

The "pleasant surprise," in the mean time, was standing, hat in hand, before Miss Evelyn Hartley. Carl Stein noted the flush of angry vexation shading the face of the astonished heiress. "She imagines this a personal pursuit," he quickly decided. "I received advices from Heidelberg which decided me at the last moment to take this vessel. My private preparations are trifling! I had already sent my books and papers over!"

Evelyn Hartley's self-possession had returned. She turned her frankly-honest eyes on the German savant, as if in haughty wonder at his labored explanation.

"It promises a fair passage!" she murmured. "You are a gainer by your sudden resolve, Doctor!" There was no doubt as to the evident desire of the western beauty for solitude. At the side of the vessel her steadfast face was turned backward to the land of liberty, and the book lay idly in her folded hands.

"An ideal Evangeline!" thought Stein, on whose ears the formal word "Doctor" grated unpleasantly punctilious as he was in his stubborn German etiquette.

Evelyn was annoyed at Stein's appearance. To meet him, in Europe, was the natural sequence of his three

years supervision of her advanced studies. The queries of her old guardian returned to her disturbed mind!
A dull anger took possession of her, as she observed
the professor was secretly watching her every movement. It was not long before the coterie of Columbia's keen witted sons were deprived of the pleasant
occupation of a cold, staring study of her points! Satisfied that the flow of her mother's platitudes indicated at least normal vigor, she was soon lost to view.
Stein, quick-witted and cautious, took himself to a
solitary study in gray and white. For an hour he sat
staring at the whirling band of screaming sea-birds
in the foamy wake. The stolen papers pressed upon
his bosom, and a sense of his treachery and cowardice
weighed on Stein, as he marked the vanishing of the
girl he was secretly following.

"I was too abrupt! I should have softened the surprise. I could not be sure until I had the schedule
and I must know her surroundings." He paced the
deck in gloomy self-communion. The steady light of
his gray eyes was unshaken and his tread defiant, for
he growled: "Is she on her guard? Fox does not
like me! I shall win at last! I must conquer! It is
for the Cause. This ocean path leads on to victory,
and to be patient is torture!"

For the sweep of the wild winds singing their shrill
menace in the tautened wires of the rigging was no
bolder than the rushing storm of pent-up thoughts,
dark and sinister, surging through the brain of the
dauntless materialist! The "City of Paris" sturdily
breasting the green surges of the Atlantic was bearing
in the Hartley hegira an invading army to dissipate
the peaceful autumnal "dolce far niente' of Admiral
Horatio Walton's life. The unbroken calm of his do-

mestic tranquillity dated from the fortuitous demise of
the spirited Italian countess who had brought a graceful social tempest into his varied existence. To a long
waltz followed by a moonlight stroll on a Neapolitan
balcony with a young Austrian attaché, he owed the
effective, if sudden, removal of a lively black-eyed tor-
ment.

On the particular June morning when Evelyn Hartley's arched brows contracted ominously at the sudden
appearance of Carl Stein as a fellow-voyager, Horatio
Walton was deliberately breakfasting at the United
Service Club. The mechanical precision of his morning social guard mount was only interrupted by resent-
ful glances at an envelope wherein he had replaced
the cablegram announcing the embarkation of his
niece and her mother.

The old sailor's carefully trimmed gray whiskers bris-
tled in anger. His *Times* lay neglected at his side
and the club steward gazed earnestly in his direction,
fearing a cyclonic outbreak of the admiral's temper.

"I wonder if Caroline retains her watchful regard
for her precious self. There is no possible advantage
to me in her visit. But if the girl is manageable and
presentable there might be—by Jove, there's Beauford
—the very man!" Admiral Walton's hailing-sign was
effective, for a tall, good-looking man of twenty-eight
approached with a pleasant nod.

In a few moments the new-comer had fathomed the
secret of Walton's anxiety.

Beauford, whose name as Lord Alfred Beauford, the
yachtsman, hunter, and dilettante explorer was a welcome theme for the London journalists, showed the
varied experiences of his life of adventure, in a hard
glint of his blue eye, a touch of the tell-tale crow's

foot, and a cynic line here and there accentuating his handsome face.

"Of course there'll be bother—no end! But your duties should be light. Representative head of family and all that! Localize them, and you can keep up your own set. They will soon make their way into the set that opens its arms to rich Yankees."

"Exactly, but that is not in the plan. Caroline wants to take a nice place in Yorkshire for two or three seasons. She never cared for London. The girl is serious! Moreover, they will be on the continent a great deal. It's there I come in as cicerone and family mentor! I heard you are going on a long tour. Would you let the Priory?"

Beauford flushed at the direct inquiry.

"There never has been a stranger at Jervaux yet! I must think it over, Admiral! I have had a fancy for a ride through Thibet, Kashgar, and there working along the Russo-Chinese frontier, out to the Pacific by Mantchuria and Korea. It would be a matter of two years or more. I've done about all the rest. I should not care to have a mob of people overrun the old place."

"See here, Beauford, I was going to write to your solicitors. My sister Caroline always fancied Jervaux Priory. Her letters, in fact, named it. Her wealth is enormous. I have carte blanche from her! She would buy a place, if I so advised, but their circle would be quiet! I would like the refusal of the Priory, if you contemplate long absence and have abjured matrimony!"

"Tell me of the late Hartley! Was he a gentleman?" The young nobleman was faintly curious.

"I don't know what you would call a gentleman in

the States,   rejoined Walton, puzzled.   "Hartley was
a fine fellow.   He began life a poor lad and ended a
multi-millionaire, a world-famed inventor, and a leader
of his community.   His charities and public endow-
ments would do credit to a prince! And he would have
further aided the working classes but his sudden death
cut off these projects in the bud.   There seems to be
no real difference of station in America.   And there the
fatal fires of discord will be fed in the envy of those
who see their equals rise to kingly power by the magic
of money."

"There seems to be no real permanence in American
society," remarked Beauford, "at least I so fancied
in my brief runs over the States.   The men are overtaxed strugglers in the money maelstrom.   The
women madly vying in display and patrician luxury
foreign to a merely commercial community. American
men are harsh, unrefined, and vastly inferior to their
women.   The weaker sex find time for the shadowy
show of their unreal social world. They struck me as
merciless in their demands, frankly unbridled in their
daring dissipations and callously indifferent to the desperate gamesters in the wild sea of speculation whose
names they bear.   It is strange their women throw
themselves so eagerly into the arms of foreigners."

The young nobleman paused.

"It is because they realize the absolute hollowness
of the pretense of a settled American society.   In a
generation the same woman may run the gamut of the
social scale. Money always rehabilitates in America,"
said Admiral Walton.   "The women have caught the
advantages of marriage into a permanently graded European society.   With their quick wit, they exchange
their gold for the highest titles they can reach, regard-

less of the results of the bargain. They know their children will have a real station protected by law. If they trusted their money to brothers, agents, and people at home, they might be robbed of it and then have neither station nor money."

"They do not get much happiness out of foreign marriages, Walton," mused the junior.

"Strange to say, Beauford, American women do not need much personal happiness! Give them precedence, get them out of America, the mere fact of their permanent translation is the crown of life's victory."

"I must say I despise the smart set of American women for their cold disloyalty to a land whose flexible institutions have raised them by happy accident to the ease of queenly place with no responsibilities. They leave their land with no regret, the men struggle on and satisfy themselves with secondary marriages at home! It can't last! The whole shabby genteel American social system of successful plutocracy has to meet its day of doom! In this last generation, the accumulated labor of thousands, piled up year by year, in the gorged pockets of the Yankee money-lords, is being transferred to Europe by the title hunting throng of American women of independent fortunes, heaped up by the men who die of paresis or snuff out their lives in overwork like poor Hartley. I must say, Beauford," the old admiral cried, in conclusion, "I don't like America. The things admirable there are unfamiliar to me! The unrest, vulgarity and sham of their society, the unscrupulousness of their press, the absolute lack of a foreign policy, the rush and rattle of their daily life, are all things distasteful to me! Most of all these heartless women throwing themselves into the arms of titled aliens! Even mature women vie with the callow heiress in this national woman treason! Their men certainly are inferior in social dash to these falcons of our day but, they are true to their gridiron flag! The whole thing has got to go by the board! Europe is pouring its worst and most dangerous classes over there yearly by the scores of thousands. Unless some national scare shall inaugurate a spasm of Russian-like repression, Yankee land will be the chosen battle-ground of the anarchist! The weak temporary pavilion of Liberty will fall and crush its inmates!"

Beauford was vastly amused as he finished his hock and soda.

"You may be right, Walton, whatever American women may have to boast of, they are both hasty and heartless! And your niece, Evelyn Hartley, is she chasing a coronet?"

"Strange to say, Beauford, I'm told she is a charming woman and has inherited much of her father's genius and force of character. God knows she did not get either from poor Caroline! I am interested in her!" The admiral showed signs of weighing anchor.

"She is not inclined to a profession, or publicity? Does she lecture or lead the world on toward better things? I have met some insufferably uncertain American cranks and freaks wildly misnamed 'earnest women!' your 'earnest American woman' is usually an indefatigable common scold!"

Beaufort was quizzing the old sailor.

"I really believe, Lord Alfred," rejoined the mariner, "that she is satisfied with being Evelyn Hartley, and, from her graceful and gentle face, her spirited letters, I think she is a woman to know."

"I should like to verify your pleasant anticipations.

There are many beautiful American women, hard, bright, and snappy. They are too eager, too restless, too self-assertive," Beauford slowly said. "Their absence of manner does not imply unfamiliarity with social customs. It only indicates their social skepticism, their morbid love of change and their distrust of the fixedness of even the most prominent position at home! It seems to me the men push each other out, and these self-crowned queens fall with them! What becomes of them in the lightning changes of American fortune, Admiral?"

Walton seized his hat and umbrella and paused for a reply. "God alone knows! I do not! I suppose they are as adaptable in sliding down the social scale as in creeping up. I have never met a superior European woman who deliberately married an American! The unquestioned merit of many American men goes for naught; and certainly the freedom of woman, as to property, movement, and personal volition should tempt a class of superior foreign women to America. Strange to say it does not! And the advantages of such attempts are evident! It is from European women of the humbler classes the American nation is recruited. There is a material betterment in the motto: 'Westward, Ho!' a social one, never! America is un-Americanizing itself rapidly. It apes foreign society rules founded on conditions which do not exist there! And it is the spirit of Yankee-land which withers the conservatism needed to build up a solidified people. With little encouragement from nature, in frozen Canada, the social plan of England is yearly perfecting! A pathless ocean seems to separate Canada and the States!"

"To what do you attribute the American social

unrest?" said Beauford gravely as the two men sauntered from the club.

"To the subordination of everything to money! Nothing is real in America but the money-getting craze,
and every human game in Yankee-land has its objective
point in a final money victory or defeat," the sailor
stoutly said. "Hartley killed himself for his money.
Evelyn will be hunted systematically in America for
her money! See here, Beauford, I expect you to
meet my sister. She's a Yorkshire woman you must
know, and don't forget to think about Jervaux."

"Most willingly, Admiral, I am curious to see your
niece also as the one American woman who is yet a
charming possibility. I shall be in town till after their
arrival and it goes without saying, I will be glad to
have you visit the Priory."

"Bright fellow, Beauford," mused Admiral Walton,
as the stately young patrician disappeared. "It is a
pity he has no definite aim in life!" Horatio Walton's
definite aim was to disembarrass himself gracefully of
the general affairs of his gently exigent sister! "I
must run down to Liverpool and meet them! Caroline,
I suppose, is more than ordinarily helpless, and Evelyn must be looked to. Her fortune, her youth can not
be too jealously guarded!"

And on the swaying deck of the great liner, near the
orphaned heiress, in patient, plotting self-counsel, the
falcon eyes of Carl Stein were reading the stars as he
dreamed of the victory of the "Cause without a Name,"
—the awful propaganda whose flag is a crimson stain!
His heart was tied by all the madness of a perverted
nature on the unspoken code whose sequence is the
doom of modern society. "Revolution—Destruction
—Annihilation."

Carl Stein's life had been a bitter struggle! His boyhood was stern and unlovely. Self-nurtured, in spite of poverty's grinding attrition, the mature intellect of the man swept the whole field of human knowledge. Despising the jingle of phraseology, the glittering varnish of self-evolved eloquence, his mind was braced to the conflict of great thought. An omnivorous reader, a robust thinker, an acute observer of his fellowmen, his heart was embittered by the passions of a high-souled scorn of self-crowned aristocracy, unslaked revenge, and a black hatred surged in his heart as he recalled the fate of his father. Moritz Stein's birth as a member of the burgher class, had held his splendid talents under the yoke of subjection to the supercilious petty nobles of his native Saxony. With eyes flashing in defiance, the ardent thinker had followed, mutely, the swaggering officers and waterfly court officials of years!

Maddened with the ills of his time, crazed with the fever of forty-eight, it was a fitting close to Moritz Stein's unhappy life, that his life-blood stained the paving stones of Dresden, when desperate Bakunin screamed "Never mind the houses! Let them be blown into the air!" Stein was dead before Michael Bakunin led the remnant of his devoted followers to Friberg! On the 10th of May, 1849, at, Chemnitz, the fetters closed on the arch-anarchists wrists. The world's boldest soul languished ten years in gloomy Konigstein —in the awful underground casemates of "Peter and Paul's" fortress on the icy Neva, or in the wilds of Siberia!

When Bakunin fled under the "Stars and Stripes" from Siberia to Japan, and touched American soil, he found, in 1861, the United States filled with the veterans of Irish, Italian, Hungarian, German, and Russian Revolution as well as the crazed fugitives of French revolt!

Even the arch-prophet of Destruction dared not to fulminate as yet his terrific creed of the utter annihilation of society, state, the church, aristocracy and accumulated wealth!

While, after wearying out England's hospitality (finding the United States not ripe for revolution), the father of Nihilism abetted the Polish rising of '63, and deserted by Herzen, Marx, Ogareff, and Kelsieff, threw himself into the arms of the International Society, the orphaned son of Moritz Stein was crawling out of the misery of his childhood.

Embittered by his father's death, struggling through the University of Heidelberg, where his splendid talents could not be concealed, Carl Stein, in the ardor of a wild youth, cast himself into Bakunin's power at Lausanne, in September, 1867.

There, in the safe retreat, guarded by the snowy ramparts of the Alps, Carl Stein learned from the lips of his father's "destroying prophet," the details of his sire's dying hours.

His legacy of hatred was increased by a mysterious influence, denying him a professorship at the University of Berlin, when the brilliant young German scholar was called later to Bakunin's dying bed at Berne in 1878. Carl Stein well knew that the hostile action was a punishment for his father's bold stand, as well as his own suspected relations with the nihilistic propaganda!

"Turn your eyes, Carl, to the United States!" said the moribund conspirator. "Here we have to fight despotism in Russia, aristocracy on the Continent, feudal conservatism in England! The Latin races are not capable of continued self-devotion! Here the army, church, and upper classes can only be reached by gradual disaffection! We must sow the seeds of Revolution and educate generations! In America there is but one engine of power—Gold!—There is no actual repression there! The tyranny is of the plutocrat alone! Without money, you can never fight the battles of the cause in America! Go there, my best disciple! Your talents will lead you into higher circles! Let your objective point be *one* great fortune! If you, Carl Stein, can find one golden heap unguarded, pour out its yellow flood in action! Money is the ammunition of your battle there! The stolen dollars, robbed from the toiler, may be, in your hands, the grape-shot of a last forlorn stand! I am wearied! Hegel's philosophy, Kant's and Fichte's dreaming will not alone overturn the social system! In America, the press, place, the ballot—all can be bought! Devote your life to the attack on one great fortune! Win it for your cause! Here, the Italian and French secret societies, the Polish, German, and Russian brotherhoods are provincial and bounded by racial lines! The 'International' has dropped into the rut of a mere squabble over hours, privileges, and wages! Revolution, utter annihilation of all the trammels of state, church and society alone will lead to the freedom of enslaved humanity. Go and trust to yourself alone. Fear, bribery, ambition, may conquer others! Son of my truest friend, you are my chosen disciple! You are as high in the councils of Revolution as man can climb! Go and light the Holy Fire."

These boyhood memories, these awful counsels stirred Carl Stein's steadfast soul as the steamer leaped over the wave! Courteous and deferential, he had disarmed Evelyn Hartley's suspicions! The lonely heiress turned to the brilliant companionship of the gifted free-lance!

When Fastnet Light cast its cheering ray over the black waters of the Irish coast, Stein communed with the stars rising from the mystic East, whence the waves of humanity have followed the sun westward.

"Can she be gained over? Strange woman! An unawakened Galatea! She would never waken to life under my wooing! Another!—One of the brotherhood!" He paced the deck in deepest thought! "She is defenseless, inexperienced! Her mother a petted self-indulgent fool! The old lawyer will delve with the property! This admiral? He will have his scheme! Pure revolution would appall her! She loves that shadowy ideal called 'her country!' To make her the priestess of a new era! To regenerate and lift up! To be a representative great American woman! Dare I counsel at Lausanne with the 'Great Council!' The fame of her fortune would precede her! Others would spread their nets! With Switzerland, our only safe base of operations, she would be too near us. In Germany, I might retain my social intimacy! The years of toil have thrown this fortune almost within my grasp! The money—the women, do we need them both. They will settle in England! I must contrive to be made one of their circle. Can I watch her from Switzerland? I must! The time is ripe! Her money, in our hands, would carry our penniless 'advance guard' into the field of action! It must be done. The millions shall be ours!"—But the stars swept on in silence!   .

CHAPTER III

"SHALL we stay here forever, uncle? I am tired of this inactivity! This house might as well be on the rock of St. Helena!"

Admiral Walton laid down his *Times* and glanced curiously at Miss Evelyn Hartley, who was nervously tapping her foot as she gazed out of a window in the Grand Hotel at London. The driving rain hid even the gloomy beauties of the Nelson Column, and the British Public, pouring by, was represented by a procession of funereal umbrellas, concealing the motley crowd.

"Open-handed mutiny," thought the wily old sailor. "I knew it would come!" His voice was coaxingly bland as he answered, "Let us confer a bit over our breakfast!"

The dissatisfied heiress turned a bright face toward him as they entered their private dining-room and seated themselves.

Three weeks had passed since the imposing retinue of the Hartleys had been swallowed up in the aristocratic privacy of the great caravansera. A thorough entente cordial had been established from the very moment when the admiral led the distinguished-looking beauty down the gang plank to the tug in the Mersey. The veteran, his manners refined and lightened by

53

travel, his mind a treasure-house of fifty years of study
and experience, charmed the lonely girl whose beauty
and freshness lit up his purposeless days. Horatio
Walton had crystallized into the classic egotism of the
London "habitué." But the influence of Evelyn Hartley's rich young womanhood swept the silent chords
of a forgotten youth! The rush of her romantic ardor
stirred his nature as the breeze of spring moves the
withered branches of a silent forest.

"Has your mother decided upon anything?" he
remarked tentatively, gazing at the anxious eyed
beauty.

"I believe, after Doctor Rheingold's exhaustive study
of the subject, she will finally decide on Askern
Waters.   She wishes to renew her Yorkshire memories but what is to become of us? I will not be
immured in that obscure corner! You must devise a
plan!"

"Have you mentioned your own feelings on this
subject to her?" quietly said Walton, as his niece
paused, a bright glow of defiant indignation bringing
the roses to her cheek.

"No!" replied Evelyn.   "Her whole life has been a
record of self-satisfaction. My dear father left her to
her own devices! She never consulted him! To consider my future for a moment, to follow anything but
her own caprices or the advice of Rheingold, would
be an impossibility!"

"Poor Hartley!" muttered Walton, as he addressed
himself to his tea-cup.   "And this Doctor fellow?
How long has he been your mother's guardian angel?"

"It is a matter of years!" shortly said the heiress.
The subject was evidently distasteful.

"Caroline is a singular being," mused the admiral.

"The same unvarying sweetness, an unshakable mental indolence, yet ever this cat-like watchfulness in carrying every point! How shall we act in this, my child? It is useless to take your mother into our councils!"

"If she were settled in her own establishment, we might travel," quickly responded Evelyn. "You could go abroad with me. It would be easy to find some business pretext of your own, I can not see the United Kingdom while under her dominion. I long for storied France, and old Germany, and Italy, always Italy! Every lake of Switzerland is pictured in my mind! You must remember this is my first voyage. The world I have longed to see lies before me!"

The admiral bent his calm blue eyes kindly on the impulsive girl's face. "Give me an hour to think it over. I will take a run down to the club. This afternoon we can have a conference. Then I will see your mother."

Horatio Walton hesitated to tell his niece how wide the gulf was in heart between himself and the handsome hypochondriac whose social day was limited to a few formal appearances. Years of absence had only intensified the differences which had held the brother and sister apart in long years of increasing indifference.

"Take me away, out into the real world! The world of life and light, of thought and olden story! I will not offer up my youth on the altar of this monumental selfishness!" said the girl as the admiral took his leave.

"By Jove! I must make a diversion here," reflected Walton as he stepped into his cab. "There is the energy of a Maria Theresa now in Evelyn's fresh heart.

She shall be free from the clinging trammels which tied down her father's nature with the inertia of this dead weight of selfishness!"

Horatio Walton fumed over his cheroot as he looked over his letters in the club smoking-room. "Ha! A letter from Beauford! Here may be relief! Victory!" he gayly cried, as he finished the nobleman's note. "Now! Jervaux Priory is only seven miles from Askern. If I can interest Caroline, she may find occupation for her shallow pride in queening it in one of the finest places in the county! That will give us our freedom!"

The sailor was cheerful as he indited a few lines. "I will prepare the way, and the rest can be left to her own vanity."

Evelyn Hartley was impatient when, on his return, Horatio Walton boldly ventured upon a momentous interview with the exacting invalid.

"Leave all to me, my child. I will return in victory!" he cried in parting, bearing the hopes of the young heiress.

With a gently dissimulated interest in her affairs, Walton laid the subject of the lease of the "Priory" before his sister. He urged it long as she furtively watched him.

"Just the place for you, Caroline. You see Beauford says his solicitors are authorized to let it for one year, or two, if so desired. There you will have every advantage! It's the very spot I would have chosen for you! Beauford will do anything I ask him personally to make it agreeable!" He waited the effect of his discourse. "Shall I write him on your behalf?"

The sailor was on the tenter hooks of impatience.

"I do not know! I can scarcely face the subject so

quickly. I must have Doctor Rheingold's opinion," placidly replied the listener.

"We can not linger here forever in this gloomy hotel," answered Walton. "I certainly can not leave Evelyn alone here with your secluded ways of life! My affairs call me abroad for the winter and I must soon leave you!"

There was a steely protest in the glitter of Caroline Walton's eyes.

"And Evelyn will be almost useless to me in this land, strange to her. It is so inconsiderate of you to leave me helpless when we have been so long separated, Horatio!"

The cat-like voice purred on unheeded.

A grave frown bent the sailor's eyebrows.

"Do you intend to tie Evelyn to your side forever? Have you no thought of her daily life—her future?"

Walton's voice was cold. He feared not the battle after the first gun!

"My daughter will remain in her proper place—near me, to render my existence as tolerable as I can hope," answered the widow, drawing the folds of her Indian shawl closer.

"Have you ascertained her wishes?" said the admiral, with kindling eyes.

"I have never considered it necessary to yield to my child," replied the lady with austerity.

Admiral Walton's answer was to touch the bell.

"Wilson, please ask Miss Hartley to favor me with her company a moment," he slowly remarked.

The look of horror was still on Mrs. Hartley's face when Evelyn entered.

"I have sent for you, my child, to tell you that I shall be called to the Continent and shall probably pass the season and winter in Italy, Switzerland, and Germany. Your mother proposes, I believe, to remain indefinitely here. Do you wish to go with me?"

With an unflinching look of quiet determination the heiress answered, "Certainly, uncle, if you desire it!"

"I do most heartily," cried Walton, as he observed the symptoms of hysterics gathering on the face of Mrs. Hartley, convulsed with an honestly expressed rage.

"Let us retire, Evelyn!" firmly continued the victorious conspirator. "Wilson, you might as well summon Doctor Rheingold!"

"The breach is not widened, my dear niece! It is only your declaration of independence!" said Walton, as the escaping pair reached Evelyn's boudoir. "You must not complicate your position by discussion. Leave all to me. You may as well choose your route in Murray now. It will be a revelation to your mother to face the realities of life!"

With a frightened face Mrs. Hartley's maid begged an interview on behalf of Doctor Rheingold.

"Show the gentleman in, Wilson!" quietly said the admiral, glancing warningly at her as he spoke.

Standing erect in his quarter-deck attitude, Horatio Walton buttoned his Prince Albert in a most formal manner. An exquisite courtesy froze the bustling excited visitor as he hurried in.

"In what can I be of service to you, sir?" placidly questioned the admiral. His perfect self-possession, the evident lack of interest disconcerted the eager Teuton.

"I came to see you, sir, on behalf of Mrs. Hartley," he stammered.

"In regard to what subject, may I venture to ask?"

the sailor said with a cold gleam of his keen blue eye, standing at ease, his eye-glasses in hand, every line of his body, every detail of his costume indicated the man of "savoir faire."

"In relation to Miss Hartley, I am requested—"

"Pardon me, sir!" coldly remarked the listener. "I believe you are Mrs. Hartley's private medical adviser, and in charge of her health. As Miss Hartley's guardian, I distinctly object to any interference on your part in her affairs. My solicitors will forward any correspondence to me, my address will be always found at my bankers."

With an appealing glance at the heiress who was mutely regarding Nelson perched on his column, the medical man beat a hasty retreat.

The tidal train of the next evening bore uncle and niece to Dover. Evelyn Hartley was troubled, in her inmost soul as she saw the "silver streak" before her.

Though the dreamland of romance, arts, and arms lay before her, there was a bitter drop in her cup of happiness. Mrs. Hartley, who had never ceded a point in her life, resolutely declined to communicate with her child.

"Do not grieve, Evelyn," dryly remarked Walton. "Your mother has not forgotten her own comfort. I saw Beauford a moment at the club when I stepped in to register my foreign address. Caroline has taken Jervaux Priory for a year, and Wilson told me your mother had telegraphed for your old tutor, Doctor Stein, at Lausanne, to aid them as general adviser. She has also written a lengthy letter to Judge Fox. I flatter myself mine will reach him first. Let us take our vagabondage lightly! All we have in life is what we gather from day to day."

"And does Lord Beauford leave England?" asked the girl, with a faint show of interest.

"Oh, yes! By the way, we will meet him at Rome or Naples! He will have some delay in arranging the details of his proposed trip to Kashgar and Pamir. The English ambassador at Petersburg must obtain some necessary papers to allow the party to pass through Russian territory. An English face is a poor passport in Central Asia now, if military purposes are suspected! Alfred is a nice fellow and I think you will get on well together. The Waltons and Beaufords are distantly connected by some old marriage. Is this man Stein a man to be relied on? Does your mother trust him?" Horatio Walton was skeptical as to the disinterestedness of all distinguished foreigners.

"He always smoothed over the little ripples in the quiet of our old household," the girl remarked, with a sigh. "Father respected and trusted him. Stein is a demigod in the eyes of Doctor Rheingold. And you know his influence over my mother!" Evelyn Hartley spoke with a bitterness which aroused the admiral.

"I wonder if—" the old sailor ceased abruptly as a pair of dark, earnest eyes quickly flashed an inquiring glance upon his face. The loud cry of "Dover" saved an awkward question, and the travelers were soon intent on the reflection of the great port lights of Calais, gleaming out far over the uncertain waters which defied Napoleon's futile enmity to Albion.

"This is a singular journey, uncle," said Evelyn, as she sought a rest where the maid and valet were watching a pyramid of the absolutely useless impedimenta of the British traveler. "We have no objective point yet. Shall I be a burden to you?"

Horatio Walton laughed as he said, "Let us take a

week in Paris to consider. It will serve to reward you for three weeks of window-gazing in London. I can find out by wire with regard to my Italian business. We are happy wanderers."

On the threshold of the great unknown world, trusting Evelyn Hartley, happy hearted, placed her hopes in her guardian, to whom the Continent was a second home.

As Walton paced the deck, a glow of satisfied feeling illumined his world-worn breast.

Dead to all human passion save avarice and the easy privileges of his social rank, Horatio Walton secretly rejoiced in the estrangement between mother and daughter. "In the future, no one shall reach her heart save through me, if I can win her confidence!"

With an uneasy conscience, memories of days dead and gone, of certain old affiliations with Carbonari and Red Republicans rose up before the man of romantic career. Born with a genius for intrigue, Horatio Walton's early adventures had carried him into strange company.

"Basta!" he cried, as the lights of Calais gleamed out flaming white disks on the darkened waters. "The women are dead and gone! The men scattered or caught in the mills of the gods! I am safe! The past is forever buried."

While the delighted eyes of Evelyn Hartley rested for the first time on the varied splendors of unfamiliar Paris in the Lyons train, Carl Stein was hastening to respond to her mother's summons. The revolutionist had been chafing daily at Lausanne, awaiting the arrival of the last necessary member of the highest council of a league whose name (even in whispers) shook with terror haughty heads though crowned and anointed.

A high Austrian court position held the last member tied to glittering formalities, until he could join the eager circle scattered around the Lake of Geneva, and meeting by stealth. For even in free Switzerland imperial gold was lavished on spies who watched the children of Bakunin. In lonely dells, in obscure haunts, or scattered over the lake in pleasure boats, the tireless conspirators poured out to each other their morbid imaginings or distilled the poison of their perfected creeds.

"It must be a serious quarrel which has divided this family circle," mused Stein, his head pillowed on a rug as the train rushed through the lovely valley of the Loire. His eyes gleamed with a coming triumph. "I shall make the separation permanent," he slowly resolved. "The American princess of Mammon must be kept on the continent. Her nature, emancipated from the selfish weakling, whom nature's laws gave her as a mother, will brook no future control.

"If Rheingold plays his part, the heiress shall find her nearest friend in me. Mere money, ease, and the paltry pleasures of society will satisfy that old figurehead guardian. Yes! I will play the ambassador. In siding with Miss Evelyn, I shall disarm her last suspicion! Fate, kindly fate, is bringing her nearer to me. And the glittering prize, the treasure destined for the Cause, is easier to grasp!"

There was a delicately expressed sympathy in the patience with which Professor Carl Stein listened to Mrs. Hartley's recital when, the dust of travel removed, he was ushered into the presence of Doctor Rheingold's patient.

Firmly declining an invitation to visit Jervaux, to which splendid retreat the opulent widow was soon to depart, Carl Stein accepted the task proposed, of drawing back the errant daughter to the tutelage of her mother.

"I confide entirely in you, Professor," concluded the unyielding invalid. "You may use carte blanche as to your movements and expense. Confer with Doctor Rheingold. He will take the burden from me! And remember that the doors of Jervaux Priory will be open to you as a home! To your efforts for me, you can add your own representations to Judge Fox. This is a delicate commission and Doctor Rheingold will represent me. Your old friendship will render your association in this most effective. I leave all details to you!"

"My presence in Switzerland for some weeks is imperative but I will trace your daughter's movements and you will find me loyal in your cause, madam," said the adviser. "Without intrusion I shall seek out Miss Hartley and you shall be at once informed of her feelings and surroundings."

Two nights later, Carl Stein, a cipher telegram in his pocket, was speeding back to Lausanne. The convocation only waited for him.

"She will be drawn into my power! I must now win the hidden secrets of her heart. As for the future, this weakling Rheingold shall unwittingly serve my purposes." For as the physician parted from the departing emissary, Stein suddenly grasped his hands and whispered, "I see your future campaign to the very end. When I demand help from you, shall I have it?" and the startled body physician quailed before Carl Stein's eagle glance as he murmured, "Yes!"

Professor Carl Stein was in a particularly good humor as his fiacre bore him through the Place de la Concorde

at Paris on his way to the Lyons station. His
cold eye rested curiously on the glittering equipages,
and the stream of pedestrians moving along the river
bank. "Just in time! I can telegraph for an answer
at Lyons and find where the 'Alpine Club' meets!
After the council I can follow my roving commission!
I can fan the quarrel adroitly. I care not where egotistic vanity may leave the empty-headed widow!
She is incapable of a great thought, an unselfish action!
Her life has been one act of fetich worship! But
this earnest-eyed girl! She can be swept off her feet
by a wave of feeling! Shall it be love or a high
ambition! Patience! Time has been my best friend!"

He started as a woman in rags, bearing a thin-faced
child in her arms, avoiding a dashing equipage, was
nearly cut down by his modest equipage. In the splendid "britska" a dreamy-eyed sultana lifted her painted
brows as he threw a few silver coins to the frightened
wretch.

"So it is ever! Vice in gilded chariots rides down
honest want! Has Time no remedy?" he snarled, his
brows contracting as the devil of revenge awoke in
him. His cheerful mood vanished as his eye fell on the
obelisk cleaving the air on the spot where a Capêt's
sacred blood splashed the stones while the drums beat
in derision of the Abbe Edgeworth's parting words,
"Son of Saint Louis, ascend to Heaven!"

"Here the people had once their will! They had the
courage of despair!" mused the embittered German.

"Will the day come again when numbers will bear
down their oppressors! Alas!" he sighed, "there was only
the brief struggle of a few aristocrats! Revolution then
meant an amelioration! When the great army of toilers rise against the invincibly armed hordes of aristoc-

racy now, they will be mowed down by the perfection of murderous machinery! With the wealth, the war material of the world, the means of communication in the hands of the tyrants of the throne and the brutal money kings, there is but one agent, the nameless terror of dynamite!

"Bakunin was right! The ultra-nihilists are logical! Thrones must be emptied by assassination! Palaces wrecked! Wealth must shudder in its bed of doom! First, individuals, then the sordid oppressors of the poor, last the whole social system! Will the touch of fire, petroleum's hidden work, Nobel's awful portable volcano, not sweep the rats in terror before the day of doom!

"The Nineteenth Century must have its climax!" he groaned. "The days of 'forty-eight' were days of aspiration, of heroic sacrifice! But it was too near the bloody travail of ninety-three! The experiment of American liberty has failed! Money grinds the defenseless poor under its heavy wheels! The tryanny of Europe continues! The continental world stands in arms waiting some fretful tyrant's nod! England rots to its downfall! And the hour is ripe! Let this year of eighteen ninety lead on to eighteen ninety-three! If a generation has to die, better die in a wild struggle, sweeping away the oppressors in one holocaust, with their revolted slaves, than to fight each other at the beck of half-insane despots! It will come! The twentieth century will open in the crash of the wildest storm mankind has ever breasted!

"Yes! Bakunin!" cried the maddened dreamer, "your black pall of utter annihilation shall cover the grave of modern society! But two things remain to achieve," he muttered, as he forced his way through the throng

at the station," the first is to bring America into line
with European revolution. The brutality of the Yankee
plutocracy will do its destined work! The other, to
baffle and entrap the wily Roman Church! Through-
out the world its shaven minions preach peace! Its
arm is long! It knows no time! Its policy is eternal!"

Carl Stein gazed on Notre Dame's twin towers rising gray and hoary in majestic outline.

"All this must come down! Naught but Bakunin's
prisoned curse of dynamite will overthrow these
temples of priestly craft! For fourteen centuries the
paltry fables of Rome have been doled out there
to the hungry human heart!"

The screaming whistles broke the spell as the
anarchist mechanically threw himself into the first
vacant seat!

"On, onward! Let the work go on! Death in the
struggle of humanity is the open gateway of eternal
freedom!"

Moody, bitter and with memories of the injuries of
his orphaned youth, Stein's robust nature exulted in
gloating passion, as he read the few lines of a dispatch at Lyons.

To-morrow night.   Territet.

The shades of evening were softly veiling the splendid panorama of the Alps as the anarchist stepped
from his train almost under the shadows of the Castle
of Chillon. The dreamy lake, from gleaming sap-
phire-blue put on its mighty mantle of gray fog, when
Carl Stein scaled the dizzy crags of Territet, on the
inclined railway. A thousand feet above the lake, a
lovely summer resort was the appointed place of rendezvous of the Alpine Club. Under the guise of con-

tinental journalists, the assembled conspirators of the International, the Latin secret societies, the Repub-licans, anarchists, and the Slavic assassins of nihilism could safely meet in the unfrequented inn.

In the guise of tourists, several loiterers eyed the traveler as he bent his steps toward the broad porti-coes of the quaint old chalêt, planted on a beetling crag overhanging the lake.

Stein's arrival was secretly noted, for a grave-faced steward approached. "The reunion will be one hour after the *table-d'hôte*. It will be held in the banquet-ing hall above. The excursion to the mountains will then be arranged."

The professor bowed in silence. His quick eye had caught the highest sign of the Council. The man who summoned his strange confederate on this calm even-ing in eighty-nine dreamed not of a guillotine which loomed up before La Roquette in days to come.

Yet, Ravachol was doomed to die under the trian-gular knife!

As the sun sank and the blackened shadows of Chil-lon's massive walls were hidden in the gloom of night, Carl Stein's eyes were fixed on the time-defying towers, in whose vaults beneath the lake Bonnivard dragged the chain of tyranny for hopeless years!

"Eternal spirit of the chainless mind!" cried the anarchist in Byron''s impassioned words. "Must the many drag forever the fetters forged by the flinty-hearted aristocrats? Yes! Bakunin! The half century of agitation, fifty years of secret propaganda, the never-ending presentment of Misery's cause to a callous world, all are in vain! It has been all fruitless! Now may the red levin of the sudden stroke bring terror to the world's drones behind their guarded lines of

hirelings, within their palaces watched by pliant lack-
eys! The hour for general action has come! Over
the field of the future struggle we must fire the warning picket shots of our battle to the grim Death!"

Two hours later the lonely crag was deserted by the
chance travelers who had watched the sun sweep over
the chiseled summits of the Savoyard Alps and glitter on awful Mont Blanc, crowned with its eternal
snows. The lake lay throbbing below the exquisite
shores of the Pays de Vaud in an unbroken monody
of the wind-waked song of Freedom.

One by one the qualified members of the "Alpine
Club of Journalists" gathered. To even the acutest
detective the presence of the polyglot assembly would
have occasioned no surprise.

Switzerland's crags and lakes are over-run with the
world's curious idlers. From the English "Milord" in
state, to humble "burschen," knapsack on back, there
is every note in humanity's social gamut ever present.
With no despots to protect, no grinding monopolies
to guard, no upstart class lording it over the humble
citizen, its unviolated hospitality covers the world's
wanderers.

The stolid Swiss, fearless and sturdy, dread not
their great neighbors, standing in embattled ranks,
trembling in mutual fear.

In the quaintly ornamental banqueting room of the
Inn, two score of Revolution's trusted leaders gazed
on the pallid face of the chairman. The world could
never dream of the haunting horrors of the prison which,
for seven long years, held Prince Davidoff under the
water level of the Neva!

To the old ex-aristocrat was assigned the duty of
guiding the Children of Revolt in their triennial delib-
erations.

Admitted one by one, they were scrutinized and tested by a committee of five in the outer room. In little knots, they communed in whispers, around the board, awaiting the call to order. Men with silvered locks, whose youth was wasted in Austrian prison cells, in the narrow chamber of Adrian's mole, or in Siberian huts—desperate souls chafing under the burning wrongs of Cayenne and Noumea, slaves who had shuddered in Poland under the knout, all were gazing in common enthusiasm at the old chairman, whose flashing eyes alone told of his past vigor.

At the hour of nine Davidoff passed the strange assembly in review, giving each a paper—to be read and returned in half an hour. Each group would choose its spokesman. For every European nation was represented, and a dozen were chiefs of special missions. In every variety of garb and personal appearance, the conspirators gathered around long tables, whence the clink of glasses and clouds of rising smoke gave an air of idle enjoyment to the scene. White veterans of the field, heroes of mad attempts, leaders of great outbreaks, and some who had drawn the awful "black lot " busied themselves with the papers, but one woman was present.

Seated by the waxen-faced president was a young woman whose resolute face shone out in the light of the great pile of birchen logs blazing in the huge fireplace.

With her short hair, dark eyes, and animated face— Vera Sassulitch resembled a Bohemian student! Her sister heroines, Sophie Perofska and Louise Michel were far distant! One lying in the nameless grave where the hangman laid her after Alexander's murderers died, together, one defiant band; the other was musing

on the shores of a South Sea island, dreaming of
Paris, once more flooded with flaming petroleum! The
womanly hand which struck down Trepoff, was accentuating in gesture her impassioned whispers.

Before the half hour had expired, Carl Stein had
fixed in his memory every word of the circular.

At a signal from Prince Davidoff, each reader handed
back, in silence, the secret circular. Slowly approaching the fire, the old prisoner of state saw the red
flames lick up the last fragment of the incriminating
papers.

It was a Congress without records. The weighty
matters resolved on were to be later disseminated,
piecemeal, by the secret press, and hidden correspondence bureau.

"Brethren," said the Russian. "Our assembly for
to-morrow is at ten. The session will be held at the
Eagle's Nest. Let all be ready for that hour. We
will now separate for consultation." Before the huge
wooden clock struck ten, the room was deserted by the
gathering. In their apartments, long after midnight,
the associated groups toiled for the morrow's executive session.

Sole representative of his special propaganda, Carl
Stein revolved the great issues before his awakened
mind.

For the first time he had met the associated chiefs
of the Impending Revolution. The control of the
lonely spot had been secured to the Cause by placing
a trusty agent of the General Committee in the occupation of inn-keeper. Even the attendants were of the
working orders of the "Cause without a name!" and
Eagle's Nest, a grove surmounting a convenient knoll,
was safe from the observation of strangers. Its little

observation chalêt was ample for the temporary accommodation of the committee.

"Can these graded elements of human dissension be welded into a compact body?" thought Stein, recalling the order of sequence of the qualified. From militant labor unions, socialistic clubs, organized communists, and advanced anarchists, the extreme was reached in the last section of recognized nihilists. Over all was the secret executive committee of the International. To this body alone was given the right of independent communication, with the head of each of the other bodies. The anarchist paced his lonely room.

Stein's tenacious memory retained the order of proceedings for the morrow. They were "Territorial Reports, Finance, The Situation, Europe, America, Asia, and Africa as Fields, The Future Work and Relations with Governments, The Church, Journalism and Secret Societies."

The work in its final phase, comprised, A Plan of General Action—The Next Meeting Place and Triennial Passwords and Signals, and the Assignments to Duty.

"All this is a matter of mere detail in the arrangement of this meeting. There is but one question before the revolutionists of the world now," thought Stein, as he smoked his last cigar before closing his eyes in dreams of victory. "It is to choose between the reconstruction or destruction of modern institutions. A fair share of the benefits instead of all the burden-bearing of society is denied us by craft or force. The penniless agitator in a shiny coat is no match for the bourgeois, his pocket laden with gold, backed by army, navy, and police! The labor unions,

workingmen's guilds, socialistic clubs, reform societies
and even the communists have for their uttermost
demand, some partial concession in lighter labor, higher
pay, easier taxes, political voice, or a small dole of land
ownership.   These are the men who must be dragged
on to action!   They must be pushed into the conflict!
Their attempt is to ease the yoke until they can bear
it—ours is to cast it off forever—to move as freely in
the light of liberty as Hapsburg, Guelph, or Hohen-
zollern!   Communism is the dead-water stage of
human development!   Its easily reached creature comforts blunt the aspirations of the soul!   It is the Nir-
vana of ignoble mediocrity.   It provides the quails and
manna which revolted the stagnated Israelites! Plato,
Sir Thomas More, Robert Owen, Saint Simon, Father
Rapp, Louis Blanc, Fourier, Barere, and Enfantin, have
failed in making the resultant load of union less than
the sum of the individual burdens. The Utopian folly
of Pantisocracy, the unfruitful seclusion of Brook
Farm, prove the failure of the philosopher to nourish
Humanity on a weak gruel of diluted communism. To
the Shakers, the Oneida Community, to the robust
Mormons, under the lion-hearted Brigham Young,
belong the only successes of communism. With all their
imitators, these schemers only open the door to a morbid social life, the acquisition of cheap land or the in-
dulgence of unrestrained lust! Communism," Stein
sneered, "is the condition of the half-developed savages
of the South Sea Islands! It is the division of primary
animal comforts in a tropic wilderness. For what do
we fight? The devoted sons of the red flag!" He
cast his last glance on the unanswering stars as he
threw himself with wildly beating heart on his couch.
"For the world's treasured heritage of human achieve-

ment. For a division of the power, place, honors, wealth, franchises, luxuries, and treasure wrung from the producer, robbed from the masses by conqueror, priest, noble, king, and money autocrat! And in sight of the battlements of wealth and power, striding over the blood-stained paths of the past, the anarchist reaches out his hand to destroy the whole rotten fabric of to-day! It shall not be reconstruction! It can not be! It must be destruction! The twentieth century shall be ushered in by the crash of falling thrones. One decade remains! Our motto, 'No Quarter,' our weapon, dynamite! 'Terror' in the Old World is our means of attack! And in the new! To grasp at money, to control votes, to ally ourselves with party, to get a hold on officials, can we thus prepare for the bloody fields of nineteen hundred! For in the United States, neither haughty nobles, a powerful church nor a strong army daunts us! Our adherents flock there every year! Money must be ours, and then, welcome the fight in the open!"

The anarchist's dreams were of the millions gathered up waiting the loosening hand of one untried and undeveloped woman nature! Evelyn Hartley's fortune haunted the slumbers of the German enthusiast.

It was only when the purpled shadows of the dying day fell to the east of Eagle's Nest that the wild-eyed conspirators closed their dark labors at the hidden rendezvous. The party of moderation vaunted the progress exhibited by the carefully presented reports, while the radicals demanded action. There were knitted brows, shouts of dissent, and the tumult of hostile difference when the final consideration of the plan of action was forced on the motley assembly. Attached to no special group, Carl Stein listened, with a curling lip to the fatal differences of creed between the chosen depositaries of the reactionary power of the world. The anarchists and nihilists urged a series of personal and class attacks upon obnoxious rulers, active enemies, military and police headquarters, demonstrations in great cities and vengeance upon greedy money lords!

To adjourn in disagreements for three years meant the downfall of active terrorism! Victory was wavering in the balance, when a singularly handsome and spirited man of thirty sprang to his feet. His dark, impassioned face, his ringing voice, his reckless eloquence kindled an ardor of sudden enthusiasm. In the undress uniform of an Austrian officer, he was the type of a leader fit to guide a forlorn hope. "Who is he?" eagerly asked Carl Stein, for the speaker had held haughtily aloof during the detail work of the day. His voice roused the German to a mental madness. "Stanislas Oborski, a Polish count, an officer of Honveds and an aide-de-camp of the Austrian Emperor," was the reply of an excited French delegate. In a wild speech the extremist swept his hearers along. "Listen!" he cried, "the night is falling! We shall turn our feet away to face the work of three long years! Shall these golden months be wasted? Who talks of moderation? Let him join the dull-eyed Chinese, the crouching Hindoo, the apathetic Japanese or the droning Mohammedan chanting, the hymns of that arch hypocrite, the camel-driver of Mecca—whose sensual creed has besotted two hundred millions of men! Who talks of moderation? Even as we speak, in Russia, Austria, Germany, England, France, and Italy, twenty-three millions of armed men (the flower of Europe are ranged under the standards ready for a general war of nations. One hundred million of helpless

workers will be exposed to fire and sword. Ruined
homes, starving women, devastated states will be the
result of the gigantic game of steel, gold, and blood!
War is the sport of princes, it is in the wild carnival
of death their thrones are firmer planted. While
these despots, less than a score, lift the finger of a Nero
the human brutes struggle in the arena of the battlefield for the approving smile of a conqueror drunk
with victory. While the masses wield the steel and
from their drudgery, provide the gold, the fields of
Europe will be soaked in the blood of the unprotected
masses. To serve such masters is human villainy.
Away with such servile baseness! I was born an alien
to my kindred. I wear the livery of one of the three
imperial thieves who divided Poland! When the grasping Prussian and the flinty Russian were glutted with
spoil, our patrimony went to Austria. I only haunt
its palaces to revenge our Polish wrongs. My father's
mother died under the lash of a Russian regimental
butcher, in the market place of our Palatinate! Let
the men now herded like sheep be led away from the
shambles. Destroy, break down and punish! The
gilded flies of place and fattened worms of wealth will
be shriveled up in the red fires of revenge? Who has
paved the road to Siberia with skeletons! Who have
thrust natives into the yawning common grave lit by
the torch of war? For whom do you toil? For self-
elected masters! I say to the serf, the peasant, the
wage-laborer, the prisoner, the oppressed, strike back,
strike hard! William the Silent, Henri Quatre, the
great Buckingham, Louis XV., the American Lincoln,
Russia's haughty Alexander, Lord Mayo, England's
haughty Indian viceroy, Garfield, the ruler of fifty
millions, Carter Harrison, were struck behind the lines

of your enemies. Welcome the knife, the bowl, the torch and the bomb! There is not a potentate, a money prince, a palace or fortress safe from your attack! The poor are your brethren! The time is ripe! Let the plan of a general attack on the hydra be decreed! Begin the attack in these years over the civilized world! And the bells of the opening century will ring in your victory!" An awful secret haunted each breast as the conspirators stole away. On the hill, in a sudden friendship, the Polish renegade smiled grimly as Stein cried, "I am with you to the end!"

CHAPTER IV

TWO BIRDS OF PREY—BY THE TIBER—LA BELLE AMERICAINE

THE golden sunlight leaping along the majestic summits of the Pennine Alps lit up the sleeping lake below the lonely inn. Its glittering lances smote the gray canopy of mist as Carl Stein gazed upon Vevey, Clarens, Montreux and castellated Chillon mirrored in the sapphire waters of the lake. His throbbing temples were heated with the mad tide of his blood, coursing as wildly as the rushing Rhone breaking away to the sea!

A sleepless night attested the fire and force of the words poured forth by the handsome Polish renegade who lingered at the foot of a Hapsburg's throne!

Gazing with eagle eyes into the blue vault, his soul exalted in the excitement of the loosening of an avalanche of destruction, the lonely German anarchist felt no concern for the future. He exulted in the first trembling movements of the storm, to be loosed in all its fury, on the shaken European autonomies before the first day of the twentieth century!

Little did he care that he stood alone, the realization of Emerson's terrific description of the rejected human outcast, "a houseless, fatherless, aimless Cain, the man who hears only the sound of his own footsteps in God's resplendent creation!"

A sound as light as the footfall of the panther fell on his ear! He turned his head slowly.

77

Beside him stood Stanislas Oborski, in all the dark beauty of his splendid youth!

"They separate to-day! Only a few chiefs of groups remain. Whither go you? Come with me to Vienna! I would see more of you!" The desperate noble had recognized a soul as daring as his own.

"Brother!" said Stein, "I am to have a private conference with the chief before noon. Wait till then! If I can not go on your way, I will meet you soon on my return from Italy!" The two Birds of Prey knew each other by instinct.

They wandered in converse till the avocations of the day called the sleepers on the lake shore to life!

On the terrace, trifling with a Galignani over his coffee and cigar, Carl Stein uttered a joyful exclamation. For at Rome, the list of the "Hotel de Russie" bore the names Admiral Horatio Walton, Chevalier, etc., and Miss Evelyn Hartley. In grave contemplation he revolved his plan of action slowly. "I might go to Constance, to Bregenz, with him, and then over the Brenner and meet Miss Evelyn—"

A sudden inspiration smote him! "The very man!" he cried, starting from his chair, as the superb figure of the Austrian officer met his eyes. Oborski was gracefully saluting Prince Davidoff whose distinguished air marked him as a "personage."

"Could I trust him? Whom can I trust?" he cynically mused, forgetting that he had forfeited the trust and esteem of the sons of men himself! "Let me think! It would add one great general to marshal our flagging cohorts! This man is a born leader!"

The remaining members of the Alpine Club were scattered in knots of allied comrades over the hills, while Oborski and Stein watched the pseudo-journalists disappear, hour by hour, to meet the waiting trains and boats! Their diverging paths led the disciples of distinction far away to distant haunts of murder hatching. A numb feeling chilled all hearts for the tidings they bore to the farthest corners of the future field were the stern orders for a series of violent demonstrations, individual reprisals, and terrifying attacks, taking advantage of all local causes of quarrel!

The great simultaneous opening of a bloody destructive warfare was to wait the signal of the secret Great Council through the veteran Davidoff.

Each departing group had its special orders, its rallying point and code of signals!

To detached agents of the highest rank, men like Count Oborski, fearless souls of the mould of Stein, was given the dangerous work of exciting and bringing on collision when the times were ripe for dynamite's horrid work.

"My son!" solemnly closed Davidoff's secret orders to Stein, "seek not in the United States to ally yourself unto parties! No people, given a ballot, dare own the ultimate purposes of our creed! Secret societies, reckless politicians, the disappointed and unsuccessful, are your aim! Watch all strikes, incipient riots, exciting political junctures and times of distress! A noted man struck down, a millionaire's private car blown to pieces, a monopolists' pleasure yacht burned, a police scare, a conflict with the militia, all these are incidents of our propaganda! In times of stress, a few intelligent and desperate men can embroil the two great classes, the rich and the poor!

"Seek to break the integrity of the centralized union of States! The American ballot is useless to us, unless you can control the election of one State

governor by massing the whole Socialistic vote!
Then, act boldly. If a member of our order he will
find a way to protect, to pardon, perhaps to throw the
arsenals and munitions of a state at our disposal in
Nineteen Hundred. Example is contagious! Opposition breeds contention! That will bring about repression! We will answer with aggression, with startling
secret vengeance, or open terrorism! The resulting
tumult will lead to destruction, the ultimate logical
result!

"Stein, we must destroy the State, to make the
future freeman! Read and study Bakunin's Geneva
speech of '68—'The first lie is *God*—the second is
Right.'

"Once penetrated with a clear conviction of your
own 'Might,' you will be able to destroy this mere
notion of '*Right*.'

"Waste no time, Stein, when you have challenged
your American wage-workers, to tell you why two
hundred arch-millionaires hold sixty millions of American citizens, in a lower slavery than the Czar does
his timorous, ignorant subjects!

"You Americans have not the excuse of ignorance,
or the shield of cowardice! They are a restless sea,
pent-up now!

"Teach them to move! One effort and the resistless masses will spurn the scum of their enslavers and
retake the priceless millions on millions stolen from
them in bonds, lands, franchises and capital's unearned exactions!

"Your course is forcible possession first, then division! Who owns your railroads? Not the sweating
fools who built them and gave away lands, franchises
and monopoly's exactions to the thieves in power!

Whose are the broad lands your citizens en mass acquired as a national property? They are held by the "Barons of Boodle!'

"Go! America's great battle is to be the Water loo of the tyrant Capital. Be it yours to open the fight! If you should fall, you will be the Arnold Winkelried of the modern human race! Die in harness —not in the trappings of a slave! Let your masters die with you and precede you to the gloomy Styx!"

The pallid old prisoner of state was Hell's high-priest as he delivered this invocation to the Furies!

With the intent to visit his proposed victim, to establish an active secret correspondence with the most deadly of American "destructionists" and to draw Oborski to his heart in closest ties, Carl Stein went forth to Constance, with the splendid noble, weaving webs, dreaming dreams he dared not make known to mortal!

Carl Stein's simple preparations for his Roman pilgrimage needed but one day at Lausanne. While he secured his papers and prepared for a leisurely visit to the Italian capital and Vienna, he keenly studied the dashing nobleman to whom he was strangely drawn. "Let the brethren separate," gayly cried Oborski, "while I pay my homage to the shade of the mighty Gibbon. For twenty years he studied the tort-uous path of unceasing revolution which led to the Decline of the Roman Empire, that great community where patrician vice and the luxury of wealth rotted away the antique man! The same poison affects now the over-pampered nations of modern Europe! Thought, principle, leading to bold and aggressive action, is needed to overturn the modern system of the world. Even as Luther, Zwingli and Calvin threw down the

tottering walls of spiritual Rome!—Mazzini, Marx,
and Bakunin are their modern prototypes in this civic
warfare! They prove how the final conflict to the
death is forced on us by repression and coercion!
Mazzini cherished the idea of general amelioration
and improvement, retaining the fable of God! His
dreamy mind shunned the logical results of self-defense!
He feared to meet armed brutality with an anonymous
assassination! He could not see that our tyrants are
self-sentenced and any suffering man is a natural executioner! . . . Marx aimed to redistribute and equalize
the burden of modern society, yet finding compromise
futile, saw the liberty of man in the red flames of the
commune! Negation of religion, a denial of the rights
of aristocracy and capital must lead on to the struggle
to break our chains forever. Philosophy, thought, and
action lead up to the 'fierce divine light of Freedom,
shining on the altar whereat Bakunin alone remains
the High-Priest of vindicated Nature!

"It is to men like you and I the leadership is given"
of the hosts, who, breaking their chains, will destroy
our foes!

"The road is clear! we must storm the heights!"

As the train dashed through the beautiful vistas of
the Canton of Vaud, Carl Stein marveled at the fasci-
cinations of the versatile Polish Palatine. Arts, romance, languages, literature, poesy and the graceful
enthusiasm of his rich youth and ardent nature made
Stanislas Oborski a star of fascination. Traveled and
cultured, with the graceful elegance of Viennas' exclusive salons lending its charm, he was an arch-jesuit
lurking in the anterooms of the most ceremonial court
of Europe.

"Come to me at Vienna, my brother, after your Italian pilgrimage is done! You can, in a few days journey, see the effects of the artful divisions of the Slavs by the Teutonic modern policy. Ah! Our Slavs are ripe for anarchy, for nihilism, but the adroit division of Poland between Prussia, Russia and Austria, prevents our Czechs being cemented to the reactionary party of Russia. Old Pogodin was right! The great Slav convention of Moscow in 1867 was a failure. Panslavism died under the repression of the iron Russian Czar, and the adroitness of the Austrian Emperor. While Germany beats our Polish brethren into its ranks, and Russia enslaves them, Austria flatters us with place and power! Austria aims to seduce each warm-hearted Polish leader. I am tied to the frivolities of a court! Revolution, to be successful, must be bloody and general! The world must be wrapped in flame! The line of our enemies will break in some weak spot! Russian nihilists are selfish in their local efforts! The Jews are the dead weight of the world, bearing no generous burdens of the great social movement! The Germans aim to break down mere militarism, the French are erratic, the Italians and Spanish not to be trusted, and revolution in Great Britain is an impossibility. A few less hours, a little more wage, and the stolid British toiler grunts in comfort at his trough!

"It is in America that the bold, bright, fearless masses whose fathers died by thousands for the abstract principle of *black* emancipation must break their *own* chains by an onslaught in the name of Humanity! I could welcome a death in that great struggle, with men like you at my side! And yet, you will smile when you meet me in Vienna, and see me, an Oborski, a lackey like the rest, with only a bit more gold lace than the palace menials and a few more medals on my breast."

In sunlight and shade, while threading the mountain chains, and sweeping over the matchless blue waters of Constance, Carl Stein was swept along by the swift tide of the handsome noble's enthusiasm!

"Who could resist such a man?" thought Stein, as he plunged into the shaded cañons of the Tyrol where Andreas Hôfer died for liberty! The scheming anarchist was on his way to plot for the empire of a human heart! To gain the confidence of "the beautiful Miss Hartley," the fame of whose millions was augmented by the queenly beauty of the young daughter of the West!

"I must not tarry! Such a glittering prize will be fought for by the nobles of continental Europe. American gold regilds to-day the faded scutcheon of even the haughtiest of the nobles."

Resolute and clear-sighted, just, even to his foes in his intellectual judgments, Carl Stein felt that his middle age, his severe intellect, his lack of the smaller agréments of fashionable life, as well as his past relation, barred him forever from aspiring to be a suitor!

As he swept down the slopes of fertile Lombardy, and his delighted eyes gazed upon the richness of Upper Italy, he knew that the romance of the land would appeal to the unawakened heart of the heiress.

"If I had Oborski's years, his graces, his personal fascination, I might enter the lists"—and the idea of another possessing Evelyn Hartley seemed to the man, who had watched her splendid nature round into classic lines, to be the desecration of a shrine!

For, in her young spring-time of beauty, the fair American was an exquisitely lovely Psyche, whom all worshiped but as yet none had dared to love!

To her, Eros was as yet the dainty spirit hovering
in her dreams!

"If she drifts out on a sea of pleasure, she is lost
to the higher life, lost to the great Cause, and the
silken curtains of Love's rosy bowers will shut out
the cries of the toilers who drudge in her far away
industrial army."

Carl Stein was conscious of the deference paid to a
prosperous exterior. As he descended from his carriage, in the courtyard of the "Hotel de Russie," his
entrée in Rome was that of a visitor of distinction.
Thanks to David Hartley's legacy, his state of gentleman was no burden to him. Under the lights of the
court, where the ilex trees shaded his table, he listened to the plash of the fountains and the echoing
songs of light-hearted students, wandering in the
moonlight on the heights of the Pincian far above.

In a reverie of delight, for the spell of classic Rome
was upon him, he was awakened by the clash of a
stately carriage in the court. He was revolving his
social début in the city by the Tiber, for he knew that
the admiral and his lovely ward were still at the
hotel. In arriving late he had only learned that the
visitors he sought were by right of Admiral Walton's
rank and cosmopolitan social position, guests at a
Quirinal dinner.

Gazing idly at the carriage, he noted a tall, distinguished Briton, with the patrician seal of England's
best blood stamped on his handsome features, busied
in handing out a lady whose rich attire and distinction invoked the frank admiration of the graceful Italian jeunesse dorée who saluted, hat in hand. There
was no mistaking the clean-cut features of Admiral
Walton, resplendent in his uniform and flushed with
the evening's pleasures.

"It is the beautiful American, Alphonse!" said a
young attaché near him, dropping his eyeglass, as
the vision of loveliness vanished up the marble stair,
"and the Lord Beauford, her English admirer! Her
fortune is immense. Alas! The Lord Beauford is
the 'ami intimè.' They ride in the Borghese Garden
daily!"

"I must be about my work," muttered Stein, as he
sought his apartments. "Love may lock the gateway
before me! This may need the noble Count Palatine
Oborski's help! I shall watch the Englishman!"

There was a frank pleasure in Evelyn Hartley's
glance of welcome as Doctor Carl Stein, with punctilious ceremony approached the beautiful neophyte
in the beau monde, under the marble arcade where
she sat at dèjeuner with the admiral on the morrow

"I greet you by the Tiber, where we have so often
wandered in thought!" said Evelyn, a bright smile
lighting up her face.

Lord Alfred Beauford acknowledged with reserve
the presentation of Doctor Carl Stein of Heidelberg.

"Deuce take the fellow! I hope he will not cut in
on our ride," muttered Beauford as he tugged at his
tawny mustache. "Some one of these German dreamers, eloquent over an upturned arch or the foot of a
broken statue!"

"Do you make a stay in Rome, Doctor," cheerily
queried the Admiral. He was glad of the new arrival
to share his duties as cicerone. The glow of youthful
romance had long since faded from Horatio Walton's
mind! A perfectly well-ordered life was his.—He
enjoyed the freedom from daily avocation, and a little
dabbling in intrigue, watching the schemes of epicurean

diplomats, crested with star and order—the sly plots of Cardinal and Monseigneur, and the dangerous skirmishes veiled by soft Italian eyes.

"I have some researches at the Vatican library to make, Admiral," guardedly remarked Stein, "I am relaxing a little. I have been in England also!" He glanced meaningly at his pupil.

"Then you can tell me all the news after dinner," said Evelyn brightly, as she rose. "Will you dine with us this evening?"

The doctor bowed in acceptance as Lord Beauford hurriedly said, "Pray, Miss Evelyn, allow me to remind you of our ride at three! I fear it will be our last for some weeks!" The nobleman spoke dejectedly. Under Stein's bushy brows his eyes eagerly watched the heiress.

"Do you leave us then, so soon, Lord Beauford, for the Asian ride?" She spoke with regret and concern, but no sentiment.

"Thank heavens! she is free as yet!" thought Stein. "She is waking to the social world, its varied panorama, not as yet to the master passion!"

"I have to run over to Venice to see my chosen comrade for the Khivan trip! He has a bit of a fever! By the way, he's a jolly good fellow. An American, too,—'Phil Maitland.'"

Evelyn started in glad surprise. "Of Harvard?" she asked anxiously.

"Certainly!" said Beauford, "and from your region —Cleveland, is it? Here's his picture! Do you happen to know him?"

The beauty laughed as she returned the photograph.

"He was my father's ward and the Prince Charming of my days in short frocks! I thought he was in China. I am sure he has not heard of our loss!"

"Very possibly," said Beauford, with interest. "Phil has been in the South Seas and Borneo and came home via Brindisi to go with me! We are 'old "shikarees"!' We met first in India, tiger shooting!"

"I wonder if he would know me now!" mused Evelyn. "If he has ever seen your face, he could hardly forget it," neatly answered Beauford, with a bit of a blush, as he caught Stein's eye. "I must nurse him up. I am afraid his sickness may delay us too late for this season, and I've some awkward letters from my solicitors about some law business. If he does not mend, I shall take him over to Adolf Schwartzenburg's castle in Hungary. I am going there hunting."

"Do you then think your trip will be given up?" The American heiress' cheeks bore a deeper tint of rose as she met Beauford's eye.

"It depends on the lawyers, Miss Evelyn. If we delay a year, I shall pass the winter in Vienna. It is very gay there! Admiral, you have friends ⌐here! Why do you not think of it?"

"Decidedly I will! Alfred," said the sailor. He was easily led in the golden path of ease and luxury surrounding his charming ward.

Cunning Carl Stein held his breath. "All things come round," he muttered. "Do you happen to know a Count Stanislas Oborski in Vienna, my lord?" he casually asked.

"A splendid soldier, and the handsomest and noblest exemplar of the old Polish families. His high rank in the Austrian service was given him because his fine old place at Jordanow, closes the only pass in the Carpathians where the Russians could break in! He is an old friend and a daring rider. Have you met him, Doctor?" Lord Beauford was interested in the reserved German.

"We are intimate! We have traveled together in Switzerland!" said the anarchist. "He has asked me to visit his home on the Arva."

"By all means go! It's a royal old domain!" said Beauford. As he saluted the fair American, wandering down the Corso with the Englishman, Stein satisfied himself of the extent of the growing intimacy.

"She is safe yet! It looks well! As yet only a congenial companionship. He evidently admires her. The electric spark is hidden in the clouds as yet. Cold and phlegmatic English nature! He is a formal 'proper' man of rank! Love has never smote his harp of Life! The sounding strings are silent! And Evelyn, grand, noble, her eyes opening to the glories of the new existence of 'high life', her womanly heart is yet untroubled!" He was free to soliloquize in safety.

"Certainly, Beauford's polished aplomb and social qualities will draw them much together, and he owns the fine old seat of Jervaux Priory where Rheingold is now languishing over the silly-minded widow! But yet—" thought Stein.

"Beauford is not the man to sound her nature!" decided Stein as he bent his steps toward St. Peters. "Mightier far than strength of nerve, or sinew, or the sway of magic potent over sun and star, is Love! When her royal soul is awakened from its original slumber it will be to the glowing noon of a matchless womanhood, or to the wild rush of a passion not to be bounded by conventionality. Sympathy and high purpose might effect the one, the fascinations of a romantic lover, the other! I can soon tell if Oborski is pitted against this Beauford!

"But here I am at Peter's fane! I must have an

excuse for lingering near them. If they go to Vienna, with the Englishman chafing to be off to the lonely trip over 'the Roof of the World,' Oborski may, in the splendors of a stately court, arouse that dormant love of factitious social precedence and patricianism which enslaves the younger American women! I must see Cardinal Rampolla and get my entrée to the Library and archives of the Vatican."

In a half hour of conference, Doctor Carl Stein's superb credentials and letters from the Palatine Oborski, as well as the flavor of his literary name, placed him on the road to the favors of the Prince of the Church.

"You are Catholic, my son?" remarked the suave magnifico.

"Your Eminence," artfully replied Stein, "my life has alternated between the occupations of student and master. As yet my belief is as vague as the clouds, as broad as the sea!"

"Doctor Stein, I am glad to meet you as a scholar, —sad to know your probable adherence to the later traditions of grand old Heidelberg. First, Catholicism, then Calvinism, now Materialism ; finally—what will be your religious teachings there? You—pantheist, atheist, materialist, come to the treasure-house of Mother Church for the garnered knowledge of nineteen hundred years! What have your ecstatic national philosophers accomplished? Philosophy, once the handmaid of Religion, is now its deadliest enemy! You spurn the God-inspired truth of the Church to lean on Plato and Aristotle. You have nothing tangible, modern, but the methods of Bacon and Descartes and Comté with their imitators! Mere methods! Do you know where Spinoza, Hobbs, and Locke, lead to? Pure atheism! And whither does the Idealism of Kant, Fichte, Schelling, and Hegel tend? Toward the anarchy toward which the civilized world is being drawn by this materialistic current in the face of your boasted intellectual freedom!"

"I am a student, not a political economist, your Eminence!" replied Stein gravely.

"Be it as you will, my son!" rejoined the Cardinal, toying with the tassel of his red beretta. "Scholarship in Germany gave us Hegel and his mad devotee, Bakunin, and his disciples will achieve the ruin of the modern world, unless men like yourself come to us and drink here of Catholic conservatism! Look at the evolution of victory in the Catholic policy in Germany! Even the man of Blood and Iron was baffled by the unshaken faith and waiting power of the church! Turn your eyes on modern Italy—a political wreck—a financial ruin! The only really reigning sovereign to-day is Leo XIII. for the wisdom of this august Vicar of Christ· alone prevents a general European war!

"Your German materialism has drifted into anarchy and fathers the world's ulcer of nihilism! There are but two active powers to save modern civiilzation from the Red Terror! The one is our broad Catholic conservatism, the balance-wheel of the whole world, aided by the strange reinforcement of Russian military energy. Stamping out nihilism in the blood of its adherents—not of their victims!

"Even now," continued the cardinal, "the Greek Church secretly yearns to come back to us—its orthodox heart beats warmly toward reunion!

"In that blessed hour," said the enthusiastic churchman, "the benign force of God's anointed would shine in peace on a world, disarmed! A world wherein no sword would break the strained peace of armed Europe!

"Germany is wearing itself out in militarism! Its citizens fly to America! Under stern repression, the anarchists of the world flock into the open doors of the United States! Unless the evil is counteracted, by the united powers of Russian repression and Catholic wisdom, when the torch of anarchy is lit it will wrap the world in flames "

"Do you think the time of an active attack on the order of existing things has been reached, Your Eminence?" queried the crafty anarchist.

"It is near!" the cardinal sadly replied. "Men of rank, bitter malcontents, unbridled natures, enthusiasts of the higher classes are scattered over the whole world! The secret reports of the church enable us to feel the pulse of the world monthly. There is nothing to shake or break, in the slavish calm of the East, or in the darkness of Africa, or the barbarity of the South Sea Islands. Practical military anarchy has been the rule in the Latin-American republics since 1820, when they deafened their ears to the warning voice of Mother Church! It is in heaving, convulsive Europe, and fevered America, the chosen home of Freedom, that the desperate attack of the anarchist on property, society, the home, the family government, yea, even God, will soon drench a world in blood!

"I do not gainsay the mechanical and material triumphs of the nineteenth century! I do maintain that the collective morality of the age is wrecked!"

"And will the church take part in the struggle you fear?" Stein gravely questioned

"The Cossack will guard his mighty sweep of Empire from the Baltic to the Pacific, from the White

Sea to the Dardanelles! The Holy Church, recogniz-
ing the necessary interdependence of capital and labor,
insisting on peace, will rally to the defense of an
imperilled social system, every loyal child of its communion! You know our attitude toward secret societies! Their amazing development in the United States
baffles the police, as well as the thinker and law giver!

"To the Catholic Church is given the police of the
human mind in the twentieth century, and even if the
shock of battle be terrible (as the warfare will be
cruel, unusual and bloody), from the sea of human
woe, the grand old Rock of Peter will rise, at once a
monument, a fortress, and a refuge!

"Doctor Stein," said the cardinal rising. "In the
Dark Ages—Holy Church preserved the heritage of
human knowledge, of classic love, and fostered the
arts! In the Red Revolution of the Twentieth Century, it will preserve by its unflinching adherence
to the Right, the worthy social institutions found
necessary for man and man! We are ready to meet
it! The proud men who, drunk with Bakunin's fantastic expansion of Hegelism, are to themselves a law,
a rule, a God;—who are mob, judges, juries and
executioners at once—who are the fallen angels of
this cycle, will yield yet to us! The darkness of
anonymous and cowardly anarchistic fury must
yield to the Light which shines from Calvary! You
are a generation younger than I! You may live to
see the horrid scenes of the great anarchistic general
revolution. I will not see the final victory of the
Right, but the propaganda of Hell will fail. The
Hosts of Heaven will fight for us! No one ever threw
himself yet against the Rock of Peter without God's
vengeance! Where is mighty Napoleon's empire? A

memory! A bloody vision of the Past! And the Church, serene and great, was never as grand as now, when the eyes of the world turn instinctively to the Fisherman's successor for guidance, sympathy, and help! The Church will throw its invincible mantle over the hearth and home!"

As Doctor Carl Stein drove past Adrian's mole, he wondered if the keen-eyed cardinal spoke prompted by secret reports of his dark belief? Did the vigorous churchman know of the threatened general attack on life, property and society! "We watch and spy on them! why not they on us?" And, brave as he was, Carl Stein trembled at the memories of Netchayeff, whose infamous betrayal of Bakunin's dark plans, brought two hundred of the secret brotherhood into the hands of the hangman or under the knout! "These priests are wily, they have gold, they work on woman-hood's credulity. May there not be a modern 'Netch-ayeff' in our midst?"

And Carl Stein, as he arrayed himself for the din-ner party of his intended dupe, passed in review every face at the secret meeting by the shores of blue Lake Leman! "We were quadruple the apostles in number! Was there even one Judas?"

"Human nature! alas! ever untrue to its highest self-imposed obligations!" The gloomy anarchist failed to see that the spy and traitor to their dark purposes would only in the extreme verify their own doctrine of personal freedom and unrestrained human volition! Treason to the truth itself, would verify Bakunin's code of the absolute destruction of all things—even conventional human character.

While the afternoon sun threw a warmer glow on the cardinal's red vestments as he watched the Ger-

man savant leave his presence, the old dignitary made
a few notes.

"Dangerous—to be watched—past history suspicious"—and affixing the name of Carl Stein, folded
it in the credentials the student philosopher had presented.

Under the witching influence of these sunny hours,
Lord Alfred Beauford rode through the arched shades
of the Borghese at the side of Evelyn Hartley. A
strange cameraderie drew them together. Beauford
was alone in the world! The aspiring American
maiden doubly so by the embittered alienation of her
vain and egotistic mother. As, in the weeks of the
rapidly growing friendship, with womanly frankness,
Evelyn Hartley unveiled her unsullied feelings to
the calm patrician, this gentle trust opened to him
vistas of a bright, clear, brave womanhood. Unconscious of the keen interest of the veteran traveler,
warmed with the fresh feelings of the realization of
her varied studies, the lonely heiress gave him her
confidence and led him on to the knowledge of a different femininity than the coldly conventional good
"society form" of his own circle.

The instinctive distrust of innocence led her away
from the jaded epicurianism of the admiral. His self-
restraint, his veteran coolness, the induration of his
heart was as evident as the perfect polish of the
manners which were his social armor.

Already, though his fires of life were waning, Horatio Walton dreamed of being the arbiter of his ward's
destiny, and under the silver-gray olives planned to
broaden and extend his influence. Certain pleasures
had not wholly lost their zest, the control of money,
with its sense of concrete power, yet allured him,

and the sailor clubman furtively regarded each day's
unfolding of the nature of the lovely girl, now blos-
soming into its fruition!

In Alfred Beauford, Evelyn met the haughty
selfrespect and high pride of an elevated nature.
Confined within the limits of caste, stately and undemonstrative, the young noble had yet the real glow of
manhood on his brow, and to an irreproachable manner, added a certain respect, dignified courtesy, and
deference which was a mute flattery to the daughter
of a self-made American inventor.

Past moss-green fountains, through shaded alleys,
down into dells where a ruined marble faun peeped
through the neglected foliage, on out by the red, dusty
woods where, basket on back, the sullen peasants
trudged, the nobly mated couple rode.

Bits of old adventure, glimpses of travel, stories
of his world-wanderings, made Beauford's conversation
a mosaic of varied romance. It was with heightened
color and dreamy eyes, the handsome American guided
her tired thoroughbred through the maze of the evening Corso on the Pincian. Music floated away on the
thin air, and the sun threw his last rays on the dome
of St. Peters. All unconscious of her growing fame,
Evelyn Hartley rode, ignoring the admiring glances
of cavalieri, tourists and the flaneurs of fashion who all
well knew by Rumor's tongue, the potency of the
Hartley millions.

Suddenly an exquisite face in a carriage caught her
eye. A woman of twenty-five, robed in deepest black,
was leaning forward with an eager smile of surprise.

Turning her head, Evelyn Hartley saw Lord Beauford bowing to his horse's mane. The curve of the
Corso swept the equestrians away and the heiress only

noted a duenna-like companion in the carriage bending her head in conference with the beautiful stranger. "She is very lovely," murmured Evelyn Hartley, as her escort followed with his eyes the now distant carriage.

"Isabel Ventnor was the reigning beauty five years ago and her appearance on 'presentation' was a social event! I did not know of her arrival. When she married General Dunham and went to India, all was bright before her. Dunham died a few months ago, a victim of the Indian climate. I was not aware of her return!"

"You know her well?" hazarded the heiress. Something in Beauford's voice touched her heart.

"We were nearest neighbors. Lord Ventnor and my father were fellow-diplomats together. I have not seen her since I went to South America. I was absent from England when she married. Poor Isabel! You surely saw the Hall. It is only three miles from Jervaux! I beg pardon," said Beauford, "I forgot that you have not yet seen my Yorkshire home!"

"No! I was away when my mother leased your country seat!" The girl's heart smote her at the estrangement which left her homeless.

"You will see the finest place in Yorkshire when you go there. I presume Lady Dunham will reside at the Hall. You will surely like her. A superior nature!" Beauford was musing as he turned his horse's head down the incline.

"And am I also a superior person? Is that the reason?" Evelyn Hartley wished to rouse her friend from his passing cloud of sadness.

"You are so different—I beg pardon, Miss Hartley," stammered Beauford, "from all the American women,

I ever met! I feel sure you and Isabel will get on well with each other! As a rule, our people really hold mos. of your sisters off a bit;—they are often unusual types of character to us!"

"And your friend will be glad to see you, Lord Beauford," Evelyn answered.

"After many years! It is strange! As I leave to-morrow night for Vienna, it will be only a glimpse. If 1 can arrange my affairs, Maitland and I will go to the far East as soon as he can enjoy it! I do not wish to wait till Central and Farther Asia has fallen under the hands of the syndicated hotels and Thomas Cook and Son! You are more likely to be near Isabel than I. I presume you will reside with your mother this winter?"

"I may remain on the Continent!" confusedly said Evelyn. "I have a wish to see German civilization at home. I have been largely indebted to its poets and authors for my later hours of soul-communion. I can not seem to get in accord with French thought! There is an unrest in the national character which disconcerts and baffles me! And if your friend does not immediately mend?" she said, as they turned into the Hotel de Russie gardens.

"I will go out alone! I have little to call me back to England. But I shall certainly see you before we leave!"

There was that in his hopeless manner which told of a haunting sorrow, a passionate longing, "wild with all regret." To the American girl it called up the kisses "by hopeless fancy feigned on lips that are for others,"—"the days that are no more!"

While Evelyn Hartley in state entertained the brilliant anarchist, at a dinner, served cozily "en famille"

—in their private dining-rooms, the Admiral falling a
victim to Stein's versatile and sparkling conversation,
the heiress, bit by bit, unraveled the purport of the
professor's visit, half tourist visit, half concealed
embassy.

With an intuition surprising to the scholar, Evelyn
Hartley said as they watched the far-off light gleaming from immortal Angelo's dome, "I have submitted
the question of my future residence during my minority and the period of the trust to my guardians in
writing. I feel, Professor, that my education should
have ended at the nursery door were I to tie myself
to my mother's incessant caprices. The great world
opens its arms to me! The world of Thought! The
grand chorus of Homer, Dante, Shakespeare, Goethe,
Cervantes, Milton, Racine, is borne along by throbbing hearts to-day! I have entered the portals of the
treasure houses of antiquity! My eyes have rested
on the castles of the great Italians. The roar of London, the fever of Paris, the dreamy beauty of Sorrento,
the awful silence of the Colosseum, all have swept away
the veil of distance, the eclipse of my pent-up childhood."

"Wherever the human heart has beat in aspiration,
where the dust of ages lingers in the ruined palaces of
the Cæsars by the storied Rhine, in the great scenes
of the awakened life of man since the Dark Ages, were
lit up by the Renaissance, there is my place!

"Not sitting with folded hands linked to an alien
soul in a tyrant body! I will be of the great world!
I will feel the sweep of its mighty aortal current! I
will joy of its joys! It may be sorrow of its sorrows!
But I shall have lived my life! I am the inheritor of
my father's spirit! The luxuries of intellectual life

denied him, the mingling free handed with the world, on the equality of mental capacity, which he could not reach, are his last and greatest gift to me! His life was a sacrifice to the unyielding demands of an egotistic companion! I have his confidence, his secret counsels binding my living soul to his dead heart! I am subject to no tyranny of selfishness. My life is a high and holy trust. I will live it as an American woman should!

"The trammels of obsolete customs, alien laws, selfish legislation and conventional fetichism shall not doom me in my golden days to sit in shadows, nor with folded hands!

"I shall have the answer of Judge Fox in a few days; with the written sanction of Admiral Walton. I shall fix my residence for the winter in Germany, Switzerland, the Low Countries, Austria or wherever my wandering life studies may lead."

"And later?" Professor Stein eagerly queried.

"When I have fulfilled my father's wishes, I shall return and carry out, at home, the grand unfinished work of his maturer years. This is a declaration of independence, Doctor Stein!" said Evelyn smiling.

"Shall I intimate these views to Mrs. Hartley?" the professor cautiously asked.

"It is as well! I thoroughly appreciate that she has returned to her highest ideal of earthly happiness. To be received as a long absent but repentant member of an English county family! The divergence of the roads is slight. It leads afar in time. I naturally divined the object of your summons to England. I am an American woman and, in heart and spirit, will so remain! There is nothing admirable in life which the institutions of my own country do not give me!

It is only in my own land that woman has received a recognition of her undoubted right to social and intel-. lectual as well as legal equality. Find me a statute on our books degrading woman, it will have the ear marks of radical religious or feudal brutality and injustice; Our women ask for no thrones! They will not be pampered favorites or silenced drudges! They demand a life wherein their sex brings no penalty, and their womanhood is no bar to the exercise of head and heart! Whatever concerns the community is the heritage of Duty to be equally divided between the men and women of America! 1 would not take the glitter of a coronet with its dead weight pressing on my brow. I ask for the freedom of God, of country, of the higher life, of all that is meant by the aspirations of a woman's heart! My life-shall be my own!"

As she turned and left the room, Admiral Walton said calmly to Professor Stein, as he offered a cigar, "My niece. has my full support in her decision, Doctor. Caroline can inflict her imperious self-will upon her servants and attendants. There is no modern warrant for the sacrifice of a human soul. It would save discussion if you would intimate to Mrs. Hartley that the views which I know are shared by Judge Fox. Caroline will not be lonely a moment! She will be busied in the affairs of the one being on earth she loves — herself!"

As Carl Stein walked home under the stars shining on the seven hills where the captive kings of the world were gathered to grace the Roman holiday, he saw the fact of Evelyn Hartley's emancipation. "She drifts toward me! Into my labyrinth! But no ordinary meshes will hold this bright, brave young being! It is an affair of the highest school! To conquer, to enslave a human heart! But for the Cause, her millions shall be poured out! I swear it, even on the ruined altars of mighty Rome!"

There was a dreamy light in Lord Beauford's eyes as he busied himself in preparation for a visit to Lady Dunham.

On his dressing-table the picture of a radiant woman looked up at him. The miniature could not give the splendid tenderness of her violet eyes or the golden wealth of hair shading her fair brows, back to him! He held the costly trifle in his hand and gently laid it on a faded rose which fell from the envelope. Isabel Ventnor's face was pictured in his heart. There was one last look of her eyes which still haunted him! Through silken lashes they were gemmed with sparkling tears! He started, for a voice seemed to whisper, as once, "Good-bye, forever!"

And now, that Death had strangely given back her freedom, the young patrician dared not ask his heart the question of the future. For across his doubting mind, the face of Evelyn Hartley passed, glowing in the bright enthusiasm of her noble soul.

With a sigh Alfred Beauford lifted a letter from the heap of easily recognized trifles. It was in the formal flourish of his solicitors. He opened it, and as his eye ran over the formal lines, a spasm of agony distorted his habitually impassive face.

"This is the end of it all!" he groaned, throwing himself into a great chair. His eyes were riveted to the last paragraph.

"We regret to inform you that the long-threatened proceedings under the 'Incumbered Estates Act,' have been entered upon. We trust your Lordship will aid us in every way to endeavor to prevent this family property being lost forever. It is not without a sense of duty well done, we call your lordship's attention to the fact that the enormous expenses of your father's diplomatic career were the origin of this sad situation. It is not to your own actions or our remissness that the loss of Jervaux Priory can be traced. The lease of one year to Mrs. Caroline Hartley will remain valid, but unless arrangements can be made to discharge the settled incumbrances, a forced sale at the end of the tenant's term will be decreed."

The young noble, for the first time since his manhood, felt the moisture of unshed tears trembling on his eyelid.

"It must go! My life goes with it! What need to tell it to Isabel? The wild horses of Ruin and Despair race faster than human thought! She will know it soon enough!"

And "Good-bye forever" seemed to be voiced once more in the silence as Beauford buried his face in his hands.

BOOK II

CHAPTER V

AFTER MANY YEARS!—A GOOD SAMARITAN—STEIN'S PUP-
PET PLAY

DARKER shadows hovered over Alfred Beauford than
those falling on the deserted by-street from crumbling
palace and lonely church as he slowly sought Lady
Dunham's apartments. The gloomy shades rested on
the young noble's heart!

"I must go! I will look on her face again! But it
will be 'adieu, forevermore!'" he murmured as he read
her few lines. "I shall be here for the winter! I
expect to see you at once. Come to-night." In past
days his heart would have leaped up at the very name
"Isabel," traced in the womanly hand he knew so
well.

"What is there left me now?" he bitterly thought.
"The services are closed to me! Diplomacy has been
the ruin of my house! A profession!" He revolted
at the idea of a hand-to-hand struggle with the thousands of surplus university men of his land.

"To accept some mere pittance and to see Jervaux
Priory the home of some 'Golden dustman!' I will

104

leave England forever! Somewhere in the great East
I will hide myself! To lift the burden hanging over
the estate is impossible!

"Thank God! A duty lies near me! I'll run up
and stay by Phil, poor old chap! From Venice I can
write to Miss Evelyn. What I have to say to Isabel
is soon said. Eighty thousand pounds! They might
as well ask me to move the Rock of Gibraltar into
the dales of Yorkshire!"

His frank manly face was pale, his eyes set and
stern as he toiled up the marble stair of the palace,
whose princely proprietor nursed his poverty at a
distance. The stranger lords of ease, the petted children of fortune dwelt in the great house where the
Orsini and the Colonna, rival gallants, had played the
social comedy for the hand of fair patrician heiresses.
Cardinals in state and priceless lace had swept the
silent halls with their robes, tragedy dark-browed
lingered in the ghostly echoes of the marble pile.

No sadder heart ever beat within the massive walls
than the ruined English noble carried to his tryst with
the lost love of his first youth.

As Lord Beauford entered the waiting-room, draped
with old tapestries and hung with 'cinque-cento' armor,
his listless mood was broken by magic.

Fairer than of old, with gentle womanly eagerness,
Isabel Dunham drew aside the portiére of her brilliant
salon! Standing on the threshold with beaming eyes
of light, her soft draperies clinging to her exquisite
form, the woman he once loved held out the blue-
veined hands he had once kissed! Bewildered, under
the spell of her voice, waking his heart echoes, dazzled by the flash of jewels, Alfred Beauford saw not
the tenderness shining in her face! He only heard
the sweet low words.

"I knew you would come, Alfred!"

Seated by her side, with a few broken words of welcome, he dimly recalled the day of their parting. Even in the meeting by the Tiber! For her golden hair fell over brows as girlish, her blue eyes in their sapphire depths bore no trace of the passing years! The cadence of her voice, the very faint perfume of the Parma violets! It was the same Isabel!

"Have you been ill? You are looking worn!" cried Isabel, her woman heart awakened to a vague danger threatening the present. It was no longer that future toward which she had looked since her foot turned homeward from India.

"Thanks! I am not exactly myself! I was on the eve of leaving Rome. But for this visit, I would be already on my way to Vienna. I have a friend lying ill there."

"You will return at once, I hope?"

Lady Isabel tried no art to quiet the tremor of her voice.

"It is improbable, I fear," slowly said Beauford. "I was on the eve of a three-years' voyage to Central Asia when Maitland, my chum, was stricken down. His condition is serious. As he is an American, and far from his friends, I must join him at once! Philip may be able to go on. I shall, in any case, not return to England. Should the worst happen, which God forbid, I shall yet go on to the East later."

"And has England no place in your heart, Alfred?" impulsively said the anxious woman.

"Tell me of yourself, Isabel," answered Beauford. "As for my future, it is as vague as the way of the winds or the path of the storm. 'The old order changes, you know, and to my father's service for

the Crown, we owe the ruin of our house. My foot
will never cross the threshold of Jervaux Priory, as
master, again! I shall try to lose myself," he faintly
smiled, "in the heart of Asia! For I am doomed to
be the last Beauford."

"Can nothing be done? Is there no way to avert
this?" questioned the beautiful young woman, in whose
kindly eyes tears were trembling. The story of impending disaster then had reached her!

"The case, alas! is a hopeless one!" answered Alfred,
whose eyes told him that Isabel Dunham was suffering also for the sins of the fathers now visited upon
their children.

The woman he had once loved rose and paced the
room with swift strides, pressing her hands to her
temples, and only in the graceful richness of her
womanly form she differed from the shy girl who
lingered under the old oaks of Ventnor to meet him
in the dead days of the past.

"But you must tell me of yourself, Isabel! I would
know of your future, your plans, your life to come!"
Beauford started as she answered. Her voice was
strangely muffled.

"I do not wish to speak of that now." she said,
and he could hear the choking back of a sob. "It will
be all so new, so strange, so lonely! There must be
some way found—your friends—"

"Pardon me," said Beauford, rising, and his voice
took on the icy coldness of the hauteur which comes
of the proud heart's keenest pangs. "I must beg you
to spare me. There is no one who has the right to
go farther than the impending ruin. Humiliation,
shame would follow which I could not bear! Thank
God! I will leave no one to divide my legacy of sor-
ow!"

"Forgive me, Alfred!" Lady Dunham murmured, as she turned her head away. "It seems so hard to lose you, to hear that we shall have a world between us still! Grant me, for the old days, one favor—the last, perhaps!"

"I will do anything," quickly answered Beauford, whose heart was beating wildly, "if you will now tell me of yourself, your future. What may I do that you wish?"

"Promise me that you will not go away—out to that strange far-away world, until you have seen me once more! I have much to say to you! I would tell you some things which I have waited for years to impart. I could not write you. Will you do this? I will not ask you to linger. If your friend is the Maitland who met General Dunham in India, on his hunting tour, he is a man who is worthy of your care. I only ask you not to go till I see you!"

"I will promise, Isabel," said Beauford gently, "for in my words to you, I can feel I am speaking my farewell to Jervaux—to Ventnor!" His voice quickened. He spoke with a strange hard accent of regret. "A woman's hand might well do me a last service— and—of all women, you!"—There was a silence until she said, speaking as if in a dream, "I shall be here for the winter. You will write me of your movements, of your friend, and, as I will do your bidding at home, we must meet!"

"It is well! I shall write. Perhaps even better thus"—her companion said, speaking as if alone. "Now, you owe me your confidence!" There was brightness in her grateful smile as Isabel Dunham briefly sketched the history of the passing years, her plans of continental residence and ultimate return to

England. "As much alone as you are, I have promised Colonel St. Leger to share his wife's loneliness here, till he returns on his promotion and retirement next year. This is my only present plan," concluded Lady Dunham, whose self-control was regained. "You must tell me now of your friend, the beautiful Miss Evelyn Hartley. All Rome knows of her fabulous wealth, her loveliness is already a proverb."

"I shall ask Admiral Walton to bring her to you, Isabel. As he and you are friends, and her mother has taken the Priory for a year, you should know each other. Miss Hartley is the admiral's niece. You would like her, for she is not the type of the bold American heiress whose lance, golden-tipped, rings sharply on the armorial shields of our land!"

"You do not fancy Americans?" softly said Isabel, with half-closed eyes.

"It is a noble land. I admire its institutions. I dislike its people individually, and I confess without reason. The need of rest, of a personal atmosphere, the nimbus of quiet and reserve is unknown to them. In the wild rush of achievement in the last century, the general excitement seems to be carried into their hearts and homes. But this girl has a sunset calm on her noble face."

"I must know her—for your sake!" answered Isabel Dunham, and as her voice trembled in spite of herself, her dreaming eyes noted a bright star falling athwart the blue-black skies of the Campagna. In its golden trail, went out the hope of a life! Isabel Dunham shivered slightly as the thought came to her lonely heart that never again that brightness would light up the blackness infinite beyond.

There was a spell upon them both, for when they

parted with clasped hands, each could feel the life-
blood throbbing in the bounding pulses of a love
done, parted by fate.

"She is wonderfully lovely, the Indian sun has kissed
into a richer bloom the English roses on her face,
but—" mused Alfred Beauford, as his eye noted the
lonely ilex waving on towering hills above him in the
silent night, "her story is an incomplete one! It began 'When I went out to India!' To see me! To tell
me something! What can she tell me that my heart has
not learned in the wild night rides in South America,
on the lonely decks of the ship in the South Pacific.
The story of a woman's fatal instability, of Ventnor's
cold and heartless ambition, of my father's shattered
fortunes, the story of five lost years, of a loveburied
in the tomb of the Past!

"To a man ruined, going out as a wanderer, the
kind 'nepenthe' of silence were better!" And the
sweep of the night winds echoed his last words, "Too
late! Too late!"

Beauford had thrown himself down to sleep, racked
with emotion before fair Isabel Dunham turned from
her mirror. Seated alone, with her golden hair sweeping her delicate face in its loosened folds, she dreamed
the dreams of old days. She was looking at Isabel
Ventnor, once more, the violet-eyed girl who wandered in the shadowed forests of Jervaux with its
lord, the promise of his youth written on his brow.
There under the silver flood of light, with a beating
heart, the beautiful English patrician heard voices
speaking to her gently of the old days. It seemed so
strange, so sad, this midnight vigil. Gazing at herself
with her hands resting idly clasped before her, it was
the ghost of lovely Isabel Ventnor in the glass, which

moved its lips and whispered, "This girl has a sunset calm on her noble face."

It was not of the fair American she thought as sleep came to her tired eyes. It was of a man whose accolade of sorrow and suffering marked him as the prey of Fate. "If I could keep him, if I dared to call him back to tell him that my gold would be poured out to keep the stranger's foot from his hearthstone, would it atone for the past?"

In the unreality of kindly visions of the night, gentle Isabel Dunham found surcease of this new sorrow. It was on the shadowy wings of sleep, her loving heart was borne out over the bounds of sentient sadness, away from the burden of the day. The angel of Forgetfulness touched her throbbing temples. In all the dreams which blessed her rest, she saw no shadow of parting, no sentence traced by the finger of Fate.

Before the anxious Beauford had reached Venice, Isabel Dunham's face was shaded with a paleness telling of a struggle between mind and heart. For, face to face, she had spoken calmly to the girl whose empire over her lost lover's heart she never questioned. In gallant old Admiral Walton's courtly chat, she found leisure to note the noble beauty of the American stranger. Winning and spirited, breathing her pure soul's freshness into the listener, Evelyn Hartley unconsciously disarmed her unsuspected rival. By natural sequence, the history of Beauford's early life followed the American's relation of these later days.

"And you know his friend? Truly the world is shrunken nowadays!" remarked Lady Dunham.

"If Philip Maitland has forgotten his little playmate, I have never ceased to think of him. We hope to meet, for Admiral Walton designs a tour to the

Tyrol and the Swiss lakes. So we may meet at Vienna,
if Lord Beauford takes Philip to Schloss Schwartzenburg."

The girl's frank eyes met Isabel's without reserve.
The rapprochement of youth and glowing womanhood
drew them to each other, aided by the invisible glamour
of a net-work of tender interest in the calm-faced
English noble. "We cannot but be friends," gently said
Isabel Dunham at parting. "We shall be neighbors
next year. My place is the nearest to the Priory and
I will show you all the beauties of Beauford's place.
I know it well!"

Lady Dunham was surprised at the sudden flash
of crimson dyeing Evelyn Hartley's cheeks. "I may
not go to England. It is quite probable I shall
remain on the Continent," said the American as she
took her leave. "But you must come to us. I shall
hold the admiral responsible!"

"He has not spoken yet," thought Lady Dunham,
as Evelyn Hartley's footfall died away. With an
effort at self-deception she gazed upon the violets sent
as Beauford's parting token. In her bosom a cluster
of the fragrant blossoms rose and fell upon a heart
strangely lightened.

For though she feared that the beauty of the west
might shine her down, in her heart the loving woman
could not give up the heart-treasured romance of the
past.

Never to be the same again after christening of lips
pressed in first love is the one man who can never be
wholly another's!

A part of the soul's history, sacred, never to be the
property of any one, is the consecration of the sacred
passion lingering in a woman's heart. In the inmost

shrine of her being, Isabel Dunham tended the altar whereat none might minister but the man whose heart was first her own!

Evelyn Hartley was strangely silent, as their carriage swept around the Corso. The passionate pleading music unlocked her heart. "No wonder that he finds her the fairest of all! Her face is a dream of loveliness!" she mused. With a sudden impulse she turned to the gallant admiral who was gayly exchanging salutes with bright-eyed Italian maids of honor, "Lord Beauford has certainly chosen a wonderfully lovely woman." Walton, hat in hand, carelessly replied, "Isabel is even handsomer now than when she took London by storm! I presume they will wait a season, 'pour les convenances.' But there's no doubt of the marriage. It will join two historic properties. An old dream of the Beaufords."

Though Evelyn Hartley was dreaming of Philip Maitland, lonely and sick nigh unto death in Vienna, this cold reference to Beauford's marriage jarred upon her strangely. Gallant, sincere, accomplished, and high-souled, the reserved young patrician had become insensibly a part of her daily life. "He is a man of another world than ours, a land of sound old conservatism, of ripened manners, of stately and honest pride. In our land, men do not seem to have the time to follow any of the pursuits which make up the high class gentleman. The leisure days are yet to come!" And with a sigh Evelyn Hartley noted the knot of blush roses Beauford had sent in parting, fading one by one!

Lord Beauford woke from the strangest visions of the night to find himeslf surroünded by the chattering crowds of the Milan and Venice station. The breath

of crisp, fresh, salt air from the Adriatic restored him.
The wildest imaginings had thrilled his over-excited
nerves. Under the old oaks of Jervaux he walked
again with Isabel Ventnor, her eyes glowing with the
light of love! "It is all a dream, you are my own
forever," she whispered with loving lips. "We shall
never be parted!" And on the threshold of his father's
halls, the calm-browed American met him, with a
smile, greeting his home coming. "You are waited for,
Lord Beauford!" she cried in her deep, earnest voice,
"Isabel and I have been watching—watching!"

In the chilly gray morning the canal gleamed deep
and cold, the mute gondoliers were Charons watching
funereal barges. Mechanically, Beauford followed his
man to the steps. A grave, professional looking man
with anxious face edged toward the careworn noble.

"Do I address Lord Beauford?" he queried.

Alfred bowed and started as the stranger remarked,
hurriedly, "I am Doctor Valeri. Your friend is at a
dangerous juncture. We had telegraphed to hasten
you. You had left Rome. It may be soon too late for
you to aid!"

The startled Englishman marked not the glories of
the Canalazzo, the sculptured palaces bearing the proud
escutcheons of the masters of the sea, the balconies
whence laughing beauties had showered roses on the
passionate lover swinging on the swelling flood of
emerald in the witching moonlight. The land of Juliet
seemed to him shaded with misery. His ruin—the
baffled heart waves of his second parting from Isabel,
and he was going on, in the coffin-like gondola to
Philip Maitland's death-bed. "I should warn you,
milord, at once, that nothing but the extremest good
fortune can bid us hope for your friend. He brought

a Roman fever here and the marsh malaria has lit its
fires once more! I am told he has property and is a
man of importance in his country. I shall leave the
dispositions as to his preparation for the future to
you. I will fight for his life. But you, his only
friend, must prepare him for death."

Alfred Beauford's impassive face never changed but
his heart was heavy, as he whispered "Poor old Phil!
It's a forlorn hope then!" As the gondola grazed the
marble steps of an old palace, once a warrior's princely
home, he became alert.

"Hobson! I shall want you to send some telegrams
at once!" "His only friend!" The word awakened him
to a sense of duty. With an Englishman's reserve, he
had learned little of Maitland's private history. In
this sudden trouble, the Greek-browed playmate's
face came back to him.

"I will telegraph to Miss Hartley, and to Walton.
The kind old admiral will bring her up! There may
be papers—a will—last wishes! Yes! It is my duty!"

"Can I stay here? I must be with him—to the
last," said Beauford, as the two men ascended the
stair.

"There are two sisters nursing him who relieve each
other! I am very glad you will stay, milord," answered the courtly Italian.

Beauford felt a choking in his throat as he stood by
the bed where, white and ghastly, Philip Maitland
lay, his eyes gleaming with a strange light! With
burning, fevered lips he muttered words none could
follow.

At a sign from the doctor the patient-faced woman
at his side glided into an inner room. The murmur
of consultation broke on Beauford's ear, and his heart

sank as Maitland's wasted hand nervously fingered the draperies of his bed.

On his knees beside the sufferer, Beauford whispered: "Phil, speak to me. It's Beauford."

And the sick man, with trembling lids, sank back in a vain effort to rouse himself at his comrade's voice.

A touch as light as a falling snowflake roused him, and the sister resumed her place at the patient's side.

Lord Alfred's hasty dispositions were soon made.

"Doctor Valeri," he said, with an earnestness almost startling, "Maitland is all I have left! Spare nothing! Call in your professional friends! Let me aid in every way. I will be here night and day!" The good doctor sadly smiled approval as the young noble penned his telegrams. "That will make Walton all right, I know the old sailor's heart. As for Miss Hartley, if she is the woman I hold her to be, her heart will be touched by Phil's lonely struggle with death. He had penned these words:

Maitland's condition is desperate. If you know anything of his affairs, come at once. It may be too late.

While Hobson departed, Lord Beauford listened to gentle Sister Louise, to whom the physician gave the orders of a general to his last leader. "Call on me in any way! My man will be at hand," urged Beauford, and the nurse's beautiful dark eyes shone on him with a grateful flush of womanly sympathy. The young man's eager heart went out to her at once!

Taking her hand Lord Beauford said, "We will work for him together."

"And aid me with your prayers, Sister," the physician murmured, raising his head from his note-book,

The twinkling stars were mirrored in the blue Adriatic and the songless gondoliers sped along like shades of night, in the dusky shadows, when, with a sigh of relief, Beauford opened a dispatch.

Coming to-night.   Meet us.   Thanks for your prompt kindness.

It was signed Evelyn Hartley.

"Then she is still the friend of other years," the Englishman gratefully thought, as he watched the taper faintly gleaming where the sister hovered, in anxious care, over the strong man laid low!

Poor Maitland's gaunt frame, his pale cheek and caverned eye-sockets, proved the desperate onslaught of the insidious enemy.

"He has youth, a strong will, and unsapped vital forces to aid him," said Doctor Valeri, when they stood by the sick man at midnight. The daring rider, the hardy traveler, the handsome young American athlete, could not be known in the still form over whose angular limbs the drapery fell in a ghastly suggestion of the last rest. The feeble tide of Life ebbed to and fro, and Evelyn Hartley's graceful form was familiar for days by Maitland's side before the doctor dared to give Beauford further hope. Admiral Walton's ready suggestion and assistance cheered the little band of helpers. It was idle to dream of any approach to active interference for the sake of the future.

"If he recovers his mind, we may endeavor to gain his wishes," said Valeri, a week later, "but now— only these noble women may be trusted with his fate."

As the days passed in the uncertainty of the seemingly hopeless struggle, Alfred Beauford's undemonstrative nature warmed to an enthusiasm foreign to

his race and blood! Doctor Valeri, tireless and as
true as steel, faced the impalpable foe. And Beauford,
gazing on Evelyn Hartley, knew, day by day, how
sweet and low her voice could be, how unshaken her
constancy, and how warm the womanly heart beating
in a bosom untroubled by the storms of Love! A
graceful presence, bright and brave in her young,
fresh-hearted enthusiasm, the man of a conventional
world saw the noblest side of womanhood!

There were brighter words of encouragement daily
from the assiduous medical man, and a happy circle
gathered to hear Sister Louise report a continued gain
in Maitland's strength. Ten days after Evelyn Hartley brought cheer and hope with her as handmaids,
Philip Maitland opened his eyes to reason. Through
the casement the strains of the band on the Place St.
Mark gently floated, in tender melody.

Sister Louise, with a smothered cry of delight bent
over the sick man's couch.

"Do you know me?" she said as softly as the falling
leaves of the forest drifting down.

"You are an angel. You are watching over me,"
replied Maitland, his hand falling back in exhaustion,
for he had striven to rise as the music swelled out in
its love plaint.

In this hard world of ours the devoted women in the
modest guise of the Sisters of Charity, lingering by the
bed of pain, praying with the unfortunate, closing the
eyes of friend and stranger, are the epitome of unselfish
womanhood.

Panic affrights them not, pestilence appalls not!
War in its grim ravages may not stay their hands
stretched out in peace. Wherever the human heart
suffers, whenever the soul is whelmed in the storms of

sorrow, these blessed ministers of charity are at the sufferer's side. 'In an agnostic age, in a world often callous to the cry of misery, no one has failed to hail these self-devoted workers as worthy of the reward toward which they strive. Braver than the soldier, great in heart, meek and unobtrusive, bright, pure and true, with steadfast step they thread the scenes of human woe, followed by the gratitude of strangers, the love of countless thousands. They are the earthly treasures of the Church!

"Thank *her*, not me," said Doctor Valeri, turning to the gentle nun who blushed under Evelyn Hartley's grateful embrace, and Lord Beauford's hearty greetings. Only the faint glow of the sea-shell's pink upon her delicate cheek told the happy watchers that Sister Louise was a woman, after all, at heart!

On her knees the thankful nurse intoned her murmured prayers to the Mother of Sorrows! The Gentle Star of the Sea!

"I shall stay until he awakens," anxiously said the doctor. "You must be near him, Lord Beauford, you alone! He knows you best of all!"

Through the open door, Admiral Walton, joined the waiting friends, while the Italian lingered until slumber should break its spell!

All started up as Beauford knelt by his friend's bedside. Valeri's lifted finger held them motionless as the agitated watcher said gently, "How is it, Phil? You know me now, old fellow!"

"Have I been here long? You are so kind!" replied Maitland. "Did I get hurt? I am so weak!" He gazed around in astonishment.

"You have been very ill, but you are all right! We will soon have a pop at the tigers," cried the overjoyed Briton. "Now, Phil, tell me who this is."

There were trembling tears in the sweet Sister
Louise's watchful eyes as Maitland gazed at the noble
face of the American heiress. His wasted hand stole
feebly out of its cover.

"Eve Hartley?" he softly said.

Beauford broke down as the stately girl stooped
and kissed his burning brow.

"Your little playmate, Philip!" she whispered.

"Don't leave me, Evelyn!" the sick man cried, as
his eyes roved from one friendly face to another.
"Where is your father? Why is he not here? Ah!"
He closed his eyes in pain as Alfred Beauford laid
his finger on his lips.

A week later Doctor Valeri delivered an oration
which electrified the coterie who were now tired of
watching the shifting shadows of the day, break and
quiver on the dark flood below the meadows.

"I see no reason why you should not be able to
travel as far as Vienna now," said the physician,
addressing Maitland, who was propped up in a nest of
pillows. "I have written a colleague who will meet
you and see you safely off to Schloss Schwartzenburg.
You need the forest hills, keen dry air, the song of
the birds, and the huntsman's chorus!"

"Can he part with you, with Sisters Louise and
Gertrude? Is it safe now, Doctor?" anxiously inquired
Lord Beauford.

"The recovery from our fevers is rapid when a radical change of climate aids!" answered Doctor Valeri
smiling. "I will have several campaigns yet here of
the kind and my field-marshals must aid me!" The
happy Italian glanced tenderly at the meek sisters,
whose dark eyes were glowing under the white badges
of their calling. "Besides, I will trust everything to

Miss Hartley who tells me that Admiral Walton will escort her to Vienna."

"Is this really so?" joyously exclaimed Beauford, turning to stately Evelyn Hartley whose expressive face was tinged with a deeper rose than its wonted hue.

"I have many things to recall to my playmate, the good fairy of my sick-room," said Maitland, whose hazel eyes and clustering golden beard lit up a face less white and pale than in the crisis. His eyes danced merrily. "Beauford, they won't let me talk much! Miss Evelyn has a five-years' budget of home news for me! I am privileged to listen."

"If we go to Asia it may be our last meeting for two years. I wish to know the belle whom I left a child under governesses." Maitland's tender glance was not lost on Beauford. "We will delay a few days at Vienna," added Maitland, "as I wish to meet Professor Stein also."

"Will he join you there?" quickly asked the nobleman.

"He is arranging some business for me in England," gravely answered Evelyn Hartley, "and our winter plans may turn upon it. He will make an admirable cicerone in the city of the Hapsburgs."

The words "business in England" sounded like a knell in Lord Alfred's ear for, in his eager sympathy he had ignored the demands of his solicitors for a conference with a trusted representative on the subject of the future of Jervaux.

"I shall be obliged to remain some time in Vienna myself!" he slowly remarked, "I have friends whom you will like!"

"And it is an old snug harbor of mine," heartily

cried Admiral Walton. "Mark me, Vienna will be the
last citadel of exclusiveness. Steadfast and haughty,
facing clouded futures, the exclusive Court of Vienna
has heed to form and rank! The 'personally con-
ducted' are not the arbiters of Viennese salons!"

"I must telegraph at once and have it out with the
lawyers there. It is only honest," bitterly mused Beauford, "for I may have to give up my Asian trip with
Maitland. I must tell him all! When? Perhaps at
Vienna!"

When a notable gathering at the station attested
the interest in the handsome young American's con-
valescence, but two faces, grown strangely dear, were
absent. Sisters Louise and Gertrude, in their convent
cells, sent up prayers for their departing charge whose
splendid thank-offering was already devoted to their
works of mercy. "You will send us your picture when
you are entirely restored?" shyly said Sister Louise,
in parting. "And ours?" With a gentle laugh, she answered: "we ceased to be women when we became
Sisters. We are all alike! You may remember us!
That will be a picture you will have always with you"

In long later years, Philip Maitland, when his tall
frame was reknit, his feet treading distant paths, could
close his eyes and fancy that the gentle footfall of his
kindly nurse was waking the silence, that her eyes
were shining on him in his dreams. "I shall have your
picture always in my heart, Sister Louise! You are
right!" he said, as he took her hand for the last time.

"It is a gallant gentleman, the young American!"
soliloquized Doctor Valeri as the shrieking train
dragged them from his sight. "And the beautiful one
with the eyes of the doe, shall it be him she will
love? Or the English milord? A noble youth, he

too, can not resist that most gracious presence. She
needs but the Italian warmth to be a wonder, a perfect
beauty of our later day!"

The staid physician himself was not insensible to
Evelyn Hartley's spell, the entrancing thrall of an
ardent woman's graceful self-denial and winning
charm!

"When she comes back to Vienna, I must see how
she has chosen! May the sunlight linger always on
her fair brow!"

The sun streaming in the windows of a splendid
apartment on the Josephplatz brought a touch of the
inherent brightness of Vienna to Philip Maitland's
face as he lay a week later watching Alfred Beauford
hastily disposing of an accumulation of letters. The
merry notes of a quickstep resounded in the great
square where a regimental orchestra was delighting
the mercurial loungers.

"Beauford, where are our friends?" said Maitland,
tossing away a Galignani. "They are at Schönnbrun
for the afternoon. Stein and Count Oborski are show-,
ing them the wonders of the Imperial palaces,"
answered Beauford, locking his dispatch box with a
sigh.

"Do you feel well enough to go on to Schwartzenburg's place, Phil?" abruptly queried Beauford, as he
lit a cheroot and paced up and down the room.

"Are you tired of me? Do you wish to get away?"
said Maitland, twisting over to get a fair look at the
Englishman.

"It's not that, Phil," continued Beauford in a quick,
constrained voice. "I wish to see you comfortable at
Schwartzenburg. I may have to run over to London
on some business, and return by Rome. You will not

be able to go home for a couple of months at any rate. I will tell you all when I return! But I am forced to leave you there. So, if you will arrange your plans with Walton and Miss Hartley, we can leave tomorrow."

"There is nothing wrong—nothing serious, I hope!" exclaimed the American. His intuition told him of a disaster to Beauford.

"I may as well give you the chance to shape your future, Phil," said the patrician, taking a seat at his friend's side. "It is all up with me! Our Asian trip is off for the present. A sudden culmination of impending troubles will leave me a wanderer, dependent on my own efforts!"

"Explain!" demanded the astounded listener. Before Count Oborski's splendid drag with its lithe-limbed Hungarian steeds merrily dashed up, Philip Maitland knew that the storm had broken dark and menacing on his friend's defenseless head.

"I must think! I must find a way to help you!" cried Maitland, in the gravest concern. "I owe my life to you, to your manly chivalry in staying with me to the last! Is there no relief possible?"

"None!" gloomily answered Beauford, "unless I find an Aladdin's lamp! I have been working with the solicitor's agents for these last days. "I will give you the particulars later, when we are alone!" The speaker paused—for Evelyn Hartley's musical laughter came ringing up the stair. A new pang was added to his sorrow as he bitterly thought, "And she must know that I am soon to be a beggar! The one woman I ever—"

He caught the waiting look in Maitland's eyes and hushed the thought uppermost in his mind.

"And your plans, if the worst really happens?" Maitland's deep voice trembled with feeling.

"I may try sheep raising in Australia or ranching in your wild West! To linger here, 'en . evidence,' a ruined English peer were madness!"

"Does Evelyn Hartley know of this?" persisted the listener.

"Not a word!" replied Beauford, "but I fear the proceedings, which are public, may reach her mother! Of course Evelyn would know at once then!" Maitland bit his lip as he noticed how naturally the friendly name dropped from his friend's lips. Ingratitude of human selfish passion! The fever convalescent did not think of the dim watches of the anxious nights when Beauford and Evelyn Hartley, listening to his own labored breathing, forgot the platitudes of the salon!

Hobson (overjoyed at the visit of congratulation) appeared with several cards.

Philip Maitland was able to receive Admiral Walton, Professor Stein and the romantic noble, whose dark eyes burned as he gallantly escorted the American heiress.

On palace duty for one week as Honorary Equerry, Stanislas Oborski was magnificent in the bravery of his corps of the service. Graceful and animated, he looked the fitting descendant of the proud Polish chiefs who boasted that they would uphold the falling heavens on their lance points!

When the buzz of congratulation had ceased, Oborski cordially remarked, "I hope Schloss Schwartzenburg will set you up, Mr. Maitland. The prince has one of the show places of Hungary. You will only miss one graceful charm to aid your recovery!" He inclined his head toward Miss Evelyn. "But you will have the nightingales, and—memory!"

"You are romantic, Count!" measuredly said Beauford.

"It is all that is left to a ruined Pole! To be true to the land of life and love, of song and poetry! The land wet with the blood of heroes! Ah! You smile! I am a member of the Austrian Household! I am not cast for Thaddeus in the Bohemian Girl! I only wait to hear the command 'Charge!' and ride down on the Russian butchers! Listen! I have treasured a letter from my grandfather written, in his own blood, from the depths of a Russian prison! The fairest of our Polish women have died under the knout! I am a man without a country! In the whole world I have no home! There is one word which to the Pole replaces Liberty! Life! Love! It is Vengeance! My romance is of a future wherein empires will roll away as blackened scrolls! When the blood of the tyrant will mingle in the dark stream of the victim's gore! When you are ready for the chase, after I have shown Miss Hartley the lions of Vienna, I may run over and see you! I am at home over there, thanks to the princely bonhomie of Schwartzenburg."

"You are very kind," slowly answered Maitland, "I may leave for America as soon as I can travel!"

Carl Stein started! His panther eyes gleamed in pleasure! One obstacle removed! Beauford was frankly amazed, while Evelyn Hartley bent her serious eyes on Lord Alfred.

He crimsoned, for in the girl's frank face he could read her thoughts.

"Then the Tiber will yield a fairer game than Cashmere's rose-scented vales! It is the olden charm of Isabel!"

"Have you given up Asia, Lord Alfred?" Evelyn ventured.

"I may change my plans materially," replied the Briton, with embarrassment.

"Then I'm out a tiger skin!" genially added Walton. "I say, Beauford! Try a Norway cruise with me!"

Carl Stein cut the gordian knot of cross purposes with a direct question. "And Miss Evelyn?"

"Oh, I am not fond of yachting! If Mrs. St. Leger and Lady Dunham can be persuaded to visit Vienna, then archæology, court balls, music, some German studies, and few excursions in this land of old chivalry, will busy me! I am promised Professor Stein's kind assistance in my studies!"

"I shall be too happy to show you the most delightful society of modern days. Our Court at least is not invaded by the vulgar crowd." Oborski's plumed shako swept the floor as he bowed to the heiress.

"Philip!" murmured Evelyn, as a chance offered, "you must see me before you go home. I have a special charge for you. I have some very important business with Judge Fox. You alone could prudently see him on my behalf!"

"Count on me in any way! I promise," hastily answered Maitland.

"What can have happened?" mused Maitland as the merry party drove away. He did not know of the bitter and final estrangement of mother and daughter —of Stein's artful riveting up of the now impassible barriers! Rheingold as physician, spy, was already, the secret jailer of the hypochondriac woman, and with suppressed glee, Stein had returned, still sealed, Evelyn's letters to her mother.

"My lawyers and my physician can receive any necessary communication!" was her cold response.

"What does this mean, Phil?" said Beauford, his hand laid in friendly cordiality on Maitland's shoulder.

"I am going to become something better than a wanderer. I shall stay in America. Beauford, if you can not arrange your affairs, I have a home there open to you! Come to me!"

Beauford shook his handsome head in dogged resolution. "I shall seek a new life among strangers!"

As he walked to the window he little knew that the man he had saved from the fever's deadly grasp, designed an effort to save Jervaux Priory from a sale under the decrees of law.

"I must get away alone, and find out if this ruin can not be averted! There must be a way, if I have to impound my last acre!" Phil Maitland gazed at his friend whose face bore the silent seal of bitterness riving his heart in twain.

"Shall I begin to pack, sir," inquired the nimble Hobson.

"Get all ready! We take the morning train!" said Beauford, as he addressed a brief letter to Isabel Dunham.

"I am sorry for Lord Beauford," artfully broke in Stein, as Admiral Walton grumbled at the young man's declination of the yachting tour. "His place was one of the finest in England."

"What do you mean, Professor?" asked Evelyn Hartley, as Count Oborski guided his splendid steeds up to the entrance of the Grand Hotel.

"Jervaux Priory and the estates will be sold under the law before a year," bluntly answered Stein. "The late lord's ambassadorial splendor has ruined Lord

Alfred. It was made public through the proceedings when I reached Yorkshire."

"Both will soon be out of the way! The road is clear for Oborski!" thought Stein. He would have lingered, but Evelyn Hartley, pale-faced, and with a strange light in her eyes, sought her room and was invisible until after the gentlemen separated.

CHAPTER VI

'ALL the Americans are a little light-headed, I fancy," commented the Chief de Bureau of the Grand hotel as he entered up a charge of two hundred and thirty-six crowns for a cablegram sent by Miss Evelyn Hartley to Judge Wilkinson Fox of Cleveland, Ohio.

The Viennese clerk had personally dispatched several registered letters, and it was now one o'clock in the morning.

"I hope the great heiress will remember me!" the drowsy cashier murmured. "I suppose all this could wait! A week would bear these tidings on safely but Love rides fast! His winged courses are not swift enough for the wild sweep of passionate youth!"

Late as the hour was, Evelyn Hartley sat in silent commune by her boudoir fire long after Count Obórski and Carl Stein had touched glasses in a red pledge of their dangerous brotherhood.

"I must have a friend!" the heiress sadly mused, as she sat at ease, her unbound hair sweeping in splendid folds over her shoulders. "I cannot speak to Beauford! I can read now the silent agony of his face. Besides, he would think me unwomanly,"—a rosy flush tinted her noble face. "Walton! Is there a heart under the polished marble of his social exterior? Has 'good form' eaten out the last bit of friendliness lingering in his nature? He lives in a world where the gilded chariot crushes those who are overthrown by fate. It is a mad race to keep in the course! Judge Fox is too distant! Lady Dunham! Can two women work together to avert this ruin? And, of all women, ourselves?

"My mother must not know! Stein is a dangerous counselor. He is my mother's ambassador and Rheingold's friend. Ah! For an hour of my father's noble spirit to guide. Philip! Would he understand? Can I tell him all? And yet he is manly. Beauford saved his life! He shall do my bidding, and gratitude as well as honor will seal his lips. He shall report to me the result of Lord Beauford's final efforts, disclose the legal snares, and he must find me a way to save Jervaux. Beauford must not wander away to unknown wilds in this mental torture! I must use Philip! For if he were to return to America, I would be powerless!"

There were smiling angels guarding Evelyn Hartley's rest that night, and when her beautiful dark eyes opened to the light of another day, Maitland and Beauford were speeding away to the castled crags of Schloss Schwartzenburg, and the breath of Transylvania's pines swept, balsam laden, in freshening incense on the fevered brow of the American.

"What's all this I hear from Stein about Beauford's trouble? Has he spoken to you of it, Evelyn?" cautiously asked Admiral Walton, laying down his Galignani and contemplating with pride the stately beauty of his niece who was gracing his late breakfast.

"It seems that his estates are endangered, uncle," answered the girl, busied with the tea service. "Lord

Beauford is most reserved but his air of distress
haunts me! He has not referred to it."

"It's a shame!" bluntly cried the sailor. "Our old
England is daily losing the noblest features of its
national life! Peerages are handed over to the eager
upstarts, old country families disappearing and the
union of blood and land weakens daily! The secret of
our marvelous hold on the empire of the modern
world has been the distribution in the service of church,
crown, and state of men representing a sound aristocracy. In the army, navy and foreign service, our
best blood has done yeoman service. Beauford's father
was a case in point. Mark me, Evelyn, the very recognition of these higher qualities by a grateful Crown
has united them.

"England's ignoble days will come with the rule of
mere money." The veteran waxed wroth. "Men who
are the architects of their own fortunes dare not risk,
will not pour out the golden hoards they have scraped
together! A higher patriotism, a broader culture,
nobler thoughts, and a distinctive moral elevation
clings around a sound aristocracy. Your anarchists
and socialists will never drag down the institutions
of England while the gentry are loyal to the Constitution."

"And what say you of the United States, uncle?"
the girl calmly queried.

"The nobler days of your Republic were its times
of storm and stress, its early struggles, your Revolutionary War brought out Washington, Hamilton, Jefferson, Jay, Adams! Your period of southern and
western development—Clay, Benton, Sam Houston,
Andrew Jackson, Fremont! Your geat Civil War
showed in its lurid light great characters—Grant, Lee,

Sherman, Joe Johnston, Sheridan, Stonewall Jackson!
Your struggles evolved Sumner, Calhoun, Webster, Alexander Stephens! Your statesmen, soldiers, thinkers,
are all men of emergency! It is your foul battening
days of the dollar rule which create your monopolists,
your land-sharks, your brutally vulgar money-kings.
Any measure of social recognition or continued success is impossible in an aristocratic government, for
your Fisks, Goulds, your mere money sharks of every
class. Thank God! all is not for sale in England
yet! I am an old man, Evelyn!" cried the admiral.
"You may see a terrific struggle of anarchy in the
United States! There is a desperate personal envy in
the hatred of your toilers for these swollen money
monsters, thrust forward out of the common herd by
robbery!

"Beware lest the rapidly foreignized mass of American voters becomes fretful and thrusts into its elective
place, men representing socialism! Your native citizens have been singularly good humored and patient!
I can see the signs of imminent danger in America!"

"In what?" calmly replied the startled heiress.

"In the absolute inability of this heaped up wealth,
ground out of your poor, to protect itself! In the
helplessness of your land sharks, syndicate swindlers,
trust bandits, and monopolists to guard their giant
accumulations! You have a trifling standing army, an
ill-assorted National Guard! Some day, these franchises,
monopolies and trumped up titles will be swept into the
common coffers—the vulgar state palaces of your fantastic money barons will go up in flames! Why, your
best people seek Europe now for ease, quiet, study, refinement and safety! The mad race of social vulgarity in
display must end in the 'States!'" growled the admiral.

As he affixed his monocle, he growled: "I'm really told there is no such legal status as 'gentleman' in America! Remember what a gifted despot said: 'Equality is a monster! It fain would be king!'"

"You are mistaken, uncle," firmly said Evelyn. "We have unrestricted political movement, a free press—an ideal Constitution!"

"Bah!" answered Walton. "Some positive affront to Labor, the result of Asiatic immigration, European importation, or the last screw of the labor tyrants will wrap the land in flame. Look at your miniature war in Homestead in your iron regions. It burned itself out! Some graver issue will call your alert, fearless, excitable, people into a tumult, whereupon sectional division and the evolution of great and crafty leaders will break up your Republic into petty fragments. I tell you modern organized manufacturing debases a high-souled people! The old craftsmen were artists. *Your* wage workers are helots! There is more difference in caste to-day between employer and operative in America than divides Brahmin and Pariah in India. The absurd antics of your socially prominent women, mostly thrust up by prosperity from the working class, fosters this growing hatred. As for your organic chartered liberties, the same great-souled woman despot I quoted, remarked: 'The best of possible constitutions is worth nothing when it makes more people unhappy than happy—when brave and honest folk have to drudge, and only the rogues are in clover, because their pockets are filled and nobody punishes them!'

"There you have your American situation of to-day in the words of the great Catherine. It will be a sweeping labor revolt, loosening class jealousy and turning foreign communists loose to plunder the community which will bring up a sharp and bloody revolution in your land. I look at home with pride and confidence to our conservatism in church, state, home life, and graded society. Admiring your rapid—even feverish development, I can see liberalism in religion go on through indifference and materialism to agnosticism. Your welcome to the immigrant debauches your lands and fills it with Europe's refuse, making American citizenship valueless. Your outcast tramps' vote helps to govern your millions of unrepresented mothers and wives! You have carved liberal principles into license. The German grinding-mills have filled your land with glib agitators who bite as well as bark! You have no superior classes to protect you, to stem this tide. You are all grubbing for money together. The man who owns a rolling-mill works as hard in the office as the slave who bundles scrap in the sheds.

'The only difference is that he is at the right end of the mill! His wife wears huge diamonds and perhaps has a traveling court of adventurers in Europe, while he grinds his own life at home into the mill with the blood and bones of his 'fellow-citizens!"

Walton ceased with a sneer at the Republic where the hard Almighty Dollar is God! "Perhaps you are right! I quote again, 'The rich have an astonishing power over humankind, since kings themselves end by respecting those who have made money!"

' You spoke of our women denied the vote, Admiral. Look at your own land!" hotly remarked Evelyn.

"The case is different. The interests of our women are voted on and practically guarded by a select class of the nation who have something at stake! In your large American cities, the rabble certainly rules!"

"Are honor and worth really needful? and if so, surely one should not restrain the desire of emulation and clog it with an insupportable enemy—equality?

"In your land, Evelyn, no position is permanent! You know too well why! In your shifting social scale a line of Beauford's of five-hundred-years' destinction in their country's service is impossible. You produce Denis Kearneys, Tammany coteries, carpet-bag governments!"

The old man sighed as he prepared for his constitutional "Would to God I could help Beauford! But eighty thousand pounds is not hanging on every bush."

"Is that the sum needed to save Jervaux Priory and the estates?" said Miss Hartley.

Walton lit his cheroot at the door. "So I am told," he said. "And it is a shame! Half the rent roll saved and laid away would free the estate in twenty years. It is as safe as a life assurance."

"What is the occupation of a penniless peer? What is his future?" said Evelyn hastily.

"God bless my soul! I never thought of that! Poor Alfred!" cried the admiral as he sought refuge in flight.

While the gay world of Vienna wondered at the impressive beauty of the already famous American heiress, as she sat in her box at the opera that night, even Stanislas Oborski's brilliant word-play palled on her ear. She was dreaming of the methods by which David Hartley's Trust could be handled to realize a certain large sum of money. "I am sure that Judge Fox could find a way if I could see him. He has insisted on some foreign investments." And the beautiful dark eyes grew very serious as the music swelled and wailed in its melodious intensity.

Forgetting the mimic agony of the lovers on the stage, she wandered in mind to the doomed oaks of the ruined peer's stately home. It was her money which engrossed her thoughts. Beside her, his romantic eyes filled with speaking light, the impassioned Polish noble keenly watched her, and plotted for the golden prize. In the rear of the loge, calm, his steady eyes watching the human pageant unrolled before him, Carl Stein, the canker of burning hatred of society in his heart, dreamed over his terrific creeds of general rapine and stealthily conjured up future meshes to ensnare Miss Hartley's money.

Admiral Walton's aristocratic exterior and glittering orders caught the merry eyes of Vienna's laughter-loving, intrigante, feminine free-lances! He dreamed of golden fires of love relit! Ashes of the past, dead embers of time fanned into a last flickering flame!

Miss Hartley's resolute face was bowed over her dispatch box for an hour while her cavalier finished the wee small hours over wine and Strauss waltzes in the court far below her.

The morning sun glittering over the firs and crested pines of the Transylvanian hills, a week later gleamed on Beauford's pale face as he walked down the great avenue of lindens with Maitland. "You are all right here, Phil," he thoughtfully said. "Forester Franz and Steward Obermeyer will make a Yäger of you in a fortnight. I will be back then. I must go over to London and as Isabel Dunham will be at Vienna on my return, I can finish my adieux. Miss Hartley writes me the ladies will join her before my return."

Maitland's cheek was redder than the returning

flush of health, the kindly gift of the pine forest air, when he said simply, as the wagonette drove up, "Can I be of any service to you, Alfred? Even temporarily?" He dared not frame his offer in more explicit terms.

Beauford's lip trembled. "You are a good old boy, Phil. You can help me! Keep on gaining as you have! When I come back, you can run down to Trieste, perhaps, and see me off—for I shall not linger within gossip earshot of my ruin bruited abroad, or lag superfluous' on the social theatre of giddy Vienna!"

"Have you settled whither you will go?" earnestly questioned the tall American.

"It don't matter much as long as it is a fair spread of longitude. Any far corner—or in fact, the longest voyage will do! Probably the travel will be the greatest element of an effacement of the past. It matters little where my feet wander! I only know they will not turn back to old England!"

With a wave of his hand Beauford was gone! Maitland, wandering slowly back to the Schloss, seated himself under a giant spreading elm. A rustic seat under its friendly shade had sheltered happy lovers from olden time. The solitary man read and read again a letter clearly inscribed in Evelyn Hartley's frank, firm hand. Its closing lines arrested his attention, and he pondered sadly as he folded the closely filled sheets.

"You must find out for me the details, every circumstance of this entanglement. I rely on you!"

"Brave, beautiful, kindly Evelyn!" mused Philip Maitland. "May you never know the sacred isolation of a broken heart! Beauford's pride will buoy him up to the very death! I can not break in upon his manly grief."

As he threw down his pen, vainly striving to write a fitting response, an hour later, in his great vaulted chamber at the Schloss, he paced the room, and paused at the open casement. The splendid panorama thrilled his romantic soul.

"Schwartzenburg's very heart life is wrapped up in this grand old domain they say! I know how heavy Alfred Beauford's heart will be as he turns his back on beautiful Jervaux! I would give five years of my life if I had Evelyn Hartley's money!"

While Maitland's eyes were bright and his sinews nerved themselves to their wonted elasticity in the pictured hill of the Austrian's princely domain, Miss Hartley was secretly happy at Vienna. Her first great victory of womanly art thrilled her with happy auguries of the future.

Admiral Horatio Walton, in company with Lord Alfred Beauford, was the secret agent of a sudden commission of the extremest importance in London The old "viveur" was not loth to spend a week in England and privately determined to keep an eye on Beauford and fathom the depths of his troubles.

"Shall you go down to Yorkshire, Walton?" said the careworn young noble.

"Most likely," answered the admiral with caution.

"I'm heartily glad, as you can relieve me of one awkwardness. My visit might otherwise annoy Mrs. Hartley. I hope you will go with me!"

"Certainly!" cried the overjoyed sailor, who secretly fancied he might bear back to the blue Danube the olive-branch of peace.

There was a singular reserve of quiet expectancy hanging over Lady Isabel Dunham and Evelyn Hartley as they leisurely enjoyed the continued attentions of Count Oborski and the all-accomplished Stein. The American girl's heart was beating in anxiety to hear the response of Judge Wilkinson Fox to the dispatches now grown vitally important to her. As yet she had not given her heart's confidence to her gentle companion. Alfred Beauford's name was avoided, with a tacit reserve. The lovely Englishwoman, alone at night, gazing on the sparkling stars murmured to her own heart, "Next week! He comes! But only to part. It may be forever!"

"Can it be that Evelyn Hartley is engaged?" mused the fairest of Anglo-Indian widows as she observed the American girl's feverish unrest on the arrivâl of the through post. Isabel Dunham had not caught up fast Indian mannerisms. The daughter of the Ventnors was above the contamination of garrison manners. General Dunham's pride in Lady Isabel's faultless social bearing gladdened the haughty veteran to the last.

"If I could read her thoughts," the beautiful widow pondered, "I might tell whether Alfred Beauford's love may yet be mine!" Drawing from her breast a golden heart-shaped case, she gazed fixedly at a face pictured therein. "It is never too late for love, Alfred! If you knew the past, even now in sorrow and trouble the star of love might light us to a home in the happy New World, beyond the blue ocean's faintly drawn horizon! Does she love him! Her American correspondence must hold the key!"

Closing the case with haste, Lady Isabel threw herself in a velvet cushioned chair, as the *Chef de Bureau* entered the grand salon. It was a sunshiny morning, a week after Lady Isabel's arrival, when the cashier himself sought Miss Hartley with a handful of important letters.

"Permit me," he bowed, as the graceful American swept into the salon, arrayed for a drive. It was a famous expedition arranged by the courtly Oborski. Stein, Mrs. St. Leger, whose easy Indian indolence rebelled against too much sight-seeing, that keen critic Stein and the dissimilar, but not yet rival, beauties.

"If mademoiselle will kindly sign the receipts."— the polite cashier delivered several registered letters. As the heiress signed the receipts, Mrs. St. Leger, fair and forty-four, faded and *rusée*, swept in, arrayed in war-paint of skillful make-up. A deliberate social campaigner she always "came on the ground" up to every requirement of the code. Oborski, brilliant and with a dash of the barbaric romance of the Slavic noble in his air, entered, followed by the alert and self-possessed Professor Stein. The polished scholar, never flurried, he moved on his orbit without haste or rest. His keen eye, ever calculating personal horoscopes, caught the expression of Evelyn Hartley's face. It was shaded by an intense anxiety. "If I could get a glance at those letters," he thought. His mental flashlight was only quick enough to note the Cleveland stamp on a heavy envelope, and the London appearance of several documents bearing the ear-marks of the stilted law scriveners.

"I deeply regret," said Miss Hartley, raising her deep, frank, dark eyes to Stein's face as if he alone were the ruling intellect, "that the most important business dispatches will claim my attention for the day. If Count Oborski can understand what a deprivation it is, I will be pitied, and shall I say—forgiven for my desertion!"

The wild Hungarian steeds were champing their silver bits beneath the open windows, and the grooms were significantly loud in their attempts to restrain them.

"I will pay the fine of my disobedience. If Mrs. St. Leger will kindly preside, shall I learn of your adventures at dinner if you will be my guests?" While the social element graciously acquiesced, bowing to the stroke of Fate, Stein mused, "Her mother's ultimatum, I suppose, through the lawyers! And I presume, her first annual statement. I must try and reach her correspondence!"

The smiling anarchist was grave under his mask of merriment all day, as he displayed his cultured erudition, in guiding the less æsthetic pleasure seekers. "If it were a private apartment, a palace even, I might reach it; but in this public, well-organized hotel, it would not do! My bribe would be so high, it might ruin me by attracting the attention of the secret police!"

Miss Hartley, in her boudoir, sat down with a beating heart, as the break rolled away, to study the problem of a secret coup of magnitude.

Her doors were locked. Her maid was sent away on an errand of some hours.

"I must think, plan, act alone! and no one shall know but—Philip! I can surely trust the friend of my childhood."

In an hour the ardent girl completed her Portia-like studies. The chaff of her correspondence was laid aside in the traveling dispatch-case, hideous with Chubb's locks. Two documents occupied her in their study for a silent hour. "Dear old friend!" she murmured, as she read for the last time the explicit answers and professional utterances of Judge Wilkinson Fox. "How noble, how prompt, how delightful. It will conceal my identity, and if Philip will serve me, I can act without discovery." With her Baedeker's map spread out, the heiress studied, pencil in hand, and blushed rosy red in the knowledge of her own secret.

"Yes!" she cried, with decision, "Munich is the nearest place of safety. All the others will be under my eye here. I must now send my telegrams and some money. It all depends on Philip's willingness to serve me! He can not refuse! Who ever knew a loyal American gentleman to abandon a country-woman's cause in a strange land? No! He would never think of a denial! He is *his* father's son and I am *my* father's daughter!"

She was surely the embodiment of David Hartley's mental energy, as five minutes later she left her hotel, in simple costume, and nestling in the comfortable shadows of a quiet coupé.

Arrived at her bankers, Miss Evelyn Hartley was so business-like as to astonish the staid gray-haired manager. "I suppose this is a mere bagatelle to the great heiress! How rich these Americans must be!" he said as he received her checks.

"I am to telegraph this two hundred pounds at once, in the name of our bank to its London address. Certainly. It will be available there early to-morrow. And the incognito of Mademoiselle is a matter of honor! The Kaiser, even, trusts our house!" he proudly remarked, with his hand on his breast, "and the other money, in Bank of England notes, and French gold. Five hundred pounds! I shall send it to the hotel by a special messenger in an hour."

The startled clerks rubbed their eyes as their chief escorted the daughter of the West to her carriage.

There was the sparkle of buoyant hope in her speaking eyes.

"To the Telegraph Bureau," she ordered, and her heart beat gayly as her slender fingers traced the lines of three short messages. The nimble keys were clicking before the handsome stranger closed her purse. Magic of money! Delightful and concrete power! The eternal charm and witchery of gold! For the first time in her life, Evelyn Hartley, as her stately head rested at ease, felt the haughty impulse of wealth moving her every pulse-throb!

Her dead father, a general whose legions were embattled gold battalions, lived again in the flash of her dark eye.

"Thanks to my ready gold! I can hide my hand until I know if I can save Jervaux, that grand old manorial estate!"

With a few turns in the Prater, Miss Hartley was able to face the curious crowd of refined loiterers who watched every movement of the great American heiress.

The innocent schemer clapped her hands in delight as she regained the friendly shelter of her rooms. All breathed of friendly rest and silence. Even the maid had not returned.

"I must keep a record of this little campaign," the happy woman murmured as she drew her journal with its mysterious locks from her dispatch-box. Leaning her fair cheek upon a rosy hand, she blushed as she transcribed her messages. "I must destroy these slips! How fortunate I learned something as dear father's volunteer secretary! Whom have I in the world to trust?" The lonely beauty's heart lingered fondly over the memory of the ardent man now lying under the great marble pillar by blue Lake Erie's distant shores.

"He was a man of men!" the orphaned girl cried, as she kissed his picture. She read encouragement in the kindly eyes now fixed forever. "Here is the record 'safe,' " Evelyn said as she relocked her dispatch-box.

Carl Stein would have bounded in rage, cool as he was, had he read the messages which were to draw into action the Hartley millions to keep Lord Beauford in his ancestral rights. The words to the solicitors were simple. "How fortunate I gained that from uncle!" thought Miss Hartley. Before the London fog of another day was choking peer and street-sweeper with impartial grip, Beauford's astonished solicitor read the following lines.

Two hundred pounds remitted to send your agent to Munich. Meet X. Y. Z. at Hotel des Quatre Saisons. Full credentials from me there. Act immediately.

"I think my plan a good one!" mused the novice at intrigue, as she arrayed herself to receive her guests.

"If this Mr. Edgar Alton is trusted with Judge Fox's enormous London financial dealings, he can surely aid me, and shield my name."

Before Evelyn Hartley's dinner guests had separated, Edgar Alton, in his London chambers, was as startled as lonely Philip Maitland under the Schwartzenburg lindens.

Come to Munich. Hotel des Quatre Saisons. Meet my agent, Philip Maitland, who will have the Judge's letters to me, and also my instructions, confidential. Preserve absolute secrecy. Answer,

"I suppose I must go!" reflected the keen-eyed American financier. "Sharp old boy, Fox. Always looks ahead. He gave her this cipher for just such turns. I'm glad to meet Phil Maitland again. But how the deuce is he mixed up in this deal?" With national promptness. Alton dashed off his answer.

Take tidal train. Arrive to-morrow night. Will observe strict silence.

"There is some reason for that girl's high spirits!" crafty Stein decided as he observed the joyous exaltation with which Evelyn Hartley queened it over her table. It had been a day of unalloyed pleasure. Lady Dunham, with quick wit, noted the chivalric empressement of Stanislas Oborski's courtesies as he tenderly gazed at the heiress.

Evelyn Hartley's frank cordiality did not deceive the wary Stein, though the Vienese noble was secretly triumphant. "She is thinking of someone else! I must get that Englishman out of the way!"

"When does Lord Beauford return?" Stein asked in a pause of the merriment.

Evelyn Hartley's face glowed with a tell-tale blush as she said: "My uncle will be here in a week. I have not heard from Lord Beauford."

A lightning flash from Isabel Dunham's eyes searched the face of the fair American. "She speaks the truth!" the happy widow felt. Her heart beat in thankful relief. Carl Stein, deceived by his suspicions, noted her blush. "It is the nobleman! He must be tricked away!" was his mental judgment.

But Philip Maitland was already snugly ensconced in the Vienna night train. "It must be something very important. I hope there's nothing wrong at

Cleveland. Well, thank heaven, I am on the mend now! Can it be that sleek social tabby-cat, her mother?" —These cogitations interested Maitland, as his head pillowed on his rug, he smoked at ease and watched the forest branches waving in the blue night as the train dashed along. He read her words again. "Come at once. You must go to Munich for me on a private matter. It will take a week. No one must know. A carriage will wait for you at noon to-morrow at the Votiv-Kirche." The simple signature "Evelyn" was a word of command to him.

"I suppose she does not care to be watched! Who is annoying her? Not Beauford or her uncle; they are in London! Can it be that cool fellow Stein or this magnificent wooer Oborski? I suppose half the Viennese jeunesse dorée are watching the rich stranger now. I'll go to the 'Schwartzen Adler' on the Ringstrasse and keep dark   Evelyn evidently wishes to tell me her own story. I will treat her as a sister."

Yet as the handsome young American in yager costume dreamily thought of the woman whose trust was so frankly placed in his loyal honor, there was a flutter at his heart *not* indicative of calm, brotherly affection.

"By Jove! I hope she has not promised herself to that romantic figure Oborski. True, he is highly placed at Court, and blue blood only flows in his veins; but all the Polish nobles I ever met were at the last only reckless dreamers, fantastic scallawags! David Hartley's daughter mates with no such adventurer if I can help it! As for Beauford—the case is different!"

And yet, as his eyes closed the American was not enraptured with the idea of an English marriage for the Cleveland heiress! There was no enthusiasm in his contemplation of that possible important social event!

Miss Hartley was satisfied with her day's work as her guests separated for the night. Stanislas Oborski, minister of pleasures, was fain to be satisfied with the announcement of Miss Evelyn's private preoccupation for several days. "You will not miss me for Lady Dunham is an enthusiast already on Vienna." Professor Carl Stein had already developed a singular penchant for the society of Mrs. St. Leger. "This duenna will surely share the beautiful Isabel Dunham's secrets. I fancy Lady Isabel will watch Lord Beauford closely. From a woman's watchful jealousy I may find means to lime my bird to the twig! The American heiress stands in Lady Isabel's path. To carry out my role of Mephisto I must indeed master this blooming military Martha before I can lead the helpless Marguerite of my passion play up to the love mirror where Oborski's face will be burned into her heart!"

The polished erudition and unfailing courtesy of Professor Stein had in fact, swept Madame St. Leger from her feet. She was only accustomed to the banal pottering of Anglo-Indian miltary dawdlers. She was as wax in the hands of the vigorous and all accomplished Stein.

While the two men walked homeward through the streets still filled with revelers, under a deserted arcade, Oborski whispered to Stein: "I had a summons from Davidoff to an extraordinary council here as soon as five of the Grand Executive can be gathered."

"I knew it," said Stein coolly. "I have seen the chief!"

Oborski started. "Then, Stein was his superior in the red propagánda!"

He gazed anxiously around. They were now safe from eavesdroppers. "What is the object?" he humbly queried. Stein faced Oborski in the pale moon-light. "Do you believe in wasting the golden years of anarchy's flowering youth in detached acts of violence? In mere disjointed outbreaks of sporadic revenge?"

Oborski's face was convulsed. "Anything to repay to the Imperial family of the Romanoffs the ruin and devastation of Poland! Revenge, personal, bloody, terrific, is their doom!"

"Precisely," answered Stein, in a chilling voice, "and for ten years the heroes of anarchy have followed to Siberia or the scaffold, the martyrs of this policy of narrow revenge. Is the sandy plain of Poland to be the *only* battle-ground of the twentieth century? Romanoffs spawn quicker than the red death can remove them. To one Cæsar another succeeds! On this narrow platform we have struggled vainly. Can you not see that horror and scorn follow the *personal assassin?* Our battle is against the dominant classes! Your Polish blindness of the mole leaves you groping! We must lift the banner of the Brotherhood of Man! We must widen the field of action! We should over-throw the tyranny of wealth, aristocracy, militarism, monopoly, and light the fires of revolution over the world! Bands of frantic conspirators, gloomily nursing petty local wrongs will never awaken the down-trod-den masses! Look at the world to-day. It is not alone in frozen Russia that tyranny exists! Italy's toilers, Germany's peasants, England's down-trodden workmen, Ireland's outcasts, the French artisan, the

Belgian miner, America's groaning wage-workers, all these sweat under the yoke of Capital, the sign of the modern demon, Plutocracy, which grinds men's bodies and women's souls in a grip more merciless than the Czar's iron-mailed hand of despotism! No! Oborski!—a few mad tracts, a little dabbling in the portable terrors of the bomb and infernal machine, a noisy howl against royalty does not reach the hearts beating in unison with us wherever money has made man its slave! Look at barbaric lands,—the East, China! We have no coherent masses of proselytes there to bring in! We must make anarchy broader, less volcanic, recruit its ranks, restrict needless ferocity, and win over thousands to join us in a broad uprising, a conflict wrapping Europe and America in a sweeping revolutionary flame! We had the impulse in 'forty-eight!' The yearning, the upheaval! We must select a field where wrongs affecting the whole of modern society can be thrown into the scale to fill our ranks! True, we can, by combined effort in Italy, Spain, and the weaker nations, bring on the European conflict! To turn the scale in France, Germany and England, we must arouse the workers of the world! Russia, on which we have wasted our first attack, by sheer inertia of ignorance, will drag along fifty years behind our general advance. No!" said Stein, his eyes flashing like steel sword-points. "We must merge labor-unions, secret societies, socialism and anarchistic uplifting in one organized protest against the tyranny of Money. We seek victory, not martyrdom! Victory is only possible where political power is reachable by the laboring masses, where money, courage, numbers, and a free press and a weak army can aid us! Where no nobility, no reigning family, no hereditary rulers can smother our kindling fires! Your land was sacrificed to the greed of three tyrants! My beloved Germany groans under ten thousand corrupt noble masters and a rotten system. Aristocracy is strong in Germany and England! France needs only the electric impulse of an outbreak elsewhere to break into flame! We must get power—move on, consolidate, organize and fight on broad ground. It can only be done, where I go to perhaps lay down my life for the Cause!"

"It is?" said Oborski, astonished.

"In the land of unredressed wrongs, the United States!" answered Stein solemnly.

CHAPTER VII

AT MUNICH—BEAUFORD'S ADIEU—A STRANGE MARRIAGE—
CALLED BACK—THE DARK ANGEL'S WING—STEIN'S SUM-
MONS—COUNT OBORSKI'S WOOING

"FRITZ! Take this key and bring me a glass of 'Goliath'!" Count Oborski's brow was gloomy as he threw himself on his splendid couch. He was alone! The determined face of Carl Stein haunted him! Though the scholar was now wending his furtive path to his discreetly chosen lair, the noble's nerves were shaken. "Stein his superior now! Did the aspiring German dream of impressing his lofty views upon the anarchistic leaders!" Even the valet's footfall, as he returned with the Pole's special tonic cordial, jarred on his tingling nerves! He seemed to hear, in the silence of the night, the rushing of dark wings, the hoarse murmur of distant voices; the swelling of lurid flames danced before his eyes, and the trampling of a mighty host broke the dim silence of the lonely night.

As his eyes closed, he tried to drive away the Red Spectre, the Cause without a name. "The American. By God! she is an uncrowned queen! She shall be mine! No man must stand between us! Her money, her talent, her splendid presence! What a sensation as Countess Oborski!"

His eyes closed, in heavy sleep, clutching him as with ghostly fingers on his throat! The passionate fantastic fool little knew that his every movement was watched by his confederates! That sturdy, sleek Fritz, a beetle-browed Leporello, murmured: "*No one ever trusted a Pole!* They are all unstable as water! This fellow is a compound of voluptuary, egoist and barbaric poet!"

Lonely Carl Stein from his casement watched the stars in silence. "This secret council! I may have to leave! But passion and vanity will sweep Oborski along to the conquest of this inexperienced American girl! Loneliness will tell! I am sure Admiral Walton will fight off all English or American suitors! The splendid social parade at his niece's expense is the wine of life to the old man of the world! The cardinal point is to get Beauford out of the way! His self-poise, his restrained dignity leads her wandering on, in curiosity, to find the *real* man under all that 'good form!' And he is by no means a fool! It is undeniable the English nobility is the steadiest of our modern days! The old boast 'An English Lord is always somebody—a continental prince *may* or *may not* be a personage.' Yes! His removal is a *sine qua non* of this game of human chess! Once in Oborski's power, her millions shall back our initiatory struggles!

If he refuses—I can reach him in any spot on the habitable globe!"

There was a scowl on the face of the stern, unloved man as he slept—around the rugged crags of his char-acter no tender vine of affection, with its white blos-soms of innocent love had ever clung! Carl Stein's polished intellect reflected no blushing glow of a hu-man heart within! His dark formula of the Brother-hood of Man was rigid in its mathematical logic of fixed demonstration! Borne on by hatred and scorn of others, maddened by the coherent strength of the cultured classes clinging to creed, home, country, and the marriage tie, the anarchist never looked behind to see the dark fiends in his train! His mental vision was blind to the great and simple truth that the new Gospel must be one of Love, not of Hate—of Faith, not of Doubt—of a *clasping* not a *clenching* of human hands!

Yet as the unbending dark enthusiast slept, God's peace wrapped a resting world in slumber, even as a babe sleeps in its mother's arms. For even on the threshold of the twentieth century, with all its vex-ing problems facing the kindly and the good as well as the sons of shadow, the immortal spirit of Love is abroad among men!

> "A gentle sound, an awful light
> Three angels bear the Holy Grail
> With folded feet, in stoles of white
> On sleeping wings they sail!"

Faith, Hope, and Charity are the three blessed angel guardians of the new dispensation of Light! Unseen by Carl Stein, these smiling angels passed the dark dreaming sleeper, whose iron code of destruction, whose red-hot plow-share of the newer law, cleft every human tie which binds in this world, and shattered the golden filaments of Faith leading beyond the stars!

In intellectual pride of the Ego, Carl Stein found God only a myth, a priest's lying invention! Country— a mere shibboleth of the politician. The State, an assemblage of grasping knaves. Society, a mad masquerade, and the family, a worn-out human device!

In every fibre of his perverted system the dark poison of Bakunin rankled! He fought behind the bulwarks of secrecy and cowardice, and dared not come out into the open, face the genius of civilization, and point *one* single noble life—*one* elevating thought, a single *practical* reform produced by anarchy! He dared not, with blinded eyes, gaze on the arena of the sporadic struggle and mark the footstep of the anarchist, red with the blood of innocent or deluded enthusiasts. Dagger and torch, the bowl and the bomb, as new ministers of moral conviction!

Shuddering in the darkness of midnight, driving on—on—by the false lights of Treason, the anarchist would drive the ship of State on the black rocks of Destruction!

And after—after all—only the cold echo of Bakunin's voice from the grave—

NOTHING!

The gloomy sun lit up the façade of the Votiv-Kirche and its sweet bells were chiming noon as Philip Maitland sauntered along the marble porch. The red and brown tints of the turning leaves of the Thuringian forests tinted his cheek.

"Ah!" He sprang nimbly into a carriage, for the

face of Evelyn Hartley's maid, peering anxiously out, met his glance.

"Miss Evelyn is waiting, sir," said the abigail, "in-the Burgplatz garden."

"I was right," conjectured Maitland, as he gazed on the glowing face of Evelyn Hartley, when she lightly sprang into the carriage and directed her coachman to seek the alleys of the Prater. "It *is* Love!" In answering the earnest queries of his country-woman, Philip Maitland was busied until the leafy arches of the park trees shaded them. The carriage stopped. Maitland with growing wonder listened to Miss Hartley's murmur:

"Will you walk with me?" As they wandered along the American noted the carriage moving slowly behind in sight.

"Quite a neat bit of feminine strategy. Evelyn is a social generalissimo of no mean power." Philip concluded, "But whose watchful eyes does she wish to avoid."

An hour later Philip Maitland, seated on a rustic bench, listened to the last words of his enthusiastic charge.

Miss Hartley's cheeks were crimsoned as she paused and raised her beaming eyes to Philip's anxious face. There was an astonishment which Maitland could not conceal. He was in hesitation.

"Can I trust you? Will you be my brother in this? You can see that I can not act alone?" Evelyn's voice was pleading in its musical eloquence.

"Certainly! I will do your bidding. I will go to Munich on the next train! I will use the same discretion as if I were acting for myself. The hardest part of your charge is to keep your secret! Can I do so loyally? Is this not too grave a matter for sudden decision! Your mother! Your uncle! and Judge Fox, your trustee! Have you no duty as regards them?"

Miss Hartley proved her heirship of her father's dauntless will as she gravely replied: "Philip! I have not told you yet,—but my mother and I will lead divided lives! I owe nothing to my mother! I am following my father's wishes as imparted by his daily teaching! His happiness was sacrificed to my mother's cold egotism! They were not to be sundered! I owe to my mother respect, but not the sacrifice of my future, my heart-life, my mental existence! How should she guide *me* who cannot shape her *own* purposes to any end loftier than a pitiable self-worship! As for Uncle Walton, he is worldly, garrulous, and, while loyal and sincere, would never withstand Beauford's direct questioning. Judge Fox does know all and approves of the investment of a block of the trust funds abroad. He urged a similar course upon my father for years as his conservative mind dreads a sudden tumult in the United States. He objects to keeping all the reserve funds of the trust in manufacturing or home railway shares. City property at home is subject to the taxation and handling of machine politicians, the evolution of the saloon loafer. The old lawyer always claimed that the power to centralize our government to be strong enough for absolute safety does not exist in our laws. I have often heard him say that our feverish policy represents the changing and eagerly excited political passions of our voters."

"You are quite a political economist, Evelyn," said Maitland.

"I often listened to my father and Judge Fox in their secret councils. If I have learned anything it is from them. They jointly deplored the extensive influence of our great newspapers which are absolutely free of responsibility and control. Strange to say, our own Western States are liable to political as well as atmospheric cyclones. The storm center of national disturbance is found in the uneasy communities of the Mississippi Valley which seem to resent the payment of any interest, and become enraged under the static burden of the freight on their crops to the seaboard. Now, Philip," said the heiress, brightly, "you can easily divine that the mortgage on the Beauford estates will be charged against my share of the Trust. It is then not necessary to notify Admiral Walton, as my mother can not be affected. There is but one thing needed. It is for you to keep my secret! Will you?"

"I promise to keep it from all but my own heart!" warmly replied Maitland. His voice shook a little as he said slowly, "And you do not wish the man you are risking eighty thousand pounds for, to even know of your noble generosity?"

"Never! That would be fatal!" cried Evelyn, hastily dropping her veil. "Let us go, Philip! You need rest and you must not miss your train, if you are to meet Alton! No one must ever know we have met here! If you encounter any friends at Munich, the galleries, and your loneliness, in Beauford's absence, are an excuse! I trust you as a brother! I have only you to depend upon!" She stood before him,—bright, lovely, and thrilled with a woman's noblest feeling of self-devotion.

Evelyn Hartley did not hear what Maitland murmured as he suddenly caught her hand and kissed it!—

Long after Philip was speeding away toward Munich, Miss Hartley, in the delightful security of her own

room, felt the touch of his lips. By a sudden impulse, as she rose to meet her friends at dinner, she
broke a rose from a bouquet, to which was attached
a simple card "Good-bye."

It was Maitland's covert adieu.

Pausing a moment at the mirror to adjust the rose
in her bosom, Evelyn Hartley's eyes were dreamy as
she felt Maitland's kisses burning on the hand which
held his rose.

"I wonder if he thinks me *unwomanly!*" the heiress
murmured, in sudden alarm.

Afar, sweeping on toward the Bavarian plain, Philip
Maitland reviewed his strange commission!

"Beauford is the luckiest man in God's world!"
thought he, with a sigh. "And I am to be *her brother!*"

A general exclamation of joyful surprise followed
Miss Hartley's astonished remark. "Lord Beauford
returned!" The circle at dinner were mystified as the
steward answered a query. "Admiral Walton has not
arrived. Milord is alone!" In the drawing-room
there was an eager inquiry in Evelyn Hartley's eyes
as she extended her hand to the returning nobleman.
Alfred Beauford's pale face and haggard eyes showed
more than the fatigue of his voyage.

Miss Hartley was startled by Lady Dunham's question. "You are not ill,—suffering?" It was in a grave
voice that Beauford dispelled all doubts. "I am
merely worn with my preparations for departure.   I
am charged, Miss Hartley, with Admiral Walton's
regrets. He was suddenly obliged by important business to leave me in London, though on his way
hither with me. You will have full letters, and he
will be here in a few days!" The grave courtesy with
which Beauford met the convives was unrelieved by

any lifting of the shadows on his brow. Count Oborski's special attentions to the heiress enabled Professor Stein to note the exchange of a whisper between
Beauford and Lady Isabel.

The English beauty moved hastily to a window to
escape the penetrating glance of Stein. Her limbs
were trembling, for in her heart the words of Beauford were echoing the knell of all her budding hopes!

"I leave for Trieste to-morrow, and now quit England *forever?* I must see you to-night!" The by-play
of the salon continued, but the shadow was only lifted
when Lord Beauford took his leave.

"I hope to be permitted to pay my respects to-morrow, as I am going away, Miss Hartley," remarked
the Englishman. "Would you kindly fix an hour, as
I am afraid I shall not see you again soon!"

Evelyn was startled as Beauford spoke. The merry
circle were busied in arranging another Viennese explo-
ration. Poor Isabel Dunham was drawn into the joyous cabal but her anxious eyes strayed to where Beauford, with a face as pale as marble, was earnestly
conversing with the American heiress.

The fair-haired beauty writhed in silent agony, even
while smiling on Stein and Oborski and listening to
Mrs. St. Leger's raptures over the morrow's outing.
"Evelyn has rejected him and I lose him forever! Oh!
God! if I could hold him back!" Lady Dunham dared
not leave before the English peer had closed his formal
visit. "He will send a letter to me at once! I must
escape!" And it was no fictitious "migraine" which
gave her an excuse for retirement. Isabel Dunham
only caught the last sentence of his conversation with
the heiress.

"Of course I will run on to see Phil, but I can get a

direct train to Trieste from Schloss Schwartzenburg. I have wired to Maitland and he will meet me!" He was gone!

Beauford left the two women in dismay!

"*I* have ruined all!" thought Evelyn. "He will follow Philip and meet the solicitor at Munich! His hasty departure must be stayed at all cost!"

"And *I* shall have no chance to win him to my side," bitterly reflected Isabel Dunham. His voyage to Australia would be one of months! Under the pressure of sorrow he might imitate the fantastic Sir Roger Tichborne, whose story is hidden by the waves of the same ocean, hiding the fate of the romantic archduke John of Austria. "He is lost to me, lost forever! It is Kismet! *His* father's folly and *my own* parent's flinty heart have ruined us both!"

Miss Hartley took counsel of her heart as soon as the chevalier Oborski could be dispatched, eager to perfect his plans of pleasure. Professor Stein, as he pressed her hand, murmured meaningly: "I hope there is nothing wrong in England."

Evelyn coldly drew back from his too eager confidence.

"Ah! My bird is shy! Can it be the English lord?" Stein pondered. "But he goes! That is one cardinal point! It leaves the field to my gallant Pole! Now, he must make his running! I will pump Walton on his return."

Ten minutes after Beauford left the salon, at her desk, Evelyn indited a dispatch to Maitland.

"That will do!" the pretty conspirator decided. "If he sends the return message to me, as well as direct to Schwartzenburg, Beauford will surely await his return! I can absolutely trust Philip!"

The gentle woman paused not to question her right to dispose of, in any way, the man whose rose lay on her bosom, the silent knight whose kiss sealed, on her hand, his oath of loyal service.

Under the stars, pacing the long portico of the Hotel, Alfred Beauford walked with Isabel Dunham. A lace veil quickly caught up, shrouded her delicate face, but the eyes, shining on him in the pale moonlight, were burning lamps of love!

In her hopeless yearning, conscious of his stern strength of will, poor Lady Dunham's words faltered on the tongue.

"It is so sudden, so final, this trip. Is there no way to keep you, Alfred?" she murmured.

"I will tell *you* what the others can never know, Isabel," said Beauford. "This voyage may save my life. Absence may teach me philosophy. I could not remain here and face my ruin. I have not slept for a fortnight. Sometimes I fear that my mind is giving away."

"Will you not appeal to your friends, Alfred?" the frightened woman cried, for his voice was as cold as an echo from the tomb. "I can not! The very thought chokes me, and eighty thousand pounds is needed to prevent the final step which parts the title and the estate. My solicitors are baffled. A direct sale would bring in the sum but Jervaux is gone forever in either case. No! I must go out and walk the path of life,—alone!"

The bitterness of his voice cut her like a knife.

"You *shall* not go in ignorance of the past. You must hear what I would say!" Isabel Dunham was clinging to his arm and shaking like a reed in the wind.

Though his heart was racked, Beauford gently said: "It will spare us another pang, Isabel, if our past life goes with the rest. I walked down alone through the old oak alleys of Ventnor where we met in happier days! I think I left my heart there under the drifted leaves! No! Spare yourself, and have pity on me. Do not make it too hard for me, this going away. Tell me of *yourself*—of your future. You will go home?" He spoke sadly and his eyes rested kindly on the gentle woman whose diamond tears glittered through the lace folds

"Take me in," she gasped. "But, I can *write* what I can not say now. By the old days at Ventnor, I beg you, do not sail till you hear from me at Trieste. Will you promise? Give me this grace! It is all so sudden!"

Lord Beauford paused in an alcove and wrote a few lines on a card. "There is the name," he said, his voice sounding harsh and strange. "Alfred Burton, 'Hotel du Crôix de Malte,' Trieste. I bury Beauford at the city gates! My passage is booked for Australia on the steel fourmaster 'Restless.' The mail or telegraph will reach me at the inn."

Isabel Dunham paused at the main entrance.

"I have your word that you will not sail till you have my letter or message? That you will dispatch me on your arrival in Trieste? Something may be needed *at the last!* I can not let you go until I know this!"

Beauford bent his tall form and kissed her trembling hands. "You have my word, Isabel. All I have left to give! Now, good-night and I will say a formal farewell to morrow."

In the gloomy entrance of the shaded hall, he felt two arms around his neck, and their eyes met in speech-

less sorrow, for he had folded her to his breast and
sealed on her lips the last avowal of a lost love!
"You shall not share my ruin, Little One," he whispered.   There was the sound of a choking sob, a rustle
of robes, the lightest footfall dying on his ears, and
through an unaccustomed mist veiling his eyes, the
ruined peer saw when he raised his head, that he was
indeed alone!

A porter at the hotel wondered, wide-eyed, at the
haggard appearance of the English 'milor' when at daybreak he brushed past him as the doors were opened.
In the darkness of the night, Alfred Beauford had
wandered until dawn, driven on, unmindful of time by
the conflict raging in his breast.

Miss Evleyn Hartley feared to seclude herself further,
and it was with a serious face she joined the excursion party at the gates of the hotel in the early afternoon.   Her eye was steady as she answered Professor
Carl Stein's query in regard to Lady Isabel.

"Still suffering, Professor.   I have just left Lady
Dunham in her darkened room."

"I may be yet able to prevent his plunge into the
obscurity of an unknown fate," thought the heiress as
she dropped the fragments of a telegram from the
drag.   Maitland's answer was encouraging.   And with
her own hand she had delivered to Lord Beauford
Maitland's request to await his return at Schloss
Schwartzenburg.

"I can give him three days, luckily," said Beauford.
"I have just received news that the 'Restless' awaits
some special cargo for a week longer."

"You return here then?" Evelyn said meaningly.

"I go on direct to Trieste from Schwartzenburg. I
wish to say a long good-bye to Phil!" answered Beauford, smiling faintly as he took his leave.

But Philip's words:

All going well, both parties here. Your instructions understood. Have wired Beauford at both places,

gave her renewed courage.

Alfred Beauford turned as his carriage swept away and watching Lady Dunham's windows, saw the flutter of a white kerchief! It seemed to call him back, yet with a heavy heart, he reached the station, his thoughts turning to the lonely woman whose thin hands were clasped in unavailing sorrow as she realized that Beauford was lost to her forever!

In a spacious private apartment of the great "Hotel des Quâtre Saisons," at Munich, on this memorable afternoon, three men sat at a table covered with papers, maps, and plans. There was no mistaking the American dash and alertness of Mr. Edgar Alton, the hawk-eyed London representative of the old Cleveland lawyer. Crisp brown hair, light-gray eyes with a glint of steel in them, wiry and active, Alton was the product, at thirty-five, of a long apprenticeship in bank, corporation, and of law-office sharpness. Trusted implicitly by Wilkinson Fox, he carried secrets of import under his impassive exterior. A single man, he had probed London life in his years of residence and was an Anglo-American of power. His mysterious money movements excited the financiers of the city who could not imagine that the gigantic interests of several American railroads were represented by the self-reliant, solitary man. Philip Maitland, under a convenient alias, was an amused listener of the cross-examination of Mr. Wilkins, the London representative of Beauford's solicitors.

"I know the firm well," whispered Alton to Mait·

land, as he made a pretext of a short rest to confer with his adviser. "Ramsdel, Jarman, and Wakefield are renowned for business acumen and conservative wisdom. I think that I will accompany Mr. Wilkins to London. If the bankers of the estate confirm the schedules here presented, a sinking fund of four thousand pounds a year would extinguish the mortgage and its interest in twenty years and leave three thousand pounds a year available now to the use of Lord Beauford. But the arrangement must include his bankers to assume the trust as the solicitors may advise and direct but can not enter into the transaction. So I must get back at once to London. I am fortunately placed in having effected a great minority compromise for them in America, several seasons past. With their aid I can preserve Miss Hartley's incognito. Beauford will only know of it as an investment of American funds. His pride will yield more readily to that arrangement than a public English transaction. They must telegraph and delay him at Trieste. Of course I count on you to hold him and to dispatch to my London address all the details you gain from him. If you go direct to Schloss Schwartzenburg, he will not know of your Vienna trip! I will have ample time on the return trip to go over every detail of this matter with this sad-eyed chap who seems to be crushed with the weight of other people's legal troubles. But he is a capable fellow—is Mr. Wilkins. I'll brighten him up a bit !"

It was undeniable that the subdued, colorless, functionary, Wilkins was startled out of his London demeanor by the unfamiliar bustle of continental life. Years spent in an atmosphere redolent of parchment, in varied stages of decay, sealing-wax, raw and burned,

166 THE ANARCHIST

and chambers thicker with dust than the tomb of the
Capulets, had sapped the foundation of whatever jovi-
ality the placid Wilkins brought with him into this vale
of tears.

Over an impromptu feast of sardanapalian luxury, the
London assistant thawed, as a generous Burgundy
warmed his veins. He delivered with care to Mr. X.
Y. Z. a carefully drawn plan for the handling of the
Beauford estates, and other documents evincing the
skill of his principles. "It is one of the finest estates
in Yorkshire," proudly remarked Wilkins. "I know
it well. Joined to the Ventnor property, it would be
matchless for beauty and availability."

The astute mind of Edgar Alton discovered a plan
of saving several hours for a needed conference with
Maitland by dispatching the joyous legal assistant on
a hasty tour of the local objects of interest, in charge
of a skillful valet de place. You can meet me at the
station, Mr. Wilkins," genially said the artful Alton.
"My man will be answerable for all your things. Just
leave him your dispatch-box and you can enjoy your
brief stay now." When the two Americans were alone,
Alton proceeded to unbosom himself to Maitland,
whose standing in Cleveland was well known to him.

"I was disturbed when I received Judge Fox's very
careful and detailed instructions, for fear that Miss
Hartley's youth and inexperience had been taken advantage of. It looks to be a fairy story, though. Lord
Beauford seems to be a man of the highest personal
merit and has the shrinking feeling of a high-born
Englishman about pecuniary obligation. My last fear
was that Mrs. Hartley was desirous of setting herself up
at her daughter's expense, in someway, as a rejuvenated county-family representative. The Judge doe

not particularly fancy this German doctor's influence over her. He expresses himself cynically, as to such *extreme devotion* with no especial view of ultimate reward. From what you have guardedly said, I infer that this peculiar attraction of physician and patient has annoyed Admiral Walton, and, perhaps, led to an alienation of mother and daughter."

"You may be right!" answered Maitland musingly. "Walton is proud, and Miss Hartley certainly can not bring herself to the level of her mother's household physician, who is as much nurse and flatterer, as medical man, I should judge. I have never met this Rheingold, but I do know Alton," said Philip decidedly, "that the union of David Hartley and his wife was a failure! One of the wrecks on the shore of matrimonial error! Through all the struggles of his lonely life, David Hartley never had a heart-thrill of mental sympathy with the doll-faced beauty he married."

"Let us walk down to the Telegraph Bureau. I shall send a cablegram to Judge Fox to be answered in London. May I say that *you* approve of this investment? It is a great venture to make on one man's judgment. I presume you know even more of Miss Hartley's feelings than the judge in this peculiar affair."

"I will write a dispatch to my old friend, if you will copy it and send it on in your cipher," said Maitland, affecting not to notice Alton's searching remark. "I would like him to know that I only act as a personal representative of Miss Evelyn in this conference— *nothing more.* You can send her by registered mail from here, a full statement of what you wish her to do. I will also write her and she can then safely communicate with me at Schloss Schwartzenburg. I will

come up to Vienna as soon as poor Beauford leaves me
for Trieste. Then, as I presume you will have his
bankers stop him by telegrams to Treiste, I can play
the role of ignorance with due regard to my honor.
should he return to Vienna." ·

Philip Maitland was intently studying the ashes of his
cigar, as he concluded.

"I would give a thousand pounds to know just how
you look at the impending marriage of Lord Beauford
and this Lady Bountiful," thought Alton, as he transcribed Maitland's dispatch from his cipher book.

But Philip made no sign, and his own dispatch to
Miss Hartley was handed in, in silence.

"Now, Alton, we have a couple of hours. I will see
you to your train. Mine draws out an hour later and
I will be with Beauford at two to-morrow. Let us go
and have a quiet chat on that portico. The evening
is a lovely one."

"Tell me of your American colony in London," said
Maitland, when the newly-made friends were at ease in
their inn. "You, I presume, are in weekly touch with
Cleveland, and I get all the home news also."

"I go out but little," said Alton gayly. "Of course
I am too busy to watch the antics of the rich Americans—the 'parvenus' and 'bienvenus' who are storming
London drawing-rooms with golden scaling ladders!
As for the business representatives, we are all specialists, and spend our days at work, and our nights
in *avoiding each other*. I seldom brush against our American diplomatists who are only remarkable for their
persistent dining out and diplomatic insignificance. It
is a little galling to our overstrung national vanity to
observe that we are without real diplomatic weight
in Europe. The sinews of war are handled by the

great bankers on both sides of the Atlantic and any forty-eight page New York journal hints enough to our government, to run it for a century! Our real relations with the world are buying and selling! We have no other! Our foreign policy is a farce! It has no purpose, no continuity! No beginning nor end! Each important act of our government as regards stranger nations, is usually 'a deed without a name!' We missed one chance of a glorious national revenge, and a successful movement which would have put some lively reading in our school histories."

"When was that?" said Maitland, drily.

"It was at the close of the war of the rebellion. If we had joined the forces of Grant and Lee, of Sherman and Joe Johnston, and taking a double revenge for the attitude of England to the North and South in our Civil War, sent the exasperated *Southern* veterans under Grant and Joe Johnston to sweep Canada and permitted Lee and Sherman to take the *Northern* veterans as far as Darien, we would have made the map of North America a convenient study for *easy reference!* The fact is that if there is such a thing as 'manifest destiny,' we missed the chance of a century. On the North, the quarrel with England, in the South, the insolence of Louis Napoleon's France would have been punished! But the chance will never occur again!"

"Why not?" said Maitland, amazed at Alton's political daring.

"Because no one man is strong enough, nor can hold the people long enough to inaugurate a strong foreign policy for the United States! Besides our laws are admirably framed to allow openings for internal discussion. In the next struggle, you will see the extreme West and South, banded against the Middle and Northern States. They will divide yet!"

"On what quarrel?" anxiously said Maitland.

"On socialistic, perhaps anarchistic, movements!" gravely answered Alton. "The protected and manufacturing states are flooded with the scum of Europe—alien labor, and the human refuse of the Continent! The red propaganda is vigorously pushed in these regions. The visible results of organized capital in building up a plutocracy enrage these mouthing would-be assassins! America may be the chosen field of anarchy for its modern revolt."

"Bah!" cried Maitland, "your double-headed filibustering scheme had the ring of patriotism—of a wild spread eagleism! But the anarchist is an *anonymous coward!*"

"Maitland! It is easy to say that! You may live to see the day when you will admit an error. Cincinnati, the Kearney Riots, the New Orleans outbreak, the Homestead affair, the Rock Spring troubles, the Seattle Chinese episode, the Chicago Haymarket affair, the death of Lincoln and Garfield, and other untoward events of the past, prove how quickly black clouds may form in our clear sky. The New York draft riots demanded the return of an Army corps from the field! The elements of *disorder* are as potent as the elements of *order*. There is a free-and-easy lawlessness in the South which is appalling. It is not vitally dangerous because finally checked by a superior class, the landowners, the political rulers! But the transient character of our public institutions becomes daily more apparent, with the growth of wealth and diversity of interest. There is a direct personal envy fighting the social pretensions of the successful in the United States."

"Then you do not believe in our *first families* in the United States?" queried Maitland smiling.

"Not a bit!" stoutly answered Alton. "There is no established grade of 'lady and gentleman' in America. The one bit of sense of the French Republic of '93 was its legal status of 'citizen' and 'citizeness'. They were then face to face with an established aristocracy which they tried to destroy and which they feared, *even in its death agonies.* We have no such class. The social pretensions of our rich are only founded on transient successes which any money reverse sweeps away!"

"Is this so?" said Maitland doubtfully.

"Is it *not* so?" answered the unflinching Alton, triumphantly.

Maitland was silent!

"Look at the marriages of our heiresses with foreign nobles, English preferred!" continued Alton. "It is not that love draws across the Atlantic, but that the permanence of English aristocracy attracts the quick-witted daughters of Columbia who are secretly encouraged by fathers and mothers, even by brothers."

"Why?" sharply asked Maitland.

"Because these keen plutocrats know that the grade *attained* in America will be *kept up* by their descendants in conservative England. They *do* fear for the permanence of American society. These gold mounted unions are a confession of fear and faith!"

"And yet the *sons* of American millionaires do not marry titled foreign women?" stubbornly said Maitland, returning to the charge.

"Precisely! It is not money—or personal inferiority or any other objection than that Plutus junior can not guarantee the superior station to his proposed wife in

the United States to which she has been born, for it
does not exist!" replied Alton decisively.

"Then you are not in danger of an English alliance,"
smiled Maitland.

"Not a bit!" said Alton. "I am not a man of leisure!
We have no *respectable leisure class* in America as yet.
I am a worker! My fight is to *gain* money. If I suc-
ceed my fight will be to *keep* it!"

"That is not very lofty!" said Maitland.

"It is the formula of every great American success,
from Girard and Astor, to Vanderbilt and Gould. When
the shackle of the slave was broken in the United
States, the fiction of Southern gentility vanished! The
representatives of the 'cavalier' element are now prosaically at work, on the American plane of the equality of effort! The effort of struggling men to maintain wives and daughters who ignore them, in a fab-
ricated, unreal, queenly splendor, and their haughty
and vicious sons in gilded idleness is social madness!"

"Your remedy?" asked Maitland, almost harshly, for
his pride was cut.   ·

"I have none!" answered Alton. "I am not a political *physician!* I am simply a cold *observer!* But I
do not borrow trouble about American aristocracy!
Dissipation, foreign marriage, speculation, profusion
and folly usually bring the families, after three or four
generations back to the original dead level! Any pecu-
liarly ambitious American families are gradually singled
out for political and social reprisals and, in time, they
will be the targets for the bomb-throwers!"

"Do you believe this?" growled Maitland.

"I fear it," moderately answered Alton. "But, by
Jove, there's my man! It's train time!"

"Singular man!" mused Maitland, as he saw the

joyous Wilkins and the Cassandra-like Alton whirled away. "He is the only American I ever met who thought he was not 'a gentleman'—whatever that may be! He seems to be a capable business man!"

Philip Maitland soon forgot, as his train bore him toward the meeting with Lord Beauford, the singular views of Mr. Edgar Alton on the future of America.

"This is a little mystifying," commented Evelyn Hartley as she sat in her boudoir on the evening when Maitland and Beauford were reunited at the castle. Horatio Walton was not a man of surprises. His dispatch was ominous.

Meet me on my arrival at ten, at the hotel. Immediately! Important! Must see you alone!

"What can have happened? Has he discovered my plan? Has he cabled to Judge Fox his protest?" The frightened heiress was agitated when the valet in waiting announced the admiral's immediate approach. A single glance was enough! Walton was wearied and broken in appearance as he threw himself into a chair.

"Are we alone, Evelyn?" he quickly asked.

"Certainly!" said the now thoroughly alarmed heiress. Her eye instinctively sought for a cordial, or his particular case-bottle, which, alas, was missing! "What has happened?"

"Your mother!" he groaned, with an air of dejected misery, "I only learned it in London!"

"What is it?" cried Evelyn, aroused by his delay.

"Was married a week ago, by special license, in London, to that half-lackey, Doctor Ernest Rheingold. "

Miss Hartley walked quietly to the window and gazed out in silence for a moment. Turning slowly, she finally said, 'You need rest, Uncle! Tell me the whole story to-morrow!" Her voice was kindly, but even Walton, man of the world in every sense, dared not intrude longer on the girl's privacy. He nodded and heavily strode from the room, leaving Miss Hartley gazing steadily at the picture of her father, in its place upon the mantel.

It was in the dim watches of the night that sleep finally sealed her eyelids, and she forgot the unexpected disclosure of the disconsolate old aristocrat.

Admiral Horatio Walton was astounded at the stoic composure of his beautiful niece, during the days succeeding his return. Forced to mingle in the amusements of the growing court of the young beauty imperially crowned in gold, the old sailor could not induce Miss Hartley to discuss her mother's strange step. Puzzled by the abrupt departure of Lord Beauford, Walton betook himself to the graces of Isabel Dunham's presence, and adroitly laid siege to Mrs. St. Leger's elastic heart! The dignity of Evelyn grew into a haughty calm! It covered her hourly impatience to hear from London as to Beauford's fate! In her lonely hours, she felt a growing gratitude to Philip Maitland, whose letter announced the departure of Alfred Beauford for Trieste. "He has promised to wait at the 'Croix de Malte' at Trieste," wrote Maitland, "and I have soothed his fretfulness by promising to go to Vienna and see if I can not shape my affairs to go at least as far as Suez with him. The admiral's return will brighten your circle up and I shall rejoin it. The London banker's telegrams should precede my arrival. Announce it openly so that I may drop into the circle unnoted. It is your only sure method to guard your secret! Remember Walton and Lady

Dunham surely know all his affairs, as well as the astute Stein!"

"Surely the plan has miscarried," thought Evelyn Hartley, as she dressed for a maquerade given by the most bewitching of Viennese grande dames on the fourth day after Waltons return. "Isabel knows nothing, and Philip must await my return from the ball, for his train is late!" The American was bending her fair neck to receive a pearl necklace, when the earnest voice of Admiral Walton was heard at the door of her dressing-room.

"You must grant me a moment, Evelyn!" he cried.
"What is it, Uncle? Nothing serious, I hope!" said Evelyn, noting the anxious air of the old sailor who was resplendent as a Venetian Doge.

"Can you give me Beauford's address at Trieste? or his ship? or agents there?" The old man was excited. "I have two telegrams, one from his bankers and one from his solicitors. He must be found! He must return here. A special bank agent is on the way here with a lawyer's clerk! I must instantly forward them. I shall leave the party to Stein and Oborski. I will come later!"

Miss Hartley smiled in spite of her assumed concern! The campaign was then a success! "Perhaps Lady Dunham could tell you! I think I heard her say she expected a parting message. You will find her in the salon! Or Philip Maitland, but he only comes in at eleven!"

"I can not wait for him! I must see Lady Isabel! Wait here! I will return. This is vital to Beauford, and may change his plans!"

As he hurried away Evelyn Hartley sank into a chair and reaped the delightful harvest of a hidden happiness.

The shimmer of satin and sheen of pearls came in with lovely Isabel Dunham as Amy Robsart, and clasping her new friend's hands, the happy woman cried, "Evelyn, Evelyn! He will come back! Thank God, he did not sail before this!" The fleeting blushes on the face of the daughter of the Ventnors told a story without words. "I shall be so anxious till we get his reply."

"Probably you will be relieved of this suspense when we return from the ball," softly said Evelyn, as she caught up a dainty lace scarf.

In the salon, Carl Stein eagerly listened to the anxious admiral. "I should remain at the Telegraph Bureau, my dear Admiral, if I were you!" said the anarchist In his heart of hearts he swore· "This devil's luck must be turned! Beauford to come back! Some fortunate happening! The path must be clear for Oborski. If he comes here, it is to his death! There is no other way! At this juncture, Evelyn Hartley's millions would be his salvation! But her money must be ours! To turn the scale and force socialism in America toward the boiling point of anarchy! We must have gold! Its power alone, can give us other aid than the distinctly criminal classes. There is no compromise between socialism and anarchy! One must swallow up the defeated creed! On this, hangs the hope of a world! Will the masses go far enough under our lead?"

As he mused, Count Oborski entered, magnificent as Sobieski, and whispered with pallid lips, "The great call! You, a mission. You are to leave at two o'clock. I was told that life itself must be risked to find you!"

"Ah!" Carl Stein drew his breath hard. "I can leave the ball at once! It is well!"

"And the rendezvous? Can I aid?" humbly whispered Oborski to his superior. A rapid secret sign told the Pole that the quest was above his grade. Mandatory silence was Stein's grim signal.

"But I want *you*, on our personal affairs!" Stein muttered. "This English fool is perhaps to return! Hang on the admiral's movements! Pump him and notify me through . . ." his voice sank to a whisper. Oborski nodded, his eyes gleaming with passion.

"I will shoot the pig-headed meddler!"

"Bah! no theater duels," said Stein. "Here the ladies come! You would lose her forever! A personal quarrel would be ruin! We must have Cæsar Borgia's cunning at hand! *Is she not worth it?*"

Oborski sprang forward, for Evelyn Hartley's pride of victory shone in her rapt eyes! She was a goddess of the night! Stanislas Oborski forgot all, save the infinite promise he fondly fancied he could read in Miss Hartley's glances! The daughter of Eve was only waiting with beating heart, till, in a pause of the minuet, three hours later, Admiral Walton swept up, a happy magnifico. "Maitland is here, and I have just received Beauford's dispatch. He comes to-morrow night." Evelyn Hartley's smiles deceived the ardent Pole, and the dance went on, while miles away Carl Stein plotted Lord Beauford's murder!

BOOK III

AT CROSS PURPOSES

CHAPTER VIII

AN ANONYMOUS FRIEND—LORD BEAUFORD GOES IN FOR
DIPLOMACY—THE ANARCHIST'S MISSION—DRIFTING—
BROTHER PHILIP—COUNT OBORSKI'S GAME OF SOLITAIRE

BEAUTIFUL Miss Hartley's eyes opened dreamily next
day as the bugles of a passing regiment of Lancers
woke the morning echoes. The sunlight was streaming in at her casement and the belle of the masked
ball noted the wonder on her waiting-maid's face.

"I was afraid to waken you, Miss Evelyn," said the
Abigail, "and yet it is after noon. Here is Mr. Maitland's card, a telegram, and a bundle of letters.
Admiral Walton wishes to see you as soon as possible!"

It was only when seated at her coffee that the happy
woman recalled the events of the night. Her face was
radiant with a secret satisfaction, the glow of a victory she enjoyed alone. With Philip Maitland near,
she felt a new sense of self reliance! The return of
Lord Beauford was certain, and in her ears still murmured the delicious sound waves of the entrancing
Viennese orchestra! The pictures of the magnificent
revel returned to her, its kaleidoscopic changes, the
thrill of the murmuring, swaying throng, the flash of

jewels, rich rustle of silks, and the tender abandonment of women's eyes, yielding to the voluptuous self-forgetfulness of the night. The very wine of life seemed sparkling in the effervescent pleasure of the maskers! A slight frown darkened her brow as she caught the full significance of Count Oborski's patent devotion. "I shall take a turn over the Swiss lakes, follow the Rhine down, and after a glimpse of the Low countries, go by Hanover to Berlin. If we decide to return to Italy, then Munich, and a return visit here will lead us back to Rome! In the meantime the Count Oborski may forget, in his military duties, his sudden predilection!" The eagerness of her ardent cavalier was manifest in an exquisite offering of the richest flowers of the Danube! As the maid handed them in, the very merriest of voices announced Lady Isabel's morning visit sans Façon.

Evelyn Hartley noted the peculiar buoyancy of Lady Dunham's manner. It only needed her avoidance of Beauford's name to confirm a conjecture as to the cause of the ecstatic mood of the visitor.

"I must veil my connection with Beauford's recall," thought Miss Hartley. Dispatching a note to Philip Maitland, on the return of her maid, she ventured a careless remark.

"As I am going for a walk with Mr. Maitland, I may not see Lord Beauford. I presume he returns this evening."

"He will be here at seven, unless there is delay. His telegram only came an hour ago! I shall not go out!" replied Lady Dunham. By accident noting the flash of Evelyn's eyes, Isabel Dunham rose blushing, and sought safety in flight.

"We are such old friends," murmured the fair-haired Anglo-Saxon.

As Miss Hartley emerged from her retirement, Admiral Walton led her to a corner of the grand salon. The old veteran had paced the grand hall in impatience, for an hour.

"Before you meet Maitland, my dear Evelyn," he began almost timidly, "we must consider our course as regards this marriage. I am very much perplexed. I have held no communication with my sister yet! Have you decided upon your line of action! Stein will know at once! He is in correspondence with this Rheingold! The others will hear it as gossip!"

"I will inform Mr. Maitland!" quietly answered Evelyn. "You should speak of the subject as you wish to Lord Beauford on his return! The others will naturally refrain from addressing me!

"And you have nothing to say to your mother *yourself?*" cried the perplexed sailor.

"I feel myself now alone in the world, Uncle! I have not a word to say to any one, even you! Pray do not forget that *I bear the name of Hartley!*"

The tall form of Philip Maitland darkened the doorway and the old admiral, nursing his discontent in a chair placed in a sunny spot, saw the disappearance of the two in the crowd of merry promenaders.

"Caroline has cut the last tie binding her to her child! Respect might even replace affection, but I see breakers ahead here! Evelyn will make her own circle and soon be lost to me!" Long after the Americans were mutually enlightened as to the movements since Maitland's departure, the old sailor sat alone, studying his chart of Life.

"This splendid soldier looms up daily as a suitor! He is a picturesque sort of chap! with all his stately splendor, I distrust the fellow!" growled Walton, who had an insular hatred of foreign alliance.

"I must advise with Stein when he returns! He seems to know Evelyn's nature better than anyone! After Beauford has had his say, I will suggest a move ment!"

"In a sudden freak, she may return to Yankee land, and I am then ruined as far as my influence goes!" Next to his social comfort endangered, the wary old veteran saw a disappearance of the £. s. d. which were so freely handled by him as cicerone.

"It is your wish, then, that Beauford should not divine in any way to whom he owes his mended fortunes," earnestly said Maitland as he led the heiress to a seat in the park.

"He must not even suspect," cried Miss Hartley. "I rely on you, Philip, to guard the whole secret. You will be with him daily and can keep me au courant!"

Philip Maitland's eyes met hers. They had verified the precautions and discussed the whole subject. The half hours had passed in the freedom of unrestrained converse.

"It is time to return!" Maitland said gently. "But do you not think I am going even beyond a brother's duty? Have I any right to violate the friendly confidence of Beauford?"

Miss Hartley fixed her splendid eyes on Maitland in an enthusiastic appeal.

"For his sake! And for my sake—Philip!" Her voice had an unwonted tenderness.

"Be it so, Evelyn! But you must be guarded. It is your duty to hold me clear of responsibility. I shall ask Beauford to stay at my hotel, then his social relations will be entirely untrammeled!"

The friends were not astonished to find Lord Beauford the center of an eager circle on their return.

"By Jove! old fellow!" remarked Lord Alfred. "I have some men coming here. I have a considerable mail, and a dispatch that a document from the Foreign Office has been forwarded by my bankers! I need a few days for business."

"I anticipated that you would like to be with me! I have taken rooms at my hotel for you!" cheerily said Maitland. "Now I claim you, for I may run over to America. I am needed there."

Wily Oborski's heart leaped for joy as Lord Beauford calmly said: "I shall probably remain but a few days. I am to take the next vessel from Trieste after my affairs are under way!"

"Bravo! It will take a serious task off my hands," thought the Pole, as his dark, gleaming eyes vainly tried to read Beauford's impassive face. "She will be mine! I wish Stein were here!" He was in the dark. The departing anarchist had glided away as mutely as a Jesuit. Oborski dared not try to lift the veil shrouding his superior!

He well remembered certain very mysterious happenings in that dark order, whose creed of love and brotherly trust, is enforced by the penalty of a merciless death to traitors and meddlers!

"But Beauford's face shows no passion! Does she love him? La Belle Americaine! Does she too hunt a coronet? I could even fancy he has a penchant for the most lovely of widows! And she is of his own order also!" Stanislas Oborski was mystified as he reined his splendid charger down the street filled with Vienna's pale, proud aristocrats!

"Now Beauford, tell me all!" exclaimed Maitland, earnestly, as the friends sat èn petite cômitè after dinner. "Do you stay with us?"

"Phil, I am as much in the dark as you! Some friendly turn of the tide may have delayed my ultimate ruin! It will soon be cleared up. The two men arrive to-morrow. The Bank's agent and my solicitor's faithful man Wilkins! They will soon tell me all."

Maitland started. He must devise a plan to seal the lips of the man of parchments.

"It must be a matter of the gravest importance to warrant them in calling me back!" mused Lord Alfred.

"I am sure the news will be of a stroke of lucky fortune!" heartily said Maitland as they separated for the night.

In the friendly shelter of her rooms, Isabel Dunham, her heart racked with impatience, murmured, "Why do they not act at the Foreign Office? My appeals to Lord Ventnor, if he has moved at once should place the son of one of England's greatest ambassadors again in the line of distinction! Yet—even if it be so,— Alfred must never know of my desperate efforts. With her lovely head pillowed on a rounded arm, she murmured as she slept, "He would not know my heart! He must not! His pride would be a bar to a future offered by the woman who did his splendid youth wrong!"

Neither Maitland, Lady Isabel, nor noble-hearted Evelyn Hartley could read their own hearts clearly! The future of Alfred Beauford was the uppermost matter in the minds of these dissimilar natures. Neither of the young women were calm enough to weigh the gold of emotion with the unswerving standards of reason! The gentle hands holding the delicate balance throbbed with the pulses of rich womanhood!

But Philip Maitland, alone in his chamber, mused over the Beauford matter en philosophe. "In what does the fate of a penniless peer outweigh that of a struggling clerk, a rising genius weighed down with adversity, a poor inventor, or any other human unit?" The serious-faced American wrestled with this problem in vain!

"Is it because he represents that sacred social formula, 'The existing Order of Things,' not to be rudely shaken in the time of the Empress Queen? Wherein has Hodge the duty to be humble, and a Howard to be magnificent! Why does Tommy Atkins stand with his Brown Bess in the ranks, and face his death in silence, and his high-born officer meet the same doom, happy in the golden tassel on his sword! Cavendish, Duke of Devonshire, walks in Chatsworth Park of fifteen hundred acres, idle, and without his walls Goodman Smith plows with weary toil his acres to pay rental to a hereditary lord! Is there any foundation in reason for rank, precedence, private right in land, and its attendant riches? Is there a warrant to weld wealth, dignity, power, and feudal right into hereditary inheritances for favored mortals?" The world-worn traveler, thinking of the complex conservatism of lands where the masses stand, cap in hand, before the few, contrasted it with the eager fever of the American struggle to rise on pillars of gold above the common herd?

The question "Is Aristocracy lawful?" puzzled Maitland, to whose cultured mind equality seemed not altogether desirable! "Beauford is certainly an honor to his patrician class! His retrogression would be a particular disaster of moment to a class accepted as the leaders of English manhood! In America, as we have *no rank to fall from*, such a change would be impossible. Both systems seem to reflect, correctly, differing national types.

"The only difference I can see is that the English aristocrats rank is owned and cherished by all. The community calmly accepts the gracious sovereign's ennobling touch! In the United States the successful plutocrat makes his own crown, puts it on himself, and wears it in defiance of public reprobation or personal envy! The intangible fabric of British civic structure seems to be sacred, as a whole, to prince and peasant!"

Maitland was fain to absent himself from his hotel with a sudden devotion to social duties, when Lord Beauford received the bank's representative, and the now eagerly curious Mr. Wilkins. In London law circles, Wilkins was now vaguely suspected of mysterious continental influence. His saddened face was big with new importance. It was not by hazard, that he received a note from Maitland as he stepped from the train. Its words of delightful anticipation were:

You are forbidden to recognize any one you have seen at Munich. Before you leave, you shall be pleasantly enlightened!

The American passed Mr. Wilkins in the bustle of arrivals and an exchange of glances ratified the compact of secrecy!

"Quite a neat tableau," whispered Philip to Evelyn Hartley as he surveyed the salon of the "Grand Hotel." The dramatis personae were drawn together by an unseen influence. "They will all be sure we know nothing of this visit or its importance!" continued Maitland.

"It is fortunate," smiled the heiress, for the light comedy of tourist life went on as usual, Admiral Walton convoying Mrs. St. Leger, Count Oborski, and several attendant nobles engaging Lady Dunham and the expectant heiress, busied in knitting up her growing friendship with Philip Maitland. The experiment of the lonely girl was nearing its crucial point! Into the circles, Professor Carl Stein's return introduced a future element of restlessness. Maitland and Evelyn were uneasy. "Must watch that fellow! He's designing!" grumbled the admiral, and Oborski vainly tried to read in Stein's immutable face the secrets of his mysterious council.

No one failed to notice the start of astonishment with which the scholar received Lady Isabel's query:

"Have you met Lord Beauford yet since his return, Professor?"

"I thought he was on his way to Australia," quickly answered Stein, with a keen glance at Oborski.

The count smiled sardonically. "Vienna seems to please Milord!"

Philip Maitland noted the steely glitter of the Polish noble's eye. "Jealous!" he murmured, "All these continental grandees seem to be fortune hunters!"

"Pardon, but can you tell me where I can find Lord Beauford?" said the Chief de Bureau, approaching Miss Hartley with an obsequious bow.

Evelyn blushed slightly, but her voice was steady as she answered, "Mr. Maitland! You may be of use to your friend."

"I have a dispatch for him from the Foreign Office," said the functionary, "sent from the English Embassy. It is for personal delivery and marked 'Immediate!'"

"I think I will send a coupé down for Beauford. I know he is engaged, but this may be of interest at this special moment," whispered Maitland to the heiress.

Both of them observed Lady Isabel's sudden inter-

est in the remarks of the clerk. Maitland saw the
fan moving more quickly the fluttering laces of the
English beauty's corsage. Her eyes had an eager
light in them. Evelyn's eyes met his in quiet significance.

When Philip returned, Count Oborski and Professor
Stein were earnestly whispering in a corner.

"Beauford will be able to have Her Majesty's command in five minutes now. I presume he will come
up," said Philip lightly, as he gained a quiet moment
with his countrywoman. Ten minutes later Lord
Beauford entered the room. His usually pale face was
slighty flushed, and there was the light of a new life
in his steady blue eye. With graceful politeness he
saluted the ladies and pressed the hands of Admiral
Walton. As he stood under the grand chandelier a
nimbus of happiness surrounded his stately head. The
direct query of Professor Stein was almost rough in
its jarring directness.

"Do you leave us soon for your voyage, my lord?"

Alfred Beauford gazed a moment steadily at the
questioner.

"I may reconsider my departure, at least delay it for
some time," he answered with quiet coldness, as if
the gray-eyed German's intrusion was most unwelcome.

"Can you give me a moment, Maitland," said Beauford, turning to Miss Hartley and her escort. "I have
some people waiting my return—if Miss Hartley will
kindly excuse you!"

Evelyn blushed almost guiltily, as she bowed and
joined Lady Dunham at the piano.

The two friends descended the marble stairway and
Beauford led the way to a retired table in the café.

His manner was strangely excited as he handed his friend an open dispatch.

"Phil, old fellow, read that!" The nobleman was as impatient as a boy. "Tell me what you know of it! *Who instigated it?*" His eyes were keenly fixed on Maitland, whose astonishment knew no bounds!

It was a carefully worded dispatch from the Foreign Office, conveying the intelligence of his appointment as an attaché of the British Embassy at Vienna and intimating that special and detailed instructions would be furnished him by the Ambassador in person. Maitland shook his head as he returned it. "I congratulate you, Beauford, from my very heart. I am in the dark! How should I know of this?"

"Because there has been some unknown and powerful friend acting in my behalf! I am puzzled—bewildered." He clutched Maitland's arm. "I must return soon. I can tell you of a wonder greater than this. My bankers have mysteriously effected the arrangement of my money affairs, so that Jervaux *may* be saved! Can it be the same influence?" his voice trembled. "I might flatter myself that my father's services had gained for me this official recognition! I can not divine the nature even of this appointment. But the other, is a concrete fact. The sum of eighty thousand pounds has been lodged to my credit, which will, under a formulated plan, redeem the estate in twenty years and leave me several thousand a year as a fixed income. The strangest part of it all," said Beauford, draining a glass of sherry in absent-minded haste, "is that I am formally notified by the bank that it accepts the trust of this liquidation as agent, and that my transaction goes no farther than the execution of such papers as my solicitors approve, with the bankers as principal!"

"It is a strange turn of Fortune's wheel!" mused Maitland. He hesitated slightly. "Do you accept the arrangement?"

"I have, as regards the estate, no choice but acceptance or ruin! I am assured," said Beauford anxiously, "that no condition present or future, is laid on me. It is a matter of pure investment. As regards the Foreign Office—Her Majesty's seal is a guarantee of the official regularity of the appointment. That is an honor befitting my palmier days! It naturally calls me to action and to abandon my globe trotting! But *to whom do I owe it?*" He searched Maitland's impassive face.

A diversion occurred to the American.

"Perhaps Lady Isabel," he began, but ere he had voiced his thought the usually phlegmatic Briton had vanished. Maitland laughed as he finished his cup of coffee, and slowly mounted the stairway. As he sought out Evelyn Hartley from the encircling crowd of ardent Austrians, Philip noted the flutter of Lady Dunham's draperies on the portico and Beauford's tall form bending over her!

"I wonder if the lovely widow *does* know anything," thought Maitland as Miss Hartley artfully emerged from the lines of her friendly besiegers.

Carl Stein, gazing moodily at the double disappearance, muttered, "What devil's foolery is this now? He returns like Wallenstein! Will no friendly sprite warn him off? Led on by the thread of the Fates! I shall have to study the drama and work a scheme as deus ex machina."

"What is it? Tell me quickly!" whispered imperiously Evelyn Hartley. "Stein is watching us narrowly! Has he discovered anything?" The friendly conspirators were safe from eavesdroppers. Miss Hartley had, with a quick glance, caught the plotting anarchist off his guard.

"The banking arrangement is a success," said Maitland. "But stranger still, Lord Beauford has suddenly received a diplomatic appointment here, with the intimation of graver duties later! There is *more than one* good fairy in the world! Can Lady Dunham have exerted her family influence?"

Philip felt his companion's fingers tighten upon his arm. "Then he will stay here?" she said hastily.

"For a time, certainly!" replied Maitland gravely. It was his turn to be astonished, for Miss Hartley said, "Take me in! Come and see me to-morrow afternoon and tell me all! I shall leave Vienna at once!"

"Why?" said Maitland, pausing. He noted the agitation on her expressive face.

"Because," said Evelyn Hartley, "it would be *unbearable* for me to have Lord Beauford fancy himself under the faintest obligation to me! I shall go to Switzerland! Will you not come?"

"Women are peculiar creatures!" ruminated Maitland, as he glanced at Beauford and Lady Isabel in the distance. "Evelyn flies the very presence of the man whom her money has called back to her side!"

The light-hearted American traveler was glad to be relieved of the "brotherly duty" so lately engrossing him, and to feel himself free to contemplate the success of Miss Hartley's plan *from a distance.*

As he selected a convenient corner he watched the doorway. Lord Beauford's face was calm and impassive as he parted from Lady Dunham.

"Come down as soon as you can, Phil! I will be free in half an hour. Thanks for your promptness!

I shall now stay in Europe." His words were eagerly watched by the furtive Stein and Count Oborski's sparkling restless eyes gazed on the friends.

"She knows nothing!" said Maitland.

"As much in the dark as I am," replied Beauford, as he passed out.

But Isabel Dunham's heart was beating wildly as she instinctively sought refuge with Evelyn Hartley. The wary women natures recognized that each held a part of the golden secret of the hour! Sympathy and distrust went hand in hand in their relations, and each was haunted with a womanly shrinking from discovery!

Lady Dunham's bosom was filled with a strange new happiness, for Alfred Beauford had told her of his strange advent into Her Majesty's service.

"It is a most singular piece of good-fortune," she murmured, "And you will accept?"

"Most certainly!' Beauford had answered, looking steadily into her eyes. "I have arranged my affairs with my bankers, and I may hope to keep Jervaux in the family. To that end, I now dedicate my life."

Lady Isabel's eyes were very kindly as she said: "Dear old Jervaux! It is the one place of the world to you!"

Pausing abruptly, Beauford caught her two hands impulsively and said brokenly:

"Isabel! Tell me of this friendly magic! of the Foreign Office matter!"

"I—I know nothing of it!" the startled woman said, timidly releasing her hands.

"You are the *one person in the world* to whom I would look for the key of the enigma! Do not spare my pride! Tell me!"

The gentle disclaimer brought no conviction to

Beauford's heart! "I will see you to-morrow—after I have met the ambassador. We are observed. Let us go in!"

The tenderness of his tone lingered to thrill Isabel Dunham in her watchful vigils, long after happy Evelyn Hartley's dark eyes closed in wonder at her unknown friend's aid in rebuilding Beauford's fortunes. In her womanly weakness she dreaded Beauford's knowledge of her action, yet fain would keep him near her!

"When he is *great*, when he is *an ambassador*, when he is able to *stand alone*, and face his brother peers, he may know, but not *till then!*"

Philip Maitland and Lord Beauford sat an hour in secret council, before the waning stars called them to rest. It is so strange—so sudden, Phil!" measuredly said Beauford, as he returned from the dismissal of his visitors. "It is most singular that this dual arrange. ment permits me to remain within hail of civilization. I can make a very respectable appearance with my settled income, and, young as I am, the path of pro. motion is open. Should I live, I may yet see Jervaux clear of debt, and leave an honored name and a clear estate to my successor."

"By the way, who is he?" queried Maitland.

"Gerald Molyneux, of the 'Rifles,'" answered the nobleman, "and a right good fellow is Gerald."

"But you will marry?" impulsively said Maitland, as he turned to select a cigar with more than ordinary deliberation.

"Probably not," calmly replied Beauford.· "I will ask no woman to share my broken fortunes! I would not marry to mend them. Love weighed down with a wife's gold! Never!"

"Make no rash vows, Beauford," said Maitland smiling. "Remember Calderon's sprightly saying, 'There is no playing tricks with love!' At any rate, old fellow, let me congratulate you from the bottom of my heart! Come to me as soon as you have seen the ambassador, for I wish to know of your every movement. I will hie me back to America and take up the only career possible there, — 'making money'."

"Why not public life?" said Beauford smilingly.

"Because there is no public career in America," regretfully said Maitland. "The general sense of our people is right. The aggregate voice of America is that of wisdom! But so quickly the floods of party ascendancy rise and fall, that a representative man is on the top wave of success, dazzled and bewildered, thrown up far beyond his proper position, or overwhelmed in the crushing depths of political oblivion, before his record can be fairly established! Our power is fairly distributed; but so restless, nervous, and mercurial are our people, goaded on by an impassioned press, and inflamed by volcanic orators, that measures and policies follow with lightning changes. The United States tries every political quack medicine as presented. Thank God, the patient, rugged in youth, strong in constitution, lives! It may be different some day!" concluded Maitland gloomily.

"What do you fear?" said Beauford, with interest.

"We worship only money! We bow to concrete profit! We subordinate our lives to gain! Great fortunes are the peerages of our land! The worship of these golden calves will produce an organized revulsion of popular feeling. Envy and demagogueism may bring about a violent attempt at the redistribution of wealth with us. The Populists and others, the Labor Unions, only

seek to throw off the burdens laid on the masses by
the rich! It may be that the wealth itself will be
attacked by the final development of human brutality
and insanity—The Anarchist!"

"I pay little attention to anarchy. In the British
kingdom, these brazen-lunged theorists are forced to
be contented with a subdued open-air demonstration,
or a joint braying-match over the rights of man, end-
ing in a ball,"· laughed Beauford. "Our English
blood is not hot enough to be influenced by a few
wild-eyed loafers, who prate of natural right, reform,
and an ideal community, and never effect anything
beyond their wild invocation of the spirit of discord!

"In France, Germany, Russia, or Italy, these midnight
plotters rise to the dignity of conspirators. They will
always remain on the level of the vagrant in England,
and be promptly collared by a 'Bobby,' or ducked in the
nearest pond! It may be that the United States will
open a field to the apostles of the higher life and soiled
linen! When I see an anarchist who has sufficient
self-respect to keep reasonably clean, in life or person,
I may listen. Up to that unreached epoch, I merely
hold my nose and turn away! They have had unbounded
chances to practically set up communities and prove,
in action, either the peacefulness or advantages,
physical and moral, of the new system, but from Ros
seau and Proudhon to the last sneaking bomb-handler,
their practical efforts have been abject failures. The
Commune of Paris could not control *itself*, and would
have starved to death in the inanition of speculative
laziness, if not scattered by force! The kitchen larders
of the useful bourgeoisie exhausted, these God-gifted
men had only their *speeches* to live on! The anarchist seems to dread one thing more than the most

hated form of tyranny!" vigorously cried Beauford, in
closing.

"And that is?" said Maitland, smiling.

'Any form of useful or productive work!" triumphantly added Lord Beauford. "*That* certainly appalls
them! My only fear for America is your national
excitability and remarkable fondness for religious and
political 'crankism!' You good-humoredly tolerate, to
a certain extent, almost anything in the United States!"
continued Beauford.

"Nothing would astonish me as happening in your
'go-as-you-please' country, but there is a stratum of
tough backbone to you, after all!"

"Precisely!" said Maitland, his eyes kindling, "We
have allowed numberless experiments from practical
free-love down to compact autonomies, of foreign resi-
dents! We have thrown our doors open to the filth
and scum of Europe! We have cheapened the getting
of American citizenship so that it is hardly worth
individual asking! But when anarchy, organized, lays
its hand on property, our millions of wage-earners
will remember the years of toil and self-denial represented in their homes, their savings, and the great
institutions,—the joint product of capital and labor.
When the torch is applied by irresponsible alien fanatics, when the bomb of the coward sheds innocent
blood in our midst, the stern vengeance of our outraged
citizens will ring through the world, and terrify the
fiends who prey on the passions of the ignorant, and
rule the fool by fraud or fear!"

"There need be no grim parade of La Roquette's
guillotine or our American Ravachols and Vaillants!
Once let the cowards, skulking under the red flag,
openly attack civil order in the United States, our

citizens will vigorously and effectively blot them out, without expense for rope!"

"But they will need a lesson! A terrible one, even in the United States, and the few scoundrels, mouthing their dark threats of rapine and indiscriminate murder, will find, in startled surprise, that the rich and prosperous will leap to arms in defense of what thrift and industry has given them! Courage and nerve does not necessarily lie only under the beer-stained rags of an imported human drone. There's a bit of the blood of Spottsylvania and Gettysburg left in the North! In the South, the nerve and broad-community character which held the gray-coated Confederates, unflinching in their shot-torn ranks, through five years of a hopeless war, will avail them to master the foreign hydra!

I'm a Northern man!" cried Maitland, waxing enthu·siastic, "but I honor the undoubted Americanism of the South! There's not a nation in Europe that could carry its flag to-day over the eleven States where the Stars and Bars kissed the battle breeze, *even if we of the North stood aloof!*

"Thank God! we will stand in the future, shoulder to shoulder—we have nailed the *old* stars together with *new* ones!"

"In other words, you draw the conclusion that anarchy will not flourish in the English-speaking lands? You have to thank us for a bit of the Anglo Saxon phlegmatic staying power, after all, Maitland! Anarchy is a continental political mange. It will never flourish in either England or America, and woe be to those to fit? their coat to our shoulders!"

"I agree with the ambassador!" said Phil Maitland, smiling, as he rose to bid the happy Englishman "goodnight." It was a simple hand-grasp, but it was sig-

nificant of a union of hearts across the sea in the con-
servation of all that makes life dear, or holds an
honest home together!

Miss Evelyn Hartley found Philip Maitland a restive
guest during the sunny hours of the afternoon,
while the American waited for Beauford's return from
the Embassy. The Western beauty was ready to leave
Vienna for the presence of Beauford incited Admiral
Horatio Walton to vain conjecture as to the future of
Jervaux Priory, and the final career of the sister, whose
estranged daughter was his ward. The old sailor was
astounded at the resolution with which Miss Hartley
plotted out her future path in life. "Of course, my
dear uncle, I have open to me a return to Cleveland,
and Judge Fox will arrange my household so as to
meet your perfect satisfaction. I am ready to go home
at once!" The loss of the swelling state in which he
now shone would have been a crushing blow to Walton. He murmured, yielded, and found that the reins
of power had passed into the shapely white hands of
the girl. The earnest light of her brave young eyes
was as dauntless and unflinching as an eagle gazing
at the sun. David Hartley's proud, unconquerable
spirit, was as sure a legacy as the tender lines read in
the later days giving his last council.

"Lord Beauford," was the announcement of the
lackey, waking Evelyn and Philip from a colloquy of
the distant, yet beloved, American home, as the newly
fledged diplomat entered, his face bright with the
sunshine of the hour.

"I am so glad to find you here, Miss Hartley," he
began, "for I am obliged to be absent a few days. My
duties begin at once. I have a little matter of business
on which to confer with you at once."

'I will take a turn on the portico, remarked Maitland, eager to gain the last detail. He nodded to Beauford and disappeared adroitly.

Miss Hartley was alone with her unconscious protegé. Her heart beat a shade more quickly than its wont, when the Englishman earnestly said:

"I trust you will pardon me for speaking to you, on a subject concerning yourself alone, but my time is short."

Evelyn Hartley's cheek was pale. Was it a chance discovery? Her bosom rose and fell in repressed emotion, but her voice was steady as she calmly said, "Proceed, Lord Beauford, I am ready to hear you."

With frank directness he said, "By strange good-fortune I have been enabled to retain legal control of my estates. I have an application for a five years' extension of the lease of your mother, under which she resides at Jervaux. May I ask if you *personally* desire to use the Priory as a residence? It might alter my ideas as to the tenancy."

The girl breathed a sigh of happy relief. "I have no wishes to express in the matter, Lord Beauford. My plans include only a tour of the Continent and return to my American home. I have no present intentions, in fact *none whatever* of sharing the occupancy of Jervaux."

Beauford rose with embarrassed constraint. He quickly noted the coldness of her manner, "That ends the Foreign Doctor's reign at the Priory," he resolved, as he withdrew to join Maitland. "I shall meet you before your departure for Switzerland, as I am only going to Paris on legation business," was his adieu.

"It's all right, Phil!" said Beauford joyfully, as he rejoined his friend. "I am named here on special duty, with a hint of future employment in the East, and my two visitors leave for London to-night. The final papers will be sent to me at Paris, where I am sent. I am to have a few months of novitiate and a post will be offered me of a politico-geographical importance."

"I must smuggle Wilkins this hundred-pound note of Miss Hartley's!" thought Maitland. "Ah, yes; Beauford's man can take it! Just the fellow!"

"See here, Maitland, I've to say good-bye to Lady Isabel. Now, I claim you for a last dinner before my diplomatic entrée into public life. Meet me at the hotel."

As they re-entered the salon, Stanislas Oborski and Carl Stein were the first to publicly congratulate Lord Beauford. His surprised air amused Oborski. "My dear Lord Beauford, nothing escapes the fair chatterboxes of Vienna. Your table will be strewn with invitations for the Clubs, all know of your appointment. I hail you as a 'lion' of the winter season!'

Yet, when the strange associates were alone, as a mute signal from Stein called the impetuous wooer to a council, Oborski snarled: "Curse this titled fool! Anchored here now, in the very central circle of our field of action. Fate throws him across my path again. But I will have your advice! Your help!"

"Not so!" answered Stein. "The time presses! I do not wish to give you my last directions in this now. I leave in a few days for America, I shall stop in England and visit Rheingold on . . . ." He made a sign which startled the angry Pole.

"Is this fellow who married the mother *one of us?*"

"Precisely," said Stein, with reserve. "The mother's ample fortune will be drawn on for our purposes, in time. But I know this proud and spirited girl! Recon-

ciliation is impossible! In fact, it is better for you
and I it should be so! I go now under orders of the
Executive Council to a secret conference with the
most advanced leaders of anarchy in the United States.
There is much discontent there. Finance, tariff, and
depression, with a growing army of tramps and malcontents. If I can be assured of the fitness of the time
—general demonstrations of unrest, political revolts,
and even carefully shielded use of the torch and bomb,
may enable us to draw out our friends, to throw the
unemployed masses against the rich, and to open the
conflict!"

"Why this haste?" eagerly asked Oborski.

"Because," replied the cool German savant, "it is
only in the embittered days of great depression that
we can hope to overturn the money power in the
United States. Prosperity is a golden chain riveting
the happy slave to his puffed-up master. The time is
propitious!"

"And the grave issue on the Continent? Is my country to bleed always under the iron heel of the Russian?" said Oborski.

"You narrow the field, Count, with your racial complaint! It is the whole manhood of the world which
calls for anarchy's general light! Bakunin's harshest
theory of the personal destruction of individual sov-
ereigns, and mere repeated violence would leave the
modern anarchist, like Anacharsis Clootz, simply
madly demanding the wreck of creeds, codes, countries,
and craving unmeaning bloodshed. He lost his head
under the guillotine by insensate raving. We must
have a general change before we can mete out sweeping punishment. We must gain the power to *sentence*,
before we proceed to *execution*. Our acts must not

have the stain of individual murder on them. Let us free *one* country, then the light will flash from land to land! Now, I will be absent for several months. If you hope to rise to the higher Council, I charge you, I care not how, to bind this woman in the chains of love and passion. She is essential to us! The safety of her name, of her position, the help of her fortune—we need all! You can safely rise to the highest power in the United States as her titled and aristocratic husband. You can gain the secrets of politics— you can watch the rich in their unguarded homes, you can pass safely over the world, secure in your rank and wealth as our agent, ambassador, our general! It is a glorious career! You can be the Sobieski of anarchy! You must enslave this woman! Watch this English lord. You know how to invoke the help of the order! Davidoff will give you the final sanction! I shall know of your every movement! You must *remove* this haughty noble! I leave the task to you! I have a spy watching her trustee in America, a man in his service. If the old man were to die, we are nearer the goal. And now—"

The two scoundrels finished their plotting with lips fearful of the rustling echoes of the whispers of murder they framed!

In merry abandon, the days drifted on. Lord Beauford lingered at Paris, and Carl Stein was prudently conferring at the nearest market town with Ernest Rheingold, the smooth dissembler, whose years of wary servitude had gained him the mastery of Caroline Hartley's purse-strings. When Carl Stein landed at New York for the first time, a fund of their enemy's gold filled the coffers of the wavering conspirators in America. It was a foretaste of power, of the tyranny exerted by a vigorous mind over mean and servile intellects which made Stein the central figure of anarchistic energy in the United States. At gay Vienna, drifting daily into closer communion, there was not a day when "Brother Philip," lingering by the side of beautiful Evelyn Hartley did not reproach himself for his dolce-far-niente. His heart refused to aid his reason in answering the question he dared not ask himself, "*Is this love or am I only 'Brother Philip'?*"

"So! Milord Beauford returns to-morrow," mu_ed the magnificent Oborski, as he sipped a petite verre in his favorite corner at the club. The letters of Carl Stein left him no doubt as to the dread responsibility of his position. "This woman must not escape us, she must be ours! Act—and act if possible alone! I shall deal my stroke here later when I hear from you! Nothing shall stand between me and these millions destined to our cause."

With a gloomy brow, Oborski, whose teeming brain was fertile in invention, deliberately addressed himself to a game of solitaire. One course (a hackneyed one in continental circles) was before him ever. A duel! It might cause too much eclât! The hated rival was a diplomat now—a personage under international comity! It might estrange Evelyn, whose ardent nature was impressed by the romantic Polish patrician. Another secret plan occurred! "Let Fate decide," he muttered. "The secret plan wins," he said. "Three runs! *It shall be done!*"

CHAPTER IX

LORD BEAUFORD'S DILEMMA—JUDGE WILKINSON FOX IN-
VITES A JEREMIAD—A MOTHER'S HATRED—LADY ISABEL
SEES THE LIGHT COMING SHADOWS—A FREE FIELD—THE
COUNT OBORSKI SPEAKS

"STRANGE irony of Fate—that I should retrace the
path by which Isabel Dunham has wandered back to
meet me! That *she* should stray alone under the oaks
of Ventnor and *I* beneath banyan and palm in far
India! Have I aught to say before I go?" Lord Beauford was a changed man as he walked the deck of the
boat darting forward over the blue Bodensee. The
steamer seemed to swim suspended between blue sky,
and the brilliant depth of the sapphire lake. All the
nerved elasticity of the young noble urged him forward on his path. He was the depositary of a state
secret—a knight going out alone to battle for England's future control in the East.

From the English ambassador at Paris, he had learned
the secret of his appointment. A former viceroy of
India, the noble Earl clearly set forth, in a secret interview, the desires of the Foreign Office. A burning
agitation as to British and Russian rights in the Pamirs
was exciting Her Majesty's government.

The wily Russian adventurers, travelers, and spies
thronged the Court of Persia and were swarming over
India. The mysteriously veiled game of Russian aggression was being played under the very eyes of the

Indian government. Beauford recalled the last words
of the ambassador. "You have a difficult part, a dangerous game to play! Let no other thought but your
mission occupy your mind for a moment until you
have made your final report in London. The gravity
of the issue is proven when I tell you it may determine
peace or war! Your face and history is unfamiliar to
the local Russian agents. As a traveler, sportsman,
and man of rank, your presence is easily explained by
the search for big game which has covered many a secret
mission! Your well-known character and fitness, your
distinguished father's loyalty to the crown, have led
to your selection. But one man can be trusted to
evade the watchful muscovites. Your route from the
Pamir plateau down the Oxus to Khiva, thence to
Teheran, and by Damascus and Beyrout to Constantinople will be a solitary one. The viceroy will give
you the final cipher instructions. You will be rushed
by rail to the frontier, and with but one follower, a
plain English servant, you must thread mountain and
desert. The amplest financial assistance will be given
by the viceroy and the British ambassador at Constantinople, who will report in cipher your arrival there—
nothing more. You will, after reporting to him, take
the 'flyer' for London, and your memorized and systematic report on Russian preparation and advances
must be made up in London *without a note!* In case
of success a diplomatic post of honor awaits you.
Should you perish in this venture, it is a solitary
leading of a forlorn hope for England! As for failure—
I do not expect that of your race and your father's
son! Your return to Vienna will throw off the
mouchards of Russia's four central secret police stations in continental Europe. From Vienna you must

quietly disappear, leaving as if for a day. Catching the P. & O. at Brindisi, you are to be watchfully silent until you meet the viceroy in person."

"To whom shall I say adieu?" deliberated Lord Beauford. "I shall grasp Phil Maitland's hand. I can trust Isabel and—and Miss Hartley." Alfred Beauford pondered the question of his parting from the noble American girl, while the hours passed as he neared Vienna. "She seems an embodiment of the young life of the West—bright, brave, and true! How nobly she devoted herself to Maitland! There is the royal seal of womanhood on her glorious brows! To see her nature unfold in its perfection, to go hand in hand with her through life, would *alone* ennoble a man! And I may not meet her again. If it were not for her millions, I might ask her to hear what another perhaps may use as the golden key to her heart!

"No! There is no place now in my bosom for love! To serve England, to save my old acres from the spoiler, this must be my duty. And Isabel—am I under a new bond to her? Do I owe this 'essay perilous', to her womanly influence. I dare not tell her, for hawk-eyed Walton would force the truth piecemeal from her lips. I must seal my lips. If I do not come back in honor and success from distant Pamir, the story of my life is closed! If I do, I will have a station to offer to some other woman who may walk by my side in happier days!" Beauford's fancy recalled the earnest, dark-eyed American face, glowing in life's ambrosial morning, and yet, the trembling fingers of Isabel Dunham seemed to tighten once more on his arm!

The voices of two eager voyagers caught his attention as the train halted ten miles from Vienna. The

dusk of evening was dropping deeper shades over plain
and forest. He could not see their faces, but the
haughty, refined insolence of their tone indicated the
pleasure-loving Viennese noble, returning from a
day's hunting.

"Lucky fellow! Oborski! A cavalry brigade, a separate command—what a signal favor of the Emperor!
And he will marry the many-times millionaire American beauty! Is it a fact?"

"My dear Rudolph! Nothing is sure where a woman
is concerned! 'Souvent femme varie!' But Stanislas
is 'aux petits soins.' He was her cavalier at the
masked ball. They are a princely couple. After all,
you know, he is of one of the oldest families of Croatia
and Poland."

"I was told at the club," said the first speaker, "an
English lord was the happy man. The new attaché,
Beauford, I think."

"Bah! He is a penniless peer, and one of these
wooden Englishmen. He cannot be named in the
race with Oborski, who has a splendid estate!"

"True!" replied the second huntsman. "But Stanislas
has piled on the debts, both for his mad social extrav-
agances, and his affiliation with Polish agitation. I
wonder even that the Emperor gives him a brigade!"

"All is anti-Russian now! Set a thief to catch a
thief, you know! But I pity the woman who links
her fate to that of the magnificent Oborski. He is
headlong as a fallen angel!"

Beauford's steady blue eye burned in hostile rage,
as he sprang from the train at the station where Maitland waited him. "By heaven! That adventurer shall
never call Evelyn Hartley wife!" he swore between
his teeth.

And yet the barrier of Fate was between them!

"Phil, dear old fellow!" cried the Englishman, "you are the one person to whom I can trust my affairs here. Jump in this coupé and listen while I am on my way to the Embassy. I wish you to be my ambassador to the ladies. Hobson," he turned to his steady-eyed man of all work, "settle all and pack everything. I leave for Brindisi to-morrow." The unmoved valet caught every accent of Beauford's whisper and was off like a flash. North Polar jaunts, tropic jungles, the desert, or American frontier wastes, no path of life could lift an eyebrow of the cool man who was Beauford's shadow.

"Now, what lark's the guvnor up to now?" muttered Hobson. "I ope as how its Injy. There's a good lay off on the P. O. No bloomin' way stations! It's all one anyhow, as we've an unlimited ticket, *that's wot we have!*"

As the coupé swiftly neared the "Grand Hotel," Beauford finished his simple story. "You alone will have my address, Phil. The F. O. will forward. But I must have absolute silence to even conjectural following. Will you kindly request Miss Hartley to give me a moment to say good-bye, as I shall not come to the Hotel to-night? And—" his voice hesitated, "You must be sure to ask Lady Isabel not to fail to await me. My departure must be kept secret. After I take leave of Miss Hartley, I will wait on the portico for Lady Dunham. I particularly desire to avoid Admiral Walton. Then you must give me every minute until I am gone, for we may not meet again. I shall send Hobson away with the things and you and I can drive away from our hotel and catch the train at the rampart station, as if going for an outing. Here you are! I'll meet you at our hotel."

"Count on me for anything," said the astonished Maitland. "Your new calling seems to be both exciting and mysterious!"

"*So it is*—decidedly!" soberly exclaimed Beauford as Philip sprang out at the nearest corner.

Maitland found Lord Beauford an hour later standing in the midst of an extempore breastwork of luggage, essentials and non-essentials. Bright-faced Hobson was reducing the chaos to order.

"Maitland! I'll leave all this impedimenta here, and a week after I leave, the Embassy dispatch agents will remove all quietly. Now, if you will refuse admittance to everyone, I'll rejoin you in an hour. Can I count on you?"

"Absolutely!" said Philip, as he resigned himself to the comforts of pipe and easy-chair.

Miss Evelyn Hartley, in carriage-dress, awaited Lord Beauford's visit. "I am glad to have seen him," murmured Evelyn, "before my Swiss tour. We may not meet again for months. Has he discovered anything? Once en route, I am safe from his honest questioning eyes." With a quick glance, the heiress satisfied herself that they were alone in the great salon, as Lord Beauford was ushered in. His manner was unusually constrained, and, hat in hand, he began a formal interview.

"I beg pardon for daring to detain you, Miss Hartley, but I could not leave without informing you, as it might possibly have some faint interest for you, that I have leased Jervaux Priory for a period of years to Lord Derwentwater. In going away for some time, I feel that I should bid you farewell. I am obliged to ask you kindly to keep the fact of my departure in absolute confidence. I depart on public business, and I hope I am not indiscreet in asking your kindly silence. I shall always feel a newer respect for womanhood in thinking of your noble aid in bringing Maitland back from shadow-land! We part as friends, do we not?" He had risen and his hand was extended.

"Surely I shall see you again, Lord Beauford?" the startled woman cried. "This is not a last farewell?"

"I go into strange paths, it will be months before I shall be again in Vienna, if in years! But," he smiled faintly, "if I am correctly informed, the Countess Oborski will not, in the gayeties of Vienna, find time to remember her fellow-nurse?"

Evelyn Hartley drew her breath in a gasp of a sudden anger. Her lips moved, but with a slight inclination of her head she passed out, leaving the peer standing alone with outstretched hand! When he recovered his composure, she was gone. But he seemed to hear the faint rustle of her robes, and a sudden gloom obscured the richness of the hall! At his feet lay a glove, forgotten in her flight.

Alfred Beauford's hand trembled as he stooped and picked it up. He thrust it in his breast, and found himself at the portico's end, below which the tide of gay promenaders flowed. His heart was racked with unavailing regret. "What mad folly brought those foolish words to my lips? She is now only a gracious memory of the past! But I have sealed the gate of the barrier forever!"

When he lifted his gloomy eyes, Lady Dunham, never more radiant in her womanly charms, was at his side. The golden hair rippled away from the sweet face, her eyes were liquid in their wistful anxiety. "It is nothing serious, I hope! Alfred, speak! Is there a new sorrow for you?"

Dull and heavy were the accents of his voice as
they fell on her ear. "Nothing! Isabel—only I leave
quietly to morrow early. I go on a long journey, and
I may not see you for months. I could not go without seeing you!"

· "But you will write? I have so much to tell you,"
cried Lady Isabel, in sudden alarm. Her untold confession was struggling to her pallid lips.

"I will not be able to write a line. It is a matter
of honor to keep my destination secret! You must
not, *even to Evelyn Hartley*, own that I have taken
leave, or told you of my departure. You simply
know nothing! I may not see or hear from you for a
year. Letters addressed to the Foreign Office will
reach me, but only on my return to London! My lips
are sealed."

Lady Isabel turned into the shadows of a deep
window recess, and Beauford writhed under her hopeless moan.

"*And we shall not meet again?*" There were tears
on the trembling little hands which Beauford stooped
and kissed.

"Some brighter day, perhaps under the old oaks
at Ventnor. God be with you, Isabel—I must not
linger! Guard my departure from Walton as you
would save my honor!"

With a choking throat, he turned away, and left her
standing alone. Her loving eyes were filled with bitter tears and she did not see him go!

"Ah! My God! The vengeance of the years is cold
and pitiless!" was the lonely woman's cry as she gained
the shelter of her apartment. "He has spoken to
Evelyn! She has refused him! And *now* he is lost
to me forever!" In her agony, Isabel Dunham felt an

insane jealousy of the stately American girl burning
in her veins. In a darkened room she hid her pale
face in the friendly shadows. When Miss Hartley
desired to be admitted, Lady Dunham's message of
regret was couched in icily polite terms. Miss Hartley, startled and dismayed by Beauford's gaucherie,
sought counsel and womanly cheer from the gentle
Isabel. But the Englishwoman, stricken at heart,
guarded her seclusion, and Lord Beauford was far on
his way toward Brindisi when Lady Dunham emerged
from her retirement. There was a constraint between
the whilom friends, which even the haste of Lady Isabel's proposed departure for Ventnor Hall could not
disguise.

Suspicious of all her Viennese surroundings,
Evelyn Hartley guarded her annoyance and surprise for she felt an atmosphere of distance separating
her uncle and herself. To "Brother Philip" alone
she turned for heart's ease in her silent loneliness. The
beautiful woman's passions were sleeping, unawakened
yet by the footfall of the "Fairy Prince." Bewildered
by Lady Isabel's manifest estrangement and the artful social rumors of Vienna, Miss Hartley would fain
have questioned "Brother Philip." But, grave and
friendly, the answer of Philip Maitland gave her no
light on Beauford's sudden departure, or his behavior.

In the vigil of their last night, Alfred Beauford had
given his bosom friend certain charges in case of accident. "I can not tell you how it pains me to part from
you, Phil," said the Englishman, as Hobson reported
the last detail arranged. "I would have wished to
have been less abrupt in taking leave of Miss Hartley.
After a month has elapsed you may tell her that I was
secretly summoned away on duty. I value her good

opinion too highly to have her think that I left in sudden pique or in some intrigue." Lord Alfred was keenly eying his friend. The approaching Oborski nuptials had not been a topic of their heart exchange.

"I would gladly do so Beauford, but Miss Hartley, I believe, leaves at once for Switzerland, with no present idea of return to Vienna."

"Did she tell you so?" eagerly queried Beauford. 'When?"

"Why, several days ago!" remarked Maitland, wondering at his animation.

"Watch over her, Phil!" cried Beauford, seizing his hands. "She is a noble woman, and you owe your life to her and that white pearl of the cloister, 'Sister Louise!'"

"He has learned of her generosity in some way! I must be careful or I may spoil all," thought Maitland. "I fancy I shall turn my steps homeward, Beauford," he said, "as your absence will be long and indefinite!"

"Yes! It may lead me to the end of Life's road," said Beauford. "Phil! we have seen a bit of life together. I have no one nearer than you in heart! I have sent a letter to my London bankers, and do you have your address registered there. I shall turn up first at London, and I will wire you the moment I am in old England again. Should anything happen, you can read that letter. *It will tell you all!*"

This was Beauford's only bit of sentiment for he was bright and cheery as he sprang into the train at the Rampart station. "Stole away! Keep the gossips quiet!" was Beauford's manly good-bye.

Two days later as Maitland entered the "Grand Hotel," he was accosted by Count Stanislas Oborski, in

whose eyes an ominous glitter told of the dark passions
lurking under his suave courtliness.

"Ah! Maitland! Just the man! Have you seen Lord
Beauford? Is he still in the city. I desired to see
him! Can you give me news? And Miss Hartley.
She is not at home. But I am informed she leaves
soon for Switzerland! Is this not sudden?"

"Everything seems at cross-purposes!" muttered
Maitland, as he remarked, with cutting coldness, "I
know nothing of Lord Beauford's movements, Count.
I presume the Embassy could inform you. And I am
equally in the dark as to Miss Hartley's plans of travel.
I suggest you should use great care, however, in not
coupling her name with that of Lord Beauford!"

"Oh! Precisely! I beg pardon! You misunder-
stood me!" remarked the discomfited officer, as the
American passed him with a slight bow and mounted
the stair. "*There is some mystery here!* I am helpless without him, I must try the English widow's
stock of gossip!" But the servant returned with the
news that Lady Dunham was breakfasting at the British Embassy. "Ah, by the way, Josef," craftily
remarked Oborski, "Did you see Mr. Maitland? Is he
in the hotel?"

"He is in the small drawing-room with the great
American lady and the old admiral," softly answered
the servant, pocketing the gold piece Oborski had
slipped into his hand.

With a smothered oath, the enraged count sprang
into his carriage, and his philosophy only returned
after an hour's very deliberate pistol practice at the
club gallery. "I will force a quarrel on that American
fool after she is gone and put him out of the way!
The Englishman seems to have been refused. He is

not in Vienna!" Oborski gave special orders to his Leporello, when his elaborate dinner at home was concluded. Before midnight he knew that Lord Beauford's private baggage had been arranged for final departure, and a few gold pieces extracted further details from the hotel servants.

When Count Stanislas left the "Grand Hotel," Philip Maitland found Miss Hartley, grave and composed, pondering over a long letter in the familiar hand of Judge Fox. The admiral welcomed Maitland's arrival. His keen eye had caught the signs of a coming social storm. He was glad to escape, and over a choice bottle of Hungarian wine plot out the "probabilities" for a peaceful future course. Isabel Dunham and Miss Hartley could not deceive, by their stately indifference, the artful sailor. "Glass has fallen too quickly! Lookout for a typhoon!" he grumbled, Under the "good form" social excuse of "letters to write," he escaped to his Horatian seclusion.

"As I am utterly ignorant of American affairs. I can be of no assistance, I fear," was his last word. Evelyn bowed in approving silence. Maitland curiously watched the woman whose clouded brow spoke of grave mental dissatisfaction. Miss Hartley was learning the lesson of life! She was proving how little free will is really left, even to those favored by fortune and station! The shadows of the troubles of *others* darkened the sunny morning of her womanhood! With no reference to Lord Beauford, she handed him the letter of her old trustee. "I wished your advice before forming further plans of travel, Philip!" she said. "Read this. I feel that you may soon be needed at home, and that even I have a duty to the interests centered in me." Her rich, deep voice made Maitland start!

There was a ring in its tones he had never heard before. A spice of deliberate sadness, an incipient world-weariness, telling of pressure from without! In truth, Evelyn Hartley divined, at last, that she was the object of unknown social schemes, that her fate was linked and interwoven with that of others, and that self-interest, in its varied forms, was weaving already nets for her unwary feet! On her beautiful fresh face, radiant in its youth, an unwonted look of fixed sternness, caught from her resolute father, gave gravity to her mien.

"I hope there is no immediate trouble to harass you?" he remarked. His light manner changed as he read the emphatic lines of the old lawyer. A guarded reference to her mother's marriage, in which his reprobation was veiled by a careful assurance that the new relation would not be allowed to affect the estate, led up to the subject of his plaint of the time.

"Under the new conditions," he wrote, "I presume you will make no permanent arrangement for residence abroad. Naturally, Admiral Walton will aid and advise his sister, whose American connection seems to be permanently severed. In charge here, and actively engaged in the affairs of the Trust, your special interests will be my study. I am desirous that you should hold yourself in readiness to return, in case of necessity, and show, by your own example, your continued interest in your birthplace and the people. There is a very uneasy feeling growing up in the United States which has gathered force for several years. A period of commercial depression, financial distrust, and political skepticism is upon us! The manufacturing interests languish under overproduction. and keen wars of competition. The agricultural toilers resent freight and interest charges, and the habitual good-humor and confidence of our people seem to be gravely disturbed. Our press is inflammatory. It declaims and exclaims! It does not lead and guide as it should! The baser papers inflame the passions of classes. A long period of peace since '65 has seen great fortunes, giant privileges, even huge monopolies slowly sail out on our civic seas! Blocks of alien laborers, aggregations of foreigners, disturb our labor-market or throng our cities. The great transportation lines are finished, our army and navy absorbs but few of the turbulent, and our top-heavy public-school system is rushing out, semi-educated, the children of the foreigners who have snatched at our citizenship to compete with our own youth in every calling. Our writers, our politicians but faintly see that our public schools are used only as language instructors for this young swarm. Capital, cold and secretive, is drawing the rein tighter every day, and the great public lands have been absorbed. Now the feeling of pressure is communicated. Tramps swarm in the country, loafers crowd the cities, the last living on vice and aiding machine politics. Never was there such a multitude of false prophets, never so many political schisms. Morality is outraged by the vulgar rich, the reckless poor, and religion's voice is getting shriller and smaller daily! I speak so far only of a present *condition*. What is the future *fear?* The prating and unceasing clatter allowed in public, and in the unlicensed press, has called up a class of resistants to the duties of citizen,—of positive malcontents and active disorganizers. The howling socialists who scream at the dangers of "Centralization," call for the government, the states, the communities, and lastly the rich, to take care of all the poor, regardless of merit. This is 'paternalism' with a vengeance! The theoretical doubt as to the right of the thrifty to have and keep property, is far different from these open threats to take and distribute by force! The attitude not óf labor-unions, but people connected with labor, of a continual menace to level factories, destroy railroads, burn cities, and wipe out property, in case of any quarrel, is alarming! Neither great political party has the firmness to denounce lawless bluster, and the small sects feed on it! The timidity and unfitness of our city and state governments has been shown in several public outbreaks. Behind all this, I know there are active emissaries of anarchism fanning the flame of hate, and seeking to precipitate any outbreak, setting the embattled ranks of the poor against the rich! It is true that the influence is mainly foreign, that its work is covert, that our own people are right in spirit, but the work is unceasing! It has greatly multiplied lately. In view of the fear of our politicians, the great monied interests of the land exchange confidential reports. There has lately been observed an organized movement of anarchists, and their abettors, aided with at least considerable funds, and we have developed the fact of increased correspondence and European direction in these incipient schemes. It looks as if an energetic apostle of Bakunin and Marx was stirring up the black flood to its depths. Manufacturing properties, especially mining plants and railway interests are subject to sudden losses from riot, fire, dynamite, or skillfully united mob action. Cleveland is like Pittsburg exposed to peculiar dangers. Great money centers like Boston, New York, and Philadelphia, are now guarded by a fairly well-organized National Guard, under trusted chief officers. Centers of railroad traffic and great manufacturing places will be the first attacked, the least protected, and the hardest to safely guard. The well located armories and compact police forces of the greater cities are not found in such places. We are fated to have hesitating men at the helm in emergencies. Every malcontent and rioter has his vote, and a vigorous *young lofer's* vote may counterbalance at the polls that of an *ex-President!* Now, I call your attention to the singular lack of moral support given to the energetic police, in cases of alarm, riot, or anarchistic threatening. There seems to be a mental inertia about the better classes not at all creditable to them. The most outrageous public exhibitions of sedition have been permitted, within a year or so, and the firm attitude of the startled police authorities of Chicago and New York has been criticised most unwisely. It seems to be now admitted that the distinctly criminal classes of ultra-socialists, and mouthing anarchists are entitled to a certain minority representation and opinion! Instead of vigorously applauding the punishment of would-be murderers of the State, a storm of approval meets the unwise pardoning in a Western State, of men who would have been interned for life, in any cool community. I say the time will come when the hand raised against the public welfare must be *lopped off* to save the vital interests dear to all! Now, the President, Cabinet, and Congress can do but little! Fact must be glaringly apparent before the slow enginry of the Federal Government will move! Criminal plotting is markedly on the increase here, and Western communities gravely threaten to abandon all claims held by the rich in deference to the debtor! The security of life and property is as essentially the liberty of the rich as the franchise is a right of the citizen toiler!

"Red-handed anarchism is creeping upon us, behind the moving breastwork of reform, socialism and 'modern theories!' In these times, in the future which may be lit up with the flames of a mad uprising, united by alien criminals, as the constituted authorities will not prepare, *it behooves those interested to make ready.*

"Holders of property like yours, women of wealth, absentees and corporate partners must be willing to aid with funds, a defensive movement! Trusty citizens, beyond any taint of a personal motive, must be sought out for executive places. Should I call on you to allow me to largely use funds in your interest, you will know why! You can see the reasons of my willingness to see a block of the trust funds safely secured for a period of years on English lands! England may *admit* the peaceful foreigner, but she gives him *no voice.* He can not set the land aflame unchallenged! The better classes have a direct voice in the control of the nation's affairs as a class. That voice has never been lifted to destroy the vested rights of rich or poor. In our remarkable country, rushing on from the period of its physical development to uncertain social and political changes, the aggregate will of the people, fairly expressed in elections, is dissipated by a sort of loss by induction and resistance. When it returns in excutive action, its direction may be changed, its force be lost forever!

"We nearly lost the country itself, when a weak man, as President, faltered between the execution of the laws and the proud insolence of an excited South. James Buchanan's tombstone might have borne the inscription 'The Last President.' It is undeniable that the 'jeunèsse dorée' of the land are now raised to despise the simple, strong democracy which built us up. The feeble sons of the rich, who ape *second-class* European manners, and nourish *first-class* foreign vices, will never right the wrongs creeping into our political system. Easy wallowing in a golden trough will content these young men who pride themselves that they never could be mistaken for Americans!

"I have done. You can see how calmly I reasoned as to the safe placing of a portion of the trust funds, but you can do me a favor. Should you meet Philip Maitland, show him this letter. Let him read it. I hoped much from his youth. I feel that his country has a claim on his manhood. To be an American, not a cosmopolitan club man, to come home, ripe with his travel, and added experience. We need him for Congress here—we need him as Mayor. We should have some such man as Colonel of our National Guard Regiment here. The old veterans are passing beyond their active usefulness. Not that he would be plunged in immediately exciting scenes, but we want *some* of the *best*, as well as *many* of the *worst*, in place! We must have men upon whom we can rely! The agitators, and sneaking conspirators are making ready! Let us make them feel that the banded useful citizens can prepare also for a struggle just as sanguinary and sharp as their mad folly would have it. In a land where we have no stong military aristocracy, no resolute sovereign to smite down red-handed criminal insurrection, the simple process of the civil court ensuring private right must be backed, through life and death by every useful citizen. Old as I am, I would go out, musket in hand, to quell the lawless spoliation of any man's home, rich or poor. If I did not, I were unworthy to rest my head in a tranquil domicile of my own! Our country has its future trials! The gray smoke drifting away from Appomattox did not show behind it all the future. The social future of America, if made a social upheaval, by anarchistic madness, will be a dark and bloody one! I will see that Philip Maitland is placed, not in the path of ambition, but in the line of his duty among his fellows. As a native-born American citizen, sound in precept, and worthy in example we need him here!"

As Maitland laid down the letter, he was conscious of the earnestness of Evelyn Hartley's eye. With her fair hands folded, she had followed the play of varied emotion upon her countryman's grave face. A silence reigned for a moment, and the young man rose impatiently, and walked to the window. His heart was full of conflicting emotions. In the meeting of their eyes he felt, for the first time, that he knew why his life had hitherto been void of settled purpose. That there were higher pleasures in this world than mere enjoyment, that the well-worn syllables "Duty" might have a charm of their own, had never occurred to him! The old lawyer's words roused him to the conception of a future worthy in its purposes, lofty in its aims, and resting on broader hopes than mere ambition.

This his brain told him, and also, and more, while his heart told him that he had lingered near Evelyn Hartley in ignorance of the fact that her strong womanly nature drew him toward her of all the world. The silent charm had been wrought in the days when she lingered near his couch of sickness! His angel walked so near him that he had not seen her beauty! For the pride and tenderness, the inspiration of her glance, thrilled him to his heart of hearts.

In a moment he was at her side. "Shall I go or stay, Evelyn?" he said quietly. "Do you think my

native land, my birth-place, my compeers have such
claims upon me as are set out in that letter?"

"I believe the noblest life for an American is that
of an active and interested member of his community.
Particular actions have special reasons! Life is various now in these later days! The world has grown
strangely small, but the American who abandons his
native land deserves to be a '*man without a country!*'
It is for you to render an account of your stewardship
of life! No one can live the life of another. No one
nature can be a law to any conscience but its own!"

"I will see you to-night. I must think this matter
over alone!" said Maitland softly, as he left her, and
went forth to a self-communion of hours.

The English mail of the afternoon added to Evelyn
Hartley's preoccupations the bitterness of a new-born
hatred whose possible consequences astounded her.
Her uncle gravely placed in her hand a letter from her
mother, in which the refusal of Lord Beauford to extend
the lease of Jervaux Priory was made the vehicle of
an attack upon her daughter, which made Miss Hartley
tremble with indignation.

"I have taken steps to secure myself a fitting residence," wrote Mrs. Rheingold, "and am not in ignorance of the unwomanly and revengeful intrigues by
which my daughter has thrust me out of the home I
had selected."

"I am at a loss to understand this, Evelyn," said
Admiral Walton, puzzled "I leave the matter entirely
in your hands. I shall make no reply to the letter."

Miss Hartley's self-command alone prevented a
possible betrayal of her secret. Had the bankers or
the lawyers informed her mother of the whole story of
Beauford's rescue from ruin?

"I shall have peace, perhaps, only in America," mused the heiress, and, as she sat alone, she wondered if any association under natural laws would ever replace the family as moulded by man!

Strange compound of passion, expediency, prudence, and stubborn plodding in the tracks of those whose feet are at rest forever!

Physical laws in operation, diverse and unfathomable personal designs, and a dropping into the way of the world, segregate little knots of human beings from the rest! The family tie, the social perspective seldom binds or includes more than three generations. At that epoch, the evolved miniature tribe, branching out, mingles in minor fragments with deeper streams of blood, as rivulets, joining the brook and flowing into the creek, mingle in the waters of the great river of Life! While characteristics are lost in time, as the group is held by law and custom, leaving out the usual criminal affection for direct offspring, the family association varies its maximum of love and attraction to its minimum of scorn and aversion. Often the history is one of the neutral line of mere sufferance! Evelyn Hartley, deprived of one parent, unloved by another, mused bitterly over the algebraic signs of heart-feeling, the $+$, the $-$, the $\pm$, and the cold $\bigcirc$ of death or nothingness, from whence we all came, and into which dark and empty circle we go hence in silence! Crowded with pallid shades, yet empty, the cave of Death is the womb of Time, peopling this world with flitting and unsubstantial shades!

In the revulsion of her noble soul, against the vulgar suspicion and coarse inuendoes of her narrow-minded mother, *a mother only in the physical fact,*—the envied heiress bowed her head and wept for him who slept

by Lake Erie! Too young in the world's strange love
to know that infallibly her life-curve must intersect
in time, another, she buried her head in her hands and
sobbed over the loneliness which shaded her path!

The throbbing pulses of her youthful heart, the royal
currents of her blood, unstirred with passion, reflected
not a thrice of the unrest which strangely moved
Beauford speeding over the Mediterranean waste of
waters, which clouded Philip Maitland's self-exami-
nation in his lonely rooms, and which haunted the gay
Count Stanislas Oborski, at the palace puppet show,
where he was one of the human players in the masque
of Royalty! For even in the presence of Austria's
Emperor, the passionate noble, greedy of the rich
prize of her magnificent fortune, inflamed by her calm
personal attitude, dreamed of the dark eyed American,
and swore "She shall be mine!"

Under the roof of the great caravansera of Fashion's choicest devotees, while Miss Hartley dreamed
of her future, clouded with the undeveloped drama in
which she was cast as "leading lady," fair Isabel Dunham, explained to the astonished Mrs. St. Leger her
reasons for a sudden return to Ventnor Hall. The
Anglo-Indian army woman resented the termination of
her pleasant sojourn at Vienna. Unconscious of the
diplomacy of Stein and the Polish count, she, with
becoming womanly vanity, accepted their Grecian
friendship as real!   .

"I might even remain. Vienna is so quaintly delightful, but Miss Hartley also departs for Switzerland.and
I could not remain alone, and follow out our pleasant
plans!"

Mrs. St. Leger was right, for even Indian Colonels
have a positive, though distant respect for "Mrs.

Grundy." The sybaritic warrior, campaigning at Simla, would ultimately hear of any risquée performance, incautiously interpolated in her "resting tour!" While he knew of the extremely social disposition of his lively wife, the gallant soldier was illustrating his military character, by the tenderest attentions to the particularly dashing consort of a dragoon captain!

This absent son of Mars, chasing certain recalcitrant fanatics a hundred leagues away, would have writhed in his saddle, had he mentally "kodaked" the pair who got on so extremely well together.

"We must certainly take leave of Miss Hartley to-night," said bustling Mrs. St. Leger.

"By all means," calmly replied Lady Isabel, who was pondering the contents of a letter from her London agents.

When Doctor Ernest Rheingold, swelling with the prosperity resulting from an easy conquest of the egoistic widow, visited Lady Isabel's bankers, he made an awkward, though unconscious revelation!

"I should like, if possible, to have Ventnor Hall for a period of ten years," said the nouveau riche. "My wife, being a member of one of the old county families, is fond of this region. We would not stand on the matter of terms, I assure you. There are but two places suited to us, and we fancied a liberal offer might tempt Lady Dunham. Any proposition in reason would be accepted by us!"

"I am, of course, pleased to forward your proposals to Lady Dunham, who is on the Continent," said the banker. "In such serious matters, we should expect her to return to London. We will write at once, and advise you immediately, but is not Jervaux Priory satisfactory to you?"

"Entirely so; but our lease is a very short one."
Returned the pompous German.

"I heard," said the man of money, reflectively, "it
seems to me, I heard, that Lord Beauford had entered
into the diplomatic service. He is unmarried. He
does not propose to keep up his home establishment!"

"That is exactly what brings me to you," replied
Rheingold, with affected confidential grandeur; "I
understand he has raised eighty thousand pounds on
the estate by mortgage from Miss Hartley, and that
the rental of Jervaux would be in her hands. It would
be very distasteful to us to bear the relation of ten-
ants."

"*Ah! I observe!*" gravely replied the banker. "I
shall have great pleasure in holding the refusal of
Ventnor Hall at your disposition, until Lady Isabel
may decide. I should fancy her home-place too
lonely and expensive for her. Besides, she may
marry! Who knows? *Nothing is expected in the case
of any woman!* I have long since ceased to be surprised at anything a woman may do!"

Doctor Rheingold bowed out with great deference,
entered his carriage, in forgetfulness of the fact
that his only knowledge of the investment of the
estranged daughter was derived from the anarchist
Stein, now plotting at Cleveland.

In his furtive visits to great centers of proposed
future commotion, Doctor Carl Stein had not omitted
to visit his old home. Literary labors of a quiet nature
explained his social incognito. "Writing a book" is
the sufficient excuse for even the strangest social
hiatus! Guarded and alert in his brief interviews
with Judge Fox, he passed in victory, the keen scrutiny of the old lawyer. But from the clerk spy, now

his slave, he learned of the English investment so opportune to Lord Béauford. "I must not let Oborski know this yet. He is too passionate, too headlong! His best chance of success lies in awakening the slumbering romantic feelings of Evelyn. Beauford and Maitland gone, then Stanislas has a free field! But Rheingold must know of this. It will serve him in his domination of the mother, for her money is secured to the Cause! Rheingold shall enrich his needy relatives and be well paid for smothering his life in that woman's daily atmosphere. *The rest is ours!* Fear will hold him straight on the course! But he must know! If Oborski gains the daughter, I can open my campaign!"

And so, with a sinking heart, beautiful Isabel Dunham learned, from her banker's cautious letter, that the very honor of Lord Alfred Beauford was pledged to Evelyn Hartley. Through her tears she sobbed: "Now I know what sealed his lips in silence! Now, I can see the golden chain which binds them." She bitterly gazed at her own useless beauty in the mirror reflecting her tears. "She is not more fair than I am! *He loved me once!* My heart is weighed down by Miss Hartley's millions!" From a vision of Lord Beauford's consort queening it at an Embassy, whereat her lost lover represented the haughty "Empress of the Seas,"—forced by the merciless social hypocrisy of "good form,"—the lonely Lady of Ventnor, her fears and sorrows locked in her breast, went out to calmly part from her estranged friend. In every glance of Evelyn Hartley's eye, Lady Dunham read the consciousness of her power over the absent man whose name was left strangely unspoken!

In the mental repression of awaiting Philip Maitland's visit and his decision on Judge Fox's appeal, the stately American beauty received a formal visit from Count Stanislas Oborski with elaborate courtesy. "You will be at Lausanne for some time?" the count said, splendid in his picturesque uniform. "I may have the pleasure of seeing you there! I have occasion to visit it often!"

A secret summons to a Council of the Red Brothers was foremost, even now, in his mind. In the radiant smile of the now composed woman, happy in her departure, Oborski read the glad tidings of Hope. "She shall not have time to forget me!" he placidly murmured; but neither Isabel Dunham nor the brilliant Pole read her heart aright.

She was awaiting "Brother Philip's" farewell visit.

CHAPTER X

AT CLEVELAND—AN ACTIVE CITIZEN—PERSONAL GOSSIP IN
THE "GALIGNANI"—VENTNOR HALL—FRIENDSHIP BLOOMS
ANEW IN SORROW—UNWELCOME ARRIVALS AT LAUSANNE—
A LAKE PARTY—THE EXPLOSION—"SHE IS MINE!"

MR. PHILIP MAITLAND was in a secretly rebellious frame of mind, as he completed his toilet for his last evening in Vienna.

"Thank heaven, I have little to bother with in my run home. My old Shakespeare and a few bundles of cigars are all I need! I am of slight importance in this glittering 'Vanity Fair.' Whatever I go to, I leave little behind here. My only return for the world-wandering of years is a memory stored with quaint shadow-pictures, and a marking down of the self-valuations of humanity to the extent of say—*fifty per cent!*

"I must say farewell to gentle Lady Isabel! I fancy, poor woman, her thoughts are with the Eastern voyager! We all seem to be engaged in a game of cross-purposes!

"As for me I throw up my cards. I stand with something to lose and nothing to gain! Lucky Beauford. If he meets no mishap, the future has golden tints for him!"

Maitland strode along in the early evening, rugged in his renewed strength, for the ozone of the Transylvanian hills thrilled his every fibre. "Yes! I will take one, some one of the sketchy occupations my scattering college course has fitted me for. I have just achieved the knowledge of my own cultured semi-ignorance! My collegiate skimming alone in the labyrinths of learning has only led me to doors sealed by my mental rawness. Shall I drift into the only recognized American career, 'Chasing the Dollar?' Must I occupy that proud station of a 'leading citizen, recognized for sound business ability?'"

Ushered into the presence of Lady Dunham, Maitland was fain to soon escape, after the usual adieu de voyage. With difficulty he parried Lady Isabel's direct questions as to Beauford's departure. "I regret that I am as much in the dark as yourself, Lady Dunham," said he, rising to take his leave. "The only address Beauford gave me was 'Foreign Office, London,' and he promised to cable me on his return. I presume the more than strict code of his new calling enjoins an absolute secrecy upon him. May I hope that we may all meet happily in England?"

His voice was very kind, and, with genuine regret, he listened to her final plaint: "If you would only tell me all, I am sure he has given you some private details." The wistful longing of her eyes, the vague tenderness of her manner told the story which her womanly delicacy would conceal.

"There is such a word in life as 'too late!' I fear the fates are against her," mused Maitland, as he left the Englishwoman doubtful and disconsolate.

"A cheerful send off! One more such inspiring scene, and I am ready for the morning train!" gloomily ejaculated Philip as he sought the presence of Evelyn Hartley.

He was unprepared for the simple word "good-bye!"

It was tacitly his decision to go to America, not from an eager desire to enter into Judge Fox's spirited undertakings, but from a sense of the futility of remaining. "If I stay here, I will drift into confidential relations which tie my hands, and I will be drawn into a play wherein my lips are sealed." As he reluctantly drew near Miss Hartley's presence, he was confronted by Admiral Horatio Walton, whose face showed great concern.

"I'm told you are off for America, Maitland. May I have a few words with you before you go?" the sailor said.

"Most certainly," replied the American. "I'll meet you in the café in half an hour!"

"Thanks!" said Walton, as he resumed his quarter-deck exercise in the main hall.

Miss Hartley extended both her hands as her visitor entered. "So you have made up your mind to go home!" she said, with sparkling eyes.

"How did you know?" he replied, astonished.

"I could tell it in your face! You have decided!" she remarked with an air of conviction.

"I leave to-morrow morning," he quietly answered, "But I am unable to see my personal duty clearly defined. I am sufficiently interested to go home and observe the rapidly changing phases of the American national character. I love my country. I am not attached to a special interest or bound to any class. The homogenity hoped for by the fathers of our country is now impossible. Foreign immigration has tinged unequally our communities. Between our farmers, manufacturers, and traders, there is no real sympathy. Mean, narrow-minded, and by no means of ideal integrity, our farmers are only meritorious as a class. They lack political honor, and steadfastness. Our manufacturers are wedded to a grinding routine and look only at their own interest. Our merchants take no bold stand in our councils, for they un-Americanize their daily life as much as possible. There seems to be no time for public interests. Each one at home rushes eagerly to the personal clearing-house of the day, and prepares only for the morrow. I have little to say but good-bye. I leave Europe with but one debt unpaid, the obligation I owe to you, and to Beauford, for saving my life! I can never repay it, but I will cherish your kindness to my dying day!"

He rose, for her face grew cold at the mention of Beauford's name. "She is too proud to ask me as to his destination, or has he told her all?"

Miss Hartley arrested him with a quick motion of her hand. She saw that he was resolute and would make no sign.

"You have more than repaid me by your devotion to my interests, and your brotherly aid. I trust *you only,* of all around me, Philip!" Her voice was slightly broken. "You may be interrogated, be questioned as to my affairs."

He gravely said, "My lips are sealed forever, I might speak to you now but that I know I must guard your trust. Be the sole arbiter of your own affairs! Lead your own life, free from meddling or dictation! Should you ever need me, I will come to you. Judge Fox will have my address always. My own affairs are under his legal control."

Their eyes met and the heiress was strangely moved as he spoke in final farewell. "You will write to my London bankers. Tell me of your new life, of your home-coming. Have I your promise?"

He bowed and pressed her trembling hands in silence. When she lifted her head he was gone. A mad impulse seized her to call him back, and in sudden alarm she sought her boudoir. "What have I to say to him?" She sat long with clasped hands, and found no answer to the question. "I am alone now, in truth," she cried, and the future showed her no bow of promise!

Maitland's brow was dark as he joined Admiral Walton. The mariner was navigating unknown seas! The delightful coterie around him was breaking up, as if under some malign influence! Daily he saw Evelyn drifting away from him on the maelstrom of life. The sunny, successful German, bred in penury, stood between him and his wealthy sister! With all an adventurer's coarseness, Doctor Ernest Rheingold had blossomed out into a country gentleman of the most absurd pretension. Walton's letters from England gravely disturbed him. The admiral was a slave of that modern fetich of "good form" to whose inane worship the luxuriously idle classes of England and its pliant apes in America, sacrifice body, soul, and fortune! The wretched unhappiness of his sister would have moved him less than the social antics of Rheingold, who combined the parvenu and mountebank in the ridiculous exhibitions now delighting Walton's cool, cynical confréres at home. The rude pressure of the world confines many weak and vain natures, within the limits of the caution of daily cares!

By the accidents of fortune, this pressure vanishing, in the world, where the dollar gilds, or the yellow sovereign ennobles, these mushroom natures expand in the rich sunlight of prosperity, into fantastic social features!

"If I could only get the doctor to return to America and astound the Yankees with his display," mused Walton. "Anything suffices to create social rank in America! It is the happy hunting-ground of the bogus lord, the self-promoted valet, the befrogged, fur-coated foreign noble, and the pretender of every land. As the presumption of these insolent pretenders increases, the Yankee worship is all the more ardent! If Rheingold could be translated to the United States, I might lead Evelyn up to position, and a future! But, between the two warring Hartley interests, I will quarrel with the one and be ignored by the other. Evelyn gathers self-will and individuality daily. I'll try Maitland. He seems to have some influence!"

"I wished to speak to you of the social future of my niece, Maitland," Walton began. "I desire very much to heal the breach between mother and daughter. I know that you are intimate with my colleague, Wilkinson Fox. Now, if I could induce the puffed-up German apothecary to return to America, I could ensure

Evelyn a brilliant settlement in the highest ranks of English society. Now, there's Beauford, one of the oldest names—"

"Pardon me, Admiral Walton," said Maitland, whose eyes had a gleam lighting them, which spoke of the intense rage possessing his inmost soul. "I return at once to America! My time is extremely limited. If I can execute any *particular* commissions for you, I would gladly do so. Miss Hartley herself seems to have none. As for in any way entering into the disturbed affairs of this family, permit me to remind you that family quarrels, in any rank of society, are of absolutely no interest to others! They should be permitted to expend their storm force within the unfortunate circle affected."

"I follow a rule of life in declining to even discuss the future of Miss Hartley. Your future plans from her will naturally be affected by your point of view. It would seem to me that an American heiress, representing one of the great names of our later development, in the enjoyment of a fortune heaped up by American toilers, might find a fitting unicn *in her own land!* Something is due to the community which looks for all the nobler works of life to those whom the blind goddess has signally favored.

"I have always been struck with the cold heartlessness with which the English dispose of every social question affecting Americans! I distinctly deny that the future is golden, which leads an American heiress into the temporary honors of monied English aristocratic life. Life, fortune, and the golden years are offered up on the altar of a courtesy title, among people who covertly sneer at the women whose father's gold furbishes up your feudal rat-hole castles.

"From an American standpoint, the absenteeism of our leading young men, the slavish adoption of the English idea, and the abandonment of their country, is cowardly social treason. As to the women, they soon feel the secondary position into which they have drifted! .The American record of brilliant foreign marriages is one of social wreck and frightful scandal! The stings and arrows of their adopted English sisters make the life of the young women sacrificed to a sickly vanity, a slavery of sorrow. American absenteeism is the fatal curse of our fin de siècle days! The heavy hand of the Government should be laid in pun· ishment, and forfeiture on this mad folly sapping our social forces! There should be absolute negation of all American rights meted out to those who abandon their country! The position of American citizen honors any man! The liberal home and social life of the American woman makes our land a Heaven to the sensible, in comparison to the Hell of cold neglect, and heartlessness into which our exported young women enter! The time will come when these doubtful 'social honors' will be patent badges of disgrace! Our communities are waking up to the return of wives, heartsick; divorced, plundered in purse, and loaded down with children who precociously illustrate the impudent vices of their foreign fathers! *We can breed vice fast enough at home!* The destruction of the Atlantic passenger ferry would be a blessing to America!"

"Why do you not practice your own code?" sneered Admiral Walton, thoroughly aroused by Maitland's manner.

"*I propose to!*" calmly said Philip. "I leave to-morrow morning. If my awakening is a late one, it may yet be effective. At any rate, Admiral, let me assure you of my sincere wish for Miss Hartley's happiness, at home or abroad.   Rheingold is only one of a class of successful foreign sycophants and charlatans who slip in through unguarded doors into our wealthier families.   He is an illustration of my theory with regard to international marriages.   So you see, Admiral, I am not specially opposed to English fortune-hunters.   Your nobility have, at least, something to give in   return   for Papa Moneybag's investment.   I am not opposed to any naturalized citizens of usefulness casting their lot with us, if the transaction is a bona fide one.   But when the stranger within cur gates fattens, and waxes insolent in our midst, building up miniature Germanys, Polands, Irelands and other polyglot communities in our midst, then I cry; 'Close the gates!'   The whole nation will re-echo it in five years!"

Maitland rose to go.   Admiral Walton stopped him with a grandiose wave of his hand.

"And you tell me that an English nobleman is not a fitting mate for an American girl?"

"Usually not!" rejoined Philip calmly.   "The question of equality does not enter.   Advisability is the vital point.   As a 'bargaining Yankee,' however, I only hope that when an American girl sells herself, or is sold, *she will get the price and fair treatment!*   I do not think England has a single noble who would be demeaned by marrying Miss Hartley.   Any American woman worthy of the name—one who represents the best class at home—can be admitted to your European circles without shaking the jewels from even the English crown!   The truth is, Admiral, England is the land of Cant and your 'good form' covers many an ugly angle!"

He extended his hand.

"You're not a bad fellow, Maitland! Let us have a parting glass?"

"Agreed," said Philip, "we will drink to the fairer adjustment of the international marriage exchanges. Send over your blue-blood girls with a bit of money. Our 'stay-at-home ' men may marry some of them *if they are as sweet as their American cousins.*"

"There is no fitting circle in America for an English woman of rank," said Walton, stiffly. "Your society has no real basis!"

"Well, we must get along without them then!" remarked Philip, merrily. "Thank Heaven! *A man can get a pretty fair consort without leaving our shores!* Our men are not as hard to suit as our women! Even our Pall Mall Brigade returns, when the exchequer is exhausted, to snap up the scattering heiresses left over by the foreign Pashas who throw the handkerchief!"

Philip Maitland felt an unwonted throb in his pulses as he left the half-mollified admiral.

"1 fancy that boy has been chaffing me a bit," grumbled the old man, as he solaced himself with "t'other glass" and plunged into a solitary consideration of the growing family feud.

Three weeks later, Maitland sat gazing on the busy throng along Euclid Avenue in Cleveland. His home had reopened its hospitable doors, and a number of old friends had verified the fact that the wanderer was not wholly spoiled by brushing elbows with dukes, count, monsignores and pashas.

With insidious tact, Philip had remained long enough in New York City to so array himself that it was *possible to mistake him for an American.* His collection of foreign curios in the way of wardrobe and personal gear was rapidly gravitating into the possession of his "man," an alert compound of trans-Atlantic prejudices.

"Do you feel entirely at home, Phil?" said Judge Fox, who had availed himself of a day out of court, to breakfast with the young man.

The wary old trustee had not found Maitland to be an artesian well of information. In fact, the pumping process failed to give the desired stream.

"I am growing accustomed to the frantic energy of the human cannon-balls, projected hither and thither, in our high explosive manner. I fancy I will wake up to the high-keyed music of home life shortly."

Fox despaired of leading out Maitland on the affairs of the Hartley family. Philip gracefully parried the advances of the lawyer, and pressed an excellent cigar upon him as a symbol of golden silence!

Venturing out from his breastworks, into the open, Fox bluntly said; "Do you not propose to settle down and become an active citizen?"

"From the description you gave of the political future, I should think I would do well to join the conservatives and watch 'our active citizens.' Miss Hartley read me your views!"

"They are truth and coming shadows already darken our present! The future will be gloomy. Maitland, I have waited for your return to tell you how serious the situation is. The discontented formulate a demand on the state to furnish, not only relief, but *remunerative* employment to the masses. Capital, backed by the government, must furnish work, needed or temporarily invented, to regulate the varying wants of the laboring masses. This is proposed as a measure, demanded as a right, and followed with the menace that the 'people' so-called, will liberally help themselves by force, if this new principle is not engrafted on our 'unwritten constitution!'

"It is a frank threat, 'You shall not keep what *you* have, unless you immediately provide what *we* want!' In other words, these agitators forcibly thrust themselves, in as uncapitalized partners, with the holders of property! It is not a theory of agrarianism, socialism, or even communism. It is the beginning of the destruction of the whole system founded on 'Private Right!'

"Once admitted in journalism, in arguments, this position, advanced as it is, will serve as a cover for newer and more daring attacks! There are skilled agitators spread all over our land now, trying to force their wedges into every flaw and cranny, to widen the breach between the rich and poor!

"Let thrift, the possession of wealth and individual enterprises, be made dangerous, and our American system is a failure! I said as much to Professor Stein when he passed through, a month ago. He frankly told me that the lower classes in Europe were moving out as a whole, from under the toppling aristocracies of Europe."

"Where is Stein now?" said Philip, with some interest.

"He is moving quietly around, making studies for his labored work, 'Racial Development in America.' He holds that, as all restraining pressure is relaxed here, it is almost time to note the results of German, Irish, Italian, Semitic, Scandinavian and other foreign migrations here!"

"He is very nearly right!" grimly remarked Maitland. "The American citizens of home blood may be studied as a *vanishing class*, and their decadence pictured by Stein, as a companion volume, if he lives twenty years. Our national resultant blood recalls the story of the cask of fine brandy which, in its transmission from the vineyard to the frontier, passed through various unscrupulous handlings. Deftly withdrawing portions and substituting water, it passed through all the stages, from pure spirit to ditch water, on its arrival.—Did Stein leave his address?" Maitland regarded the lawyer curiously.

"He did not! His movements are uncertain! His progress among these peoples is hampered by their suspicious jealousy. He said he would visit Europe once or twice in the next season!"

Philip smoked in silence. "I warrant he outwitted the judge! I will wager he has some private confidences with Doctor Rheingold." Yet he made no sign. The whole situation of both branches of the Hartley fortune was a maze of growing schemes.

"Now, Philip, as I take it for granted you will be one of us, I have a communication to make," said the judge. "Situated as we are, midway between New York and Chicago, and in a center of manufacturing, railway, and steamboat interests, we are, in a measure, isolated. Treasure passes through here, oil-pipe lines and vast general interests make a show of what the anarchistic demagogues call 'heaped-up wealth.' These fools do not see that these things all represent stock in trade, or tools of trade, paid for, or unpaid for—that capital as well as labor has its lien upon them, but that capital alone, is credited with their ownership, envied for their possession, and must preserve, as well as direct, and employ all these representatives of value. All the fine-spun theories of anarchistic peerism have not turned out a ton of steel rail, built even one hut, or added a thousand bushels of wheat to the granary of the world! It is 'vox et præterea nihil!'

"The anarchistic leaders differ from the agreeable holy men of India who sit in pious contemplation by the road and wait for the faithful to feed them!

"These blatant rogues howl for their own 'unearned increment,' and loudly demand *the other man's share also!*

"Now, about fifty of the men who are trustees of this wealth" of their own and others, recognize the tempting bait here exposed to the criminal robbers! It can be heaped up, undefended here, by adroitly maneuvering rail-way strikes. Social riot can produce confusion! Robbery and arson will follow a few sporadic dynamite terroristic outrages! In this way, the wolves of modern society propose, under cover of the confusion, to set class against class, and profit by the upheaval! The robust manliness of the American labor-unions may be led by national sympathy under the rallying cries of 'Free Speech,' 'Free Thought,' 'The Rights of Labor,' and other generalities, to give a certain support to these designs! It might be a week before an external force could restore order! In the meantime the great city would be pillaged, or left a scarred ruin like Paris after the Commune Fury.

"Other unprotected, important points are similarly exposed all over the land, irrespective of party or difference in station, a chosen band, who are watching anarchism, are preparing now to teach these insensate villains a lesson! We do not act publicly, as our designs would be frustrated by the lurking enemy. All over the land we are examining the resources at the sudden call of law and order! We leave state govern-

ments, civic office, and general reform questions alone!
We are making ready to meet criminal violence of
anarchistic nature most promptly, and visit it with decisive punishment! The foul-mouthed ravings of the
devotees of the Chicago anarchists hint at the use of
dynamite and arson!"

"We will furnish rope to grip the necks of the men
of the torch and bomb. We will back our men with
breech-loaders in trusty hands! We propose the
spoilers shall find on the threshold of every American
home, stately or humble, men ready to die to defend
the right. It will be no exchange of fine-spun theory,
but an expression of the God-given right of self-
defense, which belongs as well to the *useful citizen*
as the *mouthing malcontent!*

"Public opinion and local pride holds the police up
to a state of decent efficiency. They may need backing. Nothing but systematic force, well controlled, will
do it. Our local National Guard Regiment needs a
major. Its superior field officers may retire or be
removed. We want a man behind whom the citizens
can rally as a supporting posse, should the command
and the police need our physical help as well as funds,
and moral backing. Will you be that man? I have
been asked to sound you. None but selected men can
attain such places now! I drop compliment! It is a
call of duty! Will you help in this way to further our
plans? We are willing to extend reasonable relief to
the worthy. We are willing to arbitrate, to consider
the general welfare, and to make our state the haven
of the worthy! *We have had about enough of this
anarchistic bullying.* We will stand, under the law,
and absolutely crush the terrorists! They shall be
stoned at the gates like the outcasts of Israel! There

is a time when mercy is mad folly. Nothing contents these modern lunatics. In Russia, their death cry was, À bas la tyrannie! Vive l' anarchie!' In France, Ravachol and Vaillant die howling 'Mort à la bourgeosie! Vive l 'anarchie!' The same application of cowardly assassination to the haughty Czar, with life and death at his nod, and the lawful, unguarded representatives of popular government in enlightened France! Vaillant screams under the grip of the headsman, that his body may perish, but his principles will survive! In the face of such idiotic inconsistency, we propose that in the attempted application of the fanatic Bakunin's remedy of 'Destruction' in America, *their* bodies shall perish (if the battle joins) and *our* principles shall survive! The governments of the civilized world will be forced to join hands in systematic repression! These deserters, spies, and marauders in the campaign of human progress, seek a doom which is forced on organized society as the only remedy!

"Will you do your duty to your city, to your people, to the fellow-citizens who ask you to share this labor?"

Maitland, pausing in his restless pacing of the well-remembered library, turned to the old man and soberly said, "I will, Judge; you may use my name. I am aware of my unfitness to actively enter on this duty. But I have an old friend in command of an army post near here. I can use a month there in private study, and object-lessons, then I will be able to fill my place with at least a skeleton idea of duty."

Judge Fox shook the returned traveler's hands warmly. "This is the right spirit. We will cautiously introduce other men of your calibre. You will be asked to meet our executive committee at once."

When the counselor had departed, Philip Maitland gazed around him. The old home was a memorial of the thrift and energy of a departed generation. His eye fell on his father's picture. Under the inspiration of the eyes now closed forever, he vowed to cast his lot in with the preservative movement. Thoughts thronged upon the young man which led him to wander down to where the great city lay below him, throbbing with the organized activity of a busy day.

"It is a noble trust to guard the houses of my native city in the dear old land!" The breeze sweeping from the blue lake was laden with the very spirit of freedom, and he thanked God that he stood, a free man in a free land! There came over him a thrill in thinking of the three centuries expended in conquering savage nature, and in building up the America of to-day. The labors of the dead toilers, the thoughtful wisdom of the early patriots, our foreign war, the awful price paid for the slavery crime, the slow emergence of arts, science, literature, and a cultured society from a lonely barbarism, all these passed before his mind!

"They shall never undo the triumph of Time!" he solemnly said, as he returned his steps. Passing the closed Hartley mansion, magnificent even in its deserted state, a sudden pang rent Maitland's heart. He turned his head away.

Evelyn Hartley's face was ever present in his heart.

In the vigils of the night, pacing the deck of the liner on the wild Atlantic, he had seen the way to self-denial, to a good-bye to fresh hopes, that might have made his life a paradise.

"It is my duty not to press upon her my suit! I owe my life to her and to Beauford! Master of the secret of her noble action toward him, knowing of her lingering abroad to meet him on his return, it would be mean and cowardly in me to intervene. The confidential labors I have executed in her behalf, my knowledge of her veiled kindness, all this stops me from forcing my affection upon her.

"It would be a treason to the comrade of my heart in his distant quest! And she will walk another path in life, the darling woman whom I would call wife!" And a shadow darker than the nightfall, wrapped him round, as he sought his lonely home.

While Philip Maitland entered deeper daily into the council of that necessary conservatism which lives by the failure of general "reform" schemes, Evelyn Hartley tasted all the sweetness of life's morning in roving over the land of Tell. The thrilling grandeur of God's sculpture exalted her soul as she glided over Alp-shadowed lakes, or trod the crisp glacier with springing step. Admiral Walton had relapsed into a agreeable "modus vivendi." If the heiress was not daily moulded to his will, she was safe from extraneous pressure. Lady Isabel Dunham's return to Ventnor was hailed by the country side who gathered around the peerless beauty in her home-coming. Admiral Walton's letters told him of the marked gayety of the blue-eyed beauty. His face grew stern as he read of the general exclusion of his sister and her parvenu husband. The county families would not condone the mèsalliance of a woman, received as a Walton, who allied herself to an upstart physician.

Rank and gold, great renown is needed to carry the medical practitioner into English society. The sons of Galen hover on the outskirts of the higher circles, hardly within the door.

"Thank Heaven! They must leave! As Beauford

has leased Jervaux. to Lord Derwentwater there is no lingering there. And Lady Dunham will keep state at Ventnor. I fancy the bells in the old gray church town will ring wedding peals before long!

"Another patent social failure! May and December over again! General Dunham was not the lover to bind her heart with golden chains, nor even yet the man to win her confidence and respect, while yet young enough for companionship.

"Youthful passion makes strange matches, but family ambition and cold worldly prudence also ruin countless unions. At least the woman wedded in her heart's desire may say, as Thekla, when the storm breaks: 'I have lived and loved!'

"I'm glad Beauford will be absent some time. Lady Isabel will be disposed of! I shall live to see my Evelyn, the Lady of Jervaux Priory."

The old head of the Walton family, loyal to his birth and breeding, longed to see the beautiful American a shining star in the circle dear to his loyal British heart! "She is of our old stock. Our Yankee friend's house of cards may tumble! She will be safe from the world's storms behind the guns of England's matchless fleet, ruling her chosen battle-ground, the world's high seas!"

So the days sped merrily by in the delightful early autumn of Switzerland, and Evelyn Hartley ceased to wonder at Lady Dunham's coldness. She vainly conjectured the distant scenes wherein Lord Beauford braved all danger for the "Kaisar-i-Hind," and her mind was occupied with considerations of her next year's travel, her studies of life and continental society. She was not left without gossipy news, for the lively Mrs. St. Leger, roving from one to another of England's unrivaled country-houses, practiced her army habit of letter writing on the lonely heiress.

"She may be very available on my returning pilgrimage," thought the artful military flirt.

"It will be an agreeable break in my voyage!" Mrs. St. Leger sighed, for the social furloughs of even easy-going East Indian duennas must have an end. "I will keep an eye on this little triangular puzzle which ties up Beauford and my two friends." With sly managing skill, Mrs. St. Leger entered into the counsels of both the women who now waited for news of the mysterious quest of Lord Beauford. "It is as well to keep in touch with rising people," reflected Mrs. St. Leger, who thereupon sifted in an extra touch of sweetness, in her letters to the undeclared rivals. In the self-surrender of her joy in romantic Switzerland's varied attractions, Miss Hartley failed to realize that several rencontres, each bringing a newer touch of romance into her life, brought Stanislas Oborski into closer relations with uncle and niece. The great "Hotel de Quâtre Saisons" at Lausanne was a favorite resting place of the Austrian noble. Graced with the national facility and vivacity, Oborski was a master of the middle-age legendary romance clinging to the shores of Lake Leman.

A superb linguist, an ardent and impassioned musician, he was also a practiced master in the arts of the salon.

His courtly experience in the exclusive circles of Vienna, the chevaleresque devotion of his manner, and the distinction of his personal bearing lifted him above any of the cavaliers whom the summer days added to Miss Hartley's court. His military profession endeared him to Admiral Walton, who welcomed him with a geniality peculiar to the "services!" For your fighting trade seems to be, par excellence, the career for men of parts and good blood in Europe!

Miss Hartley was secretly proud of her influence in changing Philip Maitland's career. In his dispatches of the varied affairs of the Trust, Judge Fox found time to refer to the marked emphasis of the young traveler's welcome. "He will certainly be a leader in the community. The next year will certainly see him made a Member of Congress, and he is serving on several committees of great importance to us at present. I am rejoiced at his energy, and the manly vigor with which he is entering into our home life.

"Maitland will gather a personal following of our best young men, and be an active promoter of local welfare!—I am trying to induce him to seriously take up the legal career for which his gifts markedly fit him. He is a man to make his mark anywhere."

The beautiful woman read with eager interest the letters in which Maitland confessed himself practically a stranger to his own land. "I have lived for many years," he wrote, "in the contemplation of the conventional America. I have carried the generalism of my boyhood in my heart. I find, however, that the United States of to-day is a sentient, heaving mass of personal investigators in matters of politics, society and even religion! Old parties are crumbling, old creeds are falling, and even the stately 'public functionary' of my youthful days is a thing of the past. The land I have returned to is not the land of the speech, the novel, the song, the political picture, as luridly touched up by enthusiasm! I am astounded to see class lines drawn more sharply at home than abroad, though the lines of division are on different levels. Bradstreet's and Dun's commercial agencies are the Burke and De Brett of Columbia. Managing mammas and anxious papas scan these semi-secret records breathlessly. The rank of men is determined at bank and clearing-house, and the judiciously assorted crowns, tiaras, and bandeaux of diamonds worn by the women at the Metropolitan Opera in Gotham are tide gauges of the ebb, flow, and rise of fortunes. The motto of my native land is 'Nothing but gold!' The highest superlative is 'as good as gold.' Heaven itself is, with apt financial neatness, described as being *on a gold basis!*

"Now to those who are merely quarreling over the deference due their respective superfluities, this 'gold basis' may be satisfactory! How about those who stand without the iron gates, shutting off the toiler and his womenkind from the 'Field of the Cloth of Gold?'

"While I stand ready to meet with fire and flame the anarchistic wolves who would storm the fold and destroy sheep and shepherd in one mad rush, I have the warmest admiration for America's striving bread-winners! I am amazed at the callous indifference of the money element, the purely money-handling element to the natural wants of the deserving poor. The victims of illness, of misfortune, the weaker, the friendless, are too often thrust to the wall by the burly money-changer.

"It is these people, whose daily life is a possible tragedy, to whom my heart goes out! Alas! Even a republic does not insure against *individual misfortune.* I sigh when I think of the gracious and thoughtful interest of the men and women of gentle blood in Europe in those beneath them! A general rush for gold here, robs us of consideration and reverence for

the aged and weak, blunts our tenderness to the suffering, and hardens heart, and closes hand. I am confirmed
in my belief that a purely commercial or manufacturing life does not foster the kindlier sentiments.

"Competition, class·quarrels, and self-interest have
led our successful money-makers too often, to regard
themselves as a superior order of beings.   As a rule,
the self-made men wield the hardest lash! The upstart
women have no greater sneer than 'She is a working
woman!

"When it can be realized that those who play, dis-
port themselves, and come up to the level of luxury are
lifted by the toilers, this cold taunt seems fiendish! The
pathetic side of American life is the trustful manhood
and womanhood of the workers, facing an iron-bound
destiny with fortitude, and covering daily slights with
the clinging vines of friendship and family affection!

"It is no wonder that the plaint of the toilers often
swells the chorus of frantic agitation! The most
healthful sign to me is that the insensate wickedness
of rotten anarchism is evolved from only the foreign
scum of the emigrant ships!

"One by one, these false prophets are recognized and
dropped by the serious native labor-leaders! It is the
hope of my life, should any violent eruption occur,
that these vagrant, seditious, or murderous foreigners
may meet prison restraint, or, in open anarchistic
attack, wither under the rifle blast!

"To the earnest, striving toiler, asking his full wage,
and no more, the peaceful artisan, the useful worker,
I can hold out the hand of brotherhood. If not the
architects of our national fortunes, they are the disci-
plined regular soldiers who have fought the battles of
our marvelous material progress.   The man or woman

who would cut off their natural aspirations for a gradual rise in fortune or station is untrue to the cardinal
principles of our national character.   All hail the
workers of America!

"In my stand for the right, should place of trust or
power be mine, I hope always to have the confidence
and respect of those who have been doomed 'to labor
and to wait.'

"The crying want of the hour is not ostentatious
doles, advertised charity, the cheap expedient of the
pauper soup-house, but a warm, living sympathy with
those who need it.   There is no family tree so firmly
planted in America that it may not be uprooted, and
its proudest shoots lie on the level with the atoms
from which it sprung!

"You may hear of excitement, agitation, sporadic
crimes, or tumult, perhaps, but the great tide of American feeling is not yet tinged with foreign corruption.
The aggregate sense of our people, tardily expressed,
is firmly declarative of a devotion to civil order. The
lurid tableaux of the anarchists in America will simply
amount to exhibitions of the 'auto-da-fe.' I will cheer-
fully assist in the necessary extirpation of the adopted
children of Marx and Bakunin.   As regards Americans, I feel like the gallant Henry, riding at Ivry,
'No Frenchman is my foe.'   I have learned that the
words 'My country' mean not alone rocks, trees, and
rivers—smiling plains, and towering palaces, but those
living, beating, human hearts who cluster, in love and
peace, under the far-sweeping folds of our banner."

There were symptoms of the return of winter. The
chill blasts swept from the Jura, and the season waned.
Evelyn, secretly anxious for news of Lord Beauford,

lingered at Lausanne, and Admiral Walton revolved the problem of winter quarters. "Any place on the continent, if I meet not Rheingold and my sister. It would be social ruin to be classed on the parvenu level. As for explanations, they are always awkward—and—useless!" The old sailor was a bit of a philosopher. One afternoon as he re-read a letter announcing the final departure of the Rheingolds from Jervaux, and their proposed continental tour, he conned over his Galignani in search of a hint as to some favorable haven until spring. Seated in a sunny corner of the grand porch, calmly enjoying his cheroot, his eye strayed from the journal to the lake's blue expanse. Graceful steamers swept in at Ouchy Landing, like pictured, swans, and a royal yacht, racing along the still expanse, bore the flag of the King of Gold—Rothschild.

Evelyn, dressed for her afternoon ride, was slowly approaching, when she saw, with affright, the paper fall from Walton's hand, and his head sink on his breast.

When the girl reached his side, he groaned and motioned feebly. "It is nothing! Wait! Don't alarm yourself. I have only had some bad news. Poor Alfred!"

Miss Hartley picked up the journal and her face grew ashen as she read an extended item, in the column of "Personal Mention." The reported death of Lord Alfred Beauford of fever, at Khiva, gave the paragrapher an opportunity to more or less faithfully enumerate his titles, the lists of his clubs, refer to his extended travels, briefly sketch Jervaux Priory, and to set forth *some* of his virtues and *none* of his faults.

It was the usual parting salute of a fashionable chronicle. A reference to his expected diplomatic

promotion and his absence in Cashmere and Turkestan on a hunting-trip closed the brief chronicle. The
admiral's man aided the broken old veteran to his
room, and Evelyn Hartley, seated in silence at her
casement, looking out on the splendid picture below
her, saw nothing of the brightness of the scene, for
blinding tears were raining from her eyes! The
glory of the splendid scene was darkened in the shadows of that lonely death, far away in the burning sands
of the Asian desert.

By the next evening, Admiral Walton was able to
read the laconic words of a friend in the "Foreign
Office," in answer to his dispatch.

Nothing known here. No confirmation. Russian news.

And uncle and niece were forced to wait while, gloomy
conjectures racked their minds. The through English
mail brought Miss Hartley a tender letter from Lady
Isabel Dunham. Ventnor Hall had been also visited by
the angel of sorrow, and instinctively the woman who
hopelessly loved Beauford turned in her lonely distress
to the woman whom she thought to be the woman of his
love. When Evelyn Hartley finished the blurred pages,
she folded the lines away, with Alfred Beauford's picture. "He is gone where this avowal can not reach him,
to a land without love and laughter." While Admiral
Walton mourned in secret the ruin of all his hopes
for Evelyn's future, the heiress, arraigned at the bar
of Memory, lived over the scene when she parted
in pride, and anger from the man whose glance of sur
prise and pain haunted her now?

Miss Hartley's nights of unavailing regret brought
to her no peace of mind. It was in unbosoming her
soul to Isabel Dunham that she felt drawn nearer to

him who was gone, in cheering the woman who had loved him. The faint discord between the women was stilled in the silence of that unknown grave, and a summons to Ventnor was Isabel Dunham's tender rejoinder. "You will find the Derwentwaters the most delightful people, and I would be so infinitely happier if you were near me! There is so much to explain. I can now tell you all the story of my life—the love which has never left my heart!" For, even in her sorrow, gentle Lady Isabel read the words aright which beautiful Evelyn penned to her sister in distress.

"It can only make her happier," said Evelyn, as she finished her rejoinder. She cleared up certain matters seen hitherto darkly. Both uncle and niece understood Lady Dunham's delicate reference to the absence of the Rheingolds.

"Shall we go? The path is clear now." questioned Walton, who now drifted with the tide of Fate. There was no campaign possible for the friendly old matchmaker.

This question settled itself. By previous arrangements, Count Oborski, secretly desirous of throwing his persuasive influence on the question of winter residence, had signaled his arrival on one of his mysterious trips of duty. Neither the admiral nor the endangered heiress dreamed that Davidoff, the dreaded Chief Executive of the Red Brethren, called the noble to his side, or that the spies of anarchy watched and reported their every movement to the Polish lover. Admiral Walton, gazing at the guest book, sought Evelyn with a precipitation which excited her.

"We must leave here at once, my child. It is the only way to avoid an extreme unpleasantness!"

"Why so? What has happened?" cried the startled woman.

"Because the great state chambers are filled with the appanage and personality of the Rheingold suite. Your mother and her husband are here for a stay, and, thank Heaven, grandly secluded in their rooms."

"I have an idea," said Miss Hartley decisively. "I wished to spend a week at Evian on the southern shore of the lake. We have several friends there. I do not wish to quit so abruptly this lovely region. When we move, let us arrange our winter residence. In the meantime, we can go over this afternoon ̇to Evian and we need not meet the new-comers." Even in his hurry, Admiral Walton reflected that Evelyn Hartley's lips had forgotten the sweetest word in the language of love—Mother!

"But Count Oborski comes to-day at three as our guest," the admiral interjected.

"True!" answered his niece. "He comes at three. We will take the boat at four."

With no sign or rencontre, the tourists embarked on the dainty "Savoy," under the escort of the delighted nobleman, who joined them on his arrival. The count was watchfully tender. Perfectly aware of the reported death of Lord Beauford, he followed the wisdom of his frequent counselor, Doctor Stein. "I will let her make the first reference to this welcome stroke of Fate!" he smiled, as he marked the royal beauty of the woman who seemed to be drifting toward him.

"It is a delicate juncture," he reflected as the boat sped across the lake, quivering under the impulse of her powerful engine. "One false movement might ruin me now! 'Piano, piano,'" he hummed, as he noted the great triangular wake stretching behind them on the glassy waters. In his assiduous attentions to the woman he had marked down, the Pole had no opportu-

nity to sound Admiral Walton as to the untimely death
of Lord Beauford, or to discover what mad freak had
led the English patrician alone to the dangerous wastes
of Turkestan. For not a whisper had reached Vienna
of the absent attachés movements. "If Beauford had
a secret, it died with him, justifying the old family
motto 'Loyal quand même.'

"He was a gentleman," coolly reflected the brilliant
soldier. "Schwartzenburg is terribly cut up over it!
Vale Beauford. It's the fortunes of the war of Life!"

While Admiral Walton paced the lower deck of the
"Savoy" in reminiscence of his olden days, he decided
to sound Count Oborski. "There was something very
sudden in Beauford's abrupt departure. Can it be that
Evelyn has refused him? That he threw up his hand in
the game of life in disgust. I must find out. Oborski
knows everything going on! He has the chatter of
Europe at his finger ends!" It was true, for, cast in
a "star" part of the now complex game of cosmopolitan anarchy, the brilliant court favorite, now a dashing cavalry commander, received the secret counter-spy
reports of all but the very highest grade! The only
spies not reporting to him, in his vicinity, were those
who mercilessly detailed his every action to Davidoff,
Carl Stein, and the Higher Council—a grade he was
madly burning to reach. As the boat sped on, in its
arrowy flight, Stanislas Oborski's voice grew more
velvety in its music, his eyes thrilled with a deeper
passion, for, exhausted by her chafing regret, repel-
lent of the negative influence of her mother, Evelyn
Hartley was in a receptive state of unguarded languor!
Like all of her sex, from the strongest to the weakest,
she was the prey of moods, and this autumn day it
seemed that she sailed upon an enchanted sea. There

was a gleam of satisfaction in Oborski's eyes. He had not failed to note the softened state of the beautiful American's feelings, and it made her doubly fair. "It is the golden time," he felt, in his heart of hearts. Glancing at the groves of Evian, now near, it seemed as if he were already leading her out, beyond the old life, to the Italian shores of passionate love.

"We are about to land," he whispered. "May I—"

The reference to an evening tete-a-tete was never finished, for, with a terrific shock and floods of scalding steam, a deafening explosion rent the slight vessel in its onward course, and a shattered, sinking wreck floated in fragments, whelmed soon in the hungry waters of the deep lake. Cries and yells from the shore and the struggling sufferers sounded on the air, and shoals of pleasure boats darted out to save the pleasure seekers.

When the slight fabric of the upper deck careened and plunged below the clear waters, Oborski's first glance showed him the face of the woman he sought, within a few yards. His powerful strokes brought him to her side, and while around them young beauty and laughing life sank away under the crystal surface, the cool swimmer bore up his precious burden. It was an eternity of fear and agony to her closing eyes, but, with a supreme effort, he held her up in the chilling flood, until a boat neared them.

The accident occurred almost at the landing-place of the gay resort, and scores of willing hands aided in caring for the rescued. Headlong in his daring, and as keen-eyed as an eagle, Oborski assured himself of Miss Hartley's immediate safety, and sought for Admiral Walton in the yet unfinished melée. With a glad shout of joy he marked the old veteran's triumphal landing, for the quick-witted sailor had, by the aid of a floating mass of wreckage, "held bravely up his chin!" Hundreds were busy at the quest of survivors, or aiding the rescued and injured, and speedily the members of the party of three were safely conveyed to the warmed rooms, and welcome comforts .of the great inn.

Count Stanislas was extremely exhausted. His matchless nerve and strength had carried him through. While the attendants commented on his gallant and timely achievement in saving Miss Hartley, the anarchist lover closed his eyes to dream of triumphs yet to come. "For," he murmured to himself, *'she is now mine!'* Before the stars swept to the west, escorted by the ecstatic admiral, the fortunate soldier looked into the eyes of the grateful beauty.

The tenderness of a gratitude knowing no bounds lit up Evelyn Hartley's face, and the eyes into which his fiery glances shone returned him the exquisite promise of any reward he would ask!

Long after the search had ended, and the cruel lake was lapping its beach in quiet, Count Stanislas, in the careful seclusion of his room, repeated softly: "Mine by the gift of Fortune, mine forever now! *A life for a life!*"

* * *

CHAPTER XI

BARON VON RHEINGOLD—IN THE BALANCE—AT MUNICH.— A JUNTA OF WISEACRES—ANARCHY'S WARNING—EVELYN'S SHADOWY CORONET—THE SECRET MESSAGE.— AN ASTONISHED ADMIRAL

THE consternation and alarm created by the explosion of the "Savoy" caused a wave of excitement reaching every crested nook of the shores of the Lake of Geneva. The Swiss gentry as well as the world's tourists were busied with the history of the untoward disaster for days. The rank of Admiral Walton, the fame of Miss Hartley's wealth and beauty, made them conspicuous in local gossip. Telegrams and messages poured in upon the robust old sailor who was one of the heroes of the wreck.

Miss Hartley, by the order of physicians, was secluded until the results of the mental shock, and an illness produced by the icy immersion had been conquered. The romantic appearance and gallant bearing of Count Stanislas Oborski gave a touch of chevalresque devotion to the rescue of the lovely American. The count, really prostrated, was cool enough to guard his room and allow the mental photography of Evelyn Hartley to fix his face in her heart, as he sustained her sinking form. His impassioned voice rang ever in her ears and the proximity of the scene of the wreck added daily to her burden of gratitude. During the recovery of the two central figures of this modern romance, Horatio Walton, with an eye to the future, made a cautious reconnaissance of the enemy at Ouchy. "If I were positive, it might not be the ruin of my influence with Evelyn, I would visit my sister Caroline." A dull envy of Rheingold gnawed at the old sailor's heart. He had a gentlemanly avarice spurring him on, even in his comfortable position. He decided not to visit his estranged sister, when at the Ouchy Club he learned of the state and pretentions of Baron von Rheingold. Some shadow reflect of one of the ten thousand petty baronies of Germany seemed to have rested upon the ex-doctor. His visiting card bore a crest, the marvel of heraldic research, and the Baron von Rheingold, boldly engraved, was in fact an extract from the modern Libro d'Oro. A fortunate discussion of the affairs of the wealthy strangers, in his presence, apprised Walton of his sister's permanent residence.

"This Rheingold married an American widow of enormous fortune, and is only traveling while the castle on their beautiful estate near Chemnitz is entirely refitted. It is one of the finest places in Saxony, and the superb old feudal escutcheons will give way to his blazory, which looks like a circus banner!

"They only obtained it through the ruin of the old Rittenhouse line, and the domain was purchased in his wife's name, I am told. The sum paid was princely. My brother was one of the officials necessary to the transfer." So babbled along a careless traveling German noble.

"Adolph," the other slowly answered, "our Germany is slow to admit the nouveaux riche. It is easy to see that this fellow is aping a rank he knows little of. The old families will not admit them. Saxony is not like Paris, where a full pocket carries its own welcome."

"Oh! I fancy he will enjoy his magnificence, and the widow will shine, in her own eyes, at least. They are at least a boon to the inn-keepers. The noble Baron von Rheingold's progress is as stately as one of the visits of Louis XIV. to the scene of a little war! They are the laughing stock of Lausanne, and the queerest stories are told of his social antics. His wife is less outrée than the adventurer."

Admiral Walton finished his bottle of Rudesheimer without changing a muscle. Returning to Evian, he framed his campaign. "Any place from whence we can fly to Italy will do! Munich is unexceptionable or Vienna!" And as he paced the deck of the "Savoy's" successor, he carelessly ignored the possible consequences of Oborski's successful chivalry. "The count is certainly powerful, and has the entrée of court circles, and the proud, suspicious Viennese aristocratic salons. A club companion of Schwartzenburg and Paul Esterhazy—a man admitted to the fêtés of the Lichtensteins and Metternichs, a soldier to whom the Emperor gives a crack cavalry brigade is of the 'veille roche' beyond doubt. "All in all, I would prefer Vienna, but 'My Lady Willful' must decide. I shall ask Evelyn to choose, only our picket lines must be watched toward Chemnitz. "

Count Stanislas had found time, between his French novels and hours of secret planning, to establish a secret service line among the quick-witted servants of the lakeside inn.

With deft delicacy, his offerings of flowers, his little notes of inquiry, were borne to Miss Hartley's presence, in unobtrusive quiet. He was en rapport with the maid who served the heiress. Lying behind his closed curtains he smiled, as he realized that bluff Admiral Walton knew nothing of his small correspondence and graceful offerings.

"If I read this girl aright," he mused, "she will lead herself up to a state of exhuberant gratitude. My sickness has been well spun out. To press directly on her my claims would be coarse. I have the excuse of a necessary return to my command. An ardent interview, a rendezvous in her winter resting place, the effect of an absence, and then a vigorous and effective appeal to her emotions, and a claim on her future— this will make me master of her millions.

In a week, Miss Evelyn Hartley was busied with her installation in a superb home at Munich. "I will fancy that I am 'en permanence,' uncle," cried the heiress as on her mentor's arm she passed approvingly through the fortunately secured residence she owed to Walton's practiced negotiation. "Here let us rest! The galleries, the people, the cosmopolitan movement will be to me a varied school, and you can be relieved from the constant attendance which travel demands."

The American craved rest, for on her journey from Evian, her cheeks crimsoned with deepest blushes at the significant tenderness of Count Oborski's last interview.

Pale, and with an air of almost classic distinction, his bearing was made up of solicitous courtesy, and an ardor veiled only by the proprieties. Conscious of the immense power of imagination, of the result of a maiden's introspection, gently oblivious of the debt of a life snatched from an untimely and early death, he murmured, "The duty due my Emperor *alone* calls me from your side. I shall count the hours until I may return to you. I can not speak as I would until I have received the gracious favor of an audience. Then, I shall hasten to you at Munich! *May I come?*"

The artful leading up to his decisive manœuvre soothed the woman whose heart was beating in excitement until the almost positive directness of his finale hemmed her in.

His passionate, pleading eyes were burning with a scarcely restrained passion. The full measure of her great debt weighed upon her, as almost, with a gasp, she murmured "You may come!" The ardent kisses rained on her hands left no doubt of the throbbing tide of love in his heart.

On his returning pathway to the fields of Transylvania, Count Oborski maintained a recurrent system of keeping himself daily in her mind. Notes, telegrams, the exquisite daily gifts of flowers, even "en voyage" proved the ingenuity of his lover-like devices In the welcome silence of travel, in the preoccupations of arranging her winter manage, Miss Hartley was not brought face to face with herself in solitude. It was only when the happy admiral was free to enjoy his bachelor freedom among the elastic circles of his growing acquaintance that Evelyn Hartley cast up the account of the dying year. There had been a silence guarded as to the noble soldier's evident attachment, and Miss Hartley's tête-à-têtes with her uncle were only on the beaten track of family affairs, daily amusements or the delicate topic of the Rheingolds.

The winter's snows sifting down brought to the woman, whose first romance was thrilling her heart, a final knowledge that her fate was to be weighed in the balance of life. A mass of unanswered letters, the familiar hand of Maitland, and her veteran trustee brought the question to her mind which had been resolutely put away. "What will 'Brother Philip' think?" The waiting anxiety of Lady Isabel for definite news of Beauford's still clouded fate brought back all her Vienna days. And as each busy week fled away, she was drawn nearer the time when her heart told her Stanislas Oborski would claim at her hands the ransom of a life. With the defensive tactics of womanhood, striving to retain her freedom as long as possible, she gave her days up to the galleries, to opera, dinner, rout, and ball, and ignored the finger of Fate which seemed to beckon her to Vienna. Magnifying the obligation which rested upon her, Evelyn Hartley dared not analyze her feelings and resolutely face the problem of her life. Her inevitable submission to the

seeming decree of Fate, was not inspired by a frank
confession of her love for Stanislas Oborski. In amaze-
ment at the tranquillity of her feelings, she read the
fateful telegram heralding the count's arrival. The
words were significant.

Graciously received by the Emperor. I am coming with a
month's leave. Auf wiedersehen.

Her vague desire to escape from the present consideration of the subject soon to be brought to her heart,
led her to meet all the arrears of her correspondence.
Beauford's strange destiny seemed to cloud Isabel Dunham's life with unbroken sadness. The English woman
craved the boon of final certainty. But the sphinx-
like Foreign Office, only referred politely to its
previous dispatches and enclosure.

Alfred Beauford had sunk beneath the horizon of
death without a murmur of the busy world's notice. He
was followed only by the cry of a heart-stricken
woman, thrilled with the agonies of a true lost love!
Judge Fox and busy Philip Maitland, in their letters
dwelt on the increasing bitterness of class divergence,
and the growing unrest of the American communities.
Looking to the right and left, Evelyn Hartley could
find no pretext of escape from the full and frank consideration of Oborski's wooing.

Her vigils of the night before his arrival left her at
morn, expectant without enthusiasm, and hardly doubtful of the status into which she seemed to glide insensibly.

And so a perfect, but insensible, statue, the Daughter
of the West waited for the touch of the magician, Love,
which would wake her pulseless marble to a new and
strange life. It seemed as if she were living the life

of another, and went hand in hand with herself, toward the slowly turning gates of a newer life.

The noble Stanislas Oborski, General of Cavalry, and Knight of His Imperial Majesty's highest orders, had expended a great deal of patience in framing a cipher cablegram which would bring Carl Stein back to Vienna. "He is the only cool man I know on whom I can rely, I will need a trusty friend in this marriage. There is no one in my club circles who has Stein's aplomb and nerve. He will serve to break the apparent chance element in this union. Besides, he really knows the girl's character. And as to the property and the details of American law, he is a past-master of all arts. I would be at sea without him."

It indeed cost Carl Stein a struggle to leave the spider-web of his ripening American schemes. The severe winter was augmenting the murmurs of the dissatisfied into a hoarse growl of restless envy. The professor, studying the situation at Milwaukee, prayed to the God of Storms for a bitter inclemency of weather to intensify the brooding discontent and envy.

"Curse the quick-witted employers—the easily-moved local authorities, and the self advertising charity-mongers! They are becoming wise and doling out graded relief, mapping out districts and plotting out special classes and analyzing the causes of the winter pressure! If they can throw back the main annoyance to the people themselves, herding in great cities, it gives them a point of vantage. What we do need is political workers, a strong, fearless journal and friends to maintain and push our effective secret propaganda.

"Now, even Caroline Hartley's fondness for her new flatterer, that tyrant fool Rheingold, has its limits. My hold on him is only that of fear.' Of the hundred thousand dollars she has given him, we have had eighty, he but twenty.

"Something must be allowed this vain fool for display. I presume he will now drop into the elegant private vices of a gentleman. I must find a way to reach the principal of her money. Surely Rheingold would be satisfied with a quarter of the gross amount. If I go back and help Oborski in his splendid venture, I may be able to induce Rheingold to act—to—" his very thoughts were stayed at the grim presage! He rose and poured out a glass of neat brandy. The unwonted stimulant loosened the tiger element in the man. "Bah! What is one old Woman's life in the battle of our cause? It is only discounting nature after all. Rheingold will be sure to keep the secret!

"Fear will tie him! It binds where the clasp of Love and and duty slips! But the old egoist's will! I must prepare!"

He studied over Oborski's cipher. "What can be the vital private matter?" as he indited his answer

Sail at once; meet you at Munich. Go first to Chemnitz.

He pondered upon the situation of the advanced anarchists. "I can leave the work in good hands. With some of Evelyn Hartley's money, and a large block of the mother's estate, we of the forlorn hope should not lack for ammunition in the sharp outbreak of next yera.

"It can not be delayed! It must not be! It will loosen our pulses! We can try the resources of courts. sensational journals, and shifty lawyers to screen any who are entangled in the law. This Hartley gold! With it, what can not be done with a hungry jury, a facile judge? By Heavens! I will reach it! I will not wait for age and accident to throw it my way! I will assist nature!" He smiled with a devilish grin as he journeyed toward Cleveland. It was a simple matter to gain from Judge Fox's office spy, the very last status of both interests of the trust. "It is fortunate the interests are so vast that confidential subordinates must know. I shall soon find if the old judge knows of Miss Hartley's proposed marriage. If I read her aright, and Oborski has played his cards well, she will marry first, and notify her trustee later. She is over eighteen and there is no impediment." Carl Stein gazed on the twinkling evening stars from the car window and blessed the happy chance of the "Savoy" disaster. "The devil does take care of his own!" he mused. "Oborski's luck is a crowning help to us! If he cast well and throws the funds toward us, Davidoff may bring him up into the 'Higher Council.' But will the cool old Russian cling to his muscovite creed, 'Never trust a Pole!' He must yield here. To Count Oborski must be left enough to make a brave and gallant show, besides, his wife to be has a cool head of her own!"

Buffeting the winter storms to hasten to his fellow-scoundrel, Doctor Carl Stein arranged his plan of action. "It may take some time to effect the double arrangement of the Rheingold matter, and to work on Evelyn Hartley. If I find my presence a source of suspicion, I can return to America and reappear when matters are ripe. But Mrs. Rheingold must make her will forthwith. Can I trust her fat-witted husband to handle her egoism? Once excited by suspicion or secret fear, she will be lost to me forever! He must get her power of attorney, and she must be kept alone! Flattery, continued flattery, the sweet poison of womanhood—must be her daily food.

"But Evelyn, my bold, bright-eyed, aspiring scholar, with her it is different. She is a shy falcon, and I doubt even now, if Oborski has touched her inner nature. In the prime of her womanhood, her soaring soul will be as far above him as the stars hover, hanging over the sea."

Count Oborski waited at Vienna until his anxious soul was quieted by a cipher message from the returning High Priest of anarchy. Though dated from Chemnitz, he knew from one key-word that his superior in the order had met and conferred with Davidoff, the dark chief, who lurked behind treble mysteries of high committees, and divided councils of executives, removing him from all but the great final directory labors of the rapidly increasing cult.

Will meet you now at Munich, arrive before you.

So ran the telegram's welcome words.

"This is cool wisdom," joyously thought Oborsik, "for the wandering scholar will precede me. His affected astonishment and congratulations will shield us both. I can now move on as rapidly as possible to the fruition of this golden harvest. There shall be no time for reaction if I can hold the girl to her plighted word. Stein can quietly watch when I am not 'en presence.' No devilish step must back me now! Should the Polish, German, and Austrian red brothers have the nerve to rise, I could give them the defiles of the Carpathians as a fortress. But will the Italians do their part of great campaign? Spain is ripe for a wild tumult, yet France hems it in at the Pyrenees. Once let the torch of war be lit in Europe, France and Germany would clash in fire and flame like two warring thunder clouds. Only let the struggle be general! Only

may the storm sweep afar! Then this hardy generation may evolve the man we need, the apotheosis of
dauntless Bakunin."

Count Oborski, swept along in enthusiasm, forgo t
that the one man who ever lifted himself by strength
of talent over a warring world was the genius of
modern war, the peerless Corsican !

"And Napoleon Bonaparte conquered the world for
himself! England's fleet alone stayed the progress
of the modern Genghis Khan! Napoleon knew no law
but his own will. It cost the lives of La Grande
Armée and the world's throne to prove that in the
crush between natural law and man's boldest will, the
mysterious forces of nature swept down the heaven-
defying tyrant."

Stanislas Oborski never weighed in his mind the
relative merits of a tyranny of despotism, the rule of
the Ten, the sway of the Barons, the graded obligations of a constitutional monarchy, the equalized pressure of an honest republic, or the dogmatic draconian
brutality of a communism backed by terrorism, dynamite
and proscription of the rich. In his warped nature, assassination became holy, provided only that the proper
parties reeled under its cowardly, anonymous blow. It
affected not his mental proposition to observe that in
indifferent communiteis, under varying quarrels, diverse
and widely various individuals would yield up their
lives under the heroic remedy of destruction! Oborski
had never seen the principle of *individual execution*
carried to a crucial test !

His vindictive mind was fixed on the sweeping away
of the Russian idea, and the extinction of certain
leading muscovite families. To his narrow brain, this
effected, the whole world run on golden wheels. At this

particular epoch, under the sweeping theorem of Bakunin, the wealthier and more prominent classes of
Germany, France, England Spain, Italy, and even the
every-day bustling millionaires of the United States,
were gloomily doomed to death, for the general easement
of the many! Alas! The extinction of the superior grade
would expose in every land the *next* series of survivors
to the application of practical Bakuninism! What would
happen when property, the evidence of crime, or wage-
work—the badge of slavery—would be abolished in this
human Golgotha, seemed a distant extreme to the bit-
ter-hearted Pole, a traitor to Austria, a recreant to
his order, and merely a mad wolf—a blind foe of the
Russian idea!

The abject subjection in which he stood to all men
of the anarchistic grade of the ambitious Stein and
the haughty recluse, Davidoff, the awful nature of his
secret obligations occasionally pricked him with the
disturbing thought that he had set up an unknown
circle of masters over his own destiny, and that he had
parted with the freedom of creed and conscience he
once enjoyed under the conservative Austrian monarchy.

The fact that his dignities and life might be forfeit
to the laws of the monarchy pressed on him, but, on
the brink of this secret struggle to the death, he
looked vaguely, in the results of the uprising for an
enlargment of human free-will, which would obliterate
all social claims of man on his fellow man! Creeds,
courts, laws, all differences of rank, station, and wealth,
were to go into the general hotch-pot!

"And, after the readjustment of a generation's whole
private and public life, then what?"

The proud dominion of a world by the untrammeled

children of the red flag! Gods to themselves, and knowing neither law nor force!

With sly cunning, Count Stanislas Oborski made no parade of his conquest, no mention of his intended voyage. He even trusted his secret offices of the future entirely to Stein. "I'll leave my valet here in charge, and he may expect my daily return," mused Oborski, as he made his own secret preparations for an extended absence. "My brilliant coup de fortune will dazzle the Viennese. I am safe in any event."

A half hour spent in a necessary examination of his private papers, a few notes and billets dispatched, left the count in excellent humor for the particularly rafiiné dinner he enjoyed on the eve of his departure. With a meaning look, he announced his absence for a day or more to the valet, who was a cat-like observer of his anxious present, as he had been an active assistant in that past of gilded intrigue which made Oborski the star of even the reckless Vienna gallants.

The servitor smiled faintly, and was silent. His well-assumed indifference deceived Oborski. "I will find out your quest, my gay master," was the instant decision of the doubly-bound spy, who served Oborski's doubtful superiors of the brotherhood.

An hour later, throwing his rich furred cloak over his shoulders, Count Stanislas turned to the servant. "I shall telegraph you if I need you, and my usual outfit, leave the head steward in charge of all."

The servant bowed and opened the door, as a woman's rich voice rang out, "*He is here*, and I will see him!"

"It is Etelka," whispered the startled valet.

"Here! Tell her I am summoned to the Hof Court Marshal at once. Stay. Tell her to return at ten!

By that time I will be away," he muttered as the servant darted out.

"Did she leave quietly Fritz?" queried Oborski, with some anxiety.

"She will return, and bade me say she must see you," gravely answered the man, as he added: "The carriage waits."

Stanislas Oborski only composed his startled nerves when he was twenty leagues away from the gay capital on the Danube.

"By the Fiend! I thought that mad gypsy fool was in Persia. She must not find out my whereabouts. Ah! There is the devil's work in this. I cannot hide my presence at Munich.'

The count had smoked two of the trabucos from his amber shell case, as he lay, swathed in his costly furs, before he saw the light.

"She will clamor! She will haunt the house till I return. I will tell all to Stein. I can send her a dispatch to meet me, at some quiet village. Stein can entice her into some lonely place and we will keep her out of the way, until all is over. Violence would not do! Those devils of gypsies are world-rovers! Their dark and mysterious vengeance would reach me even in a guarded palace! What is her want? The universal want of the world—high and low—Money! I suppose! But if this devil's tongue is loosened it might be awkward!"

As the cars rushed along in the darkness of the chill night, Stanislas Oborski shivered slightly. The shadow of evil deeds, the memories of unredressed wrongs unsettled his nerves!

Yet, trusting to his ready wit, and the secret aid of Stein, he sped along to the fruition of his golden fortunes.

When a veiled woman sharply rapped at the doors of the count's private apartment that night, the heavy bell of St. Stephen's was booming ten. Though muffled in black, her elastic form and quick, swaying movement sufficiently indicated the Bohemienne. The door opened and the impassive valet appeared.

"The count!" hissed the woman, pushing him roughly aside.

"Has given you the slip, my Gitaña!" said the smiling rogue, who served a rogue.

The wandering star of night, whom Oborski spoke of as "Etelka," threw herself in a chair and gloomily eyed the valet. "You are as great a liar as he! It is useless to ask you whither he has gone! I will follow him to Iceland, but I will find him. It is the order of the Tribe!" Her piercing eyes searched the servant's sunny countenance.

"Pray be civil, now, most stormy Etelka!" said the servitor. "I may do you a favor! Not for the love of your own bold, saucy face. The Vienna girls are more civil than you sprites of the wood! I detest storm and fury. But it suits me to have my master watched! I love him too much to lose him from sight, and he has *given me the the slip* as well as you! To be brief, what will you give to know where he is? You can find out his game yourself. I know you are at home in any hamlet from Cadiz to Petersburg, from the Golden Horn to heavy Hamburg! But you shall cross my palm this time!" He smiled viciously as the tortured woman seized him roughly by the wrist.

"Softly! You impudent baggage!" he cried, shaking her off. "Five hundred florins is my price! You can frighten it out of him?"

"Explain!" said Etelka, resting against a heavy

table, and toying with a long, silver-mounted Armenian dagger. "Is it worth it! How will I know you do not lie! You can set a trap! If you set one for me, the gypsy knife will find its way to your black heart!" She flashed the sharp blade before his astonished eyes.

"Listen! Don't be a fool! If you had ever any self-control, you could have managed Oborski. He is afraid of you, you handsome she-devil! I set an old yäger, a friend of mine on his track, and gave him money to follow him. By ten to-morrow, I will have a token dispatch to tell me where he is! I think he has sneaked away to marry the great American princess from over the sea, the woman who has mountains of money. Now, rave as you will, five hundred florins in gold alone will take you to him. Be reasonable and I can help you! Pay me half now and I will tell you!"

Etelka, the Bohemienne, sprang to her feet and tore a blazing jewel from her finger. "He gave me that!" she fiercely said. "I'll ransom it in the morning! Speak! Tell me all!"

"He will surely give me directions about you! He is a wary fox. Now, I will answer him that you have disappeared disconsolate and in quiet. If you wish, I will say that you come every second day to ask for his return. This will throw him off his guard. I know you are as cunning as a weasel. Guard yourself and watch him, then come back to me if you need help.

"He may order me and all his luggage to the destination he has chosen. You can spoil his game, or make him pay a rich forfeit. Shall we watch him together?"

Gypsy Etelka's dark eyes burned into his very soul. The serving man shuddered. "You will do no mad thing! Only hold me safe!"

She tossed back her willful head. Her veil thrown aside showed a face of witching beauty, with the wildness of the mountain clans in its strange loveliness.

"I trust you now, because you fear me! I will come. You shall have your gold. Beware, though, of a gypsy vengeance."

Tossing her dark scarf over her shapely head, she made an imperious gesture. The sly scoundrel held his breath as she glided out of the count's palace.

"She's an uncanny devil, she takes my breath away!" Fritz grumbled as he discussed a flask of Burgundy. Throwing on a cloak, he muffled his face. "Now for my masters—and—more gold!" He went out in the night to betray Oborski *a second time!*

While Doctor Carl Stein and Count Stanislas Oborski talked with bated breath next day, in a parlor of the "Belle Étoile" at Munich, the gypsy in a peasant disguise was speeding to the scene. Oborski's greedy valet smiled as he secreted the five hundred florins. "She forgot to ask for the ring, in her haste to be off! I will work on this gold mine, for I am to be on the scene. It is then the American! Etelka will demand a heavy price for silence! It must needs be! Let him pay! The American bourgeoise has mountains of gold!"

Far away over the wild green Atlantic, surging in its wintry wrath, lashed by the flail of the Storm King, in the good city of Cleveland, Ohio, certain good men and true, a junta of wiseacres, communed over the unsatisfactory state of the body politic. True, no distinctly anarchistic outbreak had occurred, but bloody strikes, train robberies, increasing violent crimes, and a whirlwind of lurid threats in open meeting, spoke of a dangerous underlying mob feeling. The tramp and the vagrant element were daily more sullen and morose, and the howl of bodies of alien laborers, temporarily idle, joined to the growl of the over-crowded winter slums of the greater cities.

The public was already familiar with the demand that the State should offer a general support of uncertain duration. Extremest reformers called for the graded assessment in contribution of the known rich, and wild-eyed, long-haired, enthusiasts in lyceum halls, and Sunday-night assemblies openly advocated "taking by force," and parades en masse, under the banner "Bread or Blood!" Sporadic exhibitions of singular pulpit oratory, aided the senseless clatter, in which oratorical frenzies, the duty of the rich to divest themselves at once of their accursed wealth was loudly urged by preachers enjoying substantial salaries, grad-ing up to financial fatness.

The vagueness of the reformers in distinctly declar-ing who should take, and defining the locality of dep-redation, and amount of force suited to the awkward times, was matched by the similar quandary, as to *who* should furnish the bread and *whose* blood was particularly demanded. The impassive calmness of the rich who returned to their Monday avocations, and did not shed off their riches, added to the general failure of these impassioned appeals to the turbulent!

In the junta of wiseacres, the grave-faced business men of Cleveland listened patiently to the general complaint, and joined in the consensus of opinion that "Something must be done!" In all the phases of dis-cussion, secret and public, from the imported veteran agitator up to the Bank president, gravely addressing the wiseacres, the most extended generalities marked the arguments of rich and poor. All the proposed remedies were suited to a theoretical class· of suffering, produced by certain causes mathematically set forth in different social equations, by the speakers who effectively consumed both time and patience.

When the last sober eyed capitalist had skirmished over the ground, Philip Maitland was called upon to answer for his committee. "I can not go into causes or effects," he said, in a forcible way, "but I can report conditions. The actual situation is more pitiful daily. Houses of leading citizens are placarded with threats, robberies, small and large, are increasing, and pilfering is unbounded. It seems that there is a blank in our National and State institutions with regard to the legal assistance of the deserving, unless some bridge of inferiority or taunt of pauperism embitters the dole. It certainly would regulate and economize relief to have it directed by governmental inspectors, with power to meet unusual stress with instant and generous help. This would fairly distribute the burden, and make the aid available before suffering had driven the needy to crime or despair! As this seems impossible, at the present, the strain is thrown upon individual beneficence, and when this is not forthcoming, some form of forcible demand or terrorism must finally result. As to the positive demand of the ultra-socialist, for the state to insure the individual careers of its citizens, good or bad, that is the crowning folly of hare-brained theorists. The lesson of the hour is of charity, and gentle consideration for the needy, that appeals to those who are able to give, and urges them to open heart, purse, and hand! .

"The civic duty of the hour to watch over peace and property, to sternly repress criminal violence, will be performed by the regular officials, backed by our now thoroughly alert citizen soldiery. I venture to say that your efforts in providing for distress, joined with our watchfulness in maintaining quiet, are as effective measures as can be devised at present. I have visited in a serious mood, the assemblies of the socialistic reformers. I see no evidence in their plans or demeanor of a fitness to introduce more equity, activity, or brotherly feeling into the world, than our present system of self-reliant individualism under the law, backed by a fostered sympathy between classes. In other words, the failure of every communistic attempt at practical reform leads me to distrust their theories, while the behavior of the disciples leads me to despise them as a class of loose enthusiasts led on by artful demagogues. I feel that all respectable trades and secret societies will assist in preserving order in case of trouble. Here, as in all similar cases, the apathy of the defined classes of *wealthy women* to general suffering shows that element of the sex to be less accessible to tenderness than their more modest sisters. *Fashion seems to harden the feminine heart unduly.* The demands for specific concessions, by anarchistic leaders, are no more than the black-mail of La Mafia. The general complaint of home laborers that our land is not as rich a harvest-field for them as formerly, should be heeded. Our national resources and opportunities for easily remunerative work have been exhausted by the inpouring of Europe's most undesirable classes. From them, and their succesors, arises the howl of disappointment now.

"The fact is," concluded Maitland, "in face of the growing competition of life the effort to live easily, without useful pursuits, assisting production, is daily more difficult. To those who stand idle in the vineyard of life will be brought home sturdy Captain John Smith's remark to the idle English gentry: '*Those who do not work shall not eat!*' In these later days the right to live in peace and have a quiet opportunity of bread-winning is all the State can safely assume. As to the wars and competition of classes, England and the United States offer a fair play and a broad system of justice to the individual—beyond that, the children of men must bear the natural burden of humanity and look out for themselves!

"Life is too serious to trifle away our national existence in trying to make America one vast kindergarten of individual coddling.

"The slow and mysterious mending of the general disturbances of the community are the result of time, patience, kindliness, and forbearance. It is my belief no new principle in practical government will be successfully applied until human nature drops its struggling manhood, and attains the delightful ideal of angelic purity. I fancy, however, the aggregate virtue of the human race is nearly a fixed quantity. Let us all watch at our posts of duty, and answer the challenge of marauders from any quarter with firm ranks, and a cry of 'God save the Commonwealth!'"

The junta of wiseacres, there being no further business, voted thanks to the various speakers, adjourned without doing anything, and, well-pleased, went home to its dinners!

The suffering poor, as usual, contented itself with crusts, or went without the cheerful meal the wiseacres relished!

The sun of prosperity glittered over the pathway of the noble Count Stanislas Oborski, as he went into the presence of the woman whose hand was to be the royal reward of her chivalric savior. With rare tact, he had notified her of his arrival, and bade her signify her pleasure as to his reception. Desirous of plying his arts of fascination undisturbed, he had succeeded in drawing forth Admiral Walton by the social arts of Doctor Carl Stein. The old Englishman fell easily into Oborski's snare. Too proud to question others as to his sister's daily life, he hastened to learn from Carl Stein the latest news of the newly-planted noble family of Chemnitz.

So it was, alone, in her stately home, robed richly as if for a state ceremony, that the elated noble poured forth to Evelyn Hartley the artful eloquence of his nature. Count Stanislas was largely aided by the unvarying persistence with which he had sought the American's love. Mere iteration, and the manly vigor and impulsive ardor of his wooing had awakened a certain sense of response in the womanly nature of the foreign beauty. Her passivity was a result of a final fatigue in mental resistance, and the decisive answer which could not be delayed, now that a Hapsburg had given his brilliant general the royal permission to woo, was dictated by the obligation of a life so gallantly saved.

There was a shadowy coronet circling over Miss Hartley's fair brows, when in answer to his most impassioned appeals for an early union, the heiress fixed one month later as the day when, the ardent lover might claim her hand. Born of a loveless union, nurtured almost in solitude, without a near view of the swaying transports of affection, and shaded with the trials of her opening womanhood, love was a veiled God to the lonely woman. Face to face with the rosy God she had not been, there was over her no "breath of life's ambrosial morning wherein love shook the dew-drops from his glancing hair."

Self devoted as a silent queen, she plighted her troth to the brilliant noble, and vaguely wondered what future life lay before her when the bridal veil had been lifted.

In the gallant preoccupations of his lover-like attentions, Oborski failed to note the unawakened state of the girl's innermost heart. Elate with a tangible victory, he paused not to question her lack of personal enthusiasm.

While the Polish noble discussed gravely with Doctor Stein the future opened by the approaching union, Admiral Horatio Walton listened in grave concern to Evelyn Hartley's announcement of her approaching marriage. Secretly pleased, he had yet to consider her interests. "You will surely have the fullest counsel of Judge Fox before yielding up your American citizenship," he said, thoughtful of her wealth and its future destination.

"It is for that reason I have decided to delay the marriage a month, and I wrote in fullest terms to-night."

Doctor Stein sat in profound thought in the vine-shaded arbors of the "Hotel Belle Etoile" and pondered upon the success of his schemes. "With these fortunes to draw on, I may in turn supplant Davidoff. Money is a power, at least, the golden lever to move the world. It will be so until accumulation is impossible, until one code governs men! Until then, it is the weapon of the strong. Thanks to my counsels, Rheingold has persuaded his wife to the preparation of a will giving him the share of Fortune's favors she exacted of her unloved first husband.

"*She may not live long,*" he scowled, "but the wealth will pass into the right hands." Even as he sat, in the quiet necessary to his self-commune, he was struck by the graceful air of a woman passing through the garden.

"She has the proud bearing of a gypsy queen, a true Bohemienne," he noted, as the woman, with graceful, springy step was lost in the crowd of loungers.

Etelka had located her quarry, for the count, reassured by the lies of his valet, had telegraphed to that functionary, who arrived to share his master's stay.

After the return of Count Oborski from the opera, where he dreamed of the future, while under the charm of the pleading, passionate music, the happy Pole sat in late converse with Doctor Stein. The approach of his factotum with a telegraph dispatch which he handed to Stein, aroused the lover.

"It is marked 'Important—Answer.' Shall I wait, sir?" The skilled servitor had brought blank forms and writing material.

Stanislas Oborski sprang forward in astonishment, as Stein, with an imprecation, dashed down the message.

"Furies of Hell! This is a stroke of Fate!" the leader cried, as Oborski calmly read the dispatch. It was from Rheingold and read:

Come at once. My wife found dead. sitting in her garden-chair this afternoon. Apoplexy. Business advice needed.

It was signed Baron von Rheingold.

"The will was being prepared in London. I hardly know if it could have been signed. I fear not!" hissed Stein, his set teeth lending his stony face an air of ferocity. "It is a crushing blow."

"And Miss Hartley will defer her wedding, certainly, I fear!" sadly rejoined Count Oborski, mindful of continental usages. "It throws our whole interests in jeopardy."

It was in anxious unrest and brooding dissatisfaction that the magnificent Count Sanislas Oborski strove to cheer his promised bride. Stein had thoroughly informed him of every relation of mother and daughter. In her chastened sorrow, her increased loneliness, Evelyn Hartley bade her lover await her at Munich, for Doctor Stein transmitted the request of Baron von Rheingold to Admiral Walton to come, and to bring his niece that she might be face to face once more with the mother whose voice would never again be raised in bitterness. Count Oborski, chafing alone at Munich, knew not that he was dogged at night by Etelka, now a silent spy, and in the day, by a keen gypsy lad, a strolling musician. With a sense of defeat, Count Oborski welcoming Evelyn Hartley and her uncle back, heard the astounded admiral re-read a telegraphic summons, waiting his return from his sister's lawyers. Stein had failed, for the telegram read:

Come to London at once. Your sister's previous will makes you her sole heir.

BOOK IV

THE SPORT OF THE GODS

CHAPTER XII

THE CUP OF TANTALUS—BARON VON RHEINGOLD'S STRUG-
GLE. JUDGE FOX SENDS A MEDIATOR—EVELYN HART-
LEY'S STRANGE VISITOR—FROM THE DEAD—THE PERSIAN
MINISTER.—STEIN'S QUARREL—LADY ISABEL'S MISSION

MISS HARTLEY returned in silence to Munich, shadowed with a dull sorrow which had no silver gleams
in its sable habiliments.

The constraint of her surroundings at Chemnitz, the
leering civility of Rheingold, then an expectant heir,
and the perfunctory display of the dead woman's obse-
quies, all jarred upon her nature now moved to its
depths. Every link joining her to the old life seemed
to have been severed by the death of the mother whose
lips would never utter now a word of tender regret
for her daughter's shadowed girlhood.

Caroline Hartley died in the height of the cold,
untiring egotism, and lay unmourned and unregretted
in the marble crypt carved for others! There was a
resentment in the young girl's eyes as she noted the
haughty air of mastery assumed by Baron von Rheingold. Doctor Carl Stein, with well-assumed gravity,
threw a decorous shade upon the meeting of the
unforgiving admiral with the German parvenu. Stein

vanished when the funeral ceremonies were over, and was deep in confidential plotting, with Count Stanislas Oborski before the uncle and niece soberly returned to Munich. The old soldier was reticent on the return trip. He could not twist his nature to utter platitudes which he knew Evelyn would resent in her heart. Secretly busied with his wonderment as to the disposition of the dead woman's estate, Walton, world-worn as he was, felt a haunting sadness when he realized how far apart the motive of self-interest had carried the brother and sister of fifty years ago! The half hour which he spent alone, gazing on the silent features of his sister, brought back kindly thoughts of the bright-eyed child who ran, in happy frolic, over the velvet lawns of Yorkshire to meet him, when, a happy-hearted boy, he first put a middy's uniform on! To the old sailor, worn with his most unwelcome excursion, shocked with the snapping of the last twig of the family tree of his generation, the blunt dispatch of the solicitors brought a magical change of feeling. Before Oborski had courteously handed the paper to Evelyn Hartley, Caroline Walton became a canonized saint in the admiral's eyes. "*My poor sister! She was true at heart!*" he thought, with a strange access of tenderness, and the delicious sense of easily acquired fortune thrilled his every vein, as he remarked, with a grandeur foreign to his usual manner: "I must naturally go at once to London." His eye fell on the Count's startled face. It recalled him to the convenances. "While I can not delay, do you not think Lady Isabel would make you a visit of a few weeks?" he said meaningly to the heiress. "I must make some fitting future arrangements for you." Miss Hartley calmly returned the telegram.

"Pray act at once, as you wish, dear uncle. I have asked the Baroness Driesen and her two daughters to remain with me for a time. They arrive this evening!"

Count Stanislas Oborski, with the tact of a cavalier, retired at once, after offering the admiral his friendly service. In the heightened consideration of the noble, Walton observed that he was now ranked as a personage! Accident, the freak of a woman angered at her only child, a turn of Fortune's wheel, and he the old wrinkled veteran, was presto! The object of the deference of men, the regard of society, and the smiles of blushing beauty even waited for him!

Wonderful witchery of money! Blest glamour of gold! It smoothes the wrinkles of age, and softens every asperity on life's road!

The admiral was ten years younger, as he said to the bewildered girl: "This German fellow will be simply raving! Caroline must have made her will before the marriage! I must go at once! He will make every fight for the retention of the continental property."

Oppressed by the death of her mother, weighed down with the heavy inertia of the feelings toward her accepted lover, left alone with no bounding current of hopeful heart-desire wakening her to life, Evelyn Hartley suffered her now eager guardian to depart with no congratulation upon his access of fortune. The admiral's packing was punctuated with exclamatory remarks which proved that the wine of life was bubbling in his veins! It was only when en route that he suddenly reflected his niece had been unmoved in the most joyous surprise of his life! "She is a good girl, Evelyn. A trifle cold, but an honor to her blood."

The glee with which Admiral Walton hastened to

London did not prevent him (now quick in a new business sagacity) from directing telegrams with details to await him at Paris.

While Evelyn Hartley put away her private cares, in the reception of the guests on whose gentle womanhood she leaned in her heart loneliness, in a bower of the "Belle Etoile," Doctor Carl Stein and the anxious lover sat in excited conclave.

"This is a maddening blow! Rheingold will be frantic!" said the baffled anarchist. "How far she had yielded her heart and confidence to him I knew not, but I had hoped she had already admitted him to her will! Curse her infernal egotism! *She never thought she could die!* I fear he has lavished most of her honeymoon presents on this absurd display! Now, he is utterly useless to me. I will have to go to London and verify every detail. Wait here while I send him a dispatch. I must call on him liberally for funds."

While the defeated schemer lingered at the Bureau, Stanislas Oborski felt a sudden doubt as to his own position. "Would Walton, now rich enough to shine even in English court circles, have other views for the Cleveland heiress?

"Nothing is secure in this world until under bond and seal! I must watch Evelyn day and night. This accursed delay! What if she were to change her mind? *It is the distinctive characteristic of womanhood!* Neither obligation nor honor will stay a headstrong woman's last mood!"

With a sudden inspiration, he motioned to his man, who always hovered within call.

"Tell me! Have you heard aught of Etelka? I must not have any of her mad tricks here! Where is she?"

Oborski well knew that he was under that servant espionage which never quits master or mistress by night or day. This fellow would know by the secret intelligence bureau all underlings maintain.

"Hofer wrote me she was not in Vinena—at least not in her usual haunts. He says she is one of the star singers at Petersburg—on the Islands!" Oborski winced, as the wild magic of her unrivaled gypsy songs returned to him.

"Very well " said the impassive master, "but warn me at once if she should find me out here. You have not seen her, Fritz?"

"Never since you failed to return," said the inspirational liar, whose nerve was as cool as his master's.

At that very moment Etelka was chafing in the necessary day seclusion maintained by her, over the cold faithlessness of the Polish general. Mingling in the throng at the station, warned by the valet spy, she had gazed on the beauty of Evelyn Hartley. "The lady is dream lovely," the poor girl faltered, "and has gold! But she shall never be Oborski's bride if she had all the gold of the Kaiser."

An invincible hatred of Stein burned in her rebellious blood. Day by day, crouching, spying, following deftly, she tracked the associates. Her blood was heightened by the daily recitals of the treacherous valet. The whole story of Oborski's wooing was now conned in her heart. How to achieve a victory, where to deliver the blow of vengeance, when to strike, the maddened gypsy beauty could not determine. But in her cards, in the stars, in the mystic lore of her tribe, in the oft-told fortunes of the old beldame queen she had crouched before, she saw that Oborski was still under the spell the tribe laid on him.

When she learned that the marriage was only deferred, she clenched her hands in agony of doubt, until the nails drew streaming blood from her swarthy palms. "I will send for Melchior." Melchior, king of the Carpathian gypsies, was a man of mystic power, and his dark scowl covered secrets to strike the boldest with fear. He had a fierce tenderness for the Star of the Bohemiennes, and the reckless girl knew how to set his quicksilver blood dancing in every throbbing vein.

Stein, in the haste of his departure, did not neglect to veil his movements from Walton. "I will go to Granville and Southampton and keep quiet in London. I will find a way to get the details of the situation in England. Then I shall hasten back to Rheingold at Chemnitz. He has no official news yet. But, Count, on you hangs now the awful responsibility of making no mistake." He whispered a few words in Oborski's ear which made the dauntless Pole blanch. There was more than a sybarite's ambition, more than a fortune-hunter's future depending on Evelyn Hartley's marriage!

"Should this news prove to be true, we have lost one half. See to it that you do not fail! Watch her night and day! You will have two weeks before this old man will return. Follow her every movement. Without obtrusion, fill her softened mood with your daily tenderness! The crisis of your life is at hand, it is an hour of moment to our cause! I will telegraph you my every movement. The moment of my return to Chemnitz will be signaled. We must succeed here! This girl's money is vital to our projected American struggle! Not even life shall stand between us and victory. If you need me, call. I will come on the instant!"

He was gone, and a sense of gloomy unrest fell over Count Oborski's mercurial nature. The spectre of Etelka seemed to haunt his wakeful hours, and visit him in sleep. "I will send down to Vienna and find out more about this will-o'-the-wisp." His unrest vanished when his valet returned with a confirmation of the gypsy girl's disappearance.

"Some other lover?" he mentally queried, but a strange twinge of conscience told him "No! She is only hiding her heartbreak after the manner of her tribe." And his haunting fear confirmed the voice of his heart.

Busied, day by day, in assiduous attention to the stately heiress, Count Oborski saw nothing in her manner to make him tremble for his hopes. Loyal and frank, the American's deep, dark eyes only pleaded for time, for a rest until her sorrow should have spent its force. The social sound and clamor of an approaching struggle over Caroline Rheingold's fortunes was heard, even in the clubs. The frank disclosures of Miss Hartley told Oborski of the absolute regularity of the proceedings. The admiral was clearly and legally in the line of succession, and his cheery dispatches were a history of his progress from the modest veteran in retirement into one of the gilded lions of the day.

Doctor Stein's telegrams, concise and devoid of hope, confirmed the admiral's dispatches:

No loop-hole here—the case is without a hope

were the words, to which the anarchist added:

Next address, Chemnitz.

As Walton had surmised, Caroline Hartley, in her fury at her daughter's emancipation, had provided by the advice of her solicitors, yielding only under protest, against the future by a regularly excuted will leaving all absolutely to her brother. Perhaps the handsome egoist thought that the leverage of this pleasurable document might be used to cause Walton and Evelyn (through him) to set up a little court around her retreat at Jervaux Priory.

The return of the admiral was expected, when the news of formal proceedings by Rheingold to receive an enormous sum from the Trust for *medical services* rendered to his deceased wife, before the union, introduced a new quarrel. This was heightened by his possession of the Chemnitz castle, to which, with its personality, he laid claim. .

Count Oborski, quieted in his personal fears, recognized the masterly finger of Stein in the effort to gain at least a handsome lump-sum of money from the fortunate admiral. With becoming delicacy, he avoided the subject of the "affair Rheingold" which grew daily in public gossip. The nobleman was rendered doubly anxious as to his own future when his month's leave of absence was nearly finished. His opportunities for romantic tête-à-tête were limited by the presence of the Baroness Driesen, and further cut off by the arrival of Lady Isabel Dunham. Admiral Walton, detained beyond his expectation in London, persuaded the Lady of Ventnor to accept Miss Hartley's pressing invitation. Lady Isabel was glad to rejoin her beautiful American friend—rival no more!

The romance of the *one* was closed forever by the untimely death at Khiva, and the *other* stood in the very shadow of the orange-blossoms, the plighted bride of the splendid noble!

With courtly sympathy, and delicate tact, Count Oborski advanced daily in the regard of the circle of ladies.

"He has the grand air! I must admit him a polished and perfectly accomplished man. He seems to be heir to all the talents," said Lady Dunham. *She was actuated by that vague, general approval of marriage which brings a flutter to the womanly heart,* even in Mayfair and Belgravia.

"I can certainly trust a month's absence," mused the chafing lover, as he sat without counsel in his splendid apartment at the 'Belle Etoile.' "If Stein now, could occupy the ground, 'en ami de famille' while I am away, my cheerful return to duty will really hasten Miss Evelyn's decision as to when she will keep her plighted word."

A careful review of the whole situation, received in a letter from Stein, decided Oborski's course. Stein wrote:

There is little for me to do here but await the action of the old lawyer in Cleveland. His consent to a compromise, and that of Miss Hartley (which is easy to obtain) would close all. I burn to be at my work again. But the man of law demands the report of a trusted family agent, and has cabled that a person with the proper credentials, is on the way with a plan to effect a rapid and legal closing of the whole quarrel. If Admiral Walton's new-born pride and Rheingold's fantastic presumption can be muzzled, then I may aid you. I will take what Rheingold can offer, and you must now press matters to a close! If I can help you, I will come.

"What a man!" said Oborski. "No lammergeir of

the Carpathians has a keener eye for its prey! Marvelous in energy, he has a heart of flint. Does no human feeling ever touch his rugged bosom?"

The Pole, swathed in luxury, and nurtured in a court, little knew the bitter lessons of Stein's neglected boyhood. The anarchist's heart toughened to sinew when he saw the paving-stones which had been splashed with his father's blood!

"He must come! His eagle eye will note all! There is no suspicion of our secret union in interest."

The general, with the promptness of a soldier, sent an urgent dispatch, veiled in words which Stein would interpret.

Going to Vienna. Come at once.

These brief words brought Doctor Carl Stein to the aid of the sighing lover. With prudent judgment, Count Oborski avoided any demands upon Evelyn Hartley in his tender leave-taking. He well knew the woman he had in thrall was the bound slave of her code of honor. To her plighted word he would trust all.

His graceful sympathy, and the unselfish bearing so artfully studied for his last interview, touched the heiress.

"Shall I wait for you to call me back?" he gently said. "I have tried not to break in upon your sorrow. But your own heart will guide you." The chevalric ways he had followed in the interval of her loneliness impressed his promised bride.

"But one month more," she said, as he waited for her answer. "You can claim me then. You have been very thoughtful in these dark days!"

The daily contact with the accomplished man of the

world had built up a genuine feeling of appreciation in her heart. The voice of the world hailed him as a star of Austria's chosen chivalry. Shining above all other feelings was the never-forgotten light of the obligation which was yet unrequited—the saved life which he now asked to link with his own!

Carl Stein, warned by a letter at the station, in the hands of Oborski's valet, was invisible until darkness made his entrée easy. The nobleman, with caution, waited the midnight train.

In the conference of his last night, Oborski learned of vast, wide-spread designs for the coming season, which called for money in large amounts, and for resolute hearts.

"The oppression and tyranny here, the detection of plans miscarried, fills the United States with desperate brethren of our Cause. We must have money! If they take up work, they are spied on by the rich, or their time is cheaply sold. They are useless to us. In floating vagrancy they attract the police, and are artfully thrown in jail to separate them! Money, money is the key of the future!"

The Pole's stout heart was appalled at the dark sweep of the designs imparted by his confederate and master.

In the late hours of the night, he made his way to the station, accompanied by Stein. His nerves were unstrung with the excitement of parting from Evelyn, and the grim forebodings of anarchy's red battle as painted by Stein.

As they pressed through the motley crowd, Oborski started, "There!" he cried. *"Did you not see her?"* He made a quick sign to his valet. A woman's face had caught his eye!

"What is the matter?" said Stein, eying him with deep concern.

"It is nothing!" said Oborski, now persuaded of his mistake, for his valet shook his head decisively.

Yet *it was* the face of "Etelka" lurking in the great station to meet Melchior, her mystic adviser, soon to arrive.

A king—a gypsy king, but a king, in truth, though he traveled in humble peasant garb—for wealth was his, and light feet to do his bidding, and ready knives to strike at dead of night in his cause!

When General Count Oborski closed his weary eyes, the last word he addressed to the valet on watch in the compartment was of his fancied recognition.

"It was not Etelka, Herr Graf," positively remarked the valet. "I saw her plainly. Something of Etelka's figure but another woman, with a peasant face."

Oborski slept in peace, while the servant mused upon Etelka's carelessness.

"Prying gypsy magpie! She will spoil all yet by her headlong folly. He did see her plainly. I must warn her!" The dark-skinned girl was safe for her ally could take up the daily duty of watching Stein's daily intercourse with Miss Hartley and her guests. The cultured German was the æsthetic lion of the hour, and unsuspicious Evelyn Hartley gave to him her whole heart in confidence. Great love and great grief equally seek the relief of free outpouring to those near us. In such unguarded hours, the human heart reveals itself even to the careless stranger, rather than be pent-up with its surcharged burden.

A fortnight passed away, with Stein unconscious of the wolf-hound on his track. He was nothing loth to officially spread the tidings of Miss Hartley's approaching union, and the German nobility and English virtues of rank were duly enlightened by Baroness Driesen and Lady Isabel. "She can not recoil now!" thought Stein as he sent reassuring bulletins to Oborski He closed his last letter.

There is but one strange disappointment. Judge Fox has not yet sent his messenger. Neither the admiral, Baron Rheingold, nor your fiancée have heard of such an arrival. I find Miss Hartley in a mood, however, to aid in any reasonable adjustment and avoid family scandal.

Professor Carl Stein, like all men, was utterly incapable of going below the surface of womanhood's thousand mysterious phases. The very cheerful vivacity which reassured Stein as to Oborski's future was caused by the secret knowledge of Philip Maitland's arrival in London. The admiral, with a presage of coming jealousy, wrote that Judge Fox had begged Philip to make a quiet personal examination at London, using Alton's acute wisdom and experience, gain Admiral Walton's fullest confidence and learn his wishes. Thenceforward, to appear quietly at Munich and, before external feeling could press upon her, submit all to Evelyn and finally close up the Rheingold matters on the best terms.

Miss Hartley, herself, was not aware of the real cause of the buoyancy which cheered her near friends, and delighted Stein. It was, in truth, because, near her, in her closing day of girlhood, she would have the genial presence of *Brother Philip!*

It had been with difficulty that Wilkinson Fox persuaded Maitland to leave the trying situation, for the late spring had not yet scattered the smouldering embers of discussion. True, it was, that active malevolence had abated—but the citizen's committees knew now that Carl Stein, the veiled Mokanna, was absent from the American field, and that the active outbreaks were postponed for a year, awaiting the golden amunition. Philip's anxiety to learn of Beauford's last days—to, as it were, mourn over his friend's ashes in certainty, decided him; for the marriage of Evelyn Hartley to the many-sided foreigner *seemed a sacrilege*—albeit Oborski was clearly an eligible suitor—Maitland had no wish to witness the self-devotion of another American heiress to a future of hand-tied isolation in a foreign land!

But across the ocean foam, the memory of Lord Beauford drew him like a magnet! The loyal comradeship of men begets a higher form of personal attachment than the passion-tied knots which bind the different sexes. Ecstasy cools to indifference, and stiffens into bitter hate, but the thrill knitting together men who have battled with Fate, never grows cold. For those who have clung to the same spar in a howling storm, to the bronzed companions of dangerous rides on the lonely frontier, to the men who have watched the Indian's baleful fires, together, to those "who have drank from the same canteen" in the lull of battle, a chum's face never can be indifferent!

Despite years of absence, the ring of a loved voice will bring the old days back again!

Graver, marked by the winter's labors, and with a sense of having settled into his groove in life, Philip Maitland returned to Europe, on his delicate mission, a man in heart, a brother of men in feeling, and with a nature yet untouched by the love of woman. Though he winced when the thought of Evelyn's marriage to Oborski came to him, he felt but a vague regret, no passionate desire to cry "Hold!" even were the chance his own. For, in his heart, he felt that Miss Hartley's marriage was a result of the burial of other hopes in Alfred Beauford's grave. *"She must have loved him,"* he sighed as he gazed on the heaving waste of angry waters. The ocean calmed and soothed him, even if the Storm King were abroad. He was tired of the huddled crowds on the shore, of men, *small in creed,* and *narrow in mind!* Cold of heart, vain in windy theory and ineffective, he found the public men who paltered with reform, while he despised the unkempt malcontents, who raved for a violent remedy for all social ills. He scented the failure of unwise plans.

"Reform has its failures as well as the old systems. The great Salvation Army, in over-tender sympathy, planned its great campaign against all suffering in England! 'Darkest England' magnificent in theoretical plan, brought its believers to a sudden halt when the emotional thrill had subsided. Vulgar details of a practical nature, as to funds, the unwillingness of the helpless to be helped, the difficulty of the practical management of large bodies of the undesirable, all these things leave the great discovery stranded on the shores of 'Darkest England!'

"No one can doubt the human sympathy, the righteous purpose of the Salvationists," he mused, gazing on the unanswering sea, "but the world will go on in its old way, long after the quaintly uniformed army has gone to the Last Muster.

"The advanced socialist, even the anarchists seem to forget," concluded Maitland, as he racked his brain for wisdom, "that the combined sagacity of a thousand philosophers, the warning voice of the prophets, the songs of the saints, even the crystallized learning of

Greece and Rome, never stayed one erring soul from finding sin sweet, the play of the passions delightful, and life's morning a play-time of heedless self-surrender! No one great man can actually live the practical life of a simple starveling! The human problem renews itself with each individual. Whether the drama will end as tragedy or comedy is beyond the ken of the wisest. The experience of no one man or woman has availed to save son or daughter from going astray.

"The burden of life, the heritage of toil, the evolution of the fleeting picture known as 'Character,' is a recurrent problem, varying with each individual. Thrown up as sands on the shore, by the waves of life, the individuals only acquire importance *when massed together*, and human brightness is evolved by friction alone. Under the general theorem of absolute equality and independence, laid down by the anarchist, the race of life degenerates into a solemn march, or a final halt, for the prizes disappear in the destruction of human inequality. As for the obliteration of individualism, the great world, in its varied aspects, teems with no more varied forms of tyranny than a gleaming drop of water, crystal from Nature's fountain, and flashing in God's sunlight. In its globular confine, a world to its microscopic inhabitants, the world's tragedies are compressed with its whole theory of action confined.

"Napoleon, master of the world, sweeping from realm to realm, with the resistless sword of destruction was no greater in his kind, than the savage-looking monster chief in the watery globule, who can be seen leaving destruction in his path. The wars of Cæsar are fought over in the brutal tyranny of the strong, in the infinitesimal theater of the sparkling drop!

"Science can magnify the watery battlefield a mill-ion-fold, and show us the contained horrors, but wars cannot be varied in principle between the Waterloos of men and animalculæ!

"Bakunin's mad disciples must obliterate self-inter-est—the cardinal principle of all creation, from time immemorial, and until the heavens roll together like a scroll, before the association, personal or political, of the human beast can be radically changed.

"The aggregate conditions of mankind of to-day rep-resent the aggregate will or its minimum, *the aggre-gate sufferance*. To impress and mould anew the minds and warp of men, rests alone with that *Almighty God*, who, veiled in cloud, was not seen by Bakunin!

"Against the embattled positions into which human-ity has been moulded by fate, or natural laws, by the mysterious hand of Providence, the generations of political dreamers must dash out their brains in despair!

"I doubt, to-morrow, if the red flag were unfurled in an open field, whether the mere inertia of human ties and customs, of natural pride and tribal law, would not prevent the human race from being marched, *even to victory*, by the Prophet of Destruction!"

In the study of social distress, in listening to the thousand plans of theoretical amendment for relief, Philip Maitland's faith grew, while his esteem for politi-cal discoveries vanished. It was easy to recognize a broad and growing spirit of conciliation, and a dawning brotherhood of the more enlightened peoples. As to the future, the young American, reflected that *similar con-ditions* had been met with by generations now mouldered away:—that a steady general advance marked the world's march, and that as to the defects in the varied machinery of human society, the serious thinker was cheered only by a dawning faith that "God's greatness flows around our incompleteness!

Two weeks sufficed to give Philip Maitland every detail needed for the personal settlement with Baron von Rheingold. With a joyous heart the American crossed the channel, bearing with him but one poignant regret. The details of Alfred Beauford's fate remained shrouded in mystery. A visit to his solicitors produced no other answer to Maitland's energetic demands than the calm reply, "Our sole news as to the late Lord Beauford, is comprised in the information which you can have confirmed, in its bare details, at the Foreign Office."

"Can there be any hidden mystery in this sudden taking off?" Dreams of crime, of a lingering prison life, of treachery, disturbed Philip as he swept along to the presence of the woman soon to be Oborski's bride! Admiral Walton, now the idol of the clubs, and a man of rejuvenated social attractions, lingered only a few days to allow Maitland to conclude his business before he should follow.

In fact Horatio Walton regarded the incense of the beauties of the West End with a pardonable pride, and dallied in the bowers of the fair London Delilahs of fashion.

Miss Evelyn Hartley was the very happiest woman in Munich as she sat alone in her own especial refuge, and read Maitland's one telegraphed word announcing his arrival at midnight. She welcomed Philip's arrival. Her graceful guests, the Driesens, had sought their own home by the Baltic, and Lady Isabel Dunham was now the acknowledged "star" of that local English colony, which always assumes to lead in continental watering places. Doctor Carl Stein was absent at Vienna on a visit to the triumphant Oborski. Evelyn Hartley, with folded hands, was dreaming of the pageantry of a wedding now rapidly approaching. It seemed as if she were moving in a dream. With courteous formality, General Count Oborski had addressed her as to the visit to Munich, accompanied by his friends and witnesses for the marriage. In recognition of Miss Hartley's late bereavement, the nuptials would not be the scene of such display as might be worthy of her beauty and millions, and befitting the future Countess Oborski. Awaiting the return of her uncle, and the coming of Brother Philip, Miss Hartley sat picturing the future which was dawning for her. There was no thought of delay in her mind, and her authorization for the assembling of the Count's especial guests was already in his hands.

The entrance of her maid awakened the heiress from her dream-pictures, to the momentary trifles of the hour.

"A lady wishes to see you. A stranger, madame," said the maid. With a faint curiosity, Evelyn Hartley entered her drawing-room. She uttered a cry of surprise, in sudden fear, as a woman, heavily veiled, in costume strange to her, stood before her.

With a reassuring wave of her hand, the veiled visitor said, in a rich, ringing voice: "Pardon me! Does the gracious lady speak German?"

Evelyn's presence of mind returned under the indefinable charm of the stranger's sympathetic voice. Her affirmative answer was magical in its effect. Throwing aside the veil which concealed the face, the unknown, sank into the nearest chair, and covered her face with her hands. A torrent of grief seemed to master her very being. Miss Hartley turned to ring a bell. She would, at least, have her maid as a witness of this peculiar visitation. The unknown woman turned on her a face, beautiful even in its intensity of grief. It was the very spirit of the dusky woods. A fairy "nut-brown mayde."

"I beg you—one moment alone! Do not summon your servants. *I must speak with you alone or die!*"

"What have you to do with me?" said the wondering American. "I have never seen you in my life!" she kindly added, fascinated with the strange, wild beauty of the unknown, whose pleading address illy befitted her bold and striking beauty.

"You have seen *him!*" the stranger cried, springing to the ormulu table where the portrait of General Count Stanislas Oborski displayed all his statuesque beauty of feature. "You would steal him from me?" The woman's voice shrilled through the great lonely drawing-rooms in its tension, voicing a distracted heart.

"She is mad!" Evelyn instantly decided, her fear returning, but a pride of womanhood still stayed her hand on the bell.

"Do you speak of Count Oborski?" the heiress said, with forced composure, looking in the liquid dark eyes of the stranger for the wandering light of madness. "Do you know he is to be my husband, my poor girl?"

The picture fell to the floor with a crash, and the gypsy's head lay prone at the feet of the stranger from over the ocean waste.

With one frightened glance at the prostrate woman, Evelyn turned to face the frightened domestics who appeared in a group at the door.

"The lady has fainted! Raise her gently. Place her on the divan!"

Evelyn's maid, quick-witted and alert, was on her
eturn with restoratives, when a strange tableau met
her astonished gaze. The proud Evelyn Hartley on
her knees beside the moaning stranger whose agonized
voice rang out:

"*I am his wife!* Stanislas! Have, pity!" and her
trembling lips faltered, her eyes closed, and a death-
like swoon chilled her young blood in its cold trance.

But in the doorway, stood Philip Maitland, in amaze-
ment at the strange sight.

Springing to her side, he raised Evelyn, who sprang
to meet him, with a wild cry. "Thank God! Philip!
Come back to me! Thank God for your presence!"

Her stately head was resting on his bosom.

"What means this? Explain! *I will protect you
against the world!*" And for the first time, the electric thrill of love burned in Evelyn Hartley's veins.
Resting on his breast, she faltered, as a torrent of
tears loosened the pent-up feelings of an outraged
heart:

"It means that I have been lied to! Oborski is a
scoundrel! *This woman is his wife.*

With a quick glance, Maitland saw that the servants, glad to escape, had retired to a safe distance.

"Be silent!" he whispered, as he supported her to a
chair. "Let no one know! Who is this person?"

"I know not, but she speaks the truth," Evelyn sadly
said. "Look!" She pointed to the face where sorrow
had set the seal of its torture. The hand of "Our
Lady of Pain" had struck down the dashing Etelka
in her very glow of youth.

"Where is the Count?" quickly demanded Philip,
whose very soul was stirred.

"In Vienna," faltered Evelyn through her tears of

shame and humiliation. Brother Philip read the proud
girl's heart.

"*My sister!*" he said. "Trust me in all! Your
uncle comes in two days. Let this woman be closeted
with you alone. Let no one see her but your own
maid. I will wait here and guard the salon. Find out
all she knows. Use kindness as the golden key. I
will wait! Induce her to stay here till nightfall. You
and I alone must know of this. For Oborski shall not
see her till we four meet *face to face.*"

Miss Hartley smiled faintly. "And you will not leave
me, Philip?" Her eyes, hopeless as a stricken deer,
touched his heart.

"*Never! while you need me!* I will stay and aid
Walton in this! Now, let her be taken upstairs. I
wait out of sight. Join me when you can."

With sisterly tenderness, the child of wealth led the
daughter of the Zingaras to her own retreat. As
Maitland paced the salon, his foot crushed beneath it
silver and crystal. He stooped and picked up the
picture of Oborski in its ruin. "Another foreign swin-
dler wheedling his way into the heart of an American
heiress! My God! what stupendous folly! Curse the
brute! If it were not for Evelyn's name I would have
his heart's blood! This scoundrel has been foiled by
fate! But the Atlantic ferry is bringing every week
fresh food for his fellows. The chase of coronets is a
pitiful self-sacrifice for the women of our land!"

In the half-hour of his loneliness, Philip Maitland
pondered why the wrecked lives of the sisters sacrificed
before, did not appeal to the simple followers in the
"coronet hunt." He, a man of little familiarity with
Vanity Fair, could not realize that the American
mothers and daughters roving, at will, and alone; over

Europe, fall an easy prey to the titled scoundrel, or sly schemer, while the keen-visaged fathers toiled at home, "out of the swim!"

"Have these women no brothers, no steadfast friends to advise?"

Alas! Maitland was but too, familiar with the degenerate American hangers on of the English aristocracy! The young callow brood whose *vices* alone have the development of manhood, whose hearts throb to the chimes of Bow-Bells and the triumphs of whose lives is to copy the boot-maker's and tailor's addresses of a London rake! The raffiné, flinty-hearted American sycophants, whose triumphs of life are the flattering notice of a Parisian jockey-club flower-girl, or a bow from a titled Aspasia in the Bois!

Thinking of how Fred Winthrop rode to his death at Five Forks—of dear, peerless Charley Lowell at Cedar Creek, whose Brigadier's stars shone down from heaven on his dead body—of De Long's grapple with death at the Lena – of Custer throwing away life, not honor, dying under the mad rush of the Indian foe, Maitland wondered at the later spawn of these piping times of peace! Another strain of American blood than that of these self-expatriated weaklings, thrilled in newsboy Edison's wizard brain—a sterner manhood nerved the bosoms of the bright-faced youth of the South, dying in gray rags, under the Stars and Bars with the stanchness of the young guard! "If this stagnated and self corrupted blood must rule America's hoarded millions, better that some flame of God's vengeance should sweep away this useless muck of imitation manhood!" His brow lightened, for there are other Americans than the men who amass purchased foxtails, and hoard favors gained in the "imminent deadly preach" of the fatiguing German, whose proudest boast is to have left a distinct trail of ruined womanhood behind them!—He thought of another and an humbler class! The striving manhood of an America, unknown to the men who spend their lives in England, and boast that they "know but few Americans" cheered him. From lake to gulf, and from rocky Maine to pine-fringed Oregon, a silent army is drilling in the actual warfare of life's young morning to be the *men of the future!*

Men first, *Americans* afterward, and at least a recognizable semblance of the builders of our great Republic!

"These native-born champions of the better life should win our glorious women. It is worse than Sabine rapine to see the sugared smiles of the adventurer light the foolish flame of gratified vanity in womanly hearts. The natural, healthful brotherhood of the Anglo-Saxon strain on both sides of the Atlantic will keep the future dominion of the world fairly divided! It is only to the designing reprobate that the outraged sense of America cries 'Hands off!' To the Oborskis!" Maitland ceased, for Evelyn Hartley, her face lit with a strange fire, glided quietly to his side.

"Listen!" said she. "The gypsy girl, 'Etelka,' has given to me her heart! Melchior, king of the Carpathian tribes, is here to protect her. He was present, when, under the starlight, by the greenwood camp-fire, this man took her to wife, to guard till death, while birds should sing, the sun shine, and waters run! The gypsy king will hide her here and guard her. I have made her a promise—" her voice trembled, "you can imagine it." Maitland bowed in silence. "And the hand of vengeance will be stayed. She is to appear at my call; and now, Philip, I rest in my uncle's hands, but trust to your protection and counsel alone. "

"When does the count return?" Philip gravely queried.

"Within a week," said Evelyn. "It is too late to prevent the arrival of the official guests!"

The American mused in silence. "I have it. Walton and I will take charge of all. We will have a private interview. Your sudden illness can be used as a cloak to the irrevocable breaking off of the union. I will see this Melchior. You must send for him at once. Then we can watch in private. I will, if you will permit, join your board until the admiral arrives.— Not a word to Lady Isabel of this until the affair is over! We can trust the count's silence. The gypsy vengeance will seal his tongue. I will call at once on Lady Isabel!"

"She returns to-night!" said Evelyn.

'Then, have your strange visitor safely sent home in a closed carriage. I will come in the morning! You need rest! Sleep in peace, my poor sister!"

The yearning tenderness of his heart gave pathos to his words, and as he left the salon, a graceful woman, her eyes dimmed with tears, followed him with silent blessings.

As Philip Maitland sought his quiet retreat, selected previously to avoid Rheingold's spies, he revolved the strange surroundings of unprotected Evelyn Hartley.

"Who can have twined this web of deviltry around her? Who would guide Oborski in his sly chase?" The lightning flash of his awakened fears showed him Carl Stein, the Mephisto behind the modern Faust!

"He is the villain!" Philip Maitland swore vengeance; but it was a needless vow, for, as with flashing eyes, Etelka told the story of the day to Melchior, the gypsy king drew a heavy bladed knife and kissed its blade. "He, who took your hand is safe until he weds another; but this dog who led him to this innocent lamb, *this German cur, this Stein,* who toils to entrap you, he shall die the death of the dog he is!"

Fritz had not failed to give to Etelka's eager ear, all the details of Stein's abetting in the plot to entrap the heiress.

"And this Stein would lead you out of the way, and lay his hands on you!" Melchior growled like a beast at bay, and dreamed of a day when proud Etelka should be won at last! But a film of blood hovered between him and the gypsy wedding of the dim future!

Maitland tossed in restlessness, his soul was in arms. Late in the night, he sat with folded arms before his fire. The whole mysterious play began to unroll its hidden secrets. The stars were now in the West, and the whistle of the midnight trains had sounded an hour past in the chill, midnight air.

A vague suspicion seized him: "Could the two scoundrels have lured Beauford to his death?" An intense feeling of longing to know the ultimate truth possessed him. He saw again his gallant comrade as in the bright days of their world wandering.

"I swear," he said, "I will watch the last scene here. The Rheingold business concluded, I will go to Khiva! I will find the tomb of Beauford! I will have the story of his last hours, if, even, from foes or barbarians!" and the silent room seemed filled with the very presence of his dead friend!

A loud knocking on the door aroused him. "Here is one would see you!" cried a rough voice. It was the watchful night-porter. The flickering lamp told Maitland he had fallen asleep, and dreamed of the man whom he should never see!

Giving the fire a stroke which lit up the room with the crackling flame of the birch logs, he threw open the door.

A cloaked form stood before him, and it was only when the stranger strode into the light, that Maitland almost shrieked,

"*Beauford!*"

"The same, old fellow!" heartily cried the returned ghost as his vigorous grip proved him of flesh and blood.

"Where do you come from?" stammered the American, who dared not breathe lest his friend should take flight.

The grumbling porter closed the door and muttered; "Crazy fellows—those Englishmen. All Munich is asleep! All decent people stay at home at night!"

"I come from London, my boy," jovially said Beauford, as he deliberately lit every candle of the several branches in the room.

"And your reported death?" eagerly continued Maitland, as Beauford prosaically lit a cigar. The handsome Briton was trembling with emotion, and fain would hide his uninsular weakness.

"*The Foreign Office knew, old boy, but dared not contradict it!* It was a trap telegram set afloat by Russian spies. I rode the Pamir plateau, down the Oxus, and with secret relays of guides, furnished by the secret-service department of India, worked all through the Russian lines, and cut home by Teheran and Beyroot. From Constantinople I reached London incognito, and after reporting at the Foreign Office, here I am. Admiral Walton will be here to-morrow, I pledged him to secrecy."

"And why did you rest silent under all this?" Maitland's heart was still thumping in delight.

"Orders, old fellow! I had a tough time as it was! I would have been killed if the fact was known of my plan!"

Maitland saw the light at last!

"But your solicitors?" he persisted.

"My dear boy, an Englishman is not dead till he is seven years missed at mess! I turned up inside of *one!* Beside, I had no one to mourn me! My heir was away in the Neilgherries and he alone, on his pledge of honor as a British officer, had the viceroy's cipher telegram of the truth. I left no broken heart behind!"

Their eyes met! Maitland made no reference to Evelyn Hartley. He could see that Alfred Beauford's face, worn and aged, showed a burden of care! He then knew all! And yet Philip Maitland dared not tell of the coming explosion!

"Let's have a bowl of punch! We will make a night of it," said Lord Beauford merrily. "Won't you go back with me?"

"Go back where?" queried Maitland, open eyed.

"They have made me *Minister to Persia!* I will allow you to listen to the song of the bulbul in my garden, and you can read Sadi and Omar Khayvan in the original! As a Yankee, you might attack the Shah and furnish telephones, phonographs, and a few of your national marvels to the Harem."

He spoke lightly, but the gallant champion of old England saw that Philip Maitland's eyes were glistening.

"Yes, old man! It is in the Gazette, I am to be promoted from Vienna, so that family influence will

be credited." Cock crow found them with yet later
details to discuss, and they slumbered till high noon.

Count Stanislas Oborski, in his splendid sleeping-
room at Vienna, was forgetting, next day, a last farewell
bachelor revel, when Carl Stein, with scant ceremony,
rushed past the valet whose protests were ignored.

With a rough grasp, he awoke the handsome sleeper.

"Rouse yourself, Oborski—your foolish delays have
cost you a million. The fiends of hell are loose!"

"What mean you?" angrily cried the count. "What
do you here?"

"A truce to your folly! Read this! *You will never
marry Evelyn Hartley!*" He thrust a telegram into
the hands of the astounded general. It was an
anarchist cipher from London.

Lord Beauford alive—was on some foreign quest. Just
gazetted Minister to Persia. Left for Vienna.

"By God! *I'll wait here and kill him!*" hissed .the
Pole, as he rang for his man.

"Get up, you fool! and hie to Munich. He is there
now, and the woman who bought his honor is in his
arms."

With the snarl of a tiger, Oborski sprang from his
bed. A brutal quarrel soon proved Carl Stein the
master of the infatuated noble. The set face of the
anarchist, and his withering reproaches made Oborski's blood boil. "I am not your bond slave! *Go to the
devil!*" he yelled.

And, upright before him, his yellowish-green eyes
blazing in a new light, Carl Stein made a sign which
left Oborski's silenced lips ashen pale. He bowed and
passed the triumphant intruder as one of Cæsar's
gladiators. The cry "morturi te salutant" of the doomed

swordsmen, *the sport of the gods*, died on his lips, for the awful seal of the red brotherhood closed them. He was, in all his splendor, the slave of a merciless master! Behind him—whom? The genius of Destruction!

In the very happiest circle at Munich, as the evening stars shone down calmly on the petty joys and sorrows of the human worms below, Evelyn Hartley listened in silence to the eager recitals of Admiral Walton, Beauford's guarded story, Lady Dunham's scarcely veiled ecstasy, and Philip Maitland's meaning remarks. It was as if one had returned from the dead! A secret of moment bound Evelyn and Philip together, for the noble Count Oborski, with his evil spirit, Stein, was speeding to wed his bride, and the gypsy pair were now lurking in shadows of concealment like tigers ready to spring. "Alas! They now understand each other!" thought Beauford, gazing at the Americans, but smiling Lady Isabel, her gentle heart bounding in love's delicious tumult, had found a mission in life.

"Evelyn Hartley shall not be Oborski's bride! Philip *alone* can give Beauford back to me!"

CHAPTER XIII

FOR A MILLION—THE WEDDING EVE—"WILL YOU LIFT THE LADY'S VEIL"—A SUDDEN SUMMONS—STEIN'S DISCLOSURE—LORD BEAUFORD GOES A WOOING—MISS HARTLEY'S ANSWER—LADY DUNHAM'S SURPRISE—A SUDDEN VISIT—SAVED—THE MAGIC RING.

THE clubs and gilded circles of Munich made marvel over the scanty public preparation for the marriage of the American heiress. The death of the Baroness von Rheingold, the now public quarrel as to the ownership of the Chemnitz castle and the singular attitude of Miss Hartley's circle, gave rich food for reflection to the local scandal-mongers.

"All the Americans are more or less crazy!" coldly criticised the lean-throated, faded dowagers of the German noblesse who wailed over the feast which seemed not forthcoming.

Miss Hartley's mourning, and General Count Oborski's military trust made explanation easy, but embittered regret.

Not even Alfred Beauford, now wondering at Evelyn's strange embarrassment in his presence, not Maitland, nor the now splendid sailor veteran could follow the desperate struggle for that million needed for anarchy's coffers! All over Europe, sporadic outrages kept the continental peoples in alarm, and doubtful as to whether private revenge, or the red creed was the element of terror! In hidden mechanical work-shops and chemical laboratories, the coward's weapons, were studied, practised on, and every dark refinement of deviltry applied to the discovery of methods for *removal!* Men and women of rank and wealth grew timorous of public occasions, and the halls of pleasure sheltered many a quaking heart. Even to men who would fight á la barriere without flinching, the unknown has its ghastly chilling fear! In this brooding cloud of social distrust, Doctor Carl Stein and the now reckless Oborski, hurried toward Munich. "I may as well now force the fulfillment of her promise," sullenly said Count Stanislas.

"You are right," answered the implacable Stein, who refused to forgive the brilliant lover for the untoward delay of the marriage. Maitland was gloomy for he knew the secret hold upon Beauford's gratitude in the great money obligation of the unknown friend.

In a gloomy, waiting silence, the wedding-party waited the count's coming. "By Jove! There is something wrong," soliloquized Admiral Walton, at the "Circle des Etrangers." He was now the show figure of Munich's foreign visitors. His carriage and servants, all his social appointments, indicated a stately luxury, appalling to the thrifty Germans. "Evelyn has something on her mind!" the old man concluded, as he beamed upon the fast gathering circle of his sunshine friends.

"Thank Heavens! I will soon have her off my hands! And my yacht will be in commission." He proposed a triumphal progress through all the still dear scenes of the social world. "Much," he reasoned, "was due to the proper maintaining of his rank and position." In this attitude, Admiral Horatio Walton made the breaches of good taste, which, in a parvenu, would have been called "vulgar ostentation." But in the haut monde, actions are made tolerable by the rank of those concerned.

Miss Evelyn Walton, on the eve of an exciting ordeal, in which Maitland was to be her sole support, for Admiral Walton had given up her control in his new occupations, was gravely disturbed by a haunting fear of the future safety of Jervaux Priory.

"If I marry, should I die, would it overwhelm noble Beauford, now on the very high-road of honor?" The inexperienced girl could not tell. She did not know that as Minister to Persia, a heavy secret service fund would aid him in bearing the public charges of his brilliant station.

But the embarrassment of her refined nature, impressed Beauford, always delicate, as a cold avoidance.
"I will make sure of a few days with Phil, and then,
this physical and moral transfer over, the golden prize
landed, I will hasten on to Vienna!"

It was by order of the Foreign Office that he was
secretly directed to linger in that refined, jaded, yet
provoking social atmosphere of covert abandon. Certain movements of supplies and troops, certain heavy
changes of diplomatic pawns were to be quietly
effected before the new quiet campaign against the
Bear on the Oxus would enable the Lion to show a sharp
set of claws at will!

"Count! All depends on your social nerve and
coolness!" said Professor Stein as they swung into
fair Munich. The logician and philosopher had fur-
bished up all his ingenious wit, worthy of a Grand
Master of the Inquisition, for the ordeal. "You will
meet Lord Beauford at once. His rank will place him
in your hotel, and this wedding will bring you face to
face. Be doubly careful that no tell-tale glance gives
color to your hidden hate. And, as Maitland has
naught to do but watch, beware of him, and count
your words. The old admiral is a pompous nonentity.
But, the star of every scene is your promised bride!
Throw your heart and soul into your words and glances.
Watch her like a lynx. Strange self-protecting dis-
similation of womanhood! In all the years I have
wandered through the lights and shades of intellectual
life with her, I have never seen her unfathomed nature
stirred to its depths. The vintage of her heart may
be like the imprisoned priceless liquid in the frozen
wine, the choicest elixir of Love; but be on your
guard, day and night!

"In high play, in social life as with the unknown master of fence, the crowning blunder, fatal at once, is to underestimate your opponent! In the reciprocal interchanges of courtship, woman is your wary foe, until she falls breathless in your arms, to be your bounden slave,—if you bind her with the fetters of the law!"

Count Stanislas Oborski smiled gloomily, in this perfunctory lesson. He soared in his own haughty self-esteem far above Professor Stein, whose triumphs were the cold ones of intellect and culture, not the thousand graceful victories of the "social manner." Carl Stein had all the haughty arrogance of the German scholar,—the man of the world shone with "savoir-vivre."

The stars, indifferent to the fate of millions, beside lonely Evelyn Hartley, shone calmy down on the valley of the Iser. King and court, burgher and peasant, visitor and waif of fortune were buried in the daily trifles which make up life, but Evelyn Hartley's bosom shielded a wildly beating heart. Around her board, on the eve of the appointed wedding-day, sat the circle of her home, with the splendid bridegroom supported by his inseparable friend, Stein. There were but two at the board who knew of the vital interest of the minutes ticked away musically by the golden clock.

As, with a proud glance of veiled tenderness, General Count Stanislas Oborski pledged his bride to be, in meaning silence, the heiress felt her tell-tale glances observed. They had wandered for support to the unmoved face of Philip Maitland. Lady Isabel, Lord Beauford, the polished Stein, and the admiral, were tossing the feather-ball of idle talk to and fro! No machinery yet invented but social hypocrisy will sift the required sugar-coating over the surface of society. This cotton-wool padding of small talk alone, pre-

vents the jar and crush of ill-assorted natures. Two
human beings, hidden in the stately mansion, panted
for the hour of a formal interview between Count
Oborski, as the groom, and the prospective bride, still
an American, supported by the confidential agent of
her trustee. As for Admiral Walton, resplendent in his
garb of rank and honor, he had waved away his shadowy duties to the energetic Philip. "Should you need
to consult me, I will be at hand The notaries
tomorrow morning can elucidate any technical points.
I will entertain your guests."

At the hour of nine, Count Oborski sat in the library
alone with a tranquil smile of triumph on his chiseled
lips. No ripple on the calm surface of the social gathering indicated reluctance or reserved feeling. As
the butler closed the door and left him to his reflections, he fixed his mind on the coming interview.
"Some details as to her rights under the American
law, some formalities enjoined by the trustee upon his
representative. But to-morrow, after the double ceremony is over, I shall bear her away to Jordanov.
There, she will learn the state, the ceremonies and
the duties of a Countess Oborski!" A sinister smile
of confidence played upon his lips as he waved a jew-
eled hand. "Après, c'est moi qui fait le jeu!"

Above him in Evelyn's boudoir, Philip Maitland,
stern-faced but calm and self-contained, gave the last
injunctions to Etelka. The gypsy's eyes burned
in life's highest fever, as she dropped the folds of a
heavy veil over a dark dress of Polish mourning.
Beside her stood Melchior in his fantastic garb, a long
cloak and peaked hat lay on a chair beside him. His
uneasy eyes glittered as he listened to every sound
from the drawing-room. His brown hand fingered the

heavy knife, thrust in his belt. A warning glance from Maitland recalled the chief to his promise.

"Now!" said Philip, "*remember*," as he dropped Etelka's nerveless hand. "You are to follow in silence. I will guard you. You have my word, Melchior! and patience for you! *"Your time is not yet."*

Maitland's eye was as steady as the duelist waiting for the word when he whispered Miss Hartley. "Be firm at the last. Wait till I ring for the butler. Then watch for my sign, or my words."

He offered his arm in silence to the heiress of David Hartley. In the reassuring touch of her "Brother Philip," she felt the reflected love and guidance of her only real parent, the man sleeping where the soft roar of Lake Erie's waters lulled his last rest.

Count Oborski sprang to his feet as Philip Maitland, with a ceremonious bow, relinquished the peerless woman who would dower him on the morrow, with her hand and *hoarded* fortune. "Did the heart go with it?" Looking in the splendid eyes gravely regarding him, standing in all the cold purity of her maiden beauty, Stanislas Oborski felt his mad heart bound within him.

Goddess and queen," he thought, with surging passion. "I must wake that marble to life. She shall learn to love me!" For the courtier could not lie to himself. Evelyn Hartley had passed the hardest ordeal of the eventful night. To tell Philip Maitland all— to unfold to him the reasons why she was bound to Oborski by the strong tie of gratitude, and not the bond of burning love—to hide the futile analysis of her feelings toward Lord Beauford, and to confess her failure to enter, heart and soul, into European life, was the agony of the girl's unhappy day. But firm in her reliance in Philip's protection, and the counsels of her distant adviser at Cleveland, she feared not to face the man who waited for her in this supreme hour!

But, when her task was done, she said: "After it is over, take me home, Philip. I will select companions here for my household, but my place is in America. This is a land of cold deceit."

Maitland calmly studied Count Oborski's impassive face, as he imparted to the noble general, the details of the great Hartley trust. Evelyn was rapidly regaining her composure and a look of polite attention only animated the face of the noble suitor. "All these details and matters can be looked over by the notaries, my advisers, and the American embassy at Vienna can instruct my wife in any needed formalities."

The time for action approached, Count Oborski's marked courtesy gave no occasion for any difference, and even he, became interested in Philip Maitland's clear exposition of Evelyn Hartley's rights and duties, as heiress of her father's vast estate. A sudden thought occurred to the proud and happy general. Stein, (the unforgiving cormorant) would demand, as soon as possible, a share of the golden winnings for the dark propaganda of their common creed. In a guarded question as to his future status, Oborski gave Maitland the desired clew.

"Your dealings with the estate will be hampered with some legal formalities," said Philip Maitland, with a last glance at the beautiful woman, who sat, her parted lips seeming breathless as she hung on every measured word. Touching the bell, which startled the attentive Count strangely, Maitland whispered an order to the butler.

"It now becomes my duty to ask you, formally, if you

have ever, been married," said Philip, his voice seeming unfamiliar, even to himself, as the blood surged to his heart.

"Never," said Oborski, with a curious impatience. "I have the permission of my August Sovereign to marry!" There was a cold ring in the noble's voice. "That is enough!"

"Pardon me," said Maitland, as he accepted a glass of water from the servant who closed the door. One glance was enough. Philip had darted a lightning look at Miss Hartley, whose bosom was heaving as if some sudden emotion swept over her!

"Have you the documents with you?" The American's voice was strange in its semi-hostile ring.

Stanislas Oborski sprang to his feet. An undefinable suspicion darted over him as to the presence of the grave young American.

"*I came here to claim a wife, not to be questioned like a peasant!*" hotly said the superb noble as he glared in questioning defiance at Maitland.

"You shall have her," Maitland replied, and opened the door. Evelyn Hartley glided silently to the archway, where a woman dressed in black hovered on the threshold.

Leading the unknown forward, Miss Hartley's voice was as cold as the winter winds wail, as she said, with one withering glance of scorn at the Pole:

"*Will you lift the lady's veil?*"

The maddened adventurer tore aside the sombre crape. He staggered back as his voice rose to a shriek.

"Etelka!"

Before the echoes of his exclamation were silent, Miss Hartley and the vision had vanished. Oborski sprang **toward** the door, but Philip Maitland planted himself

firmly against it. The American's eyes were blazing.

"What means this outrage? Your life shall pay for
it!" cried the Count, closing in on Maitland. Before
he could master his enemy, Maitland saw the noble
prone on the floor, for Melchior, like a tiger had
dragged him down. The sinewy left hand of the gypsy
king was clenched on Oborski's throat, and pressed to
his heart, the heavy knife menaced his life, at a movement!

"Lie still, you dog. If you speak you die!" hissed
the gypsy. "You married Etelka before the assembled
tribe. I am her protector. If you cross her path, I will
be her avenger. The gypsy doom hangs over you!"

Maitland touched the maddened chief's shoulder.

"Silence! Let him rise. Leave him to me. You
can hear what I say!"

While Count Stanislas glared in sullen rage, the
gypsy king stood ready to leap on him once more!

"Shall I call in Beauford, Lady Isabel, Admiral Walton?" said Maitland, with a meaning emphasis. "Do
you wish to have the reason of this breaking off reach
your august sovereign?"

"It is a foul plot, it was no marriage!" raged the
noble, over whom hung Stein's dread menaces.

"You lie, Polish hound!" cried Melchior, "meet me
at midnight alone at the Heigesthor if you are a man!
I will cut the truth out of your black heart! Man to
man! Do you accept the challenge?"

Stanislas Oborski was brave, but he feared a midnight
grapple with the maddened gypsy. Melchior saw
Etelka's eyes shining on him in love, as he battled for
her in this supreme hour!

"Send away this assassin!" he muttered to Maitland
"What do you wish me to do?"

"Stand at the door within hearing, Melchior!" said Maitland. Turning to Oborski he coldly uttered the death sentence of the noble's hopes.

"Mark me, you rascal! I fear you not! If you move an inch I will blow your brains out! You have seen Evelyn Hartley for the last time. Leave this house at once, without re-entering the drawing-room. Miss Hartley's sudden illness will suffice for a reported postponement. You may use that lie to save scandal. But when you leave Munich never take her name on your lips. If you do, it is your death-warrant! Go! You can dismiss your friends without scandal. I care not if you stay here a short period. But cross this threshold again and you are a dead man! As for me," he crumpled a card and threw it toward the count, "I am at your service in any way, at once! Send your seconds to Lord Beauford!" With haunting murder in his eyes, the Count crossed Evelyn Hartley's threshold—a disgraced and discarded suitor.

The sudden illness of Miss Hartley gave Doctor Stein an opportunity to leave and as Maitland whispered "You friend has gone!" he read the story of defeat in the American's eyes.

Lord Beauford, seated in the angle of the drawing-room with Lady Isabel, into whose blue eyes a tender light had wandered back, noted not the departure of Stein or the bridegroom, for a messenger had just delivered him a sudden summons.

Come to Vienna. Mail to-morrow for you, you can leave to-morrow night.

The signature "Weathersford" and the private key-words of the English embassy proved it official.

"I must hasten on to Teheran, I fear," Beauford whispered to Lady Isabel. "Here is my summons!"

"When do you leave, Alfred?" whispered Isabel Dunham with blanched cheek.

"To-morrow night!" said Beauford, his thoughts fixed on his mission.

With a sigh of sudden pain, Isabel Dunham's fair head drooped on his shoulder. The shadow of parting fell on her gentle soul like the gloom of the grave. When Alfred Beauford had called the half fainting woman back to her self-control, he whispered, "I will come to you to-morrow. Await me here!" Anxious to end the scene, he noticed with vague alarm, the disappearance of all but the admiral, who approached with a grave face.

"Pardon, but will Lady Isabel kindly join Evelyn who seems suffering." With a look of anxious intelligence, Beauford and Isabel parted. As the light footsteps of Lady Dunham died away, Admiral Walton seized Beauford's arm. "I need your counsel, Beauford. Will you come to me here at nine tomorrow. It is an affair of the greatest moment to us all!" Lord Alfred assented and wondering left the drawing-room, where Walton began his quarter-deck pace, regardless of scattered bric-a-brac.

"The whole world seems upside down! What can have happened? Is this some sudden freak of Miss Hartley, Maitland?"—The puzzled nobleman was cut short at the door in his reflections on this singular wedding-eve, by Philip, whose face was a mirror of wild excitement.

"Don't sleep till I see you. I will come to your hotel. I have to go there to send telegrams. It is very vital to have your presence here to-morrow."

"What has happened?" bluntly asked the nobleman.

"Count Oborski will probably send you his seconds

on my account. I referred him to you." Maitland's
tone was as fierce as the hail of a hostile sentinel.

"By Jove! You must make quick work!" said the
startled Beauford. "I must leave for Vienna at midnight!"

"The sooner the better! Any time—any terms!"
answered Philip.

"All right! Count on me," said Beauford, glad to
leave this house of mysteries. "He has won her at
last! But there will be blood-stains on the altar
steps, I fear—"

It was two hours before Admiral Horatio Walton
finished his conclave with Maitland. The old mariner
was aroused, and vowed not to leave a moment until
Beauford and Maitland returned.

"He may come without me," sternly said Maitland,
"for I may meet Oborski at daybreak, and one or the
other of us will leave the ground feet foremost. If
anything should happen, tell Evelyn—" the young man
paused—"*that Brother Philip died for her.*"

"Bah! That cur will never face you!" cheerily said
Walton, as he pressed Philip's hands. "Noble fellow,"
the old sailor growled, as he mounted the stairway
The house was lone, for the gypsy king and the beautiful Etelka were now on their way to Vienna. .

"I will leave her in the heart of our tribe, where an
army would not reach her," whispered Melchior, bending his lean brown arm, "the knife shall find that
traitor heart!" This was the wild world rover's
oath.

With a dull foreboding at his heart, Carl Stein
strode to Count Oborski's superb apartment. Throwing open the door he saw the Pole seated at his table,
his head bowed in his arms. When he raised his face,

Stein seized him roughly. "You have played the fool, you have lost!"

"My wife and your million," muttered the desperate general.

"Hell and furies!" yelled Stein, his eyes blazing in the green and yellow flame of the springing tiger, "who has tricked you?"

"The American!" muttered Oborski.

"You are only a handsome ass!" sneered Stein. "It is the haughty Beauford. *The minister to Persia!* Old Walton has had a hand in this. He will leave them the mother's fortune!"

"I must get out of here, but before I do, I will strike them both." Oborski's dark eyes blazed with a baleful fire.

"Fool," shouted Stein. "Your bullying will do no good."

"Will you take my challenge to Beauford. The American referred me to him?" Oborski was almost humble.

"*No!*" thundered Stein. "I have to see him at once. What caused the breach?"

"That arch-fiend, Etelka, strode in between us and claimed me!"

"And you could not outweigh the trollop's romance in your lady's estimation?" The sneer cut Oborski to the quick.

"Melchior, her lover, had a knife at my heart. It was a planned ambush!"

Stein dropped his head on his breast. "You have ruined yourself and *I know your destination!*"

Count Oborski paled as the mystic sign of the higher council met his eyes.

"Davidoff will send you on the American mission.

This failure damns you forever. You can work out
your vengeance on the American over there. I order
you to send no message to Maitland until I have seen
Beauford. I will enter here early. Be astir!"

"I have but one chance left! To work on this Englishman's pride, to prevent the marriage. I must
desert Oborski and play the family friend. Walton
and Maitland may be of use to me!" Carl Stein left
the room without a word. Stanislas Oborski's shaken
nerve was steeled now to the wildest deed.

On the broad piazza, Beauford was the first man
the anarchist encountered. His courteous greeting
showed no feeling. "May I have a half hour with you
to-morrow, my lord?" said Stein. "I have a matter of
importance to speak of."

"It must be *to-night* then, for I leave for Vienna to·
morrow," gravely replied Beauford, scenting Oborski's
expected challenge.

"Ah! I will then speak now!" the scholar quickly
retorted, and the men entered a small waiting-room.

"I presume I can congratulate you on your new relation with Miss Hartley?" remarked Stein, opening
his fire, with directness.

Lord Alfred's silken courtesy held Stein at a dis·
tance, as he coldly replied, "I am unaware of anything
binding our names together. Explain yourself, sir!"

"I am authorized to settle the quarrel between
Baron Rheingold and the Hartley estate. In your
capacity as her future husband, you should advise her,
as Maitland has power to settle, to give the Baron a
handsome settlement. He prolonged her mother's life
ten years. He will close all and retire all his claims
for two hundred and fifty thousand dollars. You
should consider his situation. The Chemnitz castle

would then be available for you and your bride, as
your home place is, I believe, leased to Lord Derwentwater."

Beauford gazed at Stein as if the now plausible professor was mad.

"Further, Rheingold merits your special consideration. He induced his wife to make no opposition to
Miss Hartley advancing the eighty thousand pounds
to save Jervaux, *even though you turned them out after
she did!*"

"Say that again!" cried Beauford, seizing the Ger
man's wrists with a grip of steel. The solid floor
seemed whirling under his feet! Stein repeated his
remark, " *I think you are mad!*" soberly said Beauford.
"You astonish me! I have nothing to say to you!"
With a supreme effort, thinking of Evelyn's name,
Beauford left the astonished German, who cried:

"Ask Maitland! He will tell the story!" Lord
Alfred paced the floor of his apartment till after midnight before the eagerly expected Maitland arrived,
weariness and excitement had told upon the American's nerves. His face was wolfish and haggard.
Throwing himself in a chair, he cried, "Have you received the count's message?

"Not yet!' answered Beauford, as he offered refresh-
ment. 'Now, Phil, tell me your plans, for I fancy
this duel will blow over."

He was eager to question his comrade!

One overmastering thought burned within his heart.
The scales had fallen from his eyes, and he knew, at
last, whose gentle hand had stayed the grasp of the
law on the very tombs of the stately line whose blood
now tingled in his veins!

The strange embarrassment of the beautiful American was now explained. *"She fancied I would never know till years had passed!"*

He listened eagerly, as Maitland slowly reviewed the field.

"Miss Hartley is now safe from intrusion. Walton is ready to 'repel boarders' I fancy from what you say the count will disappear quietly. Certainly there will be no remark. I shall wait a week until Miss Hartley has gone to England. She will have a charming refuge with that exquisite woman, Lady Isabel. Lady Dunham is a heroine! She has taken entire charge of the past scenes of Evelyn's life in Munich. Nothing seems to shake her stately nerve, and her quick wit astonishes me! We are all agreed. In the meantime, I will run up and close this Rheingold matter. Under the present circumstances, I shall use the directions Judge Fox gave me, and end the public quarrel."

"You may not have to leave Munich," said Beauford, his eyes fixed on Maitland, as if he would read his friend's very soul. The nobleman recounted Stein's reasonable proposals, omitting all reference to the disclosure of Evelyn's generosity.

"This is a wind-fall," cried Philip, leaping to his feet. "May I send Hobson to find Professor Stein now. I will meet him in the morning and close the whole matter before you have finished your interview with the admiral. This allows me, then, to sail for home in two weeks. I have had important news by to-day's mail."

Alfred Beauford watched his friend in silence, as he indited a courteous note to Rheingold's representative. Hobson departed with orders to find his man.

The young men awaited his return in expectant silence. "All right, sir," was Hobson's cheerful response. "I found the professor in Count Oborski's room. Maitland's hand trembled as he tore open the note. It was gravely courteous, and signified Professor Stein's wish to await his visitor in the hotel garden at nine o'clock. "I design leaving Europe, and hope to meet you in closing this half-way, for I can go to Chemnitz and save you a journey."

"That ends the duel matter," commented Beauford, as he handed back the note. "You can sleep in peace. By the way, let me send my man back with you!" Beauford would not express his fear of some cowardly treachery.

"I am armed and I think I could give General Oborski a *very interesting five minutes* if he is a night rambler," said the smiling American, who, however, further armed himself with a couple of Beauford's choice regalias.

The supreme moment had come! a red spot glowed in Beauford's cheek, as he said simply:

"Well, old friend, it is a crossing of paths. *You to America, I to Persia!* Phil, you must dine alone with me to-morrow. It will be our last night. I may not see you till after *your marriage!*"

Phil Maitland's hearty laughter roused the echoes! His face beamed with genial frankness as he faced Beauford.

"What nonsense are you talking? I am going *home alone* to work, to make money—perhaps—*to fight anarchists!* Things look very ugly there."

"You overrate these dangers!" said Beauford, gaining time for his next query.

"Not a bit," gravely said Maitland. "Unless our generation is willing to tamely submit to an average amount of cruel destruction by these most fiendish bomb episodes, and to let anarchy perfect its own extensive organization, we should strike now, and break up these knots of desperate scoundrels. If we do not, it will force on all civilized nations, a cold system of general repression, coupled with the severest punishment."

"Do you go to England?" said Beauford, as he thought of the Dark Ladye and the Bright Ladye wandering together under the oaks of Ventnor Hall.

"Why, certainly not! I go home by Havre direct. Beauford's heart was beating wildly. Philip Maitland's word was the voice of honor. What could have loosened Evelyn Hartley's bond of gratitude to the Polish noble! *There was, then, no other lover. She is free!* Lord Beauford was forced to speak at last.

"Phil," he said almost solemnly, "Is it true that Evelyn Hartley advanced the money which saved my old acres from the auction sale of the law?" Maitland kindly pressed Beauford's hand, as he slipped out of the door, saying briefly:

"*Suppose you ask the lady yourself!* I will dine with you to-morrow!"

The morning of Miss Hartley's wedding-day dawned cheerily, and under the brooding wings of God's peace, the whole circle, whose game of cross-purposes had reached its crisis slept safely through the anxious night. The highly-bred domestics of Miss Hartley's splendid menage sulked about their duties as the signal for striking tents had been passed from garret to kitchen.—An inexplicable air of hurry and uneasy transience pervaded the abode of the heiress.

At the Hotel Belle Etoile, several coupés filled with General Count Oborski's friends awaited that happy man! Professor Carl Stein and Philip Maitland, seated in the open air garden of the splendid hotel, were half through the negotiation which wearied both, when Lord Alfred Beauford slowly descended the marble stair. His face was pale, his ceremonious dress was faultless in its simple elegance. A carriage of elegant appointment awaited him. Through the trellised grape-vines, he could see his friend calmly conferring with the accomplished German intrigant.

"There will be no powder burned to-day!" mused Beauford. As he entered his carriage, his clean-cut aristocratic face shone with the settled purpose which was to decide his future.

"She shall call those old oaks—those very towers her own!" he pledged himself as the crowd of curious tourists envied his participation in the wedding fes-tivities of the Lady of Millions.

The happy Count Oborski was not visible. His waiting friends became impatient.

"My dear Beauford," said Admiral Walton, as Lord Alfred entered the drawing-room, "I beg your pardon, for such an early appointment, but my niece desired to see you, and I could not explain last night. I know your preoccupations, but I must have an half hour's time with you."

Lord Beauford smiled as he replied, "I am quite at Miss Hartley's service."

"Then 1 will see you later," said Walton, as Eve-lyn Hartley stood before them. Her simple morning robe only accentuated her dazzling beauty, but in her eyes was the mingled sorrow and tenderness of a Mur-illo face. A trifling incident turned the current of her sadness. They were alone at last!

"What exquisite flowers!" she involuntarily said, as the Englishman handed her a bunch of white rosebuds.

In all their dainty virginal richness there was neither myrtle nor an orange blossom.

"Before you do me the honor to consult me," said Lord Beauford, whose face was ashen pale, "if you would permit me, Miss Hartley, I would consult you upon a matter which is of vital interest to my present and may change my future."

Miss Evelyn Hartley bowed, her dreaming eyes were fixed on the blossoms she had taken from his hand.

"You are going to England. Will you not go to Jervaux Priory?" There was a strange ring in his voice. Miss Hartley raised her beautiful dark eyes in wonder.

"As its mistress—as *my wife!*" said Beauford. "I know at last the obligation you have placed me under in so delicate a manner."

"Philip did not tell you!" said the heiress, her whole nature quaking in sudden alarm.

"Not so!" said Beauford, kindly taking her hand. "He told me to ask you, when I demanded the truth of him. It was from Doctor Stein I learned at hazard, the secret of the noble kindness which called me back from a wanderer's life—which has made me Minister to Persia What do I not owe to you! I owe to you my very life! *I offer it to you.* This is a strange world. There is witchery in the very air here. If it were not for my enforced departure, I would have deferred this request until I had shown myself worthy to walk through life at the side of a noble woman! But I fancied," he hesitated, "that you loved Maitland." He ceased, for a crimson glow rushed to her pale face, as the morning sun tints the snowy peaks of the Alps.

"Pardon me!" he murmured, "I could not leave you

for years without telling you that the only return I
can make to you is the devotion of a life! Years might
pass by before I could see your face again. It is only
right that you should know!"

The sweet girl at his side was looking kindly at
him, through lashes wet with happy tears.

"I will speak to you my whole heart. I know your
country will have no nobler representative. From the
alleys of Ventnor, I can see your roof tree. I shall
walk your halls where the faces of your line look down
in pride. I am a lonely girl, Lord Beauford. I have
glanced in at the golden gates of Vanity Fair. I tell
you as a friend of my heart, that I am going home to
my own people. My life has been tried with sorrows
every hour since I touched the shores of the old world
In my far-off land, if I cannot find a love to lead me
on, I will surely find a thousand gentle ties which tell
of Home, of Duty, of the great unpaid debt we children
of wealth owe to the friendless, the homeless, the
age, the helpless and the suffering. Shall I tell you
now, that there is not a woman in the world who
would not be honored in sharing your name, in ruling
your heart, and in dividing your joys and sorrows. But
I am also a prophetess." And she smiled daintily,
through her diamond tears. "I shall come back soon
to Jervaux and call you brother. In my dreams I
can see by your side—"

"*Lady Isabel,*" said the butler, as he threw open
the doors of the drawing-room, thinking only the gentlemen were in conversation.

The most memorable breakfast of Beauford's life was
the one at which he alone infused a certain air of gayety, for Maitland frankly reported the settlement of the
Rheingold difference, and Admiral Walton was the

nimblest squire of dames to the radiant Lady Isabel. He was happy, for he was now assured that Beauford would lead Evelyn in time, back to Yorkshire as the mistress of Jervaux. Lord Alfred had gained time, while Maitland, Lady Isabel and Horatio Walton were hold-ing a secret rejoicing over the unexpected quiet of the day, to exchange a few sentences with Evelyn in the rear drawing-room.

"I am half an English girl in blood," laughed Eve-lyn, now happy in her safety and freedom. "I will always feel you my brother while I own half of Jer-vaux with you. It will be all yours again some day, but I shall claim the right to come and see who rules your fireside!"

"*You are an angel,*" warmly cried Beauford, as he pressed kisses on the fair white hands which had given him back his dear old home.

The fairy of cross purposes touched Maitland's eyes with her magic wand! "I fancy there is no uncer-tainty in their relations *now,*" he ruminated, as the bright cheerfulness of the "Minister to Persia" was especially shared by the Dark Ladye. "It is a singu-lar fate which leads a girl from Cleveland to Teheran by the Caspian, at the beck and call of love. Dan Cupid leads us with a single hair."

Maitland's remarkably acute diagnosis of the situa-tion led him to depart to close up certain details with Stein, who was to leave at once for Chemnitz to have the deeds and releases prepared. "I am glad Evelyn will wear Beauford's name. They are a nobly matched pair," he mused, "but I always thought that Lady Isabel—" His dreams vanished before this pleas-ing certainty.

Before Maitland and Lord Beauford sat at table in

their private rooms, Stein had gladly departed for Chemnitz. "I shall come directly to Vienna, when these papers are signed. I will have at least fifty thousand dollars for the cause!" said he to Oborski. "See that no damned foolishness occurs here to prejudice you still further in the eyes of Davidoff. You have played every card wrongly in the pack. You have held all the honors and come out stripped. Patch up this gossip in the smoothest way you can! I advise you to watch night and day over yourself. Melchior's knife is as keen to-day as when at your breast last night."

In his lonely room the maddened Pole strode up and down with a raging fever of unsated revenge in his veins. "If I could only strike one blow, the other can wait. I will watch that American and later he shall give up his dog's life to my revenge. The sleek, curled English fool though, with his staring baby eyes will press that Galatea to his bosom! May the blasts of hell wither them both in that embrace!"

He studied every shade of the quarrel as he tramped his room like a caged_tiger. A confidential brother Equerry had judiciously warned the few witnesses of the groom. "Oborski will be disgraced and relieved for this fiasco," he thought, and chose the early train for Vienna." A devilish flash of wit lit up Oborski's face. *I can do it to-night!*" He goes late to Vienna. The American fool will be watching at the mansion, and his hotel is a mile away. If the American leaves him, I can do it! I will send all to the station with my man early. I have never quarreled with him. I shall go on to Vienna. Once out of Bavaria I am safe! He will not suspect! Ah! It will be a foretaste of heaven!"

Under the same roof Beauford and the unsuspicious Maitland merrily dined in private. "I am sorry to leave you at eight," said Philip, "but the admiral is now eager to leave Munich. He fears the 'qu' en dira t'-on' more than a broadside. Once they are gone, I can run down to Vienna and be with you to the last."

Lord Alfred Beauford did not urge the American to stay. A second dispatch from Weathersford bore the stirring words:

Lose no time!

"I shall surely see you," cheerily cried Maitland, "for after my people leave I wish to make a little investigation at Vienna and clear up all the mystery of the count's marriage to the gypsey beauty. I am told as a singer she was raved about by imperial Grand Dukes in Russia, and probably this impulsive man married in a brief fervor of love! I have promised Evelyn to protect Etelka, at least from any first vengeance. She has charged me with some commissions for Melchior and the singer, who are as proud in their way as the Hapsburgs."

Alfred Beauford sat alone in his room as the clock struck nine. He had but one poignant regret. The old admiral had by dint of pottering, prevented his communion of an hour with graceful Isabel Dunham. "God help her! Lonely and gentle-hearted. I wish we were in England again for a season and I could brighten her life a bit. I must ransack the bazaars of Teheran for a memorial at once on my arrival." He thought of the noble and high-spirited American girl who had given him the inviolate confidence of her maiden heart. "She is a royal nature, she draws to her all that is brightest and best. Some day—some day," Beauford dreamed, "she will awake as the wild touch of a passionate love !sweeps her heart-strings! *Then*, Evelyn Hartley will be a moving charm, a glowing picture of rapture. But, never has her thought strayed toward me. She does not seek rank or name. What waits her in the golden future?"

As he pondered of this new-found sister in heart, the rustle of a woman's robes caught his attention. A light foot paused at his door, and a timid knock brought him to his feet. Hobson was already awaiting him at the station, and he was alone. He wished to avoid contact with any of Oborski's returning guests as long as possible. Even the awkwardness of meeting the disappointed suitor, he would shun, although no word or glance of ill-feeling had ever ruffled their polite companionship.

"I suppose that diplomatic politeness must veil any knowledge of this awkward episode. It is best!" decided Beauford. But, as he opened the door of his apartment, he drew back in wonder as Lady Isabel, gliding into his rooms, threw off a filmy domino. She was in evening dress and arrayed in jewels and priceless lace. Lord Beauford's blood rushed to his heart, as he stammered: "*Isabel! My God! You here— alone! Are you mad!*" The beautiful woman murmured, "I stole away from the admiral at the theatre. I could not speak to you to-day. I may not see you again! Alfred, I could not bear to part without a last word. I only knew to-night the truth!"

"What truth?" stammered Beauford, still dazed at her hazardous stolen visit.

"*That you were not to marry Evelyn!*" she said, sinking into a chair, and covering her face with her hands. "I could not let you go to Persia without telling you that I had tried to make amends for the wrong I did you once. That it was I who bade Lord Ventnor, on his family honor, hold you back from a desperate wanderer's life by naming you at Vienna. I had to hide my hand. I knew your pride. I wished to awaken your ambition! To see you in the rank your—"

A resolute knock sounded at the door. With the lightness of a startled deer, Lady Isabel grasped her domino and sprang within the folding doors of the divided parlor. In his eagerness to prevent a discovery of her rash venture, Beauford threw open the hall door with no second thought. He was astonished to see General Count Stanislas Oborski cloaked for departure, his alpine hat with its eagle feather in his left hand. "Visite de ceremonie—not hostile," flashed through Beauford's mind.

With consummate politeness the Austrian officer paused. *"Are you alone, my lord!"* With a courteous wave of his hand, Beauford closed the door in silence.

"To what do I owe the honor of your visit, General?" said Lord Beauford, in that ceremonious polite-ness which is as distant as a dying echo.

"I desired, as I presume we both return to Vienna, Lord Beauford, to tell you that an indefinite delay in my union with Miss Hartley may cause some social remark in Vienna. As you are a diplomat of the highest grade, your simple kindness in referring to Miss Hartley's sudden illness will allay that curiosity among the English of rank which would naturally be ex-cited."For years the silken voice, and keen attentive eye of the visitor lingered in Beauford's memory.

"You are comparatively a stranger to me, Count

Oborski," said Beauford, who had not asked his visitor to be seated, "but I thank you for this politeness." In his desire to prevent any possible dicovery of the now thoroughly frightened woman, who feared the challenge to a deadly encounter was the object of Oborski's sudden appearance, Lord Beauford stood with his back to the dividing line of the doors. The urbane count's glance told him that Beauford was really alone! The great hotel was silent, and the mantel clock ticked noisily as Oborski laid his hat on the table and drew out a card case. "I shall be glad to call in Vienna and explain further. In the meantime," he politely extended the card, "let me give you this!" Thoroughly lulled by the count's easy courtesy, Lord Beauford extended his hand as Oborski turned for his hat. With an involuntary glance at the folding door, Beauford's shoulder was turned toward his visitor.

"*And this too!*" hissed Oborski, as the loud scream of a frightened woman rang through the silent halls. When a dozen domestics reached the room, they started back in horror! A woman as fair as sunlight was clasping in her arms Lord Beauford, whose warm flowing blood dabbled her laces and shining silken robes, and pillowed his fainting head on her bosom.

The room was tenantless, save for the gasping man and the distracted beauty. There was no dark token of the coward who had thrust a heavy knife into Beauford's back with a force great enough to fell him.

While the maître d' hotel and medical aid toiled over the man, faintly gasping, as he lay weltering in his blood, Lady Isabel, with a sudden inspiration, begged for messengers to call Admiral Walton and Maitland. The whirr of wheels resounded as the drivers lashed their horses. "Who has done this foul deed?" gravely questioned the master of the Belle Etoille, as he drew Lady Isabel into the now lighted room where she had hidden. He recognized the English aristo·crate at once. Lady Isabel's face was as familiar as the gallery masterpieces. "*Will he live?* moaned the woman, watching the attendants lifting Lord Beauford and bearing him to his bedroom.

"I will tell you all the moment Admiral Walton arrives," resolutely said the beauty in festal robes, spotted with her lover's blood. Before Maitland sprang into the room, followed by the hobbling admi·ral, a grave-faced German physician announced, "Mad·ame, *your husband* will live. Two inches lower and the blow would have been mortal. The knife turned on the shoulder blade and has ripped open the back muscles. It was a fearful blow!" The autocratic po·lice officials stood at the door, ready to prevent the departure of anyone.

In the distance a wild whistle as the train drew out caused Maitland to whisper in Lady Isabel's ear one word. She bowed her head in silence. Philip wheeled around. "Admiral," he said, quickly, "bring Evelyn Hartley here at once. This man saved my life and I will not leave him."

"*Nor will I, until I know him safe,*" murmured Lady Isabel, whose courage had returned.

The flying night express bore safely away a white-faced fugitive, who whispered to himself in the conceal·ment of a third-class compartment, "I can leave on the Bohemian frontier at Eger, and working through Mor·avia, hide in the Carpathians till I can get help from Jordanov. *I struck home!*" the fiend exulted. "Now for America, and I will meet the other face to face." For

Stanislas Oborski had sprung into the Berlin train and
the telegrams now speeding to Vienna to arouse the
British Embassy, were fruitless as to the capture of
the criminal.

An hour later, the apartment was silent. Only the
subdued whispers of the circle around Lady Isabel
sounded faintly in the distance. Through the opened
door across the reception-room, the rays of the night-
lamp fell on Beauford's waxen face, and the profile of
the Sister of Charity telling her beads. The flow of
blood had ceased. Admiral Walton had most haughtily
informed the mâitre d' hotel of Lady Isabel's discovery of the crime. The name of the perpetrator was
withheld until the arrival of a delegate of the British
Embassy. But to her own friends, Lady Dunham,
with a shudder, described the flash of the heavy blade,
the malevolence of Oborski's distorted face, and his
mad flight. From her coign of vantage in the dark, she
could see the movements of the figures in the lighted
room. "I shall meet that hound yet!" Maitland firmly
said," unless Melchior collects his debt of gypsy hatred
first."

An hour later, Evelyn Hartley and Isabel Dunham
were alone, whispering secrets of womanly hearts united
by a tender bond at last. "He thought Beauford suc
cessful in his suit, and marked him for revenge," faltered Isabel Dunham. The friendly shadows of the
night hid Evelyn Hartley's face and if her secret heart
had a secret, it was guarded by the genii of slumber!

Two days later, the city of Munich held no visitor
or substantial burgher, as well as "flaneur" of the clubs
who did not know that the great Count Oborski was
summarily dismissed from his rank and command.
A cipher telegram at Chemnitz, announced to Doctor

Carl Stein, now in an ecstasy of rage, an anarchistic address where the quondam general, now a disgraced and foiled assassin, could be reached.

"He shall be put in the front rank of American adventure for the cause! He will be under my orders," growled Stein, "and if he is killed, then at least my personal connection with his futile plots is *covered by his grave mound!*" Stein, in the coming possession of an available sum of gold for his campaign in the United States, decided that the useless Pole should report alone at the secret anarchistic depot in New York. He so answered the telegram adding the mandatory silence signal which enforced Oborski's obedience. "I will close this matter with Maitland, it will clear me to show myself at Munich, pass on to Lausanne, see Davidoff, and then—for the turning wheels of revolution. The cause moves on! But for this fools mad passion for a gypsy stroller, the creed would have gained a million in gold equal to an army corps in strength! But, there are *other rich women* in America, I might palm him off on some widow of colossal wealth. His broad flattery and passion play can be made useful! He shall serve me seven years for his bride, and never gain his freedom! And so Carl Stein passed onward to face the enemy in the new land of the West. Defeat never hinted of despair to him! It was only another phase of the human chess-board, and he bent his brows anew to his game of life and death. A pawn of Fate himself, he moved in her blind toils!

On the arrival of the first secretary of legation of the British Embassy at Vienna, Alfred Beauford, who was now progressing toward recovery, was able to undergo the fatigue of a short but meaning conversation with Lady Isabel Dunham. The first request of the wounded man astonished the official representative of Her Majesty. *"I want a clergyman,"* briefly directed Beauford, *"An English clergyman."*

"Nonsense, man! You are not about to die," said the secretary, who had learned to love Beauford in their association. "You need no preparation!"

"I am about to prepare to live," said Lord Alfred, and the attaché hurried away with a glance of admiration at the beauty of his friend's nurse, now as happy as woman, dainty and changing, can be in this world of ours.

The interview of the invalid seemed to have been of an important character, for, though it consisted of a few sentences, it brought beautiful Evelyn in her traveling costume, Admiral Horatio Walton, in a state of mental exaltation, and Philip Maitland, with a strange look in his eyes, to Lord Beauford's sick couch.

The Minister to Persia had whispered to sweet Lady Isabel, *"You* sent me to Teheran, Iasbel? I wish you to do me a little favor?" Their eyes met and the past rolled away as a scroll! They were walking again, with the sunlight of life's morning gilding their path, under the branching oaks of Ventnor Hall!

" Will you go out there with me?"

The loving and lovely woman, to whom he owed his life, placed her hand in his now feeble grasp. He gently disengaged his left hand, and placed a worn, thin golden band in her trembling grasp.

"It was my mother's wedding ring!" he said, as her eyes shone down on him in speechless tenderness. There was no sound in the room as, at a signal from Evelyn Hartley, a half hour later, the party, soon to part at the beck and call of fate, saw the hands of the

estranged lovers joined forever! Philip Maitland remembered years later a certain beautiful, dark-eyed one, whose eyes were never raised as the clergyman, with commendable dispatch, recited the marriage service.

"Now you must surely *come to Ventnor*, if you will not *visit Jervaux*," said Beauford, as Evelyn Hartley kissed his brow. For there, before them all, Lady Isabel Beauford had kissed the lips of the man whose heart had been hers in the by-gone days.

"I will be there at your home-coming!" said Evleyn Hartley. "And *you, too*, Phil," remarked the happy groom, his eyes seeking his old comrade.

"*That depends on many things!* said Philip, gravely.

When they were alone, Isabel Beauford whispered, as her eyes shone in love upon him, and his arms were feebly stretched toward her, "Do you remember when we read 'Maud' under the dear old trees. I have the treasured copy yet where you marked,

'O that 't'were possible after long grief and pain,
To find the arms of my true love round me once again?'"

He kissed her trembling hand in a happy silence!

CHAPTER XIV

THE OCEAN TOBACCO PARLIAMENT—FROM VIENNA TO VENT-
NOR—A HARD WINTER—THE RISING STORM—THE RED
FLAG WAVED ALOFT—COUNT OBORSKI ONCE MORE—
EVELYN HARTLEY FINDS A GOLDEN KEY—AFTER THE
CYCLONE

THREE weeks after Maitland had assisted at the very peculiar wedding scene at the Hotel Belle Etoile, he saw with satisfaction the shores of England fade from view. There was a certain sense of pride as he observed the American flag waving above him as the "New York" sped over the chopping seas without a tremor. By dint of great exertion, he had reached Southampton in time to join several returning friends. They were men who were trusted members of the silent American league of Home Defenders. Among them was the distinguished statesman, Senator Atherton, returning from a mysterious tour through Europe. "If there were reporters of our 'home school' here, they certainly would have divined his mission of quiet conference with our representatives abroad," thought Philip. "But journalism, in its mechanism, varies greatly. The great newspaper of the future will be the trusted ally of the state, a true voice of the people—at once arbiter, referee, educator. It will be one step toward the millennium," reflected Maitland, "a general public opinion, properly called out by calm and disinterested journalistic appeal, is the soundest verdict of a civilized people!

"Before its mighty power, party divisions vanish, bigotry is hushed, and the aggregate chorus of approval drowns futile dissension. It would astound the hereditary rulers of Europe to realize that *nothing can withstand the cumulative force of a free and united press in a reading country!*" Maitland was happy as he turned his eyes to his native land, lying far behind the golden sunset!

"All in all, I have not thrown my time away," he reflected as he, with the deftness of practice, arranged the temporary comforts of his state-room, "I think Beauford did well to leave the case of Count Oborski with the Austrian court officials. He is out of their power now, at any rate. Alfred's orders, and his wounded condition, favored his veiled lethargy.

THE ANARCHIST 347

"By Jove! thought Philip, as he left for a stroll on deck, "the noble Pole will not intentionally run into Melchior's hands. Evelyn Hartley's gift to Etelka will be a handsome dower, should the accidents of life make her a widow. With that fellow's linguistic accomplishments, South America or Mexico will open a fair field to his exercise of his many talents.

"Yet the punishment he flees from may meet him there! He would not dare to try the United States! He is too romantic a personage to be long concealed." The returning American did not realize that on the very craft bearing him along, were a score of the fleeing scoundrels of Europe, seeking the open doors of the United States. For fifty year, this tainted stream of corruption has silently flowed in upon us, and settling in the lower levels of life, by the accident of fortune, these foul fugitives when talented or interesting, have been tossed up by the waves of fortune into rich alliance, high station and undeserved power.

As Philip paced the deck he fondly followed the friends who grew so strangely near to each other, in the exciting days at Munich.

Gazing on the low shores of Albion, where green oaks and smooth green pastures spoke of peace and homely cheer, he pictured the coming gathering at Ventnor Hall.

It was a fortunate chance that Lord Beauford's orders to repair to London, receive his instructions and then proceed by steamer to his post, had awaited him at Vienna.

Lord Weathersford congratulated that most charming of diplomates, Lady Isabel, upon this chance run to England.

"You will have an opportunity to get up an outfit.

There is nothing at Teheran but carpets and shawls. The British Residency is even more comfortable than the Shah's Palace, but you must take all with you. By all means, take two lady companions. There are only fifty Europeans there. You will be lonely."

"Why two?" said the puzzled bride.

"You should have an *ugly* one and a *handsome* one! The pretty one will surely marry off at once. The few swains there are very gallant. The ugly one will look to you to get her back to England, and will *stay!*

"Then I will not have much society?" laughed Lady Isabel.

"Only an occasional grand fête at court, or a peep at the Harem. Teheran is a beastly place. I was there in my junior days. The great plain is uninteresting, the mud houses and heavy earthen wall are not imposing. Throw away your Lalla Rookh. There is not much of the 'bulbul' and 'roses by the calm Bendemeer,' and that sort of thing. You will not miss it much! You and Beauford can read up Firdusi, Sadi, Hafiz, Djami, and my old friend Omar Khayan, and I fancy time will not hang heavy on your hands! Haroun al Raschid never wandered back to his birthplace under the snows of the Elburz but you can recall him when you masquerade as Fatima!

"All in all, you will have a jolly time, for they will send you up the gulf in a British man-of-war. The gallant officers will be your slaves. Now, your lovely American friend would be an ideal companion!"

"Alas! She returns to her home after her first visit at Ventnor and, after Admiral Walton has shown her the beauties of Yorkshire."

"Then I shall have to trust to Beauford to make the Persian days happy for you! I was young and alone there," said Weathersford. *"I had no angel in the house!"* He bowed in courtly gallantry.

Isabel Beauford's happy heart was ready for the Persian sands or lands of snows, now that her love of a life was by her side!

Maitland's parting from Evelyn Hartley returned to his mind, as the sea-gulls rose and screamed their hoarse adieu, dropping off, one by one, to the attractions of the shore.

Philip had not trusted himself to receive the willing confidence of Miss Hartley. "I know you have been sorely beset with sorrow and exciting troubles. I shall wait you at home," he said to Evleyn, "and next winter, you can enliven the long hours for Judge Fox and myself with this story of romance. You will not miss me! Your affairs are safely closed here. Alton is a splendid counselor at London, should you need him, and I can gladden Judge Fox with reporting the manly behavior of Doctor Stein in effecting the Rheingold settlement!"

Maitland treasured for years, the thrilling glance of grateful Evelyn Hartley as she laid her hands in his, in good-bye.

"I shall have gained *one thing worth all these trials*, for when I come home, you will still be my *'brother Philip?'*"

"I suppose that Admiral Walton will be the Master of Revels at the now united estates, when Lord and Lady Beauford return from London. Their court presentation will bring sweet Lady Isabel before that August Personage, whom some Americans fancy takes her afternoon nap with the state crown on her head, and the Kohinoor dangling on her finger."

It was true that Horatio Walton's local pride was

touched. Even if his beloved niece had failed to become Beauford's wife and be welded into that shining angel band of hope, the nobility of England, he had lived to see the two estates joined at last, and the local map of Yorkshire vastly improved.

"Beauford might have done far worse! Isabel is a rare beauty, and she brings her husband land and influence. I wonder why the dickens this did not *come off before?*" The old sybarite forgot, over his brandy pawnee, General Dunham snugly tucked away in a neat tomb in India, and the late Lord Ventnor's calm award of the timid girl's hand. "I shall have a jolly lark at Ventnor," mused the admiral, for that lively military pilgrim, Mrs. St. Leger, with unerring sagacity had telegraphed to the admiral. "I will come down to Ventnor and go out to India with dear Isabel.

"Admirable woman!" mused the old sailor, as he suddenly thought of his present loneliness. "If I had met some such cheery soul, what happiness I might have enjoyed. A man in *my* position might even now!"

The veteran dozed over his glass in ignorance of the fact, that several mammas had searched the columns of the retired Navy list, and, that his hale, sturdy age was admiringly pictured to various British maidens of good form, now turning eyes toward his reat financial availability as a husband!

"There is one consolation in the whole Munich episode," thought Philip, as he closed his review of the late occurrences." The chief actors are all scattered! The whole occurrence will fade away. Events in high life, political surprises, anarchistic plots, financial storms, military combinations, and the uneasy restlessness of the time on the continent will efface the Oborski episode." With a certain solicitude, he

regarded Professor Stein's sudden departure for Amer-
ica. "Can he mean to trouble the estate legally in the
United States?" Maitland was growing suspicious of
Stein's continued prowling around the Hartley family.

"Can there be any hidden skeleton! Has he any
papers or secrets of David Hartley?" For among Evelyn's last words were the doubts she unfolded of the
scholar's integrity. "*I know not why*, Philip, but I
distrust this man. He seems to wear a suit of armor
hiding his real nature. I have felt, since my father's
death, that Stein was a factor in many things which
can not be explained. Beware of him! I know not
why, but it is a woman's reason, my instinctive dislike of the hidden nature he owns. He seems to have
acted fairly and it certainly looks as if he were not
Oborski's confidant! But beware—near or far—that
man is busied with mischief."

When the smoking-room began to fill up, after the
first night's dinner of broken detachments, Philip
Maitland was already an occupant of a cozy corner.

He had scanned with idle curiosity the main salon,
and from a distance observed the good gray head of
Senator Atherton at the table of honor. The statesman's silver hair was a foil to several American ladies,
returning from the annual "beauty parade" abroad,
who were pets of the austere captain.

Near them, "as the burthened bee forth-issues from
the rose," hovered several youths, whose raiment, alone,
was faultless. In the storms of life, deciding such·
weighty matters as the model of sleeve links, the proper
roll of a vest and the swing of trousers, their wearied
heads were sustained only by rigid collars of Hima-
layan height. With rapid interest these blasé sons of
Mammon ignored the conversation of the senator and

a great London financier, and regarded furtively the ladies, their country women, with that *particular detailed stare* which is a crowning insult.

A good humored nod from the senator found Philip anchored in Bohemia. A consumptive Denver gambler, and a gentleman who wore a fur coat and carpet slippers, (with his boot legs full of diamonds), were his right and left hand supporters. A disgusted American ex-consul, and a recalcitrant Cook's Tourist were opposite, while the flower of the table was a vivacious young woman from Oshkosh, who had failed to "rival Patti. '

"Verily, my lines are cast in pleasant places," mused Philip, as he sought the upper deck. The nod from Senator Atherton caused the vigilant Purser to at once ask Maitland if he would like "to be transferred!"

As he was not seeking social distinction, nor yet an applicant for office, the man from Cleveland thanked the all--powerful official and "preferred to retain his seat!" "That is, if rude old Boreas will permit," he mentally added. The usual smoking-room comedy was on! An English ex-groom and an alleged foreign nobleman had at once recalled an acquaintance "at court!" Several lustrous-eyed men, with solitaire diamond rings of uniform magnitude, were talking of "goods" in thick voices, and the hollow-chested gambler was throwing out prehensile feelers for the "society men," as soon as the B and S had given them courage. In a corner a red-faced Scotchman in a Glengarry, was loudly disputing with a loud-voiced Celt, sporting a harp of Erin in his tie, as to the advisability of Home Rule. Diagonally, a sanctimonious shepherd of the Lord was smoothly persuading a particularly tough looking citizen, that "intemperance had killed more men than war!" Philip Maitland, with an amused smile, was recalling the trite remark that "it takes more than one animal to make up a complete show," when, the captain "having risen" (an event of moment on shipboard), the released exquisites poured in, the ladies having yielded to the heavings in their gentle bosoms caused by a slightly chopping sea. These "symphonies in pink and white" were moaning under the ministrations of their French maids, who had already reached that bedraggled state of misery peculiar to soubrettes at sea! Behind this "frangipanni" of humanity, came Senator Atherton and Horace Walford Esq., of London. Mr. Walford officially upheld Her Majesty's peace, and like every other Englishman not actually in jail, was "talked of for Parliament." He seemed to feel the doom from which he could not escape, and had already acquired the grave air of an M. P. His delightful mission of bullying some back interest out of a bankrupt American railroad, company led him to our shores in the unlovely light of a pessimist. He was carrying a great deal of London fog with him! The cordial greeting of Senator Atherton caused the watchful Briton to admit Maitland, on due presentation, to the outer ante-room of his acquaintance. In some vague way, Walford regarded Senator Atherton as a hereditary prince of the "States," as he termed our republic. A shadowy brevet of Duke of Niagara—or Lord of the Marches of Indiana, clung to the senator in the Englishman's mind, and he decided to stick to him, until he had reached the Waldorf in safety!

Many thrilling accounts of Britons devoured by "green goods" men, (a sort of Fenian,) run down by

"Buffalo specials" in the streets, or slain in encounters with the "Bandits of Wall street" he had read in a great New York journal, whose name I would not "wrap in my more rawer breath," for obvious reasons! Both the gentlemen, having passed the trials of the age of love, rum, and cards, were free to interrogate Maitland as to the state of continental as well as American politics. In their coign of vantage, they talked of the disturbed money-market of the world. Mr. Walford was eminently sound in his special branch of knowledge, and quietly remarked that the lack of confidence of the great leaders, was due to the fear of either unnecessary continental war or the future disturbances of anarchism.

Little dreaming that Atherton, (an adviser of the government), and Maitland, (a trusted home defender), were specially interested, he said: "This is a natural progress in the evolution of distrust! Agitation, murmuring, conspiracy, ultra-socialism, class rebellion, mad parliamentary misconduct, and finally practical anarchism, drives capital to its hidden holes! It draws away its support from the manufacturer. Trade is then paralyzed, demand ceases, markets are glutted; strikes occur, the workers are embittered, and fear rules the money-world. The men who now terrorize Spain, Italy and France, the adventurers who excite Germany and Switzerland are the grandsons of the men of '93—the sons of the defeated revolutionists of '48—and the youngest brood are the revengeful spawn of the unforgiving fiends of the Commune of '70. This is the era of the false prophet, in mind, in morals, in religion, in political economy! Even the family tie is not safe!

"I call your attention," said he, "to the fact that a

vicious leaven was left in Russia, by the scores of thousands of French prisoners in 1812. Their descendants and French influence have left a dangerous stamp of wild laxity, and ferocity, in the place of the old Boyar staunchness.

"I look backward to the Reformation as the hot-bed of German materialism, for the opportunity for mental license was availed of. Followed up by Rousseau and Voltaire, the free-thinker went on to the 'ad absurdum!' Now, gentlemen," said Walford, "*I hate republics!*" His listeners started at his sturdy frankness. "The first French republic, tore down the creeds of a world— your own republic in fatal weakness, has left Almighty God out of its Constitution, and the Swiss republic has given the plotting scoundrels of the world a refuge for generations! It is the cardinal point of republican freedom to *ignore God*, and *screen the political conspirator!* Then, count me in with Church and State. *Any Church—any State!*" cried Horace Walford, "is better than republican laxity of national morals!"

Senator Atherton and Maitland exchanged glances.

"Do not smile, my friends," the Englishman said, "You admit the scum of the earth to not only *a refuge*, but *citizenship*! How many of you have even pondered on Washington's remarks as to foreign influence. America is the refuge of the anæmic human filth of Europe, and its unpunished criminals. Despotic Russia (laughed at by some) gives 'permission de séjoir' tickets and selects its citizens! Here, in England, we have a marked difference between the *citizen* and the *resident!* In the United States you have thrown the kingly privilege of citizenship open to the vilest. The vote of a fleeing Sicilian bandit, fresh from La Mafia, counteracts the vote of an ex-President in your land. Alien contract labor to day debauches your home markets. The doors are pushed inward on you by this flood of undesirables! You have no natural nerve or you would stop it! Free in name, your monied class distinctives are despotic. I read in the *same New York journal* in parallel columns the other day, that a millionairess took a salad bowl full of diamonds, rubies and other gems to be reset for a ball, the pendant, being the item that a blameless woman, of decent character, had died in misery in the same city, actually lacking food, while hiding from proposals of a life of shame! You need to mix with your development of cold intelligence, in your high-pressure schools, some form of practical morality. I care not what it be—if you cultivate the heart and morals. I am told that social competition and money greed, that later luxury, and all that comes from license, is weakening the family tie in America to a great degree. You have departed from old safeguards and you live in a 'go-as-you-please' country. A church, even if conservative, sets up a public standard of morals, and a reputable aristocracy (not one of mere money) provides an example of conduct!"

"But your own church has its black sheep?" said Atherton keenly. "True! But the fault is with human nature—not the doctrine. It is better than godlessness by law!" The senator was silenced.

"Your London fast set of the nobility, rival the heroes of the Decameron," remarked Maitland hotly.

"And yet, even *you* will admit the conspicuous offenders are dropped forever, by the honorable nobility. They are the failures of the proverb 'noblesse oblige,' and the most despised men and women in

Great Britain. *Their fall buries them forever!* Now," said Walford, "I will tell you that European confidence in the American system is greatly shaken! Investments are being withdrawn, money does not seek you blindly, and you are ruining your golden prime by the neglect of holding up American citizenship. Institutions, even investments and securities reflect the character of a people and their laws.

"Do you think you are free from coming anarchistic outbreaks in America?" quietly concluded Walford. "You are very near it! The European governments will soon combine in a Universal Board of Political Health. Naturally, cool repression, intelligent measures, will drive every cowardly dynamiter in the world to your shores, and these fellows, in the face of your loose government, your trifling army, your skeleton national guard, will carry on their damnable trade of terrorism, demoralization, and destruction. German materialism, the wars of Napoleon, and French atheism, is working out now in the terrible punishment of the third generation! As it stands, America is the safest field for these blatherskite cowards! You will hear from them! Set your house in order!"

Senator Atherton and Maitland exchanged glances as the red-faced Briton consulted his Frodsham, swallowed his "spirits," knocked the ashes out of his pipe, leaving the smoking-room in an eclispe of gloom when his painfully illustrated ulster disappeared for the night!

In later converse, while the human menagerie was in full show, as the boat leaped over the curling waves, the senator and the young committeeman exchanged their fears. "I must say, Philip," said Senator Atherton, "The state of our country is to-day far from seren-

ity, or stability, in its policy, its finances, its social workings, and all its ethical relations.   It is absurd to say
that a pure national spirit pervades the land with its
sectional interests, its diverse flags, creeds, strains of
blood, and domestic habits. I do look forward with some
alarm! The once vacant land is settled! Neighbors do
not need each others friendly offices.   The rich coldly
scorn the poor.   Our idle young men of wealth drift
into vice.   There is no. dignified permanent public
service to tempt them!   *Agnosticism is fashionable,*
and we seem to have developed a worship of the body,
born of luxury.   I care not for orthodoxy, but I do
for general religious effort. Old as I am, I can remember my mother with her Bible.   I do not believe a
man ever lived who dared to tear the Bible from his
mother's hand! I shall make a secret report upon the
general European condition of upheaval!   It is for
the younger men, like yourself, to face the storm, to
fight the fight of order, and to gradually reform our
national spirit.   But an immediate system of rigid
inspection of all arrivals, and a radical change of our
naturalization laws will alone save us bloody scenes! My
last hope is in the South and West and in the support
of the country people. Our great cities are congested.

The 'machine' must go!   And, one by one, its 'pot-
house' dictators, its 'district dukes' and 'ward barons' will enter the penitentiary. . This is inevitable.
The right will triumph, for all over our scattered great
cities, *the search-light of the press is turned on these
scoundrels now!*   There is truth in Walford's remarks
about our waning family ties, and the concrete power
of gold!"

The old statesman's brow was clouded as he sought
his hiding-place in the steel-plated cupboard termed

"a palatial stateroom," in the florid language of adver·
tisement.

Philip Maitland, smoking his last cigar alone on
deck, looked up and saw one great white star looking
through the flying scud, "I will go home to my native
land, and face whatever storm menaces our homes. The
young men of our day have the blood of 'sixty one' in
their veins! If it is necessary to put sentinels on the
battlements of freedom, the call to arms will find them
there! And, please God, I shall be among them! There
will be a struggle to the death around our homes, the
scene of our purest joys, the theatre of every hope,
before the Red Flag of Destruction waves over the ruin
of the American republic!

"There is an infinite promise in the Stars and Stripes,
as holy to-day as when it waved on the sunset-field
of Gettysburg over forty thousand dead and dying!
The 'mystic chords of memory' shall stretch out from
these silent graves and awaken us, in their thrill to
nobler deeds of manhood!"

While the "New York" swept toward America, with its
motley delegation from the Tower of Babel, Miss Evelyn Hartley was the animating "star" of Ventnor Hall.
Lord Derwentwater was fain to offer the courtesies of
Jervaux, and the American heiress gazed upon the glories of the Beauford line with a sisterly pride. Even
the lively companionship of Mrs. St. Leger did not dis-
pel a lingering feeling of envy! The old ancestral pile,
with its quaint clinging stories of the wars of Round-
head and Cavalier, wore its grave and reverend crown
of dignity. The very oaks bowed beneath druidic
mistletoe were brethren of Boscobel and the glories of
cabinet, picture gallery and armory, thrilled the
romantic woman! While Admiral Horatio Walton,

and that congenial military dame, Mrs. St. Leger, made brave show in the preparation for the brief home-coming, Evelyn Hartley had time tò cast up the accounts of her heart life. Frankly and with no bitterness, she realized that a sense of personal honor alone led Alfred Beauford to offer her his name and to ask her hand in marriage. The resolute American girl could not but admire the manly tender of his hand in marriage.

"To give all 'this up," she thought, as she walked the moonlit terrace of the Priory, "would have broken his proud heart. In the sensitive mood of an indirect debtor, he would have made me the Lady of Jervaux. It would have been his only way to directly accept from me, what was next to his life, these storied scenes of his boyhood. The birthplace of long forgotten ancestors, and the very treasure-house of their ashes!" Lingering alone by the "wishing well," flitting in light and shade down "Lady Mary's Walk," studying the faintly legible inscription on old brasses or smooth worn slabs in the stately burial chapel of the Beaufords—the romance of the old entered her very soul. Generous, warm and true to her higher womanly instincts, she was happy in the union of Lord Alfred and the exquisite Lady Isabel. "There is a blessing of the olden days hallowing them, and it is fitting and meet they should walk together in happy love, side by side, where they parted in the old days." A sudden yearning for her own home possessed Evelyn Hartley. "Here," she mused, "I am out of place. It is not in the externals—it is in the invisible moving spirit of the home surroundings that the American woman is a stranger in these feudal surroundings, as well as in the maze of the gradations of rank and custom in the English social life.

"Cucullus non facit monachum," thought Evelyn, as she voiced in her own heart, the truth that a cour-' tesy title could not put an English heart into an American body! That the subtle influences of birth, blood, home, the natural surroundings of childhood, and the social sympathies of the heart, were real and moving forces was proven in the tide of rushing feeling which turned her eyes toward her home in the west! Even in the wild storms of winter, when the lake was lashed to fury and the wintry blast whistled shrill from the pathless Canadian woods of the old voyageurs, Evelyn Hartley had loved her birthplace. On the green lawns of Jervaux she saw again her stately home, on the cliffs of Cleveland, and the mist veiling her tender eyes was born of love for the silent man who could not welcome the darling of his heart home again. The sudden wish to be again a real factor in a life she was born to, to take her part as woman and friend in the onward movement of the great, busy, toiling city by the lake, possessed her, and she was glad to return and *be the thing she was*, than to linger, even in the graceful half-shadow of exotic society, and *seem the thing she was not*.

The triumphal entry of Lord and Lady Beauford to the brief enjoyment of their home-kingdom, and the bright days of joyous revel chased away from Evelyn Hartley's mind all thought of the peril she had escaped in the averted foreign alliance. "

It is only right that I should tell you," said Lord Beauford, as they walked, alone, the terrace at Jervaux, "that I am informed by the Embassy that Count Obor- ski has undoubtedly fled to America. I mention this that you should be *on your guard*. Though," he said, smilingly, "I shall feel secure as long as you have your 'Brother Philip' to guard you!"

Something in the diplomat's tone touched her heart. In the fullness and sweetness of the happiness which fate had brought to them, Beauford and Lady Isabel spoke often of Evelyn's strange unconsciousness. "Can it be that she cannot recognize the devotion of such a man!" said the now experienced Benedick. "Think of the years, the long, sad years, that fate and pride held us apart!" whispered glowing Lady Isabel. "After all, Alfred, *how little of our lives we live ourselves!* It needs the stroke of fate, the electric touch of sudden feeling—the chastening of sorrow, or some overmastering direction, to show us where the heart has always been!" Beauford gazed tenderly at her.

"I think, I feel, in some way, I cannot explain, that all will be well!" said Isabel Beauford.

"You are a kindly and a loving prophet, Isabel!" said Beauford. "Let us hope that your prophecy will be verified."

So after the brief days of rest under the old rooftrees of home, Lord and Lady Beauford went out upon the great deep to seek Ormuz and the farther India, he to uphold England's might, and the happiest of wives to throw the witchery of her love around him, in the far land of the Lion and the Sun! The honors accorded at court and the Foreign Office to the minister, and the stately farewell festivities of Admiral Walton, were the finale of the English visit. Evelyn Hartley was not ignorant of Beauford's gratitude. For ere he left his home he spoke words to her under the great oaks of Jervaux that tinged her cheeks with blushes, and brought a proud and happy light to her eyes. "I can never feel you alien in blood or foreign in heart as long as I draw breath. I owe to your noble kindness the privilege of breathing the air of my old woods. In our far-away Persian home, we shall have you always with us in heart. You will come again to us. Ventnor Hall is always open to you. Admiral Walton has promised to be honorary seneschal, if he survives the loss of Mrs. St. Leger. But come to us, and to Jervaux, where in the old garden,—where I can yet see my gentle mother, in fond memory,—the very roses will nod their thanks and hail you sister. Dear Evelyn, while we live, you have an English home in loving English hearts!"

Admiral Horatio Walton was disconsolate when letters from Judge Fox and Philip Maitland called Miss Hartley home in the early weeks of autumn. No recount of unvisited continental attractions could tempt Evelyn to recross the Channel. The alarming outbreaks in Spain, the growing danger to the general public from brutal violence, the sound of anarchistic outrage frightening even the boldest, warned her homeward. Mutterings and discontent were everywhere. Blood of the innocent stained the pavements of Paris, the very hall of the People's Chosen in Paris rang to the sound of the coward's bomb. Wild bandits of Sicily chanted "la Ravachôle," the hideous war song of the dynamiter, Switzerland was in upheaval, and restless Germany was torn with the secret agitations of the propaganda of Destruction, now showing the ghostly footprints of that curse of humanity, Michael Bakunin! The capitals of the continent were searched to the last corner of every slum for the anarchist nests, laboratories and refuges. Crowds of suspects, uneasy human vampires, were driven from the continent to London's human waste, and rigorously hunted back again! In all the growing darkness—while cloud after cloud rolled over social Europe—Evelyn Hartley hesitated not to seek her home.

The letter of Maitland, calling for her, bade her bring resolute and reliable attendants, and to use extreme care. "The Barcelona outrage, the madness of Ravachol, Vaillant and Emil Henry, the various frustrated humble plots show us that wealth has no safeguard, rank no protection; that innocence and benevolent sympathy count for naught with the mad apostles of Destruction. It is known," wrote Maitland, "that scores of desperate anarchists have been driven to us by the now vigorous concerted action of European governments. We have only our active police of Chicago and New York, who have faced these scoundrels to teach them a lesson. The lawless riots of San Francisco, Pittsburg, Cincinnati, New Orleans and Homestead show that extremest violence may soon appear among us. There is a bitter and a trying winter before us! The fatal weakness of pardoning the three Chicago anarchists by a too tender-hearted governor of Illinois, has given crime that impetus which left murdered Mayor Harrison, the ruler of the great city of the West, weltering in his blood in his own home!

"The three anarchists turned loose had barely escaped the gallows and richly merited internment for many years. The open attempt at murder of arch-millionaire H. C. Frick, as a mere representative of capital, was a precedent and a prophecy. Whatever means the logician may take to intellectually combat anarchy as an abstract science, here in your old home, as in other awakened cities, the undismayed citizens of the useful classes are beginning to strongly organize to fight as a *body militant!* The struggle will be blown from Europe to our shores! The vilest poison is working in our midst, now! The supreme object of anarchism is to embroil the great American labor-classes, the skilled as well as unskilled and crush all the higher classes by a revolt, a revolution, an uprising which will set back American civilization fifty years! But before the red flag shall wave in victory, the rifle blasts shall scourge the foul mobs of terrorists with an awful vengeance of the men who stand by home! The mask is off! So, come to us. Come home. And help with your presence, your sanction, your property contributions and your aid in works of goodness, tenderness and sisterly feeling. Wealth never stoops when it lifts up the lowly and suffering. It honors its very essence!

"Evelyn," concluded Maitland, "The American women of to-day have as much at stake in the anarchistic issue as the men. They must in every way defend the family tie and home. Sustained in the fight against anarchy's terrors, and all corruption *by our women*, the right will prevail! *There can be no higher stand-ard in a community than the hearts, lives, thoughts and code of its best women!*"

It was almost in a dream that Evleyn Hartley, richer in beauty, riper in type of womanhood, and with her noble heart unfolding like a flower from its virginal bud and blossom, crossed once more the threshold of her great palace on the heights of Cleveland.

Standing on the great veranda, gazing over the concentrated material wealth, the accumulation of fifty years of prosperity, with Philip Maitland at her side, the richest heircss of Cleveland, in listening to his secret foreboding of coming disaster, for a terrible winter approached, trembled at the bitterness of the struggle, the vastness of the stakes in the dreadful game to open! Her mind was at peace. The joyous acclaim of friends cheered her. Judge Wilkinson Fox, courtly, prudent, and able, was at her side. Her great inher-

itance was untouched by disaster. Her noble and practical mind caught the needed spirit of the hour, a spirit
of tenderness for the honest poor, the worthy and deserving. "When you are more experienced," said Judge
Fox, as he listened to her lofty plans and purposes,
"you can show yourself a noble daughter of an honored
father. In giving away *half* your great wealth, you can
be *twice* as happy! Not spasmodically, not with sudden fancy to guide, but in a broad continuous general
plan to help, lift, aid and better all those around you!
This and only this generally adopted all over our land
—a live moral effort to raise, and purify, and better,
political, moral and social life, will prevent a sudden,
vicious and widely spread attack on wealth as an
unprotected element!"

As the winter approached, the rising storm became
louder, for the stress of the human toilers became more
bitter. The voice of discontent was everywhere, and
lurking behind the bulwarks of free speech, the spies
and priests of anarchy trod the land from end to end.
The weak temporized, the vain politician trimmed his
sails, the journals catered to the sensations, and the
public mind became accustomed to the repeated bloody
outrages of European capitals. A vague and dark honor,
a cloud of suspicion, a pall of fear hung over the whole
land. As in all cowardly and merciless enemies, the
malefactors seemed always to have the best of it. It
was in the cold, icy days of this sad December, that
the whole civilized world seemed to have positivly
accepted the new order of things, that personal reprisal, class punishment, bloody official revenge, or a great
holocaust as an exhibition of the cruel power of anarchism might be looked for at any time. Philip Maitland,
now Colonel of a local regiment, each evening com-.

muned with Miss Hartley, whose splendid mansion was a congenial meeting-place for the higher citizens. The young colonel often mused upon the strange and head-long crime of the once magnificent Count Stanislas Oborski. From advices from Admiral Walton, and researches in Vienna, it was ascertained that Count Oborski's name was veiled in forgetfulness. His estates in Galicia were under crown charge, and his pict-uresque old castle of Jordanov, was guarded by a few faithful old domestics, using it as a refuge. "Thank heaven," mused Maitland, "that the scoundrel has ceased to follow up Evelyn."

In the serious preoccupations of this memorable winter, Philip grew daily nearer to the noble woman who was the star of her native city. And yet, in her charities, his committee work and guard duty, they never paused to think how their lives had insensibly run together. It was "Philip" and "Evelyn" now in their address, and a growing confidence led them closer, heart to heart. It was with a strange suspicion that Philip galloped up Euclid avenue one bitter night, and leaving his orderly in charge of his horse, hastily sought Miss Hartley, who waited him in the library.

Her eyes read the secret of serious apprehension. Springing forward, she clasped his strong right arm in her nervous hands. "There is no immediate danger, Philip? *Tell me all!*" A loving woman's tenderness thrilled in each word!

"You are safe, Evelyn!" the anxious colonel replied, "I have a dozen picked men posted in your grounds, and your alarm wire and telephone would bring a bat-talion in ten minutes. But I am astounded! There is to be an immense mass-meeting near the rolling-mills to-night! We have obtained secret hand-bills in

German, Slavic, Russian and Polish. Our executive
committee have twelve-hour reports from the principal
manufacturing cities. It seems there is a threatened
upheaval, a general collision feared all over the middle
and east. Our wisest heads are astounded! The trades
and labor-unions of the land, handled by the Irish-
Americans are reasonably quiet! *Say what you will of
the Irish, they are not anarchistic!* Sixty per cent of
our arrests or suspects are Germans, Slavs and Poles;
and the balance French, Italians and Spaniards. Now,
who will address them to-night, think you?"

Evelyn's eyes were strangely eager.

"Professor Carl Stein, and a speech in Bohemian
will follow from Ernest Rheingold, now a bond-slave
of Stein's! I am ordered to take ten resolute men in
plain clothes, and mingle with the crowd. The committee's forces are marshalled ready to move, in any
direction if an attempt should follow on the great factories!"

Maitland gazed in the beautiful eyes of his adopted
sister!

"When I am at fault, I seek wisdom in your woman
wit! Read me the riddle of the connection of *such a
man* with this scum!"

"Philip, seven out of ten of the late anarchistic 'martyrs' have been men of superior education!" replied
Evelyn, "but I will tell you a strange feeling that has
clung to me lately. The sudden appearances and dis-
appearances of Stein, his strange travels, his fevered
activity, and his fruitless mysterious studies, have thrown
a light on him! *Has he not been for years a daring
plotter, a hypocrite!* Is not this Rheingold an accom-
plice! Remember I warned you against Stein! It is
he who has woven a web around our family! It is he

who tried to ruin my life! Do you not remember it was Stein who brought into our family the man who married my mother? That he threw that dark fiend, Oborski, across my path!" Philip started as the agitated woman spoke the hated name. "Are they members of a great band?" continued Evelyn. "These men met at Lausanne! It was their haunt! The great anarchist nest there has just been broken up! I feel as if a plot were laid against me—that some day I shall see the face of the desperate wretch who tried to murder Beauford!"

With a feeling of singular unrest, Maitland sought to cheer his dearest counselor. "These scenes are too exciting for you. I apprehend no specific outbreak to-night, but I shall think of you! The street is patrolled. You have your private watchman, your burglar alarm. I shall entreat you on the first sign of active disorder to go south for a run. Say to Florida! There will never be anarchists in the old rebel states. I begin to see their unwritten community laws are *wiser than ours!* I will watch over you! I will ride past to-night! Can it be that all these scoundrels were part of an extended conspiracy! Stein is no fool! When he openly addresses the malcontents, he forfeits the regard of his old circle. He does nothing without a reason! Can it be that the times are ripe? *Stein an anarchist?* But one thing strikes me badly in his past record. He never made friendly ties, and always lived alone!

"You may be deceived here, Evelyn, but you have been right since you returned, in every judgment. If there is an overt demonstration to-night, if there is a red flag thrown to the breeze, it may end in trouble, but Carl Stein will be chased out of Cleveland forever! Under our system he will be blacklisted in other cities, and have to slink back to Europe."

With tender solicitude, Philip Maitland calmed Evelyn's fears. The little hands resting in his were cold
as ice, and he could read in her eyes a haunting fear.
"I shall pass by to-night," he repeated, as he kissed
her hands and rode down to the place of popular
assembly.

A half mile away, he turned in his saddle to watch
the lights gleaming in her splendid house on the heights.
It was the most notable palace on the avenue. As he
did, a sudden thought set every nerve tingling.

"By heavens! She fears Oborski's presence, already
suspected! She fears a mad vengeance! If there is
a secret connection, if an outbreak occurs, it would be
a time for reprisal! I must watch over her! If I live
till to-morrow, Evelyn shall go South! I will induce
Judge Fox to have his people take her down to Florida.
She does not wish to be the first to go! But if they
invite her, she will be safe, she can recover her shaken
nerves, and this thing we face, must come to a head
sooner or later! But it is nonsense. Oborski is thousands of miles away!" And yet it was with an uneasy
feeling at heart, he met the chief of Police as he
neared the meeting place.

For a moment he forgot even Evelyn Hartley as the
chief, who awaited him in grave concern, said, "Colonel
Maitland, the executive committee have just sent me
a special report on this man Stein. It appears he has
been masquerading for two years as a literary traveler,
and, under various names has addressed the disaffected
all over America. He is a perfect linguist and is now
believed to be one of the highest order of these red
conspirators. From various Chiefs of Police we find that
he has been unusually active, and also, strange to say,
very well supplied with money. He has had several

followers and associates, nearly all foreigners. This man Rheingold, used to be a physician here. Now, my orders are to try and get this man in the clear reach of the law for a six months' sentence!

If they raise any red flag here, I have two hundred men scattered in the crowd and the same number in reserve. We will tear up their red flags, give the law-breakers a good clubbing, and arrest Mr. Stein and his body guard. We will then run him out of town after his brief imprisonment. All I wish you to do is to follow this crowd, with your scattered men. We will break it and pursue it. If there is violent resistance, telephone your men in at once. You know the secret place in the ward where we have private wires.' The chief, who had two good revolvers belted on, knotted his heavy baton on his wrist and disappeared to face a hydra-headed mob with professional coolness.

Colonel Philip Maitland was busy in receiving and transmitting secert orders, and handling his skeleton detail, until the cries borne on the wind, the glare of bônfires, the streaming in of thousands of dark, stolid men to the central nucleus of the "grand stand" told of the culminating hour. Followed by one trusty man, Maitland worked his way into the seething mass. A slouch hat and heavy loose coat disguised him, and a good service revolver, and a blackjack were handily within his reach. By dint of a half hour's struggle, Maitland, using his broad shoulders, unceremoniously forced himself to a post twenty yards from the stand. There, bare-headed, his voice ringing out in wild tension, stood Carl Stein, the mask thrown off, urging the chaotic mass to strike for their rights! The yells and cheers drowned the speaker's voice.

In the rising tumult of loosened fury, all plans were

cast to the winds. Hoarse roars and gusts of feeling swayed the great throng. It was the drunkenness of incipient revolt. Already in the skirts of the crowd, a fringe of unclean human spectres, the advance guard of the human "looters" of the homes at their mercy, gathered and waited for the rush. Borne away by his exaltation, Carl Stein suddenly threw out the crimson folds of a great red flag, and waving it, cried, "I give you here the banner of the future!" There was the silence of a moment, and then a terrific shout broke on the night air!

The enormous gathering heaved and moved in several wild rushes. "To the mills." "Clean out the avenue." "Burn the 'Union Depot!'" were discordant war cries of the incoherent factions dashing forth under seeming leadership.

While Maitland madly dashed through side streets to gain his horse and send his messengers for the waiting divisions of his regiment, the night air resounded with screams of pain and curses.

"*The police are already at them,*" cried Maitland, as his horse sprang forward. And as he neared his rendezvous, the solid platoons of the police reserves were closing in to smite and break up the sullen knots of fugitives, vainly trying to make a stand.

When Colonel Maitland headed a battalion of his regiment to sweep the square, twenty minutes later, there was nothing left but the fragments of the destroyed grand stand, broken lamps, shattered transparencies, and hats and coats cast away in flight!

The anxious hour was over! The intended coup was a failure, for the fragments of the red flags (artfully provided) lay in the gutters. The jails were swarming with squads of the arrested and the *flight* of the mob was as *rapid* as its gathering!

"All over, Colonel," cried the Chief of Police heartily, as he rode up. "This quarter of the town is clear. They telephone me to call in my men, leaving only a double reserve! Will you ride back to headquarters with me?"

"And Stein, the mad fool?" demanded Maitland.

"Spirited away! We lost him. He got out of our lines! He must have had a waiting confederate, but," the chief laughed, "he will never be seen in Cleveland again! His day is done! It was a mad attempt to unfurl that flag!"

As they rode along it was through silent streets. Maitland's junior was marching the regiment to its barracks. With surprise the young colonel noted the deserted streets. "Is it so late, Chief?" he asked, for he had not marked the flight of time.

"After one o'clock," curtly said the Chief of Police, "and all honest folk should be abed. You can go home with no delay. I will not sleep till morn!" The chief was astonished as Philip spurred his horse and waving his hand disappeared at a smart gallop. For when the answer fell on his ear, "after one o'clock," a sudden fear seized him. "I told the special guard to leave at twelve, and Evelyn is alone! Stein fleeing—desperate! If Oborski—" the young rider clenched his teeth for it was in the gruesome hours of a darkish night, and the Hartley residence was cut off in its "lordly pleasaunce."

"She shall not be unguarded a moment until she leaves Cleveland, and that will be to-morrow," thought the anxious man. The skilful escape of Stein, Evelyn's brooding fears, and the relaxation of his overstrained nerves oppressed him with a sense of some imminent peril hanging over that beloved head.

"Bah, I will not be foolish! This is a boy's fright in the woods! But I will find the old watchman on his rounds, or in the carriage-house and tell him I will send a couple of good policemen up to watch till morning. Then Evelyn shall go away! Her name has been foremost. She has too much local prominence to escape malevolence."

The tired horse splashed through the soft snow and Maitland sprang off, throwing the rein over a post. A glance at the great mansion showed that all was quiet, and, half-ashamed of his fears, the young man moved cautiously down the great walk, and eagerly peering into the semi-darkness, for if the watchman were on duty, he might meet him at any time. As he passed down in front of the library veranda, his beating heart was stilled as he fondly thought, "All is peace. Heaven's blessing is with her as she sleeps." A noise within the house attracted his attention. A heavy, dull noise as of a falling piece of heavy furniture. And a moment later a woman's scream was distinctly audible. In the olden days, as a boy, Maitland had known every nook of the great mansion. He had lately looked it over. With one spring he reached the library windows. Springing back he bounded forward with his shoulder as a battering ram, and through the crash of French blinds and the window plates gained entrance to the library. Another scream rang out, as from the higher story, the voice of the woman he sought was raised in wild appeal! Up the broad stair he sprang, like a tiger in its charge, with one shout of encouragement. A faint light burned on the landing, and as he cast his eyes toward the hall-opening of the heiress' rooms, a dark form rushed toward him. Maitland fired point blank, and, with quick practice, *pulled the trigger again.* When the butler and footman rushed down from the servants' distant lodgment, followed by the boldest of the maids, now frantic in panic, they saw Philip Maitland standing sternly, pistol yet in hand, by the still writhing body of the wounded burglar! A heavy knife lay on the floor where Maitland had kicked it away, and fallen across her own threshold, in a death-like trance, Evelyn Hartley was unconscious of her rescue.

While the women bore Miss Hartley to her sleeping-room, the lights revealed the death of the would-be murderer. It was no thief of vulgar grade! A black loose cloth mask still covered the dead man's face. "Take it off!" said Philip. The excited servants gazed at each other, as Maitland, stooping over the dead marauder sternly tore off the covering. He dropped the cloth with a cry, almost a yell!

For the Count Stanislas Oborski had kept his oath! *He was "face to face with the American in his own country!"*

There, in the "sudden taking off" of a midnight malefactor, lay the missing man, of whose fate the baffled police of Vienna had no trace.

"Here, Johnson!" said Maitland, noticing the second groom in the throng, "You'll find my horse at the gate. Gallop down to the police-office and tell the chief for me there has been a crime here, and a burglar killed by me. Ask him to send four good men rattling up here in a carriage to watch this house till morning!"

"*I will watch it myself after this!* said Philip Maitland, grimly.

"What shall we do with this?" the frightened butler whispered, pointing to the stiffening corpse.

"Let it lay till the police come!" said Maitland, gazing at the distorted face of his deadly foe.

He turned away and beckoning the butler, said sharply, "Take a man and search this house from top to bottom. Report to me. Now, Wilson," he signed to the coachman, "Step over to Judge Fox's residence and tell the judge what has happened. Say that I want him kindly to come here at nine o'clock to-morrow. I will wait for him here."

After the men had departed, Philip burned to speak but one word to Evelyn Hartley. The women servants had clustered in her rooms for protection but when Philip Maitland's foot crossed the threshold, there was only the aged housekeeper seated at the table. The room was tenantless but as he turned his head, a voice which thrilled his very heart said *"Philip."* There was a moment's pause, and it was on his breast, *her heart throbbing with the bliss of a revelation*, Evelyn heard his reply! "Sleep now! *my own darling*, for your life is *mine henceforth!* I will watch here till the day."

"And he?" she whispered as she clung to the strong man who was "Brother Philip" no more.

Maitland's motion of the hand told her all, and he turned and kissed her trembling lips! *"Never to be parted any more, my Evelyn!"* he vowed, and left her to dream of what strange fates had led her to find the golden key of her heart.

"It is the strangest thing I ever heard of," said the chief, as Maitland sat with him an hour later in the library. "This man is unknown here. Though he has a sailor garb, his whole appearance is of refinement. The pistol, knife and chloroform indicate the criminal. There were others with him. We found several articles they had dropped. A strange Canadian cutter, has been seen off the shore to-night, and my police fired on a boat with six men thinking them harbor thieves. It looks like a kidnaping scheme! *Do you know this man?*" The gray-eyed chief suddenly faced Philip.

"*I never saw him in my life!*" he steadily replied, thinking of the dear one, her head pillowed in happy rest, whom he would shield.

"It is strange!" mused the chief. "By the way, you need not come down to-morrow. I will have the inquest deferred till I can find out who this man may be! They will make a general examination by noon."

"That is very acceptable, Chief," said Maitland, as the overtaxed official rose to depart, having personally posted the guards, "for *I shall be very much busied to-morrow!*"

"Any new orders from the committee?" said the official. "I wonder if Stein got away on that yacht!"

"*I am going to be married to-morrow at noon!*" remarked Colonel Philip Maitland. "I will be happy to have you call in the evening and test the regulation cake and wine!" The chief wrung the young leader's hands and was far on his way to headquarters before he reflected that he had not even asked the *name of the bride!*

"I suppose it is all right, but it was *very impolite* in me," mused the victorious chief, as he noted the arrivals of the last straggling squads of pursuers. "I believe Mr. Philip Maitland knows more than he wishes to tell. Did this swell burglar think to carry Miss Hartley off? Was it a scheme for ransom? or some plot of this Stein gang!" The puzzled policeman lit a soothing cigar. "I will wait events. Miss Hartley's name must not be dragged in! D—n these foreigners anyway! They give us seventy per cent of our unnecessary work. I must keep this quiet till after the marriage!"

There was not a trace of disorder in the Hartley mansion next morning as Mr. Philip Maitland stood gazing from the crystal window of the breakfast-room at nine o'clock. He had already received in his mail, a report from his junior on duty, and the news in the journals of the complete practical victory of the police, and the flight of orator Stein. The German professor was thought to be unsettled in his mind, by some of the writers who knew of his once proud standing. To Maitland's astonishment, there was not a word in the papers referring to the attempt on Miss Hartley's house or person.

The silver chimes of nine startled Philip, who wondered if the woman, who now knew his unselfish and devoted love, would appear to meet Judge Wilkinson Fox. Evelyn had made no sign. But when the agitated old counselor was ushered into the room, Miss Hartley's light foot sounded on the stair! Her sweet confession of how long she had imposed her every service, unpaid, on the man whose glowing eyes welcomed her, was deferred, for she placed her hands silently in Philip's.

"Will you be seated a moment," she said, in a voice whose formality astounded her visitor. "You are my trustee, Judge Fox, and I wish to ask you a very important question!" She was smiling through her tears now!

Wilkinson Fox seated himself without a word at the table, set for three *by some strange accident.*

"I am ready, at your service, Miss Hartley," he said with a glance at Philip, who was lost in wonder.

"Is there any legal objection to my being married

to-day?" the heiress said, as her eyes dropped and the rose-flush sought her cheeks.

"*At noon, precisely,*" remarked Mr. Philip Maitland in addition.

"*Not the slightest,*" said the startled lawyer. Evelyn rose and clasped Philip's hand as he sprang up. "On the contrary, I will give my official consent, if you will allow me to bring Mrs. Fox here with the minister, and let her hear Philip promise to be *my* partner for life as well as *yours!*"

"I agree!" said the lover. "Evelyn is worthy of even *that* sacrifice!"

CHAPTER XV

A REPRESENTATIVE OF THE PEOPLE—THE ADMIRAL'S SUM-
MONS—ANARCHY'S MISSING LEADER—A STRANGER AT
JORDANOV—MELCHIOR LAYS A SNARE—BY THE BANKS
OF THE ARVA—ON THE LAWN AT VENTNOR HALL

IT was several months after the wintry cyclone of riot, and covert anarchism, had swept in fitful gusts over America, before the "beautiful Mrs. Maitland," as society termed her, found words to speak of the events of the night when she found out the secret charm unlocking her prisoned heart!

The Hartley trust was in fact a thing of the past!

A death in life left a vacancy in the three, for Mrs. Rheingold's place had not been filled. Admiral Walton could not act for himself, and with consent of the courts, on the representations of satisfaction by the two interests. Wilkinson Fox, having turned over his active law practice to his new partner and his veteran assistant, was the virtual king of Cleveland. But behind him was a gracious hidden influence which softened his rigid dealings.

"I am the happiest man in the world, Queen Evelyn," the counselor often said. "Fate's decrees have been kind to us all! Your father's trust has been fullfilled in spirit and in law. We often spoke of Philip in the by-gone years. He is here to guard you, to aid you in carrying out the wishes of your noble father. No plan, hedged round with the law's intricacies could have placed Maitland where he is to-day! As I grow older I *trust more to that Providence* which overlooks us all. I cling daily more and more to faith. But I fear only your open hand. I wish to live to hand over to you intact, the Hartley trust-funds, and to see whether your course of intelligent benevolence will lead others upward!"

"It is better to *fail nobly* in a gospel of love than to *rule by the iron haud of greed and fear*," said bright-eyed Evelyn. "I have a wise adviser here!" She glanced with pride at Maitland.

"Never doubt me," said Philip. "Only let the head and heart go together! There is a science of the care of property, of the rightful handling of wealth, and its regular harvests are better than a Nile flood of emotional benevolence. To plant the right, to uproot the wrong, needs care and personal wisdom. It will not meet the call of this divine better feeling to merely leave a field here and there for the gleaners. The grandest title of the Pope is 'Servant of Servants!' To feel that the Hartley trust sustains and cheers those, without the law, who look to it, is to nobly follow out the Golden Rule!"

When Evelyn Maitland learned all the details of

her husband's private researches, she was thankful that the public naturally looked at the attempted crime as a bold attack on the jewels or funds supposed always to be in her possession. In the inquest, Philip Maitland had been spared awkward questions, and the quondam General Stanislas Oborski slept *in an unknown grave!*

The police gradually ferreted out the hidden history of Stein's nefarious occupations. In several places in the United States, uprisings or brutal outrages had marked the long and unhappy winter. Knots of five or six desperate alien anarchists, were found to be the pivots of all dangerous attempt. It was these picket posts of the red propaganda which the German schemer had planted with the funds derived from Rheingold's scheming marriage, and each little band became the centre of a mad conspiracy. The photographs of Oborski, sent from place to place, in the comity of local officials, were returned with sketches of his active participation in a number of daring outrages.

The mystery of his movements on the night of the tumult was impenetrable. But Maitland, as well as Judge Fox, believed that he had obtained an accurate description of the interior of the Hartley mansion from Stein and Rheingold, and, with characteristic Polish madness, designed to stupify, the heiress with chloroform, and while one or two of his band guarded the frightened servants, hurry her to the boat and bear her away on the cutter to the Canadian shore.

No attempt was made to seriously punish Ernest Rheingold, who slunk away from Cleveland, to reappear as a quack doctor of pretension in one of the mushroom cities of the far West. Relieved from his fear

of Stein he was harmless, as he lacked a brain to plan
and nerve to execute deeds of daring.

As the autumn approached the general American
situation had bettered, for even the conspirators began to see that anarchy offered *no charms to women.*
There seemed to be in America, as in Europe, no distinct class of women deriving benefits or greater privileges from the new creed of human rights. *From
queen to peasant, every high and holy aspiration of
womanhood clings to a home, present and prospective!*
Leaving out the dreams of ambitious women, the
schemes of the unworthy sisters, (happy after all, a
mere minority,) womanhood's dream is to rule a home,
to contribute to its stability and embellishment. The
doctrine of anarchy, however speciously gilded, sweeps
away the family tie, destroys the home, tears down
the altars of religion, and leaves woman a lonely human atom in the mad whirl of that *new higher life!*

"You are right, Evelyn," said Maitland, as his spirited wife spoke of this fatal defect in the New Dispensation. "No woman is at heart a communist! Whatever be a woman's life, whether she basks in pleasures, walks the stern path of duty, or climbs the hill
of ambition, her very nature is imbued with *individualism,* and the highest expression of her very heart and
soul is in the love which clings around a home, wherein she is the central figure!"

Evelyn Maitland's happy eyes shone on her husband
in assent, as he quoted her father's words: *"Love is
the higher law. Love alone can lead!*

"I have no further fear for our own land, now that
public opinion is aroused to the workings of the
remarkable social system which destroys, to produce
equality, and proves after cowardly bloodshed, to be

only a system of more or less infamous class reprisals! In the reduction of all existing systems, and differences, to a dark plane of nothingness, even the ablest heir of Bakunin cannot clearly point out what he proposes to build up.

'Unless a healthful individualism is allowed a safe guarantee and protection, the human race would descend to a horde of cave-dwellers, crouching, in fear, in the night of newer 'Dark Ages.' It seems that the Anglo-Saxon strain of blood rises superior to the fallacy easier than the continental races! England drifting boldly along, in sullen inertia, like one of its own huge battle ships forging ahead in a foggy sea, runs down the mad pirates, trying to board her, and never changes a point in her course!"

Admiral Horatio Walton was unceasing in his efforts to induce the Maitlands to visit England. In his letters, he boasted of the immunity of Great Britain from the ferocious assaults which continued to shock and alarm the continent. He held out as a tempting bait the return in the spring of Lord and Lady Beauford. "There is no reason why you should not come," he wrote, "America has awakened at last. You have a welcome awaiting you which is one of heartiest English cheer. It may be the last time I shall see the hawthorn in bloom, and Jervaux Priory, as well as Ventnor, will be thrown open to the friends of that wonderfully lucky and able fellow, Beauford. He is talked of for a dignity which will surprise even his most sanguine friends!

"By the way, I note that artful rascal, Stein, has been just chased out of Switzerland. He was discovered lurking at Lausanne where an anarchist club and secret press was raided. He is supposed to be lurking in

Bohemia. His pen has been the main stay of the secret press, and I am told he has largely directed the obstructionist sympathizers in the Reichstag. But he is now a proscribed man, and a wanderer. There is no fear of his daring to come to England under our new system. I presume he will end his days in some continental dungeon. But you must come to us, and I send you letters from the Beaufords. They feel every day, more and more, what they owe to Evelyn."

"Shall we go, Philip?" questioned the glowing beauty, whose mind was shaded with thoughts of the past. "There is no danger now!"

"Not a bit of danger!" answered Maitland, smiling. "I do not fear *the whole peerage* for *Miss Hartley's* money is no longer, in the continental eye, an object of schemers!"

"Philip," said his wife, thoughtfully, "I could never have realized the web woven around a young, lonely woman, unless that madman's folly had left him open to detection. I wonder how many young women of fortune realize the intrigue which follows up every movement of their lives."

"Few do!" said Maitland, "and these hidden social campaigns will be planned and often succeed, until, with a gradual emergence from feudal 'legal incapacity' women have the experience which the *practical management of their own affairs* will give."

Maitland was glad to visit England, especially in view of important affairs of the estate, for with singular persistence Admiral Walton urged the transfer of the mortgages upon Jervaux to his account.

"We will go!" said Philip, decisively, after a conference with Judge Fox. "The time of the settlement of the trust approaches, and he is an old man, and the last of your family."

"It will not interfere with your congressional duties," said the lovely young matron, for Maitland had received a nomination to Congress. In his particular case, it was equivalent to an election, as he was pledged to a remodelling of the naturalization laws, the establishment of a proper passport system, and the enactment of federal regulations with regard to the unrestricted sale and handling of high explosives.

The temper of the American people had been sorely tried. As Judge Fox quaintly said: "We have reached a period when the citizens of the United States demand something from the Federal government. Train robberies, tumults menacing citizens of different states peacefully traveling, the past operations of the James boys, the Younger brothers, and their humble imitators, unrepressed lynch law in the South, the western traffic in Chinese slaves, gigantic opium smuggling, the easy ingress and egress of Europe's now dangerous ambulatory criminals, the hasty manufacture of a foreign vote, the filling of our land with the diseased paupers of the old world—these, and a few current happening will enable you to find out why *government does not always govern!*"

All this was in Maitland's mind as he said to Evelyn, "You shall have your Washington winter, if the sovereign electors favor me, for I will not go abroad until the session closes. If I can do anything to preserve and hand down the heritage of our fathers, if I can aid in extending the privileges and lightening the burdens of useful citizenship, if I can see an effective safeguard against vicious foreign interference placed at our portals, I will have filled the measure of my ambition. But one thing I regret in entering Congress, it is to see so few men in the Lower House representing the skilled *workers of our land.* The law, capital, the farming, mining and even manufacturing and trading classes are adequately represented, but there seems to be a dearth of recognition of the millions of wage-workers. The skilled artisan rising above labor, and, though often gifted and worthy, stopping short of the station of employer seems to have no weight in our national counsels."

"From what I have seen, Philip, is it not because they expend so much of their energies in the organizations of trade guilds and more or less suspected unions, that they are not fairly represented there?" remarked his wife, as she reflected on the thousands of really unrepresented skilled workmen of Cleveland. "They are left between the superior members of the lower class of voters, and the influence of the capitalist and employer, with no real class consideration. The unskilled laborers out-number them, the rich distrust them by reason of the secrecy of their peculiar associations!"

"You are right," said Maitland, "and yet I would like to see a score of representative men in the House of Representatives of that class. We seem to jump from the *rich man* to the *farmer* with an unexplained hiatus. England has such men in the House of Commons. France in the Corps Legislatif, and Germany in the Reichstag, and right good service they have done at times. At least, these aspiring classes cannot complain, in those lands, that they *are without voice!*

"For my part, when I meet my colleagues, the man who strives for a better, broader, purer national life *is my brother*, regardless of party lines which are of use in special agreed-on lines of policy only. To make the useful in every class of citizens, our constituency, and to check imported vice and disorder, is the first duty.

"As for national repression of the red propaganda, I would like to know by what divine or human right, any dissatisfied theorist would tear down the social system of to-day, levy forced contribution and con-demning classes and individuals unheard, and appoint individual executioners to carry out the dark ven-geance of an infernal Hate!

"The seed of anarchy carries its own death within its kernels, and even in a land which has good humoredly tolerated every species of religious or com-munity folly, *it must* meet, *it shall* meet, that stern repression of the law which indicates the survival of the fittest!

"We are not ready yet to *commit national suicide* or to be destroyed in a *general suttee!*"

It was after an exciting session of Congress that the newly-made statesman sailed for England. Some of his hopes were now accomplished facts, other aspira-tions struggled in the womb of Time, but the face of the civilized world was sternly set against the mouthed madness of the anarchists. They no longer plotted in peace, their vicarious emissaries were hunted to bay, and the violent attempts at cowardly assassination were smartly and summarily punished. The sober majority of the world had awakened to the instant application of the God-given right of self-defense! "Do you wish to go on the continent, Evelyn?" Philip asked as he watched the sun sink in the broad Atlantic, and gazed at the happy woman clinging to his arm.

"Never! until I know that Stein is—*no longer there!*" replied his wife, with a slight trembling of her clasp-ing hands.

And Maitland knew that even long months of quiet
had not effaced the sudden horror of that night, when
waking from a sleep, troubled by the anxiety of the
hour, she had seen the masked marauder almost at
her side.

"His untiring hatred and daring villainy might lead
to other hidden dangers! No! Let us remain in England. You know I have a sister's right at Jervaux."

"*You also had a 'Brother Philip' once*," laughed
Maitland. "I might never have known your hidden
love for me if I had not been led to your lonely home
that winter midnight."

"*Had you no suspicion to guide?*" said Evelyn, with
interest.

"Nothing!" replied her husband, "but a feeling at
my heart that my horse could not bear me swiftly
enough to the rescue. And the strangest thing is, that
I was led on by a mysterious power. I had really no
settled plan of action. It was only a masterly call of
the spirit to go to your rescue! I never even saw
Oborski's face till the mask was off, but *I fired as at
a mad wolf!*"

"There *is* such a strange dual faculty of the human
intellect as telepathy, I believe in my heart," softly
said Evelyn. "Finer faculties, greater gifts, senses yet
undeveloped may come to us in that gradual improvement which, after all these sharp reactions, seems to
be influencing the world."

"I am not so sure as to the telepathy," said Maitland, with careful skepticism, "but of one thing I am
assured! *It is that without love, life is not worth the
living!*"

There was no disagreement between them as they
left the wheeling sea gulls to their airy flight, and went

below to ponder over the details of Admiral Walton's festivities on the return of the laureled Beauford.

For Walton, superbly splendid with that wealth which had softened his heart toward the Yankees, was a very Fadladeen as a master of etiquette, and had read up his Lalla Rookh to appropriately welcome the returning "fire worshippers" with Persian display.

The cup of Admiral Walton's happiness was running over when he welcomed his stately ward at Ventnor Hall. One glance told him that Evelyn had quaffed from the magic fountain! That in her fitting union with her ardent husband, she had found the highest earthly good. There was a romantic tenderness in the wedding tour of the happy Americans. They were "looking backward" and many scenes of their European life took on new lights in view of their discoveries at Cleveland.

By dint of the admiral's daily over-reaching influence, Evelyn Maitland was the temporary chatelaine of Ventnor Hall. Greetings were exchanged with Lord and Lady Beauford who were returning via Constantinople and Vienna.

"I presume Beauford will bring us any later news of 'The Lost Leader,' that unruly human intellect, 'Stein.' I have privately warned him of the character of all those affiiliations and-he will be wary. The more so as I hear Earl Weathersford will retire with signal marks of Her Majesty's favor, and that Beauford is very likely to be named at Vienna."

"It is a singularly rapid promotion, is it not?" said Maitland.

"Ah! my dear boy, all is for the best in this world, if we only trust to time! While Isabel could not bring him money, she has brought him the interest of her uncle who is in Her Majesty's government. It is as easy to write *'Vienna'* as *'Copenhagen'* and I believe his lucky star is in the ascendant! Now, Maitland," said the old sailor, as they walked under the oaks, from whence both Ventnor and Jervaux Priory were visible, "It had been a dream of my life to see these historic estates united. I fancied that with Evelyn's money Beauford could buy Ventnor Hall. But Dan Cupid has tied the two estates together with golden chains!

"Now, I am growing old. I naturally have no right to all of Caroline's money. It was half English, half American. Transfer that mortgage on Jervaux Priory to my interest and let me leave it to the little Persian lad, who is named Horatio Walton in my honor! It is the whim of an old and childless man! To Evelyn returns all the rest, which, by the folly of her mother might have gone to the adventurer. I wish my gift, inter vivos, to be that settlement on the little heir of the Beaufords! I would like to see an old sailor's wishes carried out in his life-time. I have no love for the lawyers! They are human sharks!"

Maitland smilingly assented, and with the aid of Judge Fox's agent, Admiral Walton was enabled to announce his splendid endowment when Lord Beauford, with his lovely wife and a picturesque retinue of Asiatic incapables, arrived to show an admiring tenantry the most fortunate infant in Yorkshire!

In the first interval of the rejoicings which stirred the local British heart, on the return of the diplomat Maitland eagerly begged details of the Vienna situation. "It is believed," said Beauford, as they sat alone, "that Oborski's servant secured, by his order, all his jewels, plate and private papers. The town house and Jordanov estate, will go to a distant heir, but a flood of pressing claims, and many obligations await the legal proof of Oborski's death. From what you tell me, I apprehend it will be years before a final settlement is made. No one knows in Vienna that the dashing count died by your hand. The secret shall be locked in my bosom. I imagine that this scoundrel valet joined his master in America, and when Stein is run to earth, this fellow Fritz will be not far off! Stein is now proscribed in the various continental countries of importance. He is doomed either to fret out his life in foreign exile, or fall into the meshes of the law! His complicity in the Lausanne incendiary agitation has closed his open career! I would not advise you to take Evelyn abroad! There is no telling what moment the desperate villain may appear! He could easily work his revenge through others, for he is high in the order. I will hear of his appearance, for I have made special request of our secret agents to locate him. The Viennese authorities want the valet, but he is unlikely to risk his safety."

"Beauford," said Maitland, gravely to his friend. "Let us never bring up these characters to poison the present happiness of the two women who knew them. Let us seal that past!"

And in the golden prime of life, with honor, wealth, and youth to bless them, the friends, reunited in happiness, banished the dark shadows of the anarchist from the sunlight of their happiest days.

It was on an exquisite summer evening, while the revels still made Ventnor Hall, a picture of English hospitality, that a band of gypsies made merry in their green-wood camp in far Galicia, by the swift rushing Arva. The romantic river glen, with its sighing pines and larches, was a fitting retreat for the score of swarthy

Romanies whose tents and dancing camp-fire accentuated the foreground.   Beyond the stream, perched on
a beetling cliff, the old castle of Jordanov frowned
against the sunset skies.   It was the home of the
missing Count Stanislas Oborski, and it was here that,
with his brigade of matchless horse, he once held the
main defile of the Carpathians, now tipped with a
ruddy sunset glow far in the south.   In this defile of
the Arva, a resolute battalion might withstand a division of the gray-coated Russian invaders!

In picturesque confusion, the men and boys lolled at
ease, while the women, from childhood to wrinkled
age, with one exception, toiled for their masters.   In
haughty indifference, wrapped in costly shawls, and
her hands flashing with gems, the magpie spoil of her
lover, Etelka leaned against a mossy rock, and listened
to the pleadings of Melchior.

The chief was thin and stern of face as if some over
mastering passion burned within his fiery soul.

"I will delay no longer! There are no tidings of him
here; he will never return!" cried Melchior.   "It is a
year, and he has made no sign! Remember your promise!"

"*When his head lies low, and not before!*   I gave my
word!   You have it yet!   Is he dead?   Where is his
grave!   Then, if he laughs no longer at my misery, I
am yours.   But if on the earth, you must find him and
kill him, before I am your bride!   Remember your
oath!"

"Have I not tried all! The men I sent as spies were
flung from the gates!" growled the baffled suitor.   He
would not sue at the feet of this haughty one were she
not the daughter of a queen!   And well the Romany
knew of the dark charms and weird mysteries imparted
by fierce Queen Esther to her wayward child!

"The servant has been seen hovering near here! He is concealed in that castle now! Wait but a moon more and then I will ask you to watch the castle nc more. I might go up myself!"

"Never!" cried Melchior, for dark stories were told by the frightened peasants of lawless Jordanov's wild woodsmen!

"I will wait! I will do your bidding till then! If he comes not you are mine! I will work your will for one more moon!"

She laid her brown hand in his palm and the en-chantress smiled!

Melchior watched her throw herself down, tiger-like, on a great fur robe, and gaze into the fire, leaping in red tongues up, under the forest arches. With a mut-tered oath, he seized his staff, and followed by a little band, set out to picket the one winding road leading to the Jordanov crag.

In storm and dark night for seventeen days, the velvet-eyed gypsies crouched behind the crags from dusk till dawn. Their camp was hidden by a huge bend of the river bank, and from either flank they could reach the single trail unseen.

In the lonely Carpathian forest there were none to dispute the green-wood with the brown men! From the richness of forest fruits, and game, they derived an easy support.

Etelka sprang wildly to her feet, roused from vain dreams, when in the gray of a later dawn she knew that the trap had been sprung!

"Come!" said Melchior, "you shall know all! I have a prisoner here from whom we will force the truth." By the blaze of a torch, the gypsy girl, panting for vengeance, bounded forward as she saw by the flicker-ing light the face of Oborski's valet. Fritz was bound, and at his side stood a burly Romany, knife in hand. Etelka's eyes shone in the light like a crouching panther. She rapidly gave Melchior his orders in the weird tongue of the Children of Mystery. With her hands supporting her swaying hips, she bent toward him, for he had sunk down in fatigue. "*The truth, quick,* or it will be cut out of your lying heart! Where is Oborski?" The prisoner gazed at Melchior, whose right hand gripped his knife-hilt.

"*Dead—in America, the far land beyond the sea!*"

"And whom led you here to the castle?" Her voice was ominous.

"*Stein, his friend*—you know the man!" The prisoner groaned and his voice faltered.

"What does he there? The truth! Quick!" Melchior's knife glittered in the air!

"He came to remove the jewels and treasure which I bore away from Vienna. Oborski told him alone its hiding-place! He has it now. I was to spy the road and send him a signal by a peasant who comes to the river at daybreak. *It is a token he gave me!*"

"And then?" Etelka began to see the anarchists inmost design.

"I was to have my share and the peasant would guide him out by one road while I was free to go in peace."

"Listen, you dog!" hissed Etelka, "You shall bring him to us! You shall have your share, *and we—shall have ours!*"

In the early sunlight of a golden morning, the prisoner stood at the ford of the Arva and by his side in a cloak muffling his face, Melchior, with eager eye, watched the delivery of a packet to the stolid messenger who was in waiting. The boor leaped from rock to rock and waded the riffles of the icy Arva. When he was lost to sight, Melchior led the shivering valet back to the dense coppice, where a half dozen armed followers were a sinister body-guard of Etelka, now robed in her quaintest garb of gypsy wealth.

"I do not fear your lying! *I hold your life here!*" The knife was flashing at his throat. "When comes he?"

"At noon," the trembling prisoner faltered.

"Then do you show yourself here, and motion him over. My men will have crossed behind him but you shall beckon him here! You stand within instant range of a dozen guns. If you have told the truth you shall have your share, if not, the raven fattens on your flesh!"

In wait, like the crouching man-eater of the jungle, the gypsies lay as the sun slowly crawled to high noon. On the prisoner's face an awful agony worked, a sudden convulsion as, when the sun lit up the deepest pools of the flashing stream, the peasant, leading a heavily laden mule, slowly descended the crags. On the other side of the glen a white kerchief fluttered from a clump of bushes as the ambush closed in behind Stein, who walked with the springy stride of health and vigor. Etelka, with cruel eyes fixed on the trembling servant, whose face was ashen, said, "*Now! dog! remember!*" And as Stein boldly essayed the crossing, the valet, with unbound arms advanced, pushed by the muzzles of four guns. His knees were loosely bound.

When the burly form of the German was within ten yards, a man trode out from the greenwood twenty yards away. Stein cried quickly, "*Who is —*" The sentence never was finished, for Melchior, bounding from behind a rock, buried his deadly blade to the hilt in the back of the anarchist!

"*Traitor!*" he gasped as his head fell back. Two men were already at the head of the mule, and the frightened peasant staid not to look behind as he plunged into the forest.

Tossed in a rushing whirlpool of the Arva, the mangled corpse of the murdered anarchist drifted on to be borne into the rush of the Vistula flowing toward the frozen Baltic, and while the hideous thing that was a man was swept away, the turbulent soul of Carl Stein fled—*whither? Beyond all mortal ken!*

"Take evenly of the spoil," said Melchior, as the safe retreat of the camp was reached. "You may make such bundle as you wish. Tremble not! You know now one dark secret of the Zingari! You will be led to a place whence you can gain a village! Silence and secrecy is yours for life! *Beware the gypsy doom!*"

And when the sun went down, in gloomy shades, the night hid from sight the trampled, blood stained turf, where Bakunin's heir gave up his wretched life to treachery and greed!

In a wild feast at midnight, when the Romanies were ten leagues away, Etelka whispered as her supple neck bent under a flashing necklace of the stolen gems, and frantic mirth told of the wine madness, "*I am yours now, for he lives no longer and you have avenged me on the dog who led him away!*"

Vanishing by different paths, the band never reunited, but to all was known the reign far and wide of Etelka, as the dreaded queen of her ferocious gypsy husband.

To human eyes, Carl Stein never reappeared, and later, when in furtive council, the survivors of the

Lausanne congress met in a far distant city, the aged Davidoff solemnly said to two survivors of the great secret executive, "*Our brother is no more! By some device he has given up his life!* Time may tell us if by a sudden vengeance of government agents or in an unhappy accident. But I have thrice signalled him to every department. *He is lost to the face of the earth!*" Alone, unmourned, with not a moment's warning, the restless, warring spirit had passed beyond earth's turmoil to the dark Lethe of the Unseen! The blow had fallen!

The apostle of Destruction had met with the unmerited fate meted out to the innocent by the apostles of his own deadly creed!

It was months after the arrival of Lord Beauford at Vienna, when in a solitary walk through one of the great annual fairs, a veiled gypsy woman crossed his path. A whisper riveted him to the spot, for the tidings were of import. "Tell the beautiful American that the villain and traitor has now a comrade in the grave! The wretch who helped to plot her ruin, who was her false friend, died the death that Oborski fled from here only to meet beyond the ocean! *Give her this!*" She passed and was quickly lost in the crowd.

When Evelyn Maitland saw the token, she bowed her head in silent prayer. It was a ring which she had placed on the gypsy girl's hand in the days at Munich! The Ventnor days were red letter days to her friends. Before their lives divided, again to mingle with the refluent tide of human existence, Isabel Beauford and Evelyn Maitland agreed in heart upon the simple truism that *around the home, the purest feelings of mortals cling like ivy to beloved olden walls.* That no sudden re-distribution of human rights and duties could compensate woman for the loss of the delicious individualism of tne marriage tie, based upon religion, custom, and the evolution of social wisdom. Down in the green alleys of Ventnor, England's now rising diplomat, spoke freely as he walked with his American friend. "Maitland, you go home to your own theatre of duty and action. You may bear renewed hopes in your bosom. *Anarchy will be stayed by the solid walls of the Anglo-Germanic element of world. The Emperor William favors a general Anglo-Germanic union.* Conspiracy and anarchistic madness is either Latin or Slavic. But in their sameness of family life, literature, laws and natural spirit, *Germany*, *England* and the *United States* can find a general ground of union. Speculative politics, ideal social constructions, the vain throes of the discontented may convulse the world, but it is in the sympathetic union of *three great Anglo-Germanic peoples* that stability will be found. The right of society to organize and protect itself is an axiom, and can not be howled down! As for the rule of the fanatic dynamiter, concerted measures of the governments threatened will crush the knots of would-be murderers. *Public morality is public health*, and no better plans of human concerted action have been devised than a regulated individualism seeking a gradual betterment in station, culture, and enjoyment. That the industrious and useful shall live in terror of the vicious and reactionary would be a colossal cowardice. Society can and will protect itself. Ravachol, Vaillant, Fauch, Henry, Bourdin and their followers will lie forgotten in felon graves like their mad prototypes, Wilkes Booth, Guiteau and Prendergast. *'Their blood be upon their own heads!'* As for anarchistic clubs and circles, the constituted authorities of the world will ferret them out and destroy them! *Anarchism has no creed which gains even the monetary support of a rational mind.* Go back to your Western home in peace! Your country does not need great men, *save in its times of crisis!* It needs only the good and wise! That overruling Providence which gave you a Washington, a Hamilton, a Jefferson, and brought out from the gloom of your civil war a Lincoln and a Grant, will raise up for you men of the hour, who will lead you aright! Here in Europe, with its discordant peoples, we need men who tower above their fellows. They labor now for peace and order. We have on our side *Gladstone, the veteran Bismark, and Pope Leo XIII.*, the three greatest men of the day. It is true the real leaders of anarchism have not yet been detected. The blind assassins, chosen by lot, are mere tools. But when these veiled Prophets are forced to drop the mask, their power departs, for humanity stands aghast at *self-destruction.* For my part, I doubt not through the ages, one increasing purpose runs—the coming of the peaceful 'Brotherhood of Man!'"

Their hands met in the pledge of this faith as they entered the doors of the stately English home.

THE END

www.ingramcontent.com/pod-product-compliance
Lightning Source LLC
Chambersburg PA
CBHW051525100726
47898CB00005B/1578